W9-CET-124

INTO THE DARKNESS

Barbara Michaels

G.K.HALL &CO.
Boston, Massachusetts
1991

Published in Large Print by arrangement with
Simon and Schuster Inc.

G. K. Hall Large Print Book Series.

Set in 16 pt. Plantin.

Library of Congress Cataloging-in-Publication Data

Michaels, Barbara, 1927–
Into the darkness / Barbara Michaels.
p. cm. — (G.K. Hall large print book series)
ISBN 0-8161-5129-6 (hc.). — ISBN 0-8161-5130-X (pbk.)
1. Large type books. I. Title.
[PS3563.E747I68 1991]
813′.54—dc20 90-20241

ACKNOWLEDGMENTS

I would like to thank all my friends in the antique jewelry business who gave so generously of their time and effort to help me with my research. Special mention goes to Carol Canty of Collage in Frederick, who not only lent me her books but delivered them to my door; and to Gene Rooney of Victorian Manor in New Market, Maryland, who answered all my questions and allowed me to peer over his shoulder while he carried out the goldsmith's chores at which he is so skilled. Few friends would have gone to such lengths! If I am in error on any point, the fault is mine, not his.

I am not resigned to the shutting away of loving hearts in the hard ground.
So it is, and so it will be, for so it has been, time out of mind.
Into the darkness they go, the wise and the lovely. Crowned
With lilies and with laurel they go; but I am not resigned.

Lovers and thinkers, into the earth with you.
Be one with the dull, the indiscriminate dust.
A fragment of what you felt, of what you knew,
A formula, a phrase remains,—but the best is lost.

The answers quick and keen, the honest look, the laughter, the love,—
They are gone. They are gone to feed the roses. Elegant and curled
Is the blossom. Fragrant is the blossom. I know. But I do not approve.
More precious was the light in your eyes than all the roses in the world.

Down, down, down into the darkness of the grave
Gently they go, the beautiful, the tender, the kind.
Quietly they go, the intelligent, the witty, the brave.
I know. But I do not approve. And I am not resigned.

EDNA ST. VINCENT MILLAY,
"Dirge Without Music"

1

BEYOND THE GLASS, snowflakes swirled in patterns of blowing lace. The human figures stood frozen, as if snared in white netting; but the web was too fragile to hold them, soon they would move, slowly but inexorably, toward her, bearing a deadly gift of knowledge she could not, would not endure again. . . .

Meg Venturi's hand moved in a convulsive gesture of rejection, pushing the miniature, encapsulated world away. The crystal teetered on the edge of the table and would have fallen if Nick's quick fingers had not caught it.

"Need you express your dislike so dramatically? A simple 'no, thanks' would have sufficed." His voice was calm, but the sharp underlying edge of surprise and annoyance was audible to anyone who knew him as well as she did. The dark, finely arched brows that contrasted so strikingly with his pale blond hair were raised high, in the same expression with which he confronted a hostile witness. Nick Taggert was one of New York's best criminal lawyers, a profession in which his theatrical good looks served him well. His hair was a little longer than current fashion demanded; it was one of his best features, and he was well aware of the effect on the more susceptible women jury members when he brushed the thick shining locks away from his face. Meg teased him about wearing it long in order to cover his ears; he thought they were too big, and when she laughed and called him Mr. Spock his echoing laughter was a little forced.

Meg loved his ears. She loved everything about him—well, almost everything—she didn't blame him for resenting her reaction to his gift. It was an exquisite toy, unusual and obviously expensive. Cheap imitations could be found in any gift shop, tiny Santas or woodland scenes engulfed in temporary snow squalls when the plastic globe was shaken. This was different. The enclosing globe was of crystal, the tiny figures hand-carved and exquisitely painted.

"I'm sorry! I do like it; I love it. I didn't mean. . . ." Then a flame of anger kindled, sparked by his. "You forgot. Damn it, Nick, how could you be so insensitive? I told you about my father—about the night they came, through the snow and the dark, to tell me. . . ."

For a moment his face was blank with incomprehension. Then his blue eyes widened. "I'll be damned. Sorry, sweetheart. I wanted to get you something beautiful and unusual; buying you jewelry is like carrying coals to Newcastle, so when I saw this I was delighted; I thought I'd found the perfect gift. It reminded me of that wonderful weekend in Maine—the first long weekend we spent together, remember? Honestly, it never occurred to me that that old memory was still festering."

He went on talking, explaining, apologizing. Meg stopped listening. The imitation snowflakes behind the glass had settled, the little carved man and his little lady stood immobile. Only the figures in her mind moved, out of the winter darkness more than twenty years past.

She had been waiting at the window for such a long time, her snub nose pressed to the glass, her eager breath making patches of fog on the pane. When the headlights appeared she let out a squeal of joy. But this wasn't the car for which she had been waiting, and neither of the men who got out of it was her daddy. This car had printing along the side and a red light on top. Revolving, it sent dull crimson flashes cutting through the dark and cast a rosy glow on the carpet of snow on the ground, like the funny pink snow in the *Cat in the Hat* book. But this pink snow wasn't funny or pretty.

She knew what the car was. She wasn't a baby, she was almost six years old and she could read . . . well, some words, anyhow. The words painted on the side of the car weren't words she knew, but she didn't have to sound them out, she knew this was a police car, and the men were policemen. Not cops or fuzz or any of the other words she had heard on TV; Mama and Daddy said those weren't polite words. Mama and Daddy said policemen should be treated politely because they were the good guys. They helped people.

If you got lost or somebody bad was bothering you, you should go to a policeman, and he would help you.

So why was it that the sight of these policemen scared her? Her stomach hurt, and the patches of fog on the glass formed and faded more quickly than before. Maybe it was the snow that made them look so . . . She couldn't find the word. It was as if they'd come, not from a regular police station with ordinary walls and rooms, but out of the storm itself. They had stopped moving. They stood still, looking at the house. She had the feeling they were as scared as she was.

Then the front door of the house opened and somebody came out onto the porch. It was Mama. She wasn't wearing a coat or a scarf, and the long, full skirt of her blue velvet dress dragged behind her and brushed the snow from the steps as she ran down them. Meg was afraid she'd slip and fall; she was moving too fast, and she was getting her pretty dress all wet. Meg liked it the best of all Mama's dresses. So did Daddy. That was why Mama was wearing it, because there was a party that night. Daddy was late. But he would come upstairs to say good night and play their game, the way he always did. Always. Even when he was going out, to a party or to work, or anywhere, Daddy always came.

The snow made pretty patterns on the velvet dress, like lace, before Mama fell down. One of the policeman tried to catch her but he wasn't quick enough. She lay on the ground with the crumpled folds of blue velvet around her and the snow fell harder, like a heavy curtain, like it was trying to cover her up.

And that night Daddy didn't come.

After Nick had gone Meg bolted the door and fastened the chain. She had lived in Manhattan too long to neglect that precaution, even though her mind was on other things.

As she turned she saw someone facing her across the narrow hall. The shock was so great it set her heart thumping, yet the figure was her own—her reflection in the tall pier glass. She had seen it a thousand times, but tonight it looked different, and she studied it with the detached curiosity of a stranger meeting someone for the first time.

The new shade of eyeliner wasn't as flattering as she had believed. Instead of looking bigger and softer, her eyes were opaque, solidly black as the crayoned eyes of a child's drawing. Her pale, carefully blotted lipstick had not been blurred by Nick's kisses. He hated bright lipstick, he said it made her look older and harder—and it didn't do much for him, either. His hands had loosened the heavy mass of her hair; instead of falling in soft waves over her shoulders, it stood out in crazy disarray, like the snaky locks of a Medusa, and the light died in its blackness. She was a little vain about her hair, it was the true, rare blue-black that is seldom found in nature. An inheritance from her Italian father, her grandfather would have said. Dan was a firm believer in heredity. In the debate about nature versus nurture, he came down hard on the side of nature.

Meg turned away from the mirror and walked into the living room. It was still early. The crystal globe had not shattered, but something else had, and her attempts to mend it had failed. Nick had not blamed her. "I couldn't have stayed long anyway, sweetheart. Tomorrow is Cara's birthday, and I promised to take her and some of her friends out on the boat. They'll be raring to go at the crack of dawn—you know teenagers."

"Not your teenagers."

His eyebrows lifted. "Meg, darling—"

"I'm sorry." She twisted away from the hands that held her. "I'm sorry about everything, Nick. I don't know why I'm in such a foul mood tonight."

"It's obvious, isn't it?" He leaned back against the arm of the couch. "That call you got, telling you your grandfather was ill."

"It's just the flu. Nothing serious."

"I hope not. But you have to face facts, darling; the old boy isn't going to live forever. No, don't turn away—look at me." He reinforced the words with a gesture as fond as it was firm, cupping her cheek with his hand and turning her face toward his. "I'm glad you told me—reminded me, rather—about your father. It wasn't just the tragedy of losing him, it was the—er—the unusual circumstances, and the fact that you were at a particularly vulnerable age. It's no wonder you transferred all that dependency thing onto your grandfather. I'm no psychiatrist—"

"Thank God," Meg murmured.

"Meg, darling, you can't dismiss an entire profession because of one negative experience. You never really gave it a chance. My own analysis helped me a great deal—enough, certainly, to understand your problem. It isn't that complex."

"Oh?"

"Sweetheart, I'm only trying to help," Nick said patiently. "The fear of death, for ourselves and the people we love, is a basic human emotion. Intellectually you know your grandfather is going to die. Emotionally you can't—or won't—accept it. In your case it's doubly difficult because you lost your parents at an early age, and under particularly painful circumstances; Dan became not only grandfather but father and mother as well. It's no wonder you panic at the idea of losing him, or that any reminder of his mortality should revive memories of that earlier loss."

"I didn't panic. I haven't had one of those attacks since—" Meg stopped herself. She had not told Nick about the terrifying, uncontrollable episodes; she hadn't even thought about them for years, it had been so long. . . .

He didn't ask her to explain. Glancing at his watch, he rose, and reached for the little crystal toy.

"I'll keep it for you until you're ready to face those memories. When you are, we'll sit and watch the snow falling, together. Good night, love; I'll always be there for you, you know that."

Except when Cara wants you. Or Emily, or Nick Junior.

Remembering those words—which she had thought but not voiced aloud—Meg collapsed ungracefully onto the couch and began twisting the ring on her little finger, a gesture so habitual she was scarcely aware she was doing it. She wasn't jealous of Nick's other relationships—of course she wasn't. He and his wife had been legally separated long before she met him, and she could not have loved or respected a man who neglected his kids. Children came first.

And yet . . . Was it so unreasonable of her to want to be first with someone, not always, not to the exclusion of other commitments, but at those moments when the frightened child that lives in every human being cried out for comfort? Since that bleak winter night she had never had such total support, not from anyone. Sometimes Nick's facile diagnoses irritated her beyond measure, but maybe this time he had hit on something. After the death of her parents she had tried to find a substitute in her grandfather, but she had always known she had rivals for his love—not only Gran, but the gems that were Dan's joy and obsession. Sometimes she had the feeling that he would have sacrificed all of them, even her, even Gran, for their cold, glittering beauty.

The ring turned under Meg's fingers, catching the light in splashes of fiery crimson, kingfisher blue, and the iridescence of diamond. It was an early-Victorian posy ring; the words of the verse, or "poesy," twined around the circumference of the hoop read: *"Je suis ici en lieu d'ami."* Though she had long since been forced to move it from her third to her little finger, she continued to wear it because it was the first posy ring Dan had given her, the start of what was now a valuable collection.

"I am here in the place of a friend." That was the real reason why she continued to wear the outgrown trinket, a superstitious belief in the power of the engraved motto. A friend . . . A person who knows all your faults and likes you anyway. Dan knew her faults. He'd pointed them out often enough! And he liked her—loved her—anyway. And she would lose him too, as she had lost her father.

But not yet. Please, not yet. It was nothing serious, just a touch of the flu. Eighty-two wasn't old, not these days. Lots of people lived to be one hundred.

But Daniel Mignot had lied about his age, as he lied about so many things—even his name. He claimed to be descended from a famous European goldsmith of the same name, who had flourished during the sixteenth century. That claim would have been preposterous enough—few people can trace an unbroken lineage so far back in time—but Mignot, who had been born Daniel Merck, had no shame about adorning his family tree with equally implausible kinsmen. Through his mother he was related to the Castellanis, who had revived the lost Etruscan art of granulation, in which minuscule globes of gold are fused onto a golden surface. The technique of the Castellani family had died with them, though when their descendant was in a particularly expansive mood, he was wont to assert that he had inherited that secret along with the other legendary skills of his ancestors. His great-great-grandfather had supervised Nitot in resetting the crown jewels of France for the coronation of Napoleon; his father had taught Lalique all he knew.

Jacob Merck had probably never heard of Lalique. An immigrant from Poland, he had a hard-enough time supporting himself and his family in the teeming tenements of turn-of-the-century New York. Yet one could not help wonder whether his son's fantasy had some factual basis, for how else could one explain Mignot's passionate obsession with the complex techniques of the jeweler's craft, and his instinctive knowledge of gems? None of his stories of how he got his start made much sense, and some were mutually contradictory; but it is possible that he was telling the truth, for once, when he claimed to have been taken into custody by a suspicious policeman because he had been standing with his nose pressed to the icy-cold glass of the show window of Tiffany's store at Fifth Avenue and Thirty-seventh Street for three solid hours—during a snowstorm. The intervention of none other than Louis Comfort Tiffany,who happened to be leaving the store at the strategic moment, saved the boy from arrest. Louis, the eccentric iconoclast of the family, was amused by the contrast between the child's shabby appearance and the blazing wealth that had so enraptured him; he gave the lad his first entrée into the jewelry business, hiring him to sweep the offices.

Another of his favorite stories was that he had saved the life of a Rothschild or a Rockefeller (the names varied) during the Great War. He had been underage when he enlisted, but that didn't deter him, or the U.S. Army. He stayed in Europe until 1925, and when he returned he brought with him the beginnings of his famous collection of antique jewelry. "There is always money to be made at the death of a civilization," he would say, quoting a source he never bothered to credit. The statement was certainly true; a starving man will barter diamonds for bread. But it didn't explain how Mignot got the money to buy the bread.

The crash of '29 was not a disaster, but another stroke of luck for Daniel Mignot. Native conservatism had kept him from expanding his business; the capital he had saved was used to acquire, at bargain prices, the jewels of those who had been less cautious.

Not until the late thirties, when he had begun to expand, did he take time out to woo and marry a wife, a gentle, exquisitely pretty New England aristocrat. Her family, understandably skeptical of Mignot's genealogical fictions, protested to no avail; lovely Mary Morgan had always gotten what she wanted, and for reasons that completely eluded her bewildered family, she wanted the brash, undersized nobody who was almost twice her age. Their first daughter was born in 1937; the second came howling into the world the day after the Japanese bombed Pearl Harbor.

Daniel Mignot was among the first Americans to enlist. He claimed to have abandoned wife and children because of patriotic fervor, and who could prove he lied? Outrage and love of country moved thousands of Americans to do as he did. But in Mignot's case one is entitled to wonder.

This time it was Asia, not Europe, to which he applied his philosophy of acquisition. He was rather vague about his activities, hinting at top-secret intelligence work; by some means or other he managed to make his way to India, and was stationed there when the war ended. For centuries the subcontinent had been the market for the gem dealers of Burma, Ceylon, and Kashmir. It was hardly a coincidence that only after its founder returned from war did the firm of Daniel Mignot gain international status, right up there with Tiffany's and Harry Winston and the other giants of the jewelry business. Like them, Mignot had the big stones, the bright stones, the famous stones, but he specialized in design instead of concentrating on the gems themselves. As a designer he himself was second-rate, but he had an uncanny knack for spotting and encouraging new talent. He paid high salaries and was one of the first to list publicly the names of his top designers. By 1965 he had opened branches of his New York store in Palm Beach and San Francisco. His personal life was as happy as his business dealings were successful. Mary hated New York and disliked travel, so when, early in their marriage, she inherited the family home in Connecticut, he converted it into a mansion worthy of housing his most important gems, as he called them: his beautiful wife and his two daughters.

Then, in the space of a single night, the whole glittering edifice crumbled and fell. A year after the tragic scandal that destroyed his family Mignot retired from active management and sold the business to an international conglomerate. Even his enemies, and he had plenty of them, felt sorry for the beaten old man.

His friends pitied him too, but they knew better. Dan wasn't beaten; like the hero of the old ballad, he would lay him down to bleed awhile, then rise and fight again. However, none of them could have predicted the form his recovery would take. Some years earlier he had opened a small store and workshop on Main Street in the small town where his wife had grown up, like her parents and grandparents before her. Doting husband though he was, he must have found the exquisite perfection of his home wearing at times; in the shop he could be as "messy" and "noisy" as he liked, smoke his nasty black cigars, swear and tell off-color jokes. The shop was his toy and his hobby, a place to which he could retreat in order to practice the skills in which he took such pride.

The store was more than a toy, however, and the critics who swore that Dan Mignot never did anything unless he hoped to make a profit from it were right. The growth of the small business was so slow at first as to be almost imperceptible; Dan ran it himself, with the help of a bookkeeper—who later became his son-in-law—and a series of antiquated but knowledgeable managers, all old friends and former employees. The basis of the business was antique jewelry, bought from people who heard Dan was offering good prices for that "old junk of Grandma's." He had been building up his stock for forty years, adding the best pieces to his personal collection and stockpiling the rest for the time he knew would come —the time when the inevitable cycle of fashion would bring the quaint, old-fashioned ornaments of the eighteenth and nineteenth centuries back into fashion. The garnet parures and heavy gold chains and multicolored jewelry of the Victorians were sneered at by connoisseurs and collectors; they hadn't been sold because they were considered ugly and valueless, nor broken up for the stones, because garnets and peridots, topazes and alexandrites were worth so little in themselves—then. Mignot was one of the few to appreciate their worth, and to capitalize upon it, and when the catastrophe shook his life apart, his little hobby provided the emotional and professional foundation for a new career. Twenty years later Daniel

Mignot Jewelers of Seldon had a reputation that extended beyond the boundaries of the state and the country, and old Dan bestrode the town like a genial colossus.

In the words of one of the sentimental old poems he often quoted, he had met with triumph and disaster, and treated those impostors both the same. There was no reason why he should not have lived to be a hundred. But when the virus invaded his body he was ninety years old, not eighty-two, and he had just made a discovery that shook him to the core of his cynical old soul. It is inconceivable that Dan Mignot would have welcomed death; he had been a fighter all his life. But his defenses had been shattered, and the enemy to whom all men must lose in the end took full advantage.

The coffin was open. Meg abhorred the custom, but she had not protested; it was what her grandmother wanted, what Dan himself had set out in his will. Besides, the townspeople would have been deeply affronted if they had been denied the chance to pay their respects in the good old-fashioned way. Once a scorned outsider, Dan had become one of their own. Never mind the corporate offices in New York and the expensive shops in glamorous cities like Palm Beach and Paris and Buenos Aires; to his contemporaries in Seldon, he would always be Dan Mignot who had run the jewelry store on Main Street. For twenty years Dan had opened it every morning nine o'clock on the dot without fail. Every weekday he had gone across the street for lunch at Kate's Kafe, joining Mike Potter, who owned the hardware store, and Barb Bothwell, of Barby's Beauty Shoppe, and the other merchants who had survived Seldon's transition from a small country town to a quaint stopover on the tourist routes of New England. It was in large part due to Dan that the transition had been so painless for the small businesses and the people who operated them. They had come to mourn not only a friend, but the passing of a tradition.

On one level Meg acknowledged the tribute and found comfort in it. On another, more primitive, level she resented the intrusion of outsiders and the formal decorum their presence demanded of her. She had even bought a black dress, a color she never wore. Black was for death, black was for mourning. Glancing into the mirror that morning before she left for the church, she had recoiled from the ghostly image that stared back at her, its face white as ashes under the broad-brimmed black hat, another hasty purchase that at least had the advantage of shielding her face from curious or sympathetic glances.

Gran had not approved either. Studying the ensemble with a distressed frown, she had murmured, "Black should be a good color for you—or is black a color? I never understood about that. . . . Perhaps it's because you're so terribly pale. Anyway, it was a sweet thought, dear."

Gran looked superb in black, and was well

aware of it. The lace at her throat and wrists was the same snowy white as her thick, wavy hair. Her only jewels were the magnificent pearl choker that had once belonged to a duchess, and matching pearl earrings. She sat erect and dry-eyed, armored in the rigid dignity of her generation and social class. She was eighteen years younger than Dan, and she had known this day would come.

Meg knew she couldn't live up to Gran's sterling example, but at least her face wasn't soggy with tears. So far she had shed none. It had all happened too fast for comprehension: first the telephone, jolting her out of uneasy and unremembered dreams and heralding the bad news by its very timing; then the hasty packing and frantic rush to the airport, and the need for composure and efficiency in the face of Gran's initial helplessness. She seemed to be all right now, but the formality of a funeral had given her a framework in which to function. She'd do the right thing, the gracious thing, as long as there were rules governing proper behavior. Were there rules of proper behavior for the dark hours of solitude, when a widow was alone with her loss? Perhaps dignity and decorum became habitual if they were practiced as long as Gran had practiced them.

Meg wished she could believe that were true. Her grandmother's composure worried her more than frenzied grief would have done. She herself was behaving abnormally, and she knew it. She felt numb, armored not by dignity but by a queer detachment that enabled her to observe the proceedings as dispassionately as any journalist. Thank God for George; she could never have managed without him. She glanced sideways at her uncle, who sat between her and Gran. The word that came to her mind was "solid"; not just his six feet of bone and muscle, but his calm reliability. As if feeling her gaze, he turned his head and smiled at her over her grandmother's devoutly bowed head. His eyes were redder than Gran's. George Wakefield was Gran's son-in-law, not her born son, as the town would have expressed it; in the same idiom, he was close as kin and as good to the old folks as if he'd been their own. Never married again, nor looked twice at another woman, and it's been over twenty years. . . .

Meg realized that the pastor was praying—that was why Gran had bowed her head. Hastily she ducked her own, but she was unable to concentrate on the words. Out of the corner of her eye she could see the hands of the man who sat on her left—long, brown hands, well tended, neatly manicured. Trust Cliff to have acquired a tan so early in the summer. And how could hands so demurely clasped convey an impression of contemptuous amusement?

It wasn't his hands, it was what she knew of Cliff himself. She hadn't seen her courtesy cousin—George's son by his first wife—for many years, but when he had arrived that morning she sensed that he hadn't changed. Physically, yes, of course; he was no longer the pimply, weedy youth she had last seen, but a grown man with all his father's height and wiry build. His manners were smooth and courteous, his features as handsome as his father's, his eyes the same bright blue. But their expression was the same as that of the mischievous boy who had teased the life out of her and aroused the wrath of the entire town by his pranks until his exasperated father sent him away to school. There was none of George's warmth in Cliff's smile, only expectant amusement—as if he were hoping for a chance to laugh at someone's stupidity or clumsiness. Well, he wouldn't get his laugh from her. She was grown up too, no longer victim to his tricks.

Thickened by emotion, the minister's voice droned through the long list of Dan's charities to the town and the people who lived in it. Meg was unable to hold back a smile. Dan wouldn't have smiled, he'd have laughed out loud at the aura of saintliness the pastor was weaving around his memory. He used to claim the only crime he hadn't committed was barratry, and that was because he didn't know what the hell it was. He hadn't had much use for religion, either. Out of respect for Gran he had kept his opinions to himself, even when he discovered that the gentle, timid young pastor on whom she doted was unmarried and meant to remain so. He hadn't been so reticent with his cronies, though; Meg vividly remembered overhearing his comments on the subject of a celibate clergy. "Any man who's not interested in the most delectable object nature ever fashioned has a gaping hole where his . . ." At that interesting juncture he had seen Meg, and burst into a fit of coughing. "Where what is?" she had asked, brightly curious. "His brains," said Dan.

A hand closed over her arm and pulled her to her feet. She scowled at Cliff, who closed one eye in a deliberate wink. His lips barely moved, but she made out the words: "Don't laugh, it isn't proper."

"I wasn't. . . ." But she *had* been on the verge of laughing. The organ began to play, preventing the response she was tempted to make. She recognized the tune—"Rock of Ages"—and fought another burst of hysterical amusement. How Dan had hated that hymn! He didn't mind the loud, cheerful ones like "Onward, Christian Soldiers," but the lugubrious melodies and submissive sentiments of the other variety had offended both his ear and his pride.

Her eyes moved restlessly around the church, noting the many evidences of Dan's generosity. What an old hypocrite he had been, she thought fondly, lavishing gifts on an institution he despised. But the gifts had really been for Gran; that wasn't hypocrisy, it was the most disinterested form of love. The stained glass in the window behind the altar was one of Dan's contributions. Its unorthodox appearance had divided the town into opposed parties, one that admired the work and one that wanted to smash it. Instead of saints and scenes from Scripture it showed a vast expanse of sapphire blue scattered with stars and galaxies. One had to look at it for some time before seeing that the sweep of light had the shape of a huge hand, shaking suns and worlds from its fingertips even as it gathered them into the protective curve of its palm.

Finally the service ended. George rose to his feet. He was one of the pallbearers, and it was not until he turned to offer his arm to Gran that Meg realized there was one last rite to be performed before they could leave the church. The thought of this one roused no amusement at all, it was the part she had dreaded most.

I can't do it, she thought. I can't, I won't. It's barbaric, it's sick, it's unfair. . . . Then she saw Cliff's hand move, and she reacted, as instinctively as a laboratory animal reacts to an electric shock, rising quickly to her feet. She had walked into the church on Cliff's arm, as Gran had insisted, but she was damned if she was going to let him share this final farewell, or observe her cowardly shrinking from what lay ahead. She had no intention of actually looking at the cold mask of what had been her grandfather's face. She would rather remember him as she had seen him last—his deep-set, twinkling eyes, his wicked grin half-concealed by his bristly white mustache.

As she started to leave the pew, shaking with sentiments more appropriate to a fight than a funeral, she saw a face that reflected her emotions so accurately it was like looking in a mental mirror.

Physically the face was as different from hers as a human countenance could be: a man's face, not handsome or even particularly attractive. His features were too large for his long, narrow face—a jutting beak of a nose, a chin that matched the nose in arrogance, a tight-set mouth that bisected his thin cheeks. In the rock-hardness of his face only his eyes seemed alive; they blazed with the same fury of denial she felt, and they were staring straight at her.

Meg stared back. What was he doing there, in the front pew reserved for close friends of the family? She had no idea who he was; to the best of her recollection she had never seen him before. Though the church was packed, there were empty spaces on either side of him, as if the others who shared the pew shunned his presence.

Cliff poked her in the back. Meg forced herself to move toward the front of the church and the open coffin.

The rest of the proceedings passed with merciful quickness. At the grave site she saw the unknown man again; his harsh features stood out sharp as a cameo against the blur of other faces wearing identical expressions of grief. Only once, when he glanced at the white marble angel marking the family plot, was his angry look replaced by one that might have indicated mild derision. No one stood near him. When the brief service ended he was the first to leave, and people fell back, opening an aisle for him as if he were a king—or a leper.

Meg followed her uncle and grandmother to the waiting limousine, again ignoring Cliff's arm. He got into the front beside the chauffeur. That left four of them in the back—Gran, George, herself and Henrietta Marie, Gran's spoiled, aristocratic Himalayan cat. Henrietta had her own jeweled harness and leash—set with topazes and carnelians and other stones in the warm brownish orange shades that complemented her seal-point coloring—and she accompanied Gran everywhere, with an air of lofty condescension that drove the family wild. Meg had ventured a weak protest when Gran carried the cat to the car, but Gran had insisted; and now, seeing how they greeted one another she was glad she hadn't made an issue of it. Henrietta promptly climbed into Gran's lap, and the old lady gathered her close, careless of the hairs that transferred themselves to her black satin lap. The tightness of her grasp betrayed her need for comfort, and for a wonder Henrietta Marie, who usually voiced her disapproval of rough handling in no uncertain terms, did not object. However, she turned her head to stare at Meg, and there was no mistaking the sneer on her furry face. She had never cared much for Meg. She didn't care much about anybody except Mary and Dan, whom she apparently regarded as a useful appendage to her mistress.

Apparently she thought of George in the same light, for she allowed him to pat Gran's shoulder. "Are you all right, Mary?"

Gran straightened. "Of course. I'm a little tired, that's all."

"And that mob coming to the house . . ." George shook his handsome silver head.

"It's just our friends," Gran said gently.

"Just the whole town, you mean."

"Friends," Gran repeated. "Dan didn't want outsiders. All those people from New York, and the store managers—I hope I didn't offend them by telling them not to come. But Dan was very firm about it."

"Thank heaven for that much. I'll make your excuses, Mary, if you'd like to lie down for a while. They'll understand."

Gran shook her head, smiling, and George turned to Meg. "Same offer goes for you, honey. Everyone knows how close you and Dan were. They will—"

"No, they won't," Meg said. "Thanks, George, but I'll do my duty. For Dan. How he would have enjoyed all this!"

George's eyebrows lifted. "My dear Meg—"

Gran laughed, a surprisingly light, girlish giggle. "Meg is right. Dan would have adored every moment of it. Remember, Meg, how he used to joke about faking his death and attending the funeral in disguise?"

"That's right, he did." Meg laughed too. "He said it was the one time a man could expect to hear only good of himself—and most of it lies."

"He does love to make jokes," Gran said fondly.

The use of the present tense startled Meg a little.

It also reminded her of what her grandmother had said in response to Dan's joke about attending his own funeral. "But Dan, dear, of course you will be there."

From anyone else it might have been a macabre jest. Gran never joked about things like that, though. Wonderingly, Meg studied her grandmother's serene face. Was that what sustained Gran, the belief that Dan was hovering over her like one of the guardian angels in a Victorian painting? The picture took shape in her mind, vividly detailed and hideously inappropriate: Dan wearing wings and a halo, with his cigar jutting out of the corner of his mouth. . . . Meg wanted to laugh and cry at the same time. Shock, she told herself. We're not out of it yet, neither Gran nor I.

Several new subdivisions had sprung up in recent years, but the town itself was small and the old cemetery, like the house Dan had called The Manor, was on the western side of the original settlement. Meg had never been certain whether the name was serious or whether Dan had been poking fun at himself and his pretensions. When Mary inherited the house it was known only as "the old Morgan place," but his extensive renovations had removed all traces of its ancestry. Meg suspected that only Gran's restraining hand had prevented Dan from converting it into a genuine fake manor house, complete with battlements and towers. Where his craft was concerned he had exquisite taste; otherwise he was apt to wallow in baroque and Victorian extravagance. As it now stood the house was a hodgepodge of materials and styles, but it had mellowed with the years, and the extensive landscaping gave it considerable charm. Not for Meg, though. Whenever she saw it, drenched in sunlit summer or wrapped in the flowering of spring, she saw whirling snowflakes and the dark of that dreadful night. That was one of the reasons why her visits to Seldon had been few and brief in recent years.

The servants had gone straight from the church to the house, missing the services at the cemetery—no small sacrifice on their part, as Gran was quick to acknowledge. Giving both hands to Frances Polanski, the housekeeper, who met them in the hall, she said, "I know I needn't ask if everything is ready for our guests, Frances. Thank you for being so helpful."

Frances must be well into her sixties; she had been in charge of the house ever since Meg could remember, and she hadn't changed in twenty years. Her hair was the same insistent auburn, her figure as rigidly corseted into slimness, her round face as plump and highly colored. She treated Gran like a beloved but very young child, and she ran the household with consummate efficiency. She would have been the perfect housekeeper had it not been for one failing—a fondness for sentimental old novels that led her to adopt the mannerisms of various fictitious housekeepers. With a sinking feeling Meg realized that since they left the house Frances had switched roles. That morning she had been the devoted family servant, wiping her tears away with the corner of her apron, and calling Meg "dearie." I should have known, Meg thought dismally. On this day of all days, I might have expected Frances would turn into Mrs. Danvers.

The sinister housekeeper of *Rebecca* did not acknowledge her mistress's greeting with so much as a murmur. Face cold as a marble mask, she took the cat's leash from Gran and summoned a hovering maid with a brusque snap of her fingers. Armed with a brush, the young woman led Mary away.

Meg started to follow, knowing she wouldn't get away so easily. Frances barred the way, arms folded, eyes boring into Meg's.

"So you think you've laid him to rest."

"Think?" Meg caught herself. A discussion with Mrs. Danvers was depressing at best; in her present mood it would be unendurable. "Excuse me, Frances, I've got to—"

"Think," Frances intoned. When she was Mrs. Danvers her voice dropped a full octave. "He's not at rest. Nor will he be until the truth is known. I've had no chance to talk to you before—"

"Well, this certainly is not the time," Meg said desperately. "The guests will be arriving any minute."

"Let them wait. He waited long enough. But you never came."

Meg felt the blood drain from her face; Frances always knew how to hit a person where it hurt.

"I caught the first plane, Frances; I didn't even pack, just threw things into a suitcase. If I'd known how ill he was . . . No one told me. Why didn't you tell me?"

Under direct attack Mrs. Danvers retreated, to be replaced, if only briefly, by kindly old Hannah, the loyal servant of the March family. "Honey, I didn't know. Nobody did. It was real sudden. . . ." Her features froze and her voice deepened. "Too sudden. There's a curse on this house, I tell you. He was the first. There's two more to come."

The wide hallway was filling with people. The maids were taking coats. "Don't talk nonsense, Frances," Meg snapped. "This is no time for your morbid ideas. I have duties and so do you."

"Your first duty is to the dead. He won't rest, I tell you, not while his murderer walks free."

Meg was so furious she couldn't speak. This was too much, even from Frances. She gave the housekeeper the look that sent her subordinates at the ad agency running for cover, and Frances shrank back, registering exaggerated horror with every muscle of her face and body. Believing her reproof had produced the desired effect, Meg turned, and found herself face-to-shirtfront with someone who had come up behind her—probably just in time to hear Frances's lunatic accusation. "I'm sorry," she began, looking up.

It was the man she had seen in church and at the cemetery—the king, the leper. His expression was no more benign than it had been earlier. "Oh, don't apologize until you know who I am. I'm the one she was talking about. Dan's murderer."

2

MEG HELD OUT her hand. "How do you do."

His face wasn't designed to display emotion, but her reaction obviously took him aback, and the long pause before he responded gave her time to study him in more detail. He was wearing a dark suit that must be the one he reserved for weddings and funerals; though scarcely worn, it was several years out of date. Nice tie—heavy silk, patterned in shades of blue and turquoise—but too narrow. Also reserved for weddings and funerals? His expression was not; she had a feeling it was his normal look. Grim was an understatement. He could have served as the model for a statue of an Aztec god, one of the ones who accepted the flayed skins of victims as tribute.

The hand that finally took hers was big and blunt-fingered; the skin of his palm felt as rough as a snake's scales. "You're a cool one," he said.

"Not cool. Just numb."

Heavy lids, fringed with bristly dark lashes, veiled his eyes for a moment. It was the only sign of embarrassment or apology he displayed, but his deep voice softened slightly when he responded. "Yeah. He was very proud of you."

It struck Meg as an odd thing to say. Dan hadn't been proud of her; quite the reverse, he had never forgiven her for refusing to follow the career he had laid out for her. "He loved you," would have been more accurate, and more conventional. Was "love" a word this man couldn't pronounce? Who the devil was he? Yet when she started to ask, her throat was tight with unexpected tears and the words wouldn't come. Proud of her? Dan?

Before she could gain control of her voice he had dropped her hand and turned away, yielding place to others who were waiting to greet her.

Some of the faces were familiar, most were not. Meg responded to their murmured condolences with robotlike courtesy. It was with genuine relief and pleasure that she finally found herself facing an old friend. Darren Blake was Dan's personal lawyer, having inherited the job from his father. He was only a few years older than Meg; they had played together as children, and he had always been like a protective older brother, defending her against the rougher boys and Cliff's merciless teasing. Meg was not surprised that he had taken to the law, for even as a child he had preferred argument to fisticuffs. He was extremely shortsighted, and the thick-lensed, horn-rimmed glasses seemed as much a part of his face as his gentle brown eyes.

The clipped dark mustache he had cultivated since she last saw him gave some distinction to a face that was otherwise unremarkable, pleasant rather than conventionally handsome. The bristly hairs tickled her cheek when he bent to kiss her, holding her hands in a warm, comforting grasp.

His suit was in style and expensively tailored, but it didn't quite conceal a slight tendency toward embonpoint.

The crowd had thinned, and Meg felt she could relax her guard at last. She let out a long, shaken sigh, and Darren squeezed her hand. "Bad day?"

The genuineness of his sympathy compensated to some extent for the banality of the question. "Bad three days—week—however long it's been. I've lost track."

With the air of a man gallantly defying convention, Darren put his arm around her and led her toward a chair, capturing a glass of wine from a passing maid along the way. "Sit down and relax for a minute," he ordered. "You look exhausted."

"No, I look like hell, and I feel like it, too." Meg took a sip of sherry. "Mmmm. Just what the doctor ordered. Maybe I'll take the decanter up to my room and get sloshed."

"The worst is over, Meg."

"I wonder. If Frances goes on being Mrs. Danvers, we're in for a sticky evening." Darren looked puzzled, and she realized he was unaware of that particular family joke. She didn't feel like explaining, but she was still furious at Frances and had to unload on someone. "She's predicting doom and gloom and family curses. I really think she's gone over the edge, she said that it was my duty to bring Dan's murderer to justice! Can you believe it? And the worst of it was, the man she was talking about overheard. She meant him to. He was behind me, so I didn't see him, but she was looking straight at him."

"I saw you talking to him," Darren said slowly.

The effect of the wine on her empty stomach and weary body was more potent than she had expected. It took her several seconds to react to his statement. "How did you know whom I meant? You aren't trying to tell me—"

"No, no, nothing of the sort." Darren looked shocked. "But it's not the first time I've heard that accusation bandied about. Small towns are given to gossip, and they are suspicious of outsiders."

"Who is he?"

"I'm surprised you haven't met him. But come to think of it, he's only been in town for three years. You haven't often graced us with your presence, Meg."

"I've been busy." She had meant to stop at that; she didn't owe Darren Blake or anyone else an explanation for her absence. The mild, reproachful eyes got to her, though. "I saw Dan often, you know that; he came to New York almost every month. Gran too. Darren, if you don't answer my question I'm going to scream."

"Oh, sorry." Darren blinked. "I can't understand why Dan didn't tell you about him. His name is A. L. Riley. He took over as manager of the store a couple of years ago."

"Really?" Meg scanned the room with renewed interest, but the man was nowhere in sight. He must have gone into the dining room, where the conventional funeral baked meats were set out.

So that was A. L. Riley. Dan *had* mentioned him, not once but a number of times. He had said very little about the man's origins and background; he always claimed he didn't give a damn where a man came from or what he had done, so long as he could use his hands and his brains, and Riley had demonstrated he could and would use both. He excelled at the same skills upon which Dan had prided himself until arthritis crippled his hands: gem setting and goldsmithing, the basic arts of the jeweler. And he had a talent Dan himself lacked: more than a talent, a genuine genius for design.

If he had said more than that Meg didn't remember; she had done her best not to listen, not only because Dan tended to repeat himself, often and at considerable length, but because the subject was so uncomfortable. A tactful man wouldn't have talked about it any more than was strictly necessary; a sensitive man would have understood why she had fought his efforts to bring her into the profession that elicited such terrible memories. But then tact had never been one of Dan's attributes, and the business was an obsession with him. All his life he had been searching for an unknown genius—the ultimate designer, who, under his tutelage, might come to rival the great artist-designers of the Renaissance such as Holbein and Cellini. Once before he had found such a man. And that man had betrayed him twice over, not only dying before he could fulfill his promise, but destroying Dan's family in the process.

That man had been her father.

"Meg?"

Darren's concerned voice brought her wrenchingly back to the present. She forced a smile. "I was remembering something . . . something Dan said."

It was impossible for a man as pink-cheeked and cherubic as Darren to look sly, but he tried. "Something about Riley? Did he ever . . ." He stopped, frowning, as a fresh influx crowded into the house. "We need to talk, Meg, but this isn't the time or the place. Don't forget that we're meeting in the library at five for the reading of the will."

"Yes, all right," Meg said. Someone was bearing down on her, with the clear intent of expressing commiseration and comfort—a stout elderly woman with a face like that of a Cabbage Patch doll. "Who the hell . . ." Darren murmured, "Mrs. Allan. Head of the library board," and then he moved away. Meg squared her shoulders, pasted a social smile on her face and prepared to do her duty.

It seemed to go on for hours, but by five o'clock everyone had gone, the last diehard celebrants tactfully swept out by Darren and—not so tactfully—by Frances. Meg had passed beyond exhaustion into a state of relative peace; she was simply too tired to feel anything. Or maybe, she told herself, she was too drunk. How many glasses of sherry had she consumed? People had kept pressing them on her, and after a while she had found it easier to sip than to smile or mouth hypocritical platitudes. Dan had had a good life and a long life, but he hadn't been ready to die and she was not resigned to his loss. "Down into the darkness of the grave, Gently they go, the beautiful, the tender, the kind. . . . I know. But I do not approve. And I am not resigned." Dan hadn't been beautiful, or particularly tender, and she was damned sure he hadn't gone gently. But the poet had it right. She did not approve; she was not resigned.

Consternation replaced the pleasant blur of fatigue brought on by alcohol and poetry when she entered the library. She had been looking forward to the moment when her public duties would end and she would at long last be alone with her family and her childhood friend. Wrong again; the library looked like a theater, there were several dozen chairs arranged in rows before Dan's big mahogany desk. Dan must have set this up too. How many people had he mentioned in that will?

The servants, of course. They were present, filling the back row—Karen Anderson, the cook; the two maids; old Jeb McComber, the head gardener, who had been with them forever, Frances of course; and several others she didn't recognize. Half the chairs were occupied, and people were still coming in. Barby Bothwell and Mike Potter, Dan's old pals from the Rotary Club, several younger faces that looked familiar, but that she was unable to identify in her present state of bewilderment. And A. L. Riley. He was one of the last to enter, and his expression strongly suggested that he wished he were elsewhere. His scowl changed to an equally unprepossessing smile as he surveyed the rows of chairs and their occupants, passing over Meg with an indifference that made her stiffen with inexplicable anger. Not so inexplicable, perhaps; the arrogance in that leisurely survey was unmistakable, and when he ignored the empty chairs and went to lean against the wall next to the window she was convinced he had deliberately chosen the most conspicuous position possible.

Darren took a seat behind the desk and opened his briefcase.

His initial statement—"I must ask you to bear with me; this is not a short or a simple will"—brought an unwilling grin to Meg's face. Dan had discussed his will so often and with such relish that it had ceased to be a symbol of death, and had become a running family joke. He spent hours hunched over his desk revising the long list of bequests and the accompanying comments; when he struck on a particularly felicitous insult or well-turned phrase he repeated it, over and over, to anyone who would listen.

He'd have been delighted at the success of some of his witticisms. Several times smothered bursts of laughter interrupted Darren's reading. But the insults were reserved for his old pals, and there were more tears than mirth. He had left something to every servant, even those who had been with him a short time; the bequests to cook, gardener and housekeeper were of such generosity that Frances forgot to be Mrs. Danvers, and dissolved into sobs. There was an interminable list of trinkets or mementos to people Meg had never heard of, including a boy named Joey Pentovski, who inherited Dan's ten-speed bike, along with an admonition to let his little brother ride it sometimes.

The body of the estate went to Mary Mignot, Daniel's beloved wife—but only for her lifetime. After her death it passed to Daniel's sole surviving descendant. . . .

Meg gasped. Dan had gossiped at great length about minor bequests, but he had never discussed what he meant to do for her. He didn't have to discuss it, she trusted him completely, and he had given her so much already, enough to take care of her in comfort for the rest of her life. If she had thought about the matter, which she preferred not to do, she had known that one day—one far distant day—she would probably be a very wealthy woman. But this—it was arbitrary, unfair, autocratic. It left Gran no discretion about the disposal of the estate, and it made no provision for George, who deserved better of the man he had served so faithfully.

Gran wasn't surprised, and neither was Henrietta, who reclined regally on Gran's lap. Their faces bore almost identical expressions of smug approval. Meg glanced at her uncle. If the news had shocked or distressed him, he showed no sign of it.

Darren fixed the crowd with critical eyes and waited until the murmur had subsided before continuing, ". . . with the sole exception of the establishment known as Daniel Mignot Jewelers, at 13 South Main Street, with all its stock and appurtenances. . . ." Meg bit her lip with mounting impatience as Darren droned on through one qualifying legal phrase after another. So, fine, whoever gets the store gets the plumbing fixtures in the john and the curtains in the show window. . . . What, no mention of the dust under the rug? This was building up to another of Dan's little jokes, she knew it as certainly as if she had seen him chortling over the complex phraseology, the delay. The store was his baby, his darling—his favorite hobby as well as the visible memorial to his skill. Who . . . ?

Eventually Darren (and Dan) ran out of legalisms. One-half interest in the store to her, Meg. The other half to A. L. Riley.

The reaction wasn't as mild as a murmur this time; it sounded like a flight of wasps boiling out of a threatened nest. Every head in the room swiveled, as if pulled by a single string—Meg's among them.

Riley had moved closer to the front of the room. Textured patterns of tree limbs and leaves, stained bright emerald by the dying sun, filled the windows before which he stood. Against the brilliance of gold and green his figure stood out in dark silhouette, lifeless as an inked outline. The contrast between the rich, complex background and the still shape it framed was heraldic, symbolic; trained in art and its metaphors, Meg's imagination found sinister parallels: the Dark Angel in the Garden, Death on a summer afternoon. . . .

For a full minute he held his pose; it might have been astonishment, or defiance, or simple uncertainty that held him motionless. Gradually the voices died into silence, and then A. L. Riley spoke. "That tricky old bastard," he said. Turning, precisely as a guardsman, he walked slowly to the door and went out.

No one felt like eating the elaborate meal Frances had ordered. "For heaven's sakes, try," Gran said in her sweet, calm voice, as Meg cut her salmon into increasingly tiny pieces and pushed it around her plate. "Cook will be heartbroken if you don't eat; it's her way of expressing her sympathy. And Frances will worry about you."

"No, she won't," Meg said perversely. "Would Mrs. Danvers worry about that nameless little wimp of a heroine in *Rebecca?*"

"Who says you're the wimpy heroine?" Cliff inquired. "Maybe you're Rebecca. Mrs. Danvers doted on Rebecca."

"I don't want to be Rebecca. Not only was she a vicious bitch, but she was dead."

"Please, darling, your language . . ."

"Sorry, Gran. She was, though."

"I never did understand those jokes about

Frances," Gran said plaintively. "They don't seem quite nice, somehow. She has been so loyal and devoted. . . ."

"That's role number two," Cliff said with a grin. "Derived from *Little Women.*"

"Drop it, Cliff," George said.

Cliff's smile stiffened, but instead of retorting he shrugged and applied himself to his food. Meg felt an unexpected surge of sympathy for him. She, not Cliff, had brought up the subject. Now that she thought about it, she couldn't remember her uncle ever scolding her. Cliff had had more than his share of lectures and punishment—probably well deserved, but who could say how much was cause and how much effect?

George turned to her with a smile that contrasted sharply with the frown he had given his son. "Your grandmother is right, Meg, you must eat something. You didn't touch your lunch, and you only had coffee for breakfast. You'll make yourself ill."

"No, I won't. I haven't time to be ill." But she impaled a piece of salmon and forced herself to chew. "Gran, I know you think it's rude to discuss business at the dinner table, but I have to get this off my chest, it's choking me. When did Dan change his will?"

Her grandmother lifted delicate brows. "Meg, dear, Daniel has been changing his will once a month for fifty years."

"I know. But—"

"We'll discuss it later, dear. Try some of the carrots, they are very good, and good for you."

She had dressed for dinner, as she always did, superbly, ignoring the peculiar attire in which other members of the family might choose to appear—sweatshirts and jeans for the children, a wrinkled shirt for Dan, who hated neckties and suit coats. This evening she had outdone herself; her blue gown, with its ruffles of priceless lace, could have appeared at the court of St. James. Around her neck, at her ears, on her slim wrists and wrinkled hands blazed the sapphires that had once belonged to a queen of France. On anyone else, in such a setting, the display would have been inappropriate verging on vulgar, but Gran carried it off superbly, and Meg understood why she had chosen to honor Dan's memory with her finest gown and her favorites of all the jewels he had given her. She hated to distress her grandmother, but the subject bothered her too much to be dismissed so easily.

She did eat a piece of carrot before she spoke. "There are a number of things we need to discuss, Gran; naturally we'll postpone the business details till a more appropriate time. But this isn't exactly business."

"What exactly is it?" George asked.

"Justice, Uncle George." Impulsively she turned to him. "You weren't even mentioned in the will."

"Oh, is that it?" His face cleared. "You're a sweet girl to worry about me, but I assure you it's unnecessary. Dan was very generous to me over the years; I've never been more than a bookkeeper and accountant, really, and I was never concerned with Dan's corporate holdings—he had a separate staff of lawyers and accountants for that. All I handled was the store, and the housekeeping finances."

"All?" Meg's throat was tight; she had to swallow before she could go on. "You were much more than that, Uncle George. Without you . . ."

"It's all right, honey. Take my word for it—I have been more than amply compensated for what little I was able to do for him."

"Really?"

"Really." He smiled at her.

A slight movement from his son, seated at his right, drew Meg's attention. But Cliff remained silent, his eyes fixed on his plate. He hadn't been mentioned in the will either. Had Dan been "very generous" to him over the years, or had he coolly ignored that long relationship? Cliff had no legal claim, but surely there was a moral obligation. . . .

"Is that all that's worrying you?" George asked.

He knew it wasn't, but before Meg could answer, the door opened and one of the maids entered, ready to clear the table.

"You are finished, aren't you, darling?" Gran asked innocently.

Meg could only nod and give in. Gran had her own little ways of controlling a situation.

Meg didn't try to raise the subject again that evening. It had been wrong of her to do so in the first place, for her real concern, as all of them must have known, was not so much Dan's will as A. L. Riley's place in it. If they had begun talking about him she might have mentioned Frances's outrageous accusation and Riley's equally outrageous reaction to it. One could hardly tell a grieving widow on the evening of her husband's funeral that someone had admitted to murdering him—even if the admission had been a joke. All the more so if the admission had been a joke.

Gran always retired early, and Meg had hoped to have a chat with her uncle afterwards, but this evening the exhaustion she had been fighting all day finally overcame her. She had barely strength enough to stumble to her room.

Meg dreamed about the Salem witches. She was one of them, accused by hysterical children of bartering her soul and body to the Prince of Darkness in exchange for pleasures beyond human comprehension. And she was guilty. As she lay bound, awaiting execution, she laughed and licked her lips, remembering those dark raptures. She went on laughing even after the first weight came to rest, gently, almost softly, on her body; weight upon weight followed the first, crushing ribs and lungs, stopping her breath; and still the silent internal laughter filled her.

She opened her eyes. Henrietta was sitting on her chest. Her enormous blue eyes glared directly into Meg's. Meg stared back, disoriented and breathless. Henrietta emitted a squeak of annoyance and put an imperative paw on Meg's chin. Her claws were not sheathed.

"Ow!" Meg sent the cat flying with a sweep of her arm. She sat up. "Damn it, Henrietta—"

Henrietta rolled to the bottom of the bed and came to rest against the footboard. Lying on her back, paws every which way, she looked like one of the expensive stuffed toys that children and some women keep on their pillows.

"I'm sorry," Meg said defensively. "It's your own fault, though. You have the worst manners. . . . And how the hell did you get in here?"

Henrietta did not deign to reply, though her expression suggested she could have done so if she had wanted to take the trouble. Without bothering to turn over she folded her front paws across her stomach and closed her eyes.

Meg collapsed against the heaped pillows. From her bed she couldn't see the clock on the mantel, but she hadn't taken off her wristwatch—nor brushed her teeth nor washed her face. Her clothing had been tossed carelessly over a chair. I must have been absolutely exhausted last night, she thought.

According to her watch it was almost eight o'clock. She had slept without stirring for ten solid hours. Only on the rare occasions when she had taken a sleeping pill could she remember sleeping so heavily. She was sure she hadn't taken one the night before; she had barely managed to get her clothes off before she tumbled into bed. Surely Gran wouldn't . . .

Gran would, though, if she thought it necessary. The after-dinner coffee, perhaps. Stretching stiffened muscles, Meg had to admit it might have been a good idea. She felt a thousand percent better. But it had not been Gran who opened her door and sent Henrietta to call her to breakfast. Gran never played practical jokes. That was more like Frances, in her jolly old housekeeper role. Or Cliff. Meg would never forget the time he had crept into her room and tossed a cat—not Henrietta, one of Gran's earlier pets—onto the bed where she lay sleeping. Her screams, and those of the terrified animal, had aroused the entire household, and Cliff had been grounded for a week.

Meg followed Henrietta's example and relaxed, lost in old memories. They weren't all unhappy. The room itself, unchanged since she had left for college—never to return except for brief holidays—reminded her of the fun she and Gran had had selecting the dainty chintzes and rose-flowered wallpaper, the airy gauze that draped the bed like a princess's couch—or a bed in a high-class bordello, Meg thought, grinning as she recalled Dan's thoughtless comment. She had been almost as outraged as Gran, and Dan had promptly apologized—to Gran. He had winked at her behind Gran's back. . . .

She had been ten or eleven at the time—too young to share Dan's amusement, too old for the Winnie the Pooh wallpaper and pictures of kittens the ruffly chintz was to replace. She and Gran had picked out that wallpaper too, when she moved from the west wing where she had lived with her parents. Her room in the west wing had wallpaper printed with horses and elephants and trapeze performers, and a lamp shaped like a clown; his nose lit up, a bright red ball, when the switch was turned on. Her father loved circuses, he had started taking her when she was barely old enough to walk. . . . No clowns in the new room. Winnie was safe, Winnie was safely different. Selecting that paper hadn't been much fun, though. Even at six she was old enough to know why everything had to be different, and Gran's strained effort to be cheerful was almost as painful as tears. The rose-spattered paper was better. Two layers and four years away from the clowns. . . .

Henrietta Marie jumped down from the bed and walked to the door, reaching it just as someone knocked softly. Damned spooky cat, Meg thought sourly, and called, "Come in."

The door opened; the cat stalked out, tail waving like a banner; and one of the maids edged in, carrying a tray. "Miz Polanski thought you'd like your breakfast in bed this morning," she explained. "Hope I didn't disturb you; she said you'd be awake."

"As you see," Meg said, thinking dark thoughts about Frances. Jolly old Hannah was, in her own way, just as annoying as Mrs. Danvers.

The maid had hesitated, intimidated by her brusque tone and her sour expression. Meg couldn't remember her name; she smiled and indicated the desk. "Put it there, if you will, please; I can't eat in bed, I'm always spilling coffee on the sheets."

Reassured, the girl smiled back at her and deposited the tray as directed. Before she left she delivered a final message: "Your gramma would like you to come to her room when you're ready. No hurry, she says, just take your time."

After that, of course, Meg gulped down her breakfast and rushed through her ablutions. Choosing something to wear wasn't difficult; she had only brought a few clothes. Wrenching the black dress off its hanger, she tossed it into a corner of the closet. She would never wear it again. Gran was right, she should never have worn it in the first place. She put on a bright yellow blouse and matching Liberty print skirt and hastened to her grandmother's suite, where she was rewarded for her efforts by being allowed to assist in the endless production of thank-you notes.

At the best of times it was not an activity she would have enjoyed. At this particular time, with so many more urgent problems on her mind, it was frustrating as well as painful. But Gran was firm—and astonishingly well organized. The cards from the innumerable wreaths and bouquets had been collected, before the offerings were sent to hospitals and nursing homes, and Gran had already sorted them into categories—old friends, local business acquaintances, customers, out-of-town business contacts. Each category required a different kind of notepaper, and a different degree of formality. Mary lingered over the cards and messages, smiling, reading some aloud. When she finally dismissed Meg, the latter had a raging headache and a strong urge to run around in circles, howling like a mad dog.

When she reached the sanctuary of her room, she collapsed with a groan into a beruffled chair. That ghastly chore was over, but there were others almost as unpleasant awaiting her. Her grandmother had dismissed her with the cheerful reminder of an appointment she couldn't remember having made. This afternoon she and Uncle George, accompanied by their legal advisers and a representative of the Infernal Revenue, as Dan had called it, were supposed to inventory the famous jewelry collection. Technically, Meg already owned a good part of it. Dan had taken full advantage of the tax laws relating to gifts, and for years he and Gran had been transferring title to the most valuable pieces. Once upon a time viewing the collection had been a rare treat, for Dan was jealous of his treasures and seldom invited even his nearest and dearest into the basement room, steel-lined and -roofed, where he kept them. Not this time; it was going to be a complicated, tedious business, deciding what belonged to whom and verifying the legality of the gifts, with Infernal Revenue nose down on the trail of any possible error. These reminders of Dan would be particularly poignant, for of all the wonders that had passed through his hands, these were the ones he had cherished most, the pieces he couldn't bear to part with. Remembering the intent, glistening gleam in his eyes as he studied them, the reverence of his touch, Meg wondered whether they had not been dearer to him than any human being.

Then there was the store. Fond memories were replaced by fury as Meg considered that incredible bequest. What on earth had been on Dan's mind when he added that clause to his will? He knew how she felt about the store and the business. Was this a last-ditch attempt to force her into the position she had refused to take? Knowing Dan as she did, she could well believe it, but if he really wanted her to take over the store, saddling her with an unknown, unattractive partner like Mr. Riley was surely counterproductive. Unless . . . an unwilling grin softened Meg's face. Dan knew her so well. The conditions of the bequest were so peculiar that curiosity and exasperation—and well-founded suspicions of what his true motive might be—would force her to investigate further before acting.

She glanced at the clock. It was ten after twelve. She ought to be "freshening up" for lunch, as Gran had gently suggested. Gran had also suggested she change, which was not only unnecessary but impractical; her packing had been done in such frantic haste that she had brought only the bare necessities. If she hadn't been in such a frenzy of grief and confusion she would have realized she'd have to stay in Seldon for some time. She ought to go shopping, pick up a few changes of clothing; she ought to call her boss and tell him she needed another week's leave. He had already called twice, asking when she would be back. Sweet, kind, sympathetic Jack. . . . He had fired one employee for taking a month off after his wife had given birth to a little boy whose serious heart defect necessitated several long, agonizing operations. By those standards the death of a grandparent didn't deserve more than eight hours leave. So let him fire me, Meg thought. I hate the mean-minded son of a bitch anyway, and I don't need the job. . . . I really don't need the job. Funny, I hadn't thought of it that way before. I'll call later, while he's out of the office on one of those three-martini lunches of his, and leave a message. I can't cope with his reproaches and complaints now.

It was now twenty minutes after twelve, but Meg didn't reach for the phone. Nick had said he would call at noon.

In the frenzy of packing and rushing to catch a 6 A.M. train she hadn't had time to call him after she got the news. Instead she had telephoned from Seldon later that day. Nick didn't like her to call him at the office, but as soon as she explained what had happened he had been warmly sympathetic. He had sent flowers, not only to the funeral home, but to her—pink roses, a delicate compromise between the crimson of life and love, and the white of mourning. "A friend of yours, dear?" Gran had asked, studying the carefully formal message. "How nice. I'll let you write the note, then, but be sure to say how much we all appreciate his thoughtfulness."

Dear innocent Gran. She hadn't met Nick, but once, when Dan was in New York without her, Meg had decided the two men in her life ought to meet. Fortunately it had been a brief encounter—predinner drinks at the Carlyle, where Dan was staying—for it certainly could not have been considered a successful one. It had taken Dan about thirty seconds to comprehend the situation and condemn it; and when Dan disapproved of something he took no pains to conceal his feelings. Meg's thoughts fled from that uncomfortable memory to the last time she had seen her grandfather, on his final trip to the city.

"So. No young man in the picture yet?"

He peered at her over the rims of the glasses Gran had finally persuaded him to acquire. "I know you don't need them, dear, but they make you look so distinguished!"

"No young man. Nobody middle-aged or elderly, either."

"Hmph. That fellow—what's his name—still hanging around?"

"Nick?" He knew the name perfectly well. The pretended lapse of memory was his way of expressing disapproval.

"He's still hanging around," she said. "Don't be so stuffy, Dan. You liked him. You said you did."

"That was before I found out he was a married man. Call me old-fashioned if you want—"

"You're old-fashioned." She grinned at him, but instead of responding he only grunted and turned his attention to his plate of sauerbraten.

They were lunching at Hugo's, a small German restaurant on the East Side, which Dan claimed as his own private discovery. It had remained his own private discovery because the cooking, while perfectly adequate, had nothing to recommend it to gourmet-conscious New Yorkers. Dan liked the casual ambience and enjoyed practicing the ungrammatical German he had acquired during his "first war." Now he raised his voice: "Achtung, waiter, some salz, bitte."

That condiment having been promptly supplied, Dan returned to his earlier grievance. "I'm not old-fashioned, damn it. I'm thinking about you. There's no future for you with that guy. He'll never divorce his wife—"

"I hope not. I'd hate to be stepmother to those rotten kids of his."

Dan refused to be distracted by flippance. "You'll be thirty years old pretty soon."

"Not for two more years. I will of course slash my wrists on my thirtieth birthday if I'm still single."

Ordinarily Dan enjoyed these exchanges, sputtering loudly at her impertinence, as he called it, while secretly enjoying it. Not today. Instead of snapping back at her he pushed his plate away and said quietly, "I'd like to see my great-grandchild before I die, Meg."

It took her a moment to catch her breath. "That's not fair, Dan. Are you . . . ? You aren't . . . ?"

He didn't answer immediately, and she felt as if her heart were being squeezed in an invisible vise. Then he said pensively, "First I thought I'd tell you I only had a year to live. But I figured that might backfire."

She couldn't decide whether to laugh or throw something at him. "You tricky old devil!"

He went on in the same meditative voice, "Either you'd go out and get yourself pregnant by some jackass who wasn't fit to sire piglets, or you'd get your grandmother all worked up, or you'd call Doc Schwartz or—"

"Or all of the above. Don't do things like that to me, Dan."

"I didn't, did I? Meg." He didn't touch her, or take the hand she had extended; he wasn't given to physical expressions of affection. His voice deepened, always a sure sign of strong emotion with him, and the diminutive was one he hadn't used for years. "Mignon, I'm old. I'm damn old! Sometimes when I think about how old I am I can't believe it, you know? But I won't live forever. I'd like to know you'll be taken care of."

"What do you want me to do?" she demanded, torn between pain and anger. "I can take care of myself, Dan, I don't need a man for that. I won't marry some—some jackass who isn't fit to sire piglets just to carry on the Mignot dynasty."

"So who asked you to? All I'm asking is for you to start looking around. You know what you're doing, don't you? You're using that—that married man like a shield. What are you, scared of marriage? It's not so bad. I've stood it for over fifty years."

He gave her one of his wicked grins. Struggling for breath and for control, Meg wondered—as she had so often—whether those random comments of his were as random as they sounded. This one had certainly struck a nerve. Afraid—no, not of marriage, but of what it implied. Handing over your heart to someone who might drop it or throw it away like trash. . . .

She wouldn't let him see how much it hurt. "I thought you despised psychology," she said.

"I do. That's not psychology, it's plain common sense. You're not eating. Eat your food, it's good for you. You can't have dessert until you eat your sauerkraut."

"I don't want dessert. And I hate sauerkraut. See here, you tricky old—"

"You want dessert. You're too thin." One flick of a finger brought the waiter running. "Black Forest cake for me. You want that or the strawberry tart?"

"Neither."

"Two Black Forest cakes."

She almost hated him at that instant, for using love, pity, tenderness as weapons against her—for coming so close to the bone. "And if I am afraid of marriage," she said, not caring if the retreating waiter heard her, "I've good cause. Haven't I, Dan?"

It was one of the cruelest weapons she could have used, worse than any of his, but his face gave no sign of wounding. "I'm old, Meg," he repeated. "I'm damn old."

The box of tissues was across the room, on the bureau; childishly, Meg wiped her wet eyes with the back of her hand. Just as well Nick hadn't called while she was crying. She had made a complete fool of herself the last time she talked to him, blubbering and moaning,asking for help he had been unable to give. She couldn't wait any longer or she would be late for lunch—a deadly sin in Gran's book.

She was in the bathroom when the telephone rang.

Swearing, she dashed for it, but was too slow. Hearing Frances's voice, she cut in, "I've got it, Frances. Thank you. You can hang up."

Several seconds passed before she heard the click that indicated—she hoped—that the housekeeper was no longer on the line. Nick had listened for it too; amusement colored his deep voice when he spoke. "That, I take it, was Mrs. Danvers."

"Damned if I know who she is today," Meg said. "It's almost twelve-thirty. I had given up expecting to hear from you." She pushed back a damp curl that had fallen over her forehead, wishing she could take back that last sentence.

"I was in a meeting," Nick explained. "I told you it might not always be possible for me—"

"I know, I know. That was an explanation, not an accusation." Meg twisted the hair around her finger. "This is a ridiculous arrangement anyway, it's inconvenient for both of us, and it's unnecessary."

"What about your grandmother?"

"I was being overprotective. Habit, I suppose; Dan always treated her like a fragile flower. I suspect she's not as unworldly as she let him believe."

"Whatever you say." He accepted her rationalization more easily than she could do. "You sound much better. Everything all right?"

Meg laughed, briefly and humorlessly. "At the moment everything is all wrong."

"It must seem that way. There are always a million painful little details to deal with after a death. As the heir—"

"He left everything to Gran. Except . . ."

"Except?"

A rap at the closed door stopped her before she could explain. "It's too complicated to go into now," she said. "I'm already late for lunch."

"I understand. I wish I could do something to help. Call anytime—any evening—if you feel like unburdening yourself."

But telephone calls, especially on his terms—why not on hers?—were a poor substitute for what she really wanted; his physical presence, warm and near. She couldn't invite him to come to the house, Gran would start asking coy questions about his intentions, and then she'd have to invent some unbelievable story or admit the truth. But there was a charming country inn in Patterson's Mill, eight miles away. . . .

The knock came again, more peremptory this time. "I have to hang up," Meg said. "I'll talk to you later."

After hanging up she went to the door and flung it open. She had expected Frances; the frown that darkened her features didn't relax when she recognized Cliff.

He stepped back, raising his hands in a gesture of mock defense. "Don't shoot, lady, it's not my fault. Frances made me do it. She says you're six and a half minutes late for lunch."

His bright eyes moved from her face, examining the room behind her with unconcealed curiosity. Meg stepped out into the hall and closed the door. "I was expecting Frances herself."

"Then I forgive you for glowering." He fell into step with her as she started toward the stairs. "Sorry I interrupted your telephone call."

The candid admission that he had been eavesdropping startled her into a near stumble. Smoothly he caught her arm and steadied her. He was a head taller than she; when she looked up at him his eyes met hers without shame, and his smile broadened. "I couldn't make out what you were saying," he said. "Just the sound of your voice. I figured you weren't loony enough yet to talk to yourself—though I wouldn't blame you."

His hand did not loosen its hold; it was smooth and deeply tanned, with long slim fingers. "Your sympathy touches me," Meg said dryly.

"Oh, I'm very good at useless words of concern." He released her at last, and gestured her forward. "But in your case I might even be willing to break my rule of noninvolvement in other people's problems. Is there anything I can do?"

"I wouldn't want you to strain yourself. Or, to put it more courteously—"

"Butt out? Wait a minute."

With a sudden agile jump he stepped in front of her so that she had no choice but to stop or push him aside. "You've been avoiding me ever since you got here. There's no reason why you should like me; we've scarcely seen one another for years, and I don't suppose your memories of our shared childhood are tender ones—"

"You were a spoiled brat and a bully."

"*I* was the bully, *you* were the spoiled brat. Actually, I gave up bullying girls a while back. I really would like to help. I know—perhaps better than anyone else—how difficult this is for you. I loved the old rascal too."

Meg was moved, not only by what he said but by what he was careful not to say. They had more in common than memories of play and childish quarrels: their shared loss and the shame of that loss.

"Thank you," she said.

"*De nada*. And if you ever want to marry me, I'd be happy to consider the idea."

"What?"

"Oh, sorry. I thought maybe Dan had mentioned it. There was a time when he was all gung ho about the possibility, and of course my old man would go bonkers with joy. But don't let it bother you; it was just a thought."

"I certainly won't let it bother me." She pushed past him and went on down the hall, heels clicking angrily. He fell in behind her; she heard him whistling softly through his teeth, and felt certain he was smiling. Damn the man, he could still get to her—first softening her up by a word of kindness, then catching her off guard with that outrageous suggestion. She had been right about him in the first place; the leopard had not changed its spots.

By late afternoon she had a raging headache. Bad air was not the cause; the vault had an elaborate ventilation system, not for the benefit of the humans who might visit it, but for the treasures stored there. Some incorporated materials that could be damaged by heat or humidity: leather belts and book covers, garments embroidered with gold thread and jewels. A few gems were also affected adversely by environmental changes. Opals could crack or lose their fire, ivory tended to mold when it was damp and to split when the air was too dry.

Ivory and opal and moonstone, precious rubies and emeralds and cornflower-blue Kashmir sapphires—every known gem in every conceivable setting had passed before her that afternoon. Meg tried to focus her tired eyes on the object on the table in front of her: number 429 in Dan's inventory, a heavy gold pendant set with table-cut diamonds, rubies and emeralds, and bearing the enameled figures of Faith, Hope and Charity, their white bodies chastely draped in swirls of gold. From the bottom of the pendant hung three enormous pearls. It was one of the prizes of Dan's collection because it had been attributed to his "ancestor," the original Daniel Mignot. The style and workmanship were of the right period, late-sixteenth-century south German, but there was no certain way of knowing which of several contemporary masters had fashioned it.

The rustle of turning pages and the drone of voices, as Uncle George and the IRS man conversed, echoed in Meg's head like insects buzzing. She started as an arm encircled her shoulders, and turned her head dizzily to see Darren.

"Can't we finish this tomorrow?" he asked, not of her, but of the other men. "Miss Venturi is obviously not well."

She sank gratefully into the chair to which he led her, and took a sip of the water he poured. After a few moments her head cleared. "No, it's all right," she assured her uncle, who was bending over her. "I don't want to stop, I want to get this over with."

"You needn't stay," George assured her.

"I'd rather." Her lips set stubbornly. George grinned and patted her shoulder.

"No sense arguing with you, I know that look.

Gentlemen, we've almost finished; let's get it done."

Infernal Revenue had a heart, after all; the grim-faced young representative, who hadn't cracked a smile or said an unnecessary word throughout, stopped examining the objects with the suspicious air he had displayed, and rushed the rest of them through with scarcely more than a glance. The last half-dozen items were unfamiliar to Meg, and her flagging energy revived as they were displayed. One was particularly lovely: a necklace of opal plaques, shaped like lilies, veined and framed in diamonds, with curved emerald leaves. "Surely that's Lalique," she exclaimed.

Her uncle laughed. "Dan always said you were his best pupil. He bought this last year, from the daughter of the woman for whom it was made in 1908. It's never been photographed or displayed." Meg took her loupe from her pocket and examined the piece appreciatively. The famous signature was there, stamped on the clasp, but she hadn't needed to see it; the other signature, of design and workmanship, had been equally unmistakable.

The Lalique pendant was the last. The IRS took its leave, its bureaucratic facade cracking into a smile that was almost pleasant as it shook Meg's hand and thanked her for her cooperation. It—he, Meg corrected herself—he's probably as glad to be finished as I am.

Darren refused her invitation to stay for tea, pleading a previous engagement. "I do need to go over some things with you, Meg," he said. "May

I have my secretary call you to arrange an appointment?"

"I'll call," Meg said. "Tomorrow or the next day?"

"At your convenience," Darren said seriously.

After he had gone, George ran his fingers through his hair and sighed deeply. "Whew. As my son would say, it's been a bitch of a day. Ready for a drink, Meg? You deserve one."

"I'd rather have ten minutes of your time," Meg replied.

"How about both? I was about to lead you into my lair, so we could booze it up in private. Not that your grandmother would object if we asked for ouzo instead of orange pekoe. . . ."

Meg laughed and took his arm, squeezing it affectionately. "No, she'd just look sad and hurt. She won't be down for another half hour, so she need never know. Can you supply Scotch as well as ouzo?"

"Scotch, but not ouzo. I just couldn't resist the alliteration. Hurry up, before Frances catches us."

He swept her along the hall and into his office, a small but comfortably appointed room near the library. It was in this ambience that Meg always pictured her uncle when she had occasion to think of him; over the years he had added various homey touches, photographs and knickknacks and unfashionably comfortable furniture, like the sofa in front of the fireplace. It was worn and lumpy-looking now; no doubt some part of its dilapidation was due to her, for she had spent many hours sprawled across the cushions, talking to George. He was always ready to lay aside his work and listen, grave and sympathetic, while she complained about Cliff's teasing and her grandparents' strict, old-fashioned rules, and her stupid teachers—everything and anything, except the one subject that disturbed her most. She had known that subject was not to be discussed, even with Uncle George—particularly with Uncle George.

Apparently this was to be a business rather than a social occasion. George placed a chair for her next to the desk, and she sank gratefully into the soft leather while George opened a Chippendale cabinet to disclose a well-stocked bar. After he had handed her her drink he filled a glass for himself and sat down behind the desk.

For a moment he hesitated, obviously searching for words. Then he said, with a half-smile, "Here's looking at you, kid."

Meg wasn't sure how to respond. The conventional, joking toasts seemed inappropriate. She remembered one of Dan's favorites, an enigmatic, sardonic epigram dating from Roman times. "Be of good cheer; all men are mortal." That might have been appropriate, but it certainly wasn't very cheerful. So she simply smiled and raised her glass.

George never touched alcohol; his glass contained only tonic and ice. He drank thirstily. "The air in that vault is as dry as a desert," he complained. "Would you like something taller and wetter with your Scotch?"

"No, thanks. I expect your throat is dry because you did most of the talking. As I am about to ask you to do now."

"Don't tell me, let me guess. Mr. Riley?"

"Right the first time."

"It didn't take much insight," her uncle said with a smile. "You have a more immediate interest than anyone else, but the whole town is talking about that legacy."

"You didn't know about it?"

"My dear girl! I'd have had the decency to warn you in advance—and if I had known before Dan died, I'd have tried to persuade him to change his mind."

"Why? Do you know anything to Mr. Riley's discredit?"

"I don't know anything at all about him. That's why."

"Do you think Dan was senile? That there was—what do they call it—undue influence?"

The play of conflicting emotions on her uncle's face was easy to read. At last he said reluctantly, "I'd like to say yes to both, but I can't. Darren Blake is the person you should talk to; but I feel sure he'd have told me, and your grandmother, if he felt Dan was incapable of making a proper will."

"I feel sure of that too," Meg said. "Nor am I keen on the idea of trying to overturn that will.

Aside from the expense and inconvenience, Dan would come back to haunt me."

"He probably would at that. So what do you intend to do?"

"I'm not going to do anything until I find out more about my new partner."

"You surely can't mean to let that arrangement stand?"

"It doesn't appeal to me," Meg said, knowing he would appreciate the irony of that understatement. "Any more than Mr. Riley appeals to me. But Dan obviously thought well of him, and . . . Oh, I don't know, Uncle George, it's such a mess—and the most disturbing thing is not that Dan would leave a half-interest in the store to Mr. Riley, but that he'd leave me the other half. What was he trying to accomplish? He knew how I felt. He never accepted it, but he knew. I never could decide whether he was too selfish to care about my feelings or too bullheaded to accept them!"

"He was selfish, and he was bullheaded," her uncle said sympathetically. "The fact that we loved him needn't blind us to his faults. He had no right to force you into a career you didn't want."

"If it were just that simple." Meg sighed. "On the surface, the bequest can be viewed as Dan's final attempt to get his way. If he had left the store to me free and clear I could have sold out. As it is, I feel obliged to give this man the chance Dan obviously wanted him to have."

"You do?" Her uncle studied her in surprise.

"Meg, dear, aren't you being a little too noble? I admire you for it, but—"

"I'm not being noble. I'm just trying to be fair. It isn't Mr. Riley's fault that we're in this absurd position; he shouldn't have to pay for Dan's mistakes. I don't know what he did for Dan. He must have done something or Dan wouldn't have felt he owed him this. I don't want to owe him. I want to pay my debts, and Dan's."

"Your attitude does you credit, dear. I wish I could answer the questions you've raised, but the store was Dan's baby; I had very little to do with the hiring end of it. All I know about Mr. Riley is that he showed up one day and Dan took him on. And promoted him. When I asked who he was Dan said, 'He's a damned good goldsmith. That's enough for me and it should be enough for you.'"

"Is he?" Meg asked.

"A damned good goldsmith? I'm no judge, Meg. But he'd have had to be to satisfy Dan."

"True."

Her uncle studied her downcast face. "What is it, Meg?" he asked gently. "You needn't make a decision immediately; it will take some time to prove the will. What's really worrying you about this man?"

She hadn't meant to tell him. It sounded so absurd—Frances's wild accusation, Riley's reaction. But George had always been able to read her mind. As she stumbled through the story, she felt as though she had emptied her mind of something that lay festering within it, infecting every other thought.

His reaction was swift and comforting. "Meg, that's nonsense. Dan was ninety years old—"

"Ninety!"

"He'd always lied about his age," George said, with a faint smile. "Not that it mattered. Eighty-two, ninety—he was old, Meg. He died a natural death."

"Was there . . ."

It took him a while to understand what she meant, and a look of horrified disbelief transformed his face. "An autopsy? You know there wasn't. There was no reason for one. You can talk to Dr. Schwartz if you like."

"No, no. I don't know why I asked that, I guess I'm just being morbid."

Her disclaimer didn't have the effect she had intended; her uncle continued to look disturbed. He began fingering the objects on the desk. "Sometimes I think Frances is more trouble than she's worth. You ought to know better than to take anything she says seriously; but if she's spreading this around town . . . I'm afraid there are some people who would take it seriously."

"Surely not."

Her uncle raised his eyes from the small cardboard box whose lid he was unconsciously lifting and replacing. "You did—seriously enough to mention it to me. Mr. Riley isn't popular, and you know small-town gossip."

"You don't believe they would actually do anything . . . do you?"

"There hasn't been a lynching in these parts for centuries," her uncle said lightly. "No, my dear, I don't think they would do anything. Forget it. Or, better still, talk to Darren Blake. And I'll drop a casual word to Frances that she could be sued for defamation of character if she doesn't control her imagination."

"Good." There was no more to be said, and no time for more; her grandmother would be coming down shortly. Meg was about to rise when a gleam of warm metallic color caught her eye, from inside the box her uncle was absently turning in his hands. "What's that?" she asked. "Something that escaped the eagle eye of the tax man?"

"You have an eagle eye yourself." Her uncle handed her the box. "It's obviously old, but that's all I can tell; you know more about these things than I do. It came in the mail today."

"In the mail?" Meg repeated wonderingly. She took the ring out of its box and held it to the light.

The heavy gold of the hoop had the soft glow of age and long handling. Instead of being set with gems, the flat bezel was intricately carved and coated with enamel. Black-enameled lettering twined around the hoop.

"It's old, all right," Meg murmured. "Probably seventeenth century. Does the top . . ."

It did; the catch yielded to the pressure of her fingernail, and the top opened. Her uncle leaned across the desk. "I didn't see that. What is it, a poison ring?"

"No." Meg turned the ring so that he could see what lay inside the opened top—a skeleton, scarcely an inch long, carved with exquisite precision and coated with white enamel. The oblong shape of the bezel, she now realized, was that of a coffin.

George was fascinated. "It's beautifully made, isn't it? But what kind of person would wear a grisly thing like that?"

"It could be a memento mori ring," Meg said slowly. "A reminder of death, literally; our ancestors weren't so much morbid as more realistic than we—willing to face facts. Or a memorial ring, left to a surviving relative—son, husband, wife, whatever—by someone who died. There's an inscription on the shank, but I can't quite . . ." She reached into her pocket for her loupe and focused it. The lettering was not only small, but in ornate Gothic script and a foreign language. It took some time for her to puzzle it out. "*'Hier lieg' ich, Und wart' auf dich. . . .'* Here I lie, and . . . and . . ."

"German," her uncle said interestedly. "There's a German dictionary in the library—"

"I don't need a dictionary. 'Here I lie, and wait for you.' That's what it says."

"Strange ideas of sentiment those old Germans had," George said with a grin.

"They weren't the only ones." All at once Meg had the impression that the object she held had changed its texture, from smooth metal to something rougher and more brittle—like old bone. Involuntarily her fingers released their grip; the ring dropped onto the desk, where it bounced and rolled until George slapped his hand down on it.

"Who sent it?" she asked.

"I don't know. It came in today's mail, in one of those padded envelopes, but there was no return address."

"The envelope was addressed to you?"

"It must have been, or Frances wouldn't have put it on my desk. . . . What are you doing?"

"The wastebasket has been emptied." Meg straightened, but did not return to her chair.

"Of course. Whatever Frances's other failings, she runs the house efficiently." Her brusque questions and obvious agitation had left him more bewildered than offended. "Was this something you were expecting? If I opened your mail by mistake I apologize, I've gotten into the habit of assuming that anything on my desk is meant for me. There was no message—"

"Oh, but there was," Meg said. "'Here I lie and wait for you.' You, Uncle George."

3

HER UNCLE STARED at her as if she had made an obscene suggestion. "Me?"

"You. And '*ich*—I—'" She indicated the ring, which lay on its side with the top still up. The tiny skeleton shone pale against the black-enamel lining of its coffin.

"Oh! You mean. . . ." Comprehension dawned on him; he transferred his incredulous stare to the ring.

"I mean it's a threat, Uncle George."

George sat back in his chair. "Now, Meg," he said, in the soothing voice one employs when speaking to a frightened child. "You're letting your imagination run away with you. Small wonder, after the last few days—but whatever gave you such a morbid idea?"

Meg hesitated. She couldn't admit the truth—that the "morbid idea" had seemed to come from outside herself, like a distant, dictatorial voice. That *was* morbid. It must have been her subconscious at work, using data she couldn't consciously recall. "What other explanation is there?"

Instead of answering, George looked toward the door. Meg heard it too—the faint creak of hinges. She swung around.

The door opened. "It's a fair cop," said Cliff. "I got so interested in the conversation I leaned against the door. Relax, coz."

Meg dropped into her chair. Her uncle began, "Of all the contemptible—"

"I know, I know." Cliff sauntered into the room and perched on a corner of the desk.

"Eavesdropping is *not* nice. However, it can be very informative."

"Why didn't you just walk in?" George demanded. "You usually do."

"I wasn't sure you'd continue this absolutely fascinating conversation," Cliff admitted. Eyebrows and lips were quirked in one of his maddening smiles, but Meg realized he was not amused. He picked up the ring and held it to the light. "Charming little item. Lifelike portrait. Touching sentiment. Why didn't you tell me about this, Dad?"

"I saw no reason to. Meg is tired and overwrought. There must be some innocent explanation."

The speech was so stiff and artificial that Meg wondered whether her suggestion had surprised him quite as much as he pretended. Cliff's eyebrows edged up another half inch. "Oh, yeah? Can you think of one?"

George looked as if he would have preferred to tell his son where to go and what to do to himself when he got there, but he restrained himself. "Perhaps someone wants to sell his collection."

"So he sends you a sample through the mail, without a return address or covering letter?" He turned to Meg. "Any idea where this might have come from?"

Meg stiffened. "If you're implying—"

"If I thought you'd sent it I'd say so," Cliff replied coolly. "You're the authority on this type of jewelry, aren't you?"

"I'm not an authority on anything. Oh—do you mean the posy rings? I collect them, yes. But this isn't—"

"This has a verse inscribed on it, like the posy rings. What's the difference?"

"Clifford, I don't like your attitude," George exclaimed. "You have no business talking to Meg in that tone of voice."

"I don't mind, Uncle George. He has every right to be concerned about you." And, Meg added to herself, she much preferred Cliff's blunt questions to his smirks and insinuations. She turned to her cousin. "The posies are betrothal or wedding or friendship rings—tokens of affection. I suppose the mourning rings could be viewed in the same light, given the attitudes of the times in which they were made. Life spans were shorter, child mortality was high, people died at home instead of in hospitals. And they believed, sincerely and unquestioningly, in an afterlife. Marriage was for eternity; husbands and wives didn't think, they *knew* they would find their partners waiting for them at the Pearly Gate."

"Now that's a gruesome thought," Cliff began.

He was back in character, Meg thought. She frowned at him. "Dan bought quite a bit of Victorian mourning jewelry in the line of business, but to the best of my knowledge he never specialized in it. Some of it has become very collectible—hair jewelry, for instance."

"But this isn't Victorian." Casually Cliff slipped the ring onto his finger. It fit perfectly, and Meg repressed a shudder. He went on, "If I'm any judge, this is older and much more valuable. Not the kind of thing a local yokel would find in his granny's jewel box."

"You seem to be something of an authority yourself," Meg said.

"One picks up odd information here and there," Cliff murmured.

"Well, you're right. This is probably seventeenth century—German, obviously—and it is more likely to have come from a collection than from a hoard of family jewelry. Are you implying that it belongs in one of Dan's collections? Or mine?"

"Isn't that the most logical conclusion?"

"Nonsense," his father said brusquely. "There are thousands of people who collect antique jewelry. Time's getting on, Meg. Your grandmother will be waiting for us."

"You can't just drop the subject," Meg protested. "Maybe I'm wrong—I hope to God I am—but we ought to make an effort to investigate. I'm ninety-nine percent sure this—this object didn't come from my collection, but I'll check the inventory anyway."

"Not tonight, you won't." George rose. "You're going to have tea with your grandmother, eat a good dinner and go to bed."

Cliff got up from the corner of the desk, where he had perched. "Dad's right, coz, you've had a busy day. Anyway, it will be a waste of time. This adorable object"—he stretched out his hand, admiring the ring—"didn't come from your collection."

"Take it off," Meg said sharply.

"Must I? Don't you think it's me?"

"Cliff," his father said wearily.

Grinning, Cliff returned the ring to its box. He had always enjoyed teasing her, but Meg had a feeling he had observed her superstitious reaction to the ring. Not for any reward would she have slipped it on her finger, and it gave her a cold chill to see anyone else wear it.

"I hope I need not mention that I don't want Mary to hear of this," George said, fixing his son with a stern look.

"You need not," Cliff said, visibly resentful. Then the familiar, hateful smile came back, and he turned to Meg. "Aren't you going to ask me where I think the ring came from? No? Well, I'll tell you anyway. I'll give you five-to-one odds—"

"No, you won't." Meg headed for the door. "I'm not interested in guessing games, nor in your opinion."

Cliff didn't persist. He didn't have to, she knew what he had been about to say.

Cliff offered to accompany her to the store the next morning. It was an offer she literally couldn't refuse, short of having him bound and gagged and locked in his room. After she had turned down the suggestion that he drop her off, saying she preferred to walk, he blandly announced that he could use the exercise too. He didn't look it. He had his father's slim, wiry build, but while age and sedentary habits had thickened George's body, Cliff's was solid muscle. He was wearing casual clothes that morning, a knit shirt and form-fitting jeans, and the form they fit was definitely worth displaying.

The distance was only a little over a mile. The Manor had once been on the outskirts of town. Now new housing developments and shopping centers surrounded but did not enclose it; the Mignots owned almost fifty acres, and they had hung on to them despite the increasingly tempting prices offered by developers.

When they left the shade of the tree-lined driveway Meg reached into her purse for her sunglasses. It was a beautiful summer morning; the fresh green foliage and bright flower beds, the wide lawns and old houses looked like a picture postcard of small-town America. As they passed a white frame house whose front porch was shaded by climbing roses, Cliff waved and called out. "Hi, there, Mrs. Henderson. Nice day."

Meg saw the face squinting at them from behind the veil of roses and produced a halfhearted wave of her own. There was no response. Cliff had lengthened his stride; she had to run a few steps to catch up with him.

"What's your hurry?" she asked.

"If you hesitate she insists you come in for a chat. Don't you remember her?"

"I remember her. I must admit I hoped she had gone to a better world."

"Only the good die young."

"So they say. Why were you being so charming to the old bat?"

"I like to keep on good terms with people," Cliff said. "You never know when they can be useful to you."

"I hope you'll keep that in mind this morning."

"Why, darling, whatever do you mean?"

"You know what I mean. And I know why you insisted on coming with me. Why do you think Mr. Riley was the one who sent that ring to your father?"

Cliff began, "Logically—"

"Logic has nothing to do with it. You don't—you can't—prove anything or you would have told Uncle George. What have you got against the man?"

"He has no sense of humor."

"Damn it, Cliff—"

"I might just as reasonably ask why you're so set on defending him."

"I have this silly idea that a person is innocent until proven guilty, that's why."

"You have a weakness for the underdog, that's why," Cliff retorted. "Far be it from me to criticize such a charmingly naive view of the world. I'll leave you to make up your own mind about Riley. You will anyway. I'm afraid my own profession has made me somewhat more cynical about the human race."

"What do you do for a living, anyway?"

"You mean you haven't followed my career with affectionate interest?" His eyebrows lifted. "I followed yours. Your meteoric rise in the advertising business has been a source of inspiration to—"

"Oh, shut up, Cliff. Why can't you answer a simple question?"

"There's no simple answer, darling. I've been a bartender, lifeguard, waiter, chauffeur, deckhand, reporter, actor—summer stock and off Broadway—"

"I never saw your name listed."

"The off-Broadway role was that of the corpse in a thriller," Cliff explained with a grin. "You didn't let me finish. Musician, gigolo—they called it an escort service—construction worker, truck driver—"

"I get the picture. An all-round Renaissance man."

"My father prefers a shorter, less flattering term. He wanted me to study accounting."

"I see."

"I thought you might," Cliff said. "At the moment I am more or less employed in an insurance agency. They were very sympathetic to my request for prolonged personal leave, possibly because they hope I'll prolong it indefinitely."

Further conversation was impossible; they were approaching the town center, and Cliff had a greeting for everyone they met. Meg could only murmur and smile in reply to the people who called her by name and expressed their sympathy. She was annoyed by Cliff's attempt to suggest a parallel between his situation and her own. Rejecting his father's demands didn't mean he had to turn himself into a drifter.

When they reached the store she stopped short, gripped by poignant memories. It was exactly as she remembered it: the faded green awning, the time-darkened oak door with its delicately etched glass. The show window was draped in dark blue velvet; Dan always maintained velvet showed off gems to their best advantage. There were only half a dozen pieces in the window: a heavy gold watch chain, double-linked; a set of wedding and engagement rings, rubies in an elaborate gold setting. . . . She couldn't take in the rest of them, her eyes were blurred.

Hoping Cliff hadn't observed her brief lapse, she walked to the door, which was set back from the sidewalk and the store-front. Quickly as she had moved, he was before her, flinging the door wide. Chimes rang a familiar, silvery peal.

The interior, cool and shadowy after the bright sunlight of outdoors, looked like Ali Baba's treasure cave. Glittering gems and gleaming metal reflected the soft glow of the lamps. They were of two types, ordinary electric bulbs and fluorescent strip lighting. Another of Dan's lectures came back to her: rubies glow brighter and more brilliant under electric lights, but those same lights darken sapphires, except for the finest Ceylon and Kashmir stones. Strip lighting for sapphires. . . .

A woman behind the counter to the right looked up when they entered. For almost the first time that day Meg saw a face she recognized, and when she said, "Hello, Candy. You haven't changed a bit," she was conscious of the irony in the trite greeting. The heavy, inexpertly applied makeup didn't soften the other woman's angular jawline, or render her long, mournful face any less equine. She had painted bright crimson lips over the narrow outlines of her own.

Candy started, dropped the cloth with which she had been wiping the countertop, and banged her head on the edge of the glass when she stopped to retrieve it. Meg approached her with exclamations of concern, which only seemed to increase the other woman's discomfort. Tears flooded her eyes.

Proffering tissues and sympathy, Meg wondered why on earth Dan had hired this limp dishrag of a woman. Candy had been the class scapegoat when they were in grammar school; clumsy, homely and painfully shy, she had been the butt of cruel jokes and rude humor, to which she had consistently responded by bursting into tears. Even at that age Meg had known there was nothing so tempting to bullies as a weeping victim; exasperation with the bullies rather than affection for their prey had sometimes moved her to Candy's defense. Candy hadn't returned the favor. When the class comedians turned on Meg, Candy was usually in the front row of the giggling audience.

"I didn't realize you had come to work for Dan," Meg said.

Candy's tears overflowed. "I'm going to miss

him so much," she mumbled, smearing mascara across her cheeks with the sodden tissue.

"We all will." Meg's voice was cool. Candy's watery grief left her completely unmoved. Candy had always cried at the drop of a hat, or an unkind word. Now Candy would probably tell her friends—if she had any—that Meg Venturi was hard and unsympathetic. She was equally unmoved by that concern, but she was determined to be courteous. "Thanks for keeping the store open. It can't have been easy these last few days."

"I—oh. Oh, no." The tears stopped as if a spigot had been shut off. "He's the one you should thank. He's been wonderful. Feeling the way he did about Mr. Mignot—he's not the sort of person who shows his feelings, actually, but any sensitive person could see how bad he felt."

She was as rambling and silly as ever, but she had made one thing eminently, embarrassingly clear. He's got one defender anyway, Meg thought. Aloud she said, "You're speaking of Mr. Riley?"

"Yes. Riley."

"Is he here?"

"Of course. He's been here every day. The only time we closed up was for the funeral. In respect. It would have looked funny if we—"

"I wasn't criticizing, Candy. I was simply asking for information."

Her patience was wearing thin, and her voice showed it. Candy flushed unbecomingly. "He's in the back. In the shop. As usual. I can handle things out here, he trusts me."

"With good reason, I'm sure," Cliff said, giving Candy one of his warmest and most dazzling smiles. Her response—a faint, uncertain smile and an awkward wriggling movement—reminded Meg of a puppy hoping for a pat on the head. A female puppy, just going into heat and not quite sure what to do about it. . . . You're a bitch yourself, she told herself. She's pathetic. Give her a break.

"I'll go to him," she said, starting toward one of the doors at the back of the store.

"You can't go in there!" In sixth grade Candy had been the last one chosen when the class divided into teams for any sport, but she reached the door before Meg, the former track star. Barring it with her body, arms outstretched, she looked like a martyr prepared to die for her faith.

"Now just a minute," Cliff began.

"It's all right, Cliff," Meg said, suppressing her own annoyance. "I understand. I remember bursting in on Dan one time when he was soldering a chain. It startled him so, he singed all the hair off his left hand."

"So what do we do, wait with our hats in our hands till his Eminence decides to emerge?" Cliff demanded. "Knock on the door, Candy; or if you're too intimidated to do it, get out of the way and let me."

Candy didn't move. "He knows you're here,"

she said smugly. "The intercom is on. It's been on the whole time."

Now Meg didn't know whether to be furious at Candy, who clearly loved to see her being snubbed, or at Riley, who was doing the snubbing. He was probably sitting back there like a king in his audience chamber, smirking as he listened to Candy trying to patronize her.

"I expect he'll be out immediately then," she said. "Candy, your makeup is smeared all over your face. Go fix it before a customer comes in."

Her voice was quiet, but her tone was that of employer to employee. Candy's smug smile disappeared. She made a dash for the counter, glanced into one of the mirrors, squealed and headed for the restroom.

"Doesn't she remind you of the White Rabbit?" Cliff asked. " 'Oh, dear, oh, my ears and whiskers.' "

"Sssh. She'll hear you."

"Not likely. She's the type that turns on the faucets as soon as she goes in the john, for fear somebody will hear the toilet flush."

Cruel as it was, the appraisal was so accurate—as evidenced by the unmistakable rush of running water from behind the closed door—Meg couldn't help smiling. She seated herself on one of the plush-covered customers' chairs.

She had avoided the store over the last few years, but she had spent so much time there as a child and adolescent that every aspect of it was as familiar as her own apartment. The two doors at the back led to the office and the shop respectively. The daintily appointed powder room occupied a cubicle that was a later addition, along with the curtained alcove containing supplies for making tea and coffee. The teacups were porcelain; Dan wouldn't permit the abomination of disposable plastic for his customers. The idea was to persuade them to linger, relaxed and comfortable, while Dan wooed them with conversation, flattery, coffee and, if they liked, cigarettes. Dan had nothing but scorn for modern health fads. He had scattered ashtrays along the counter with a lavish hand, and for his favorite customers he supplied the frosted, raisin-studded rolls for which Ed's bakery was famous—warm from the oven, heavy with calories and cholesterol. Dan used to say he sold one piece of jewelry for every frosted bun. . . .

"He's taking his sweet time," Cliff complained.

"What?" Memories had made her lose track of the passage of time. "Oh—yes, he is, isn't he? You might check that intercom, Cliff. That's the switch, I think—there by the door."

When Cliff flicked the switch, faint sounds were heard—rustles and rhythmic tapping. "Why, that little bitch," he said softly. "She had it turned off. Women are the most—"

"Red light—sexist comment approaching," Meg said. "I expect she just forgot. Yoo-hoo, Mr. Riley. You've got company."

The tapping had already stopped. It was followed by other, less distinguishable sounds. Then the door opened.

He wore a heavy canvas apron over slacks and shirt; the metalworkers' protective eyeshade had been pushed up, ruffling his hair. The fabric of his shirt was worn by innumerable washings; it showed Meg that the muscles of his chest and shoulders were overdeveloped, out of proportion with the rest of his body. They would have been more appropriate to a blacksmith than a man who handled the delicate tools of the jeweler's craft. So would his hands have been. She could understand, though, why they were roughened by innumerable scrapes and scars. Dan's hands had once been that way too. No matter how carefully one handled the acids and sharp tools and hot metal, minor accidents were inevitable.

He said, "I'm sorry if I kept you waiting."

He didn't sound sorry; his voice might have come from the mechanical tape of a robot, it was completely without expression.

"That's all right. I should have called first."

"Why? You own the place."

Meg smiled. "Half of it."

"Yeah." With the slow, arrogant stride she had seen before, he crossed to the counter; but instead of taking the chair next to hers he went behind it—shopkeeper to customer. Reaching into his pocket he took out a crumpled pack of cigarettes.

"Smoking is bad for your health," Meg said.

"So I've been told." At least he didn't blow

smoke in her face. He stretched out a long arm and pulled one of the ashtrays toward him.

Cliff had controlled himself longer than Meg had expected he would. Now he burst out, "Riley, you have the manners of a Neanderthal. You'd better forget that high and mighty attitude, because you're in deep trouble. We came here to—"

"Talk," Meg said. "Cliff, kindly allow me to manage my own affairs."

Early in her business career she had learned to use her voice to intimidate people who underestimated her youthful face and small stature. The icy tone worked just as well on Cliff. It amused Riley. At least she assumed the odd curl of his lip was produced by amusement.

"Talk, huh?" He took a last drag on his cigarette and put it out. "Where's Candy?"

Candy was eavesdropping. Meg had seen the narrow slit along the edge of the washroom door. Now it opened and Candy emerged, painted like Belle Watling and simpering like Scarlett O'Hara.

"I'm sorry, Riley, I was just . . . Did you want me?"

Meg almost felt sorry for her. The question wouldn't have been so bad but for the longing look that accompanied it.

"I just wondered where you were," her employer replied coolly. "Why don't you take your lunch break now?"

"But it's only ten-thirty!"

"Coffee break, then."

"But I was. . . ." Her voice trailed away. Riley

fixed her with a dark, unblinking gaze, and waited. "Yes, all right. I'll just run across to the café. I won't be long."

"Take your time."

"Can I bring you anything? Coffee, a Danish—"

"No, thanks."

She dawdled as long as she could, pretending she couldn't find her purse, putting on a jacket she didn't need now that the early-morning chill was gone. Riley followed her to the door; when it finally closed after her he snapped the latch, and turned the sign from "Open" to "Closed."

"Now we won't be interrupted," he said, taking out another cigarette. "I don't know why it is, but I get this funny feeling you have something serious on your mind."

Cliff was mistaken. Riley did have a sense of humor—of sorts. She was tempted to reply in kind; she could play that game too, and it might be interesting to see which of them was better at it. But her own talent for sarcasm had been developed out of desperation, as a means of overcoming insecurity. She doubted insecurity had ever been one of Riley's problems. Having a face like his certainly helped. Unlike her own, which mirrored every emotion with annoying clarity, Riley's might have been cast of bronze. His heavy eyebrows shadowed deep-set eyes, making it difficult to read their expression, and his mouth had learned to give nothing away. Only the big clumsy-looking hands, constantly in motion with cigarette, matches and ashtray, suggested that he wasn't as confident as he appeared.

Hearing a harsh intake of breath from Cliff, who stood at her shoulder like a hired bodyguard, she opted for charm instead of a head-on attack. "Why, no, Mr. Riley, I haven't come to talk business. It's early days for that. I just thought we ought to get to know one another better."

"Oh, yeah?" Smoke trickled from his nostrils. One of those ancient idols, Meg thought wildly—Baal, with a fire in his belly, awaiting the sacrifice of the firstborn. "Well, okay. You can call me Riley."

"I just did."

"Not 'Mister.' Just Riley."

"Oh." So far he was ahead. Meg tilted her head and gave him a dimpled smile. "My friends call me Meg."

"Yeah." The way he watched her, eyes fixed and unblinking, reminded her of another of Dan's favorite adages. "Beware of the man who looks you straight in the eye; he's probably getting ready to stab you in the back."

After a moment, Riley went on, "I thought maybe you came to make me an offer."

The dimples didn't seem to be working. "Is that what you want?" Meg asked.

"Well, I don't suppose you're exactly thrilled at having me for a partner." Riley lit another cigarette. "It wouldn't have been my idea of an ideal arrangement either. But no—I don't want to sell my share. I'd prefer to buy yours."

Cliff gave a grunt of surprise and disbelief. Meg jabbed her elbow into his ribs.

"Do you have the cash?" she asked.

"No. But I'll raise it. Somehow."

His voice was flat and defiant, but the last word was in itself an admission of vulnerability.

Cliff had got his breath back. "How?" he demanded.

"Never mind," Meg said, cursing male egos in general and Cliff's in particular. "There's no need to make a hasty decision. The will won't be *probated* for some time." Dismissing the subject, she glanced at the contents of the display case. "You seem to be well stocked."

"Not bad," Riley said cautiously.

"That's nice. How did you price it?"

Riley glanced at the piece she had indicated, an inch-wide band bracelet delicately chased and set with topazes. "One seventy-five. It's gold-filled," he added, as her lips parted in incipient protest. "And the catch has been repaired—badly."

Cliff shifted position. "What we really came for," he began.

"Introductions," Meg said. "Get acquainted, a touch of nostalgia. All those good things." She stood up; Riley stalked her, step by stiff step, as she moved to the next counter. "Yes, very nice. May I see that tray of rings?"

With an odd, sidelong glance, he took out the tray and switched on a lamp. One of the stones glowed crimson and she smiled reminiscently. "That's a nice ruby."

"It would be if it were a ruby," Riley said.

"Spinel?"

"Right."

"It's still beautiful." She slipped the ring on her finger, turned it to admire the setting, returned it to its place. "Too big for me. What's this one—a regard ring? No, the stones are wrong. Moonstone, amethyst, ruby, another ruby . . . or is it a garnet?" She glanced at Riley in smiling appeal, but got only a blank look in response. Well, it had been a pretty crude attempt. The day Dan's granddaughter didn't know a ruby from a garnet . . . Flushing slightly, she went on. "Garnet, of course. Amethyst, ruby, emerald, topaz. Margaret!"

Her delighted little laugh invited him to share in her triumph, but it was not entirely calculated; the regard rings and their variants had always charmed her. Riley's expression changed from blank to blanker.

Cliff took the ring from her and examined it curiously. "What's all that about?"

"The initial letters of the stones spell a name or a word," Meg explained. "The most common word is 'regard'; that's why they're called regard rings. I have several in my ring collection."

"That's right, you do collect rings. Rings with messages."

Meg could have kicked him; in fact, she would have kicked him if he had been close enough. He was about as subtle as a two-by-four across the head. If Riley was innocent there was no harm done, but if he had sent the ring, he was now forewarned of their suspicions.

Blithely unaware of her disgust, Cliff went on, "You ought to have this one then, since it spells your name."

"My name isn't Margaret."

"But I thought—"

"Meg is a logical nickname for the one by which I was christened. Dan insisted on it, since he had no sons to carry on the family name."

"Mignot?" Cliff grinned. "I never knew that. Mignot Venturi. . . . Actually, it doesn't sound as bad as you might expect."

"It's not that different from Mignon, which is a perfectly legitimate female name." She spoke to Cliff, but watched Riley out of the corner of her eye. His face had not changed. Either he had known her real name, or he didn't give a damn. Probably the latter. "Dan called me by it sometimes, when he was feeling affectionate. Sort of a pet name. I hated it, though. Everybody else in my class was named Jackie or Julie or Jennie or Trish." She slid the ring on her finger and shook her head. "It's too small. I think I must have it, though. I don't own one that spells Margaret. Will you please put it on my account, Mr. Riley?"

"Just Riley. It's yours. Half the stock is yours."

"But which half? No, we'll do this by the book, for the sake of Infernal Revenue if for no other reason. You'd better enter the transaction in the ledger."

"The old ledgers are long gone," Riley said. "We're computerized."

"Oh, really?"

The front door rattled. Apparently Candy had not seen the "Closed" sign. She pressed her face against the glass, squinting, as she continued to push against the door. The old beveled glass distorted her features into a comic mask.

Without comment or change of expression Riley went to the door and unlocked it.

Candy plunged in. "I'm back," she announced.

"So you are." Riley looked at Meg. "If you have time I'll show you the new setup."

Candy held out a small paper bag, already liquid-stained. "I brought you—"

"No, thanks. This way, Ms. Venturi."

His tone was no more brusque than it had been when he spoke to Meg, but Candy's lips quivered and her eyes brimmed with tears. However, Meg's sympathies were with the pursued. How was a man supposed to deal with that relentless, demanding adoration? He couldn't even demonstrate basic courtesy without fearing it would be interpreted as encouragement. As she turned to follow Riley, Meg realized that Candy had found someone to blame for her idol's rejection; the tears in her eyes magnified her glare at Meg.

The office was even more cluttered than Meg remembered. Dan's mammoth old rolltop desk had been pushed into a corner in order to leave space for the computer and its various accessories. Filing cabinets and shelves heaped with untidy stacks of magazines and miscellany left little empty space.

"Are you the computer expert?" Meg squeezed herself into the chair in front of the console and fingered the keys.

"I'm no expert. I took just enough courses to learn what I needed to know. I hate the damned thing, to be honest. Dan was like a kid with a new toy; he loved playing with it."

It was the longest speech he had made, and the most revealing—and unless her imagination was working overtime his voice had softened when he spoke of Dan's delight in his new toy. "Show me how it works," Meg said.

Riley shoved his hands into his pockets. "Current inventory is cross-indexed according to date of purchase, price, type and source. When an item is sold—"

"Show me," Meg said softly.

Like many of her generation she was computer-literate. She was familiar, not only with the general principles, but with this particular make of computer. Riley must have suspected as much, but there was no way he could refuse her request without flagrant rudeness, and no way he could avoid touching the fingers she left resting lightly on the keys. He had to bend over her to reach them. He bent stiffly, from the waist, like a mechanical man, but the big rough hands were surprisingly deft. His fingers barely brushed hers. The screen flickered as file replaced file.

"I think I get the idea," Meg said, putting her hand over Riley's.

He recoiled as if she had touched him with a white-hot metal glove. "By type, you said," Meg murmured, punching keys. "Yes, I see. Bracelets, pendants, hair ornaments. . . . Rings."

4

"It wasn't there," Cliff said.

"You sound like a kid who's just discovered there is no Santa Claus." Meg rummaged in her purse for her sunglasses. "Of course it wasn't there. I didn't expect it would be."

"Then why did you look?"

"Where the hell . . ." Meg peered down into the cluttered interior of her purse. "You're distracting me, Cliff. Use your head. You surely don't suppose that Riley is stupid enough to leave a record of what he did? Either the ring didn't come from the shop or he wiped the entry. So I didn't expect to find it."

"That's the trouble with these damned modern inventions," Cliff muttered. "A good old-fashioned ledger would show signs of tampering. Then why did you—"

"There they are," Meg said triumphantly. She unfolded the glasses. "I was just testing him, to see how he'd react to my interest in rings. I was being subtle. Which wasn't easy, with you flexing your muscles and making not-so-veiled threats. If I may say so, it was a disgusting performance."

"Oh, yeah? Well, so was yours. You were all over him. And it didn't get you anywhere, did it? He didn't so much as—"

"What did you expect him to do, with you there?" But there was enough truth in the malicious speech to bring an angry flush to Meg's face. "I suppose when a woman makes friendly gestures to you, you grab her and throw her on the floor and—"

"Try me," Cliff said, baring his teeth. "Try me sometime."

Red-faced and equally furious, they glowered at one another. Then Cliff relaxed and shook his head ruefully. "Listen to us. Just like the good old days. I'm sorry, Meg. I made this great resolution, before I came, all about starting over and being friends. Can we give it a try?"

"All right. Just don't—"

"I know, I know. I won't—if I can help it. I'm worried about Dad, he's been under quite a strain, with Dan's death and everything; and this he doesn't need. It makes me want to go barreling in and beat the truth out of someone."

"I understand." Not only did she understand, she sympathized. Cliff's devotion to his father was one of his most attractive characteristics, especially since it didn't appear to be wholeheartedly reciprocated. "But it won't work, Cliff."

"I still think that ring came from the store,"

Cliff said stubbornly. "And that makes Riley the most logical person to have sent it."

"Not necessarily."

They were standing under the shade of the awning. Meg turned and glanced at the closed door of the store. Cliff's eyes followed hers, just in time to catch a glimpse of the face pressed to the glass.

"Candy," Cliff muttered. "That's crazy. Why would she. . . ."

Meg turned on her heel and walked away. Cliff caught up with her in a few long strides. "Okay," he said. "Maybe you're right. Maybe I wasn't exactly subtle. But you made a mistake too, picking on Candy the way you did. You should have tried to ingratiate yourself."

"What for?"

"Do I have to spell it out?"

Meg snorted. "I have no intention of trying to subvert that pathetic wimp into spying on her boss. Anyway, it would be hopeless. She's infatuated with him."

"That's why the potential is so great," Cliff argued. "He's not going to put up with that wet-lipped adoration of hers much longer. One of these days she'll back him into a corner, and he'll tell her to get lost, and—"

"Hell hath no fury, et cetera. What a contemptible, cynical view of people you have, Cliff. I suppose if poor Candy were beautiful, blond and built, her adoration wouldn't be such a burden."

"My viewpoint isn't cynical, it's realistic. We need a secret supporter—oh, all right, a spy—at the store. You aren't going to get anything out of old stone face."

"I certainly am not going to get anything out of him, as you put it, by antagonizing him. You were damned rude."

"He was rude first." Cliff chuckled. "It was his fault, Ma, he hit me first. Where are you going, by the way?"

Meg stopped. "The wrong direction, apparently," she admitted. "I wasn't thinking, I just wanted to get away from the store."

The sun was high overhead, so there was little shade from the ornamental trees that had been planted along Main Street. Most of them were Bradford pears, now in full bloom, like pale pyramids of blossom. Ahead was the gas station, the last commercial establishment in the town center, tastefully surrounded by beds of flowering tulips. The bookstore was unfamiliar; after a moment Meg identified it as the former insurance office, now repainted and restored, with bright red geraniums and trailing ivy filling the planters on either side of the door.

"Things keep changing," she muttered, glancing up and down the street. "I hate it when things change. What happened to Kate's Kafe?"

"It's still there," Cliff reassured her. "New name, new facade, but the same old Kate. Unlike you, she believes in keeping up with the Joneses. Come on, I'll buy you lunch."

Meg hung back. "I don't know, Cliff."

"If you're worried about annoying Frances,

don't; it's just cold cuts and salad for lunch, I asked before we left."

"I don't give a hoot about Frances. But . . ."

"You'll have to face them sooner or later," Cliff said gently.

"Why? Why should I? I don't live here anymore, Cliff. I can walk away anytime."

If he had argued with her, sheer stubbornness might have allowed her to maintain that point of view. His very silence forced her to admit, to herself, that she was wrong. She couldn't simply walk away, not now, not yet. Gran needed her. And there were other things. . . . Her decision was not formulated or even defined in that moment, but the seed had been sown.

"Oh, damn," she said.

Cliff laughed and put a casual arm around her. "Eloquently expressed. I promise that if you bite the bullet it will taste better than you expect."

"Kate hasn't lost her knack?"

"No. But that wasn't what I meant."

He steered her through the traffic. Nervous as she was (and how ridiculous that she should be nervous, she scolded herself), Meg couldn't help grinning as she got the full effect of Kate's latest and wildest stab at exterior decoration. A handcarved wooden sign, so extravagantly curlicued that it was practically unreadable, appeared to say, "Le Café des Printemps." Flowers painted in vivid shades of orange, turquoise and purple carried out the theme and further obscured the letters. The striped purple-and-orange awning had scalloped edges and foot-long fringe; the café curtains at the windows hung from huge brass rings. What Kate had had in mind was anybody's guess. French country, French provincial? Something French, at any rate.

The interior wasn't as bad as one might have anticipated. The fake overhead beams dated from an earlier foray into American primitive. To the miscellaneous baskets (made in Korea) and bits of brass (made in Japan) hanging from them, Kate had added strings of onions and garlic. Red-checked tablecloths had replaced homespun, but each table had its own rack of condiments, including bottles of low-brow mustard and catsup.

A huddled crowd of people were waiting for tables. Cliff pushed through them, murmuring apologies. Meg followed; she was beginning to suspect that she had been set up, and when she saw the big round table at the back of the room she knew she had. The faces that turned toward them were bright with pleasure and anticipation, but not with surprise. And there were three empty chairs. One was always kept for Kate, who popped out to join the gang whenever she had a spare minute—hence the location of the table, conveniently close to the kitchen.

Out of the corner of her mouth she hissed, "I hate being manipulated."

"Me too," Cliff said blandly. "Hello, everybody. I guess no introductions are necessary."

With a painful constriction of her throat Meg saw how the ranks had diminished over the past years. Only three of them left, besides Kate. Dan had been the oldest, but the baby of the crowd, Barby, had to be pushing seventy. She was pushing as hard as she could, and to good effect; after all, as she often said, beauty was her business. Having decided that an older woman had to choose between a wrinkled face and a thickened waist, she had opted for the latter, and her round, delicately tinted face was as delectable as a ripe peach.

Mike Potter, of Potter's Hardware, had to lean down to kiss her. Meg hugged him back, in a rush of grateful affection; he looked just the same, his height undiminished by age, his bony frame tough as a gnarled tree. His thick, iron-gray hair hadn't changed color for thirty years. Dan used to kid him about Grecian Formula. . . .

The third survivor—she couldn't help thinking of them that way—was as pink and roly-poly as Mike was thin and gray. Like Barby, Ed claimed he had to be a walking advertisement for his wares, but he didn't have to advertise; the bakery was famous throughout the state. Some of Ed's customers drove sixty miles to stock up on bread and coffee cake and biscuits—none of these newfangled things like croissants and Danish for Ed, he baked the food his grandmother had baked, and boasted that his buttermilk biscuits had to be covered to keep them from floating away.

He started to struggle out of his chair. Meg put a hand on his shoulder and dropped a quick kiss on the top of his bald head. "Don't get up, Ed.

It's so good to be with you all again, here at Kate's."

"Not so many of us as there once was," Ed said cheerfully. "But the younger generation is sure doing us proud. You turned into a real pretty woman, Meg. You know Janine's got three kids now? I think I've got some pictures of the baby—" He reached toward his pocket.

"What do you mean, think?" Barby demanded. "You'd as soon go out without your pants as without those pictures. She doesn't want to see them, Ed. Sit down, honey. Here, next to me."

They all wanted her to sit next to them. There was a certain amount of shifting and moving chairs—except for Ed, who preferred not to move unless he had to, and who sat smiling fatly at Meg, the pictures ready in his hand.

As soon as she was settled, between Barby and Mike, the waitress swooped down on them with a promptness reserved for special customers. Meg tried to order a salad, but was shouted down. Ed said she was way too thin, Barby proclaimed the virtues of Kate's seafood Newburg, and even Mike—who wasn't much of a talker, possibly because he had a hard time getting a word in, rumbled, "You need to keep up your strength, honey. This is a celebration; have something good."

Aware of Cliff's sardonic smile, Meg let them order for her. After the waitress had left she said, "I don't feel much like celebrating, Mike. Except for the pleasure of seeing you and the others."

"That's the point," Ed said. "That's the only

way to live. Enjoying people while they're with us, enjoying the memories after they're gone." His spherical face split into a wide smile. "I've got my celebration all planned. Menu and everything. I'm gonna write out some tributes for Barby and Mike to deliver—"

"Fat chance," said Barby with a sniff. "You'll outlive us all, you old goat. If there were any justice in this world you'd have killed yourself a long time ago, eating all the wrong things, getting no exercise, drinking like a fish—"

"Now I don't neither drink too much," Ed said indignantly. "A couple of glasses of wine every day never hurt a person. It's in Holy Writ."

The arrival of the waitress, with the wine praised by Holy Writ, prevented Barby from replying. As the young woman poured, a rush of warm air and the slap of the swinging door heralded the appearance of Kate. She pushed Cliff back into his chair with one hand and stretched out the other to Meg.

Kate claimed it was the moist heat of the kitchen that kept her face so miraculously unlined. She worked a twelve-hour day, six days a week, and her diminutive figure had thickened only slightly over the past few years. When Meg said, "You look wonderful, Kate," she spoke only the truth.

"I look like hell," Kate said, pushing a strand of limp hair under her tall white hat. "Don't know how much longer I can stand this stupid hat. If the French are supposed to be so damned smart about cooking, how come they invented these things? I'm thinking of going back to that early-American day-cor. Then I could wear one of them, what do they call them, mobcaps. I can't get used to this damned thing, it keeps hitting the pots and pans. What do you think, Meg?"

Mike cleared his throat. "First things first, Kate. Let's have the toast. Here's to Dan." He raised his glass.

"Is that all?" Ed asked, pouting. "You should've let me make the toast. I had a nice speech all written out—"

The three old cronies groaned in unison. "You know what Dan thought of your damned speeches," Kate said. "Mike has it right. Here's to Dan."

They drank. The ensuing silence only lasted a few seconds. Kate turned her bright, birdlike gaze on Meg. "So, what do you think? Should I change the day-cor? What's the latest in New York?"

She was quite serious, so Meg obliged with descriptions of the latest fads in ethnic foods, all of which Kate dismissed with a sniff or a toss of the head. She wasn't about to start serving raw fish to anybody, and as for those other countries—wherever the hell they were—everybody knew those poor souls lived on rice and scraps. Meg knew she wasn't really interested in food; what she really wanted to hear were stories about hookers, drug pushers, muggers and other exotic characters. Kate was an avid reader of hard-boiled mysteries, and was convinced that ninety-five percent of the population of New York City consisted of the aforementioned types.

Kate never sat for long, though; warned by some invisible time clock, she bounded up and announced she had better get back to work. "You come for supper sometime, Meg honey. Wednesday's a good night, it's usually slow; if you come about eight, I can get away and we'll have a good talk."

The others, profoundly disinterested in sushi, hookers and crime, had been talking quietly among themselves. Cliff caught Meg's eye. "Ed says he thinks he saw a ring like the one Dad received in Dan's collection."

"You told him—"

"Why shouldn't I? This is a serious matter. Dan had no secrets from his best friends."

"Like hell he didn't," Barby said. "There were plenty of things in Dan's life, past and present, he never talked about. And you can't believe Ed, he's so agreeable he'll say anything if he thinks you want to hear it."

Ed pouted, but before he could deny the accusation, Cliff laughed and said, "I think Barby has a weak spot for your dour partner, Meg."

Barby grinned. "He's a man. I like men, especially men built like Riley."

Meg's eyes turned toward Mike Potter. She loved all three of them, but Mike was the one whose judgment she trusted most. "What do you think of him, Mike?"

"Riley?" Mike pondered. "He's a hard worker. Dan had a high opinion of his talent."

"Is that all you can say?" Cliff demanded.

Mike turned a mild blue gaze on him. "Not much else I can say. Takes a while to know a person. Riley isn't exactly an open book." He thought for a moment, and then added, "He's good with his hands."

Cliff scowled. "Weren't you surprised when you heard Dan had left him half the store?"

"I sure was," Ed said. "He's only been here a year or two."

"Three," Barby said.

"Has it been that long? Time sure flies. Point is, even three years isn't long enough to explain a big legacy like that. You figure maybe he had something on Dan?"

Barby protested vehemently and even Mike shook his head. "You shouldn't say things like that, Ed. Blackmail is a crime."

"I didn't say—"

"You sure did. Not that anybody would pay the slightest attention to your crazy ideas," Barby added caustically. "How about some dessert? Meg, Kate still makes that almond cake you like so much."

They turned their attention to the serious question of dessert. Meg allowed them to order the almond cake for her, thankful that their bizarre ideas of "celebration" hadn't gone so far as a birthday-type cake with "Here's to Dan" in green icing. But Barby's attempt to change the subject, if it was that, did not succeed.

"I won't use the word 'blackmail' either," Cliff said. "But was there anything in Dan's past that would make him susceptible to pressure of that kind?"

There was an odd, uncomfortable silence. The three old people exchanged glances. Even Ed seemed reluctant to comment. It was Barby who said finally, "Everybody's got some secret he wouldn't want spread around. Dammit, this is supposed to be a celebration, not an inquest. Meg's got enough practical problems on her plate without raising up ghosts. Forget it, honey."

"I wish I could," Meg said. "One of my practical problems is what to do about the store. A partnership is out of the question—"

"Why?" Barby asked.

"Because . . . well, because I don't know anything about the man. He'd be the one in charge, the one on the spot, even if the present arrangement continued. I don't have enough information to judge his honesty or his capabilities."

"That makes sense," Mike said, nodding. "But those are things you can find out, honey. You'd have to make the same judgment about anyone you hired to run the store.

"I haven't decided. . . ." Meg stopped short, as it dawned on her that Dan's old friends had never considered the possibility of her selling the store.

"You shouldn't decide anything just yet,"

Barby assured her. "Take your time, think things through. My goodness, child, you've got all the time in the world."

As she and Cliff headed homeward along the shaded street, Meg felt weighted down by other people's assumptions.

"I'm so stuffed I can hardly walk," she grumbled. "That was a dirty trick, Cliff. Why didn't you tell me they were expecting us for lunch?"

"I was afraid you'd think of some excuse not to go," Cliff said. "You saw how much it meant to them."

"That was why I'd thought of some excuse not to go," Meg admitted. "Because it meant a lot to me too. There are so many emotional hurdles to get over . . . but I'm glad I went, glad I could join in celebrating Dan's life with the friends he loved best. Thanks for conning me into it. And now that I've thanked you, kindly tell me whatever prompted you to bring up the subject of blackmail?"

"I didn't bring it up. Ed did."

"You practically programmed him. Barby is right, Ed will say anything. It didn't do you any good, though, did it? They didn't tell you anything specific."

"They won't tell me," Cliff said. "I'm an outsider. I'll always be an outsider, even though my father was born here and my mother was a local girl. I was only seven or eight when I was sent away to school; maybe that's what sets me apart, being away all those years—but you left after high school and hardly ever came back. . . ."

"I'm an outsider too, in some ways," Meg said, wondering why the approval of a small town should mean so much to him. "At least some of the local citizens think of me that way. Who cares?"

"Yeah, right. Who cares?" Cliff shrugged. "At least Dan's old buddies accept you. I can't seem to get to first base with them. I thought I had Ed pinned down on the subject of the ring, and then Barby—"

"She was right. Dan used to say Ed could contradict himself three times in a single sentence. I don't see why you're so obsessed with that cursed ring, Cliff. I've thought of another possibility—a repentant thief."

"You don't get it, do you?"

"I guess not. What are you talking about?"

"That dirty word 'blackmail.' Face it, Meg; that's the only explanation for Dan's generosity to a man he had known for only a few years. He had a strong sense of family; why else would he leave assets as valuable as those to a relative stranger?"

Unwillingly swayed by the force of his argument, Meg was about to call it what it was—a theory, thus far unsubstantiated by fact—when he went on, "The ring fits only too well into that scenario. Blackmailers don't stop. Dan is beyond such threats now, so a new victim has been selected."

They turned into the driveway. Sunlight, dappled and diffused by the leaves overhead, made shifting patterns of light across the paving. The distant roar of a lawn mower sounded like a giant insect buzzing.

"You can't blackmail someone unless they fear disclosure," Meg said. "Are you accusing your own father of being involved with Dan in some crooked deal?"

"It couldn't have been much of a deal," Cliff said dryly. "Dad only handled Dan's personal finances. But he was close to Dan in a way no hired accountant could ever be; he was, and is, one of the family. Dan was a tight-lipped old devil, he never told anybody any more than was absolutely necessary, but if he had confided in anyone it would be in Dad. And he'd be just as anxious as Dan to avoid scandal—"

Meg made a wordless sound of disgust and protest. "Could, might, would . . . It's a pretty plot, Cliff; I've read worse. But there is not a single fact to support it. If you really believe this nonsense, you'd better stop bugging Barby and Ed and Mike, and talk to George. He'll tell you the truth, won't he? You're his son, after all."

She had not set out deliberately to hurt him. The dark color that stained his cheeks brought into sharp focus something she had only suspected until then. The alienation between father and son prevented the mutual trust Cliff wanted, and didn't know how to win. He was going about it the wrong way, but George wasn't entirely blameless; a little more warmth, a little less criticism . . . To apologize would only acknowledge the affront, but her voice softened, and she put a friendly hand on his arm.

"Cliff, you know I'm as concerned about George as you are. But right now I'm so full and so giddy from all that wine, and so damned tired, I can't think straight. I'm going to go lie down in Dan's hammock and rest, and smell the roses. We'll talk later, okay?"

He assented with a grunt and a nod; she couldn't tell whether he still harbored resentment, and as she struck off across the sunny lawn she decided she didn't care. She was weary of catering to other people's sensitivities. That was the exhausting aspect of life, not hard work; she could cope with the endless tasks resulting from Dan's death if she didn't have to spend so much time and energy considering everything she said, and apologizing for every wrong word.

A bright red riding mower buzzed toward her. The man atop it waved; Meg waved back, though she didn't recognize him. The lawn and gardens in which Dan had taken such pride required several full-time workers, but the turnover was great; this man must have been hired since her last visit.

Walls of brick and stone and antique wrought iron divided the grounds into smaller sections, concealing the utilitarian area of garage and workshops and allowing scope for Dan's enthusiastic eccentricities in regard to landscaping. There were an Italian garden and a wildflower garden and a water garden, complete with lily pond and waterfall; there was even a grotto, with imitation mosaics made out of seashells. The cultivated area ended abruptly at a higher wall, now covered almost entirely with a green curtain of Virginia creeper. Meg glanced curiously at it as she passed by. Apparently the old prohibition still held. She wondered what condition the cottage was in by now—or whether it still stood. To the best of her knowledge no one had entered it or the part of the estate surrounding it for over twenty years.

Dan's favorite part of the gardens was a small corner walled in by hedges of the old-fashioned roses he loved and shaded by two tall maples. The hammock was strung between them. Meg maneuvered herself into it and lay back with a sigh. Slowly her taut muscles relaxed. The green leaves made a shifting canopy overhead, offering an occasional glimpse of blue sky. Most of the roses were still in bud; only Therese Bugnet, the earliest bloomer, spread crumpled pink blossoms across the branches. Meg took a deep breath, inhaling the rose fragrance. That was one of the reasons why Dan had preferred the old roses; hybrid teas might bloom all summer instead of only once a season, but their waxen perfection held almost no scent.

The sound of the mower rose and fell as it proceeded on its path. It made a soothing background noise, blending with the rustle of leaves, the hum of bees wooing the roses, and the music of birdsong.

In Manhattan the pavements would be radiating heat and the air would be thick with smog. By this time she would have drunk half a dozen cups of coffee and lunched on yogurt and a bagel. Her stomach would be churning and her nerves would be jumping and people would be running in and out of the office and the phone would be ringing. . . .

Phone. Meg realized she had missed Nick's noontime call. She hadn't given it a thought till this minute. She hadn't thought about Nick for hours. She wished she hadn't thought of him now. The surroundings were so seductive, so sickeningly drenched with romance, that her responsive body pictured him lying next to her, his hands holding her, his mouth hard on hers. She pushed him away with a vigorous mental effort. That wasn't what she needed right now. Nick would, of course, claim that was exactly what she needed. He was a great believer in physical therapy.

Some kind of therapy had had its effect. Here in Dan's favorite retreat, surrounded by memories, for the first time since his death she felt no need to mourn him.

The rumble of thunder woke her in time to feel the first raindrops slip through the leaves and onto her face. She had slept heavily; drowsy and disoriented, she stared blankly at the wildly waving branches overhead. The next sound of thunder was not a low rumble but a rattling crack, like artillery. She started up, as the drumming of raindrops on the leaves grew louder. Before she reached the house she was soaked to the skin.

The kitchen door was closest. She stopped just inside, and stood dripping forlornly onto the mat until the cook advanced upon her with towels and sympathy. "Take off those sandals and dry yourself before you move one step, Miss Meg. I just mopped the floor this morning. Then you'd better get on up and change before you catch your death of cold."

"Good advice indeed," a voice intoned. Frances appeared from the butler's pantry. The housekeeper's long black gown and gliding walk told Meg—to her intense irritation—that Frances was still Mrs. Danvers. The bunch of keys at her waist jangled discordantly as she moved, and her voice was a mournful baritone. "Another death in this doomed house—"

"Frances, please!" Meg tossed the damp towel onto a chair and stepped out of her shoes, leaving them by the door. "I'm not going to catch cold, and if I did, I wouldn't die from it. Couldn't you pick another role, just for the next few days? I really don't think I can stand Mrs. Danvers right now."

Hands folded at her waist, Frances stepped aside to let her pass. "Joke if you like," she said ominously. "Mr. Dan made fun of me too. And you see what happened to him. . . ."

Meg fled. Frances didn't follow her, but she raised her voice to a shout. "Your grandma's been asking for you. Worried her half to death, you did. And her not strong. She sent me down to look for you. Mooning around out of doors with a tornado coming on. . . ."

The tirade ended only when Meg slammed the door behind her. Dan had not only laughed at Frances, he had encouraged her fantasies, claiming that she was a great source of comic relief. Dan always did have a weird sense of humor. . . . No doubt a psychologist would say that her role-playing was Frances's way of dealing with emotional crises. Unfortunately, it increased the trauma for the people around her.

The lights in the drawing room were on, but Mary was not there, though it was ten minutes past the conventional hour for tea. Meg went up the stairs as fast as she dared; her stockinged feet tended to slip on the polished treads. Aside from the personal inconvenience, a fall would only encourage Frances's superstitious fancies.

The door of her grandmother's room was open; glancing in, Meg saw the familiar form in its familiar position—seated at the dressing table, putting the final touches on her impeccable toilette. Gran saw her reflected in the mirror; without turning, she said placidly, "There you are, darling. Do hurry and change; I'm afraid I'm a little late this evening, but tea will be served in ten minutes."

Scared half to death was she? Meg cursed Frances as she hastened to her own room.

Ten minutes. She made it, by curtailing the long hot shower she had hoped for, and by slipping into a long robe of gold brocade instead of trying to slide panty hose over damp skin. Her hair was damp too, despite hasty minutes with a blow-dryer; she twisted it into a knot and pinned it at the nape of her neck, added a jeweled comb and reached, almost at random, for a pair of earrings. It was the gesture that mattered—the rigid maintenance of certain seemingly unimportant standards in the face of tragedy. They were Gran's standards, not hers; all the more reason why she should attempt to match them.

The others seemed to understand that too. They were already in the drawing room when she arrived, and both men rose punctiliously. Cliff had put on a shirt and tie; George wore his usual three-piece suit.

"Sorry I'm late," Meg said, taking her place on the love seat next to her grandmother. "And disheveled. I fell asleep in the hammock, and got caught by the rain."

"You needed the rest," Mary said, handing her a cup. "And you look very nice. Is that a new ring?"

Meg glanced at her hand. "What a memory you have, Gran. Yes, it is new; I found it at the store this morning, and couldn't resist it. I don't have one that spells 'Margaret.' "

"Spells? I don't understand."

Meg explained. Her grandmother's interest in jewels was aesthetic and acquisitive; she loved them for their beauty and gloried in possessing them, but she claimed to be too stupid to understand the technical and historical aspects. Meg had always suspected that was an act, part of the sweet-little-old-dumb-me female image her grandmother's generation affected. Dan must have told her about regard rings.

If it was an act, it was a good one; her grandmother's amused delight sounded genuine. "Isn't that clever? You have others, that spell different words? Well, I just think that is a darling idea. I can't imagine why Dan never gave me one with my name."

Meg laughed and patted Mary's wrinkled hand. The fingers looked too frail to bear the weight of the rings that adorned them—a trio of perfectly matched, flawless, blue-white diamonds, and an amethyst so big it reached to the first knuckle. "Moonstones and small amethysts wouldn't suit your style, Gran. Anyway, there is no gemstone starting with a *y*."

"Isn't there? You would know, dear." Mary passed a plate of dainty sandwiches. "Yours is very pretty. Much more suitable for a young girl than diamonds."

"Diamonds are boring," Cliff said with a smile. "Right, Meg?"

"Dan thought so. He was mad for color, the more unusual, the better. The different shades of green in tourmaline, emerald, peridot and demantoid garnet, that wonderful apricot color of imperial topaz. I guess his lectures affected me; I feel the same way. And, of course, I thought it was soooo sophisticated to say diamonds were boring." She laughed, and took another sandwich.

"These are delicious. I don't know how I can eat after that huge lunch, but I'm starved."

Mary was still absorbed in the ring. "You must show me some of the others like this, Meg dear."

The suggestion had been made in all innocence, Meg felt sure, but George was quick to react. "I'd like to have a look too, Meg. I haven't been able to locate an inventory of your personal collection. Do you know where it might be?"

"I have a copy somewhere." The sandwich suddenly lost its savor. Meg put the rest of it on her plate. "Is there a problem, Uncle George?"

"No, no." But her uncle frowned. "At least I don't think so. That collection is your private property, it shouldn't be considered part of the estate. And, if I remember correctly, no single item is of great value."

"I don't remember," Meg said. "I haven't looked at it in years."

"What inhuman lack of curiosity." Cliff leaned back in his chair. "But I suppose if you own the Koh-i-noor, a mixed lot of zircons and citrines don't thrill you."

"I don't own the Koh-i-noor," Meg said shortly. She was not about to explain her apparent lack of curiosity to Cliff, or tell him it was not so much disinterest as abhorrence, of everything that reminded her of the business Dan loved and she had learned to hate. The collection did not include individual items of great value, but in its totality it was worth quite a lot—which gave her a reasonable excuse for leaving it in Seldon. A Manhattan apartment wasn't the safest repository for valuables.

"You haven't had time," George said. "There's been so much to do. I wish I could be more help, Meg, I know how difficult this is for you."

"You've already helped enormously, Uncle George. I couldn't have managed without you. I'll check my collection first thing tomorrow, I promise. And show Gran the regard rings."

"Thank you, darling, that's sweet." Mary's face glowed with pleasure. "I'd love to see them. Are you sure there isn't a stone that starts with a *y?*"

Meg laughed and started to answer, but her grandmother went on, frowning prettily, "Dan would know. I must ask him, when I talk to him tonight."

5

"THERE IS NOTHING to worry about," George said.

Meg turned on him, the full skirt of her robe flaring out like a golden bell. "Nothing to worry about? When she's forgotten she buried her husband two days ago?"

"She hasn't forgotten. Stop pacing, Meg. You're just wearing yourself out."

Meg flung herself into a chair and stared at her clenched fists. George was being so kind and patient she wanted to scream at him. Because she knew that was unreasonable, she transferred her inimical stare to his son, who was sprawled in the second of the deep leather chairs flanking the fireplace in George's office. Cliff was so relaxed he looked boneless, and the superior smile with which he regarded her didn't make her feel any more kindly toward him.

"You really are out of it, kid," he said. "Don't you know that death is only a step across the threshold to a better world? For fifty bucks you too can talk to Dan, or George Washington—"

"That's enough," his father said sharply. "I won't have you jeering at Mary's faith."

Cliff's smile vanished. "I didn't mean—"

"All right." Seated behind his big mahogany desk, George leaned back with a sigh. "I know you'd never speak that way in her presence, but the flippant attitude of your generation angers me sometimes. Meg, your grandmother's faith is deep and sincere. The tenets of that faith assure her that Dan survives, in another, immortal form, and that he is still close to her. If that's senility, then a lot of people, of all ages, suffer from the same thing."

"But all those questions about the ring," Meg argued. "She behaved as if she had never heard of that type of jewelry. Dan must have told her—"

George's hearty laugh interrupted her. "Meg, dear, you really are looking for trouble. Dan told her the same jokes, the same stories over and over; she always behaved as if she were hearing them for the first time. Maybe she was at that; the women of her generation probably learned to stop listening in pure self-defense."

His smile invited her to join him in his affectionate amusement. Badly as she wanted to, Meg was unable to accept his optimistic appraisal of her grandmother's mental condition. Gran's deep, sincere faith in an afterlife—yes, of course, Meg could accept that; many of her friends believed just as sincerely. But none of them carried on conversations with their lost loved ones. Not in public, anyhow. However, she kept her doubts to herself. Her uncle had enough to deal with.

"I expect you're right, Uncle George," she said. "You really . . . you really think she's okay?"

"I know she is. I drove her in to the doctor this morning—just as a precaution. He says she's fine."

Meg went to him and put her arm around his bowed shoulders. "Uncle George, you are a rock at my back. Is there anything I can do for you? You worry about the rest of us, but you're the one who has taken the brunt of all this."

"It's my job, honey. And my pleasure."

"We can examine the collection tonight, after dinner, if you like," Meg offered.

"No, no, you take the evening off." George glanced at his watch. "As I plan to do. I'm going out for dinner, with an old friend."

"That's nice. Is it anyone—"

"I'm going out too," Cliff announced. "But not with the same old friend as Dad. In fact, my friend isn't old in any sense of the word. But you don't want to hear about her—"

George's "I suspect I wouldn't," and Meg's emphatic, "Certainly not" sounded like a duet. They grinned sheepishly at one another, and Cliff continued, "I'd like to make a reservation for tomorrow's showing. What time are you planning to unveil the famous collection?"

His father frowned at him. "I see no reason why you—"

"I don't mind," Meg said. She did mind, though, and it was not without malice that she added, "Early. Right after breakfast. Which is served, in case you aren't aware of it, at 8 A.M."

Cliff groaned. "I am only too well aware of it. I just ignore it."

"As far as I'm concerned, you can ignore the showing too. I want to get it over with; there are a number of other things I ought to do tomorrow."

"Such as making a will," Cliff drawled.

Meg stared at him, and her uncle, who had been studying the papers on his desk with an abstracted frown, said sharply, "What on earth put that idea into your head, Clifford?"

Cliff looked sulky. "It's logical, isn't it?"

"Yes, I suppose so, but. . . ." George glanced at Meg. "You have a will, don't you, my dear?"

"No. No, I haven't. There was no reason. . . . I mean, I assumed anything I possessed would automatically revert to Dan if I. . . ."

Observing her confusion, George tactfully interrupted. "Of course. But the situation has changed. As a matter of fact, Darren has been anxious to talk to you about a new will, he's mentioned it several times. I didn't want to trouble you with the matter just yet, since there seemed to be no urgency about it." He carefully avoided looking at Cliff, but the latter shifted uncomfortably.

"But I haven't the faintest. . . ." Meg caught herself. "Sorry, Uncle George. I sound like some bleating little female twit. You're absolutely right. I'll call Darren in the morning and make an appointment; there are a number of things I need to discuss with him."

Her uncle gave her an approving smile. "He's waiting for you to call; but he knows, as we all do, how busy you've been and how many things you have to deal with. Forget about it for a few hours, honey, and have a quiet evening."

Cliff was on his feet before Meg. He opened the door for her, but she paused.

"Uncle George?"

"Yes?"

"Wasn't there some provision made in Dan's will for how his property would be disposed of if I predeceased him and Gran?"

"Yes, of course; that's standard practice. Didn't you hear that part?"

"If I did, I don't remember. I was somewhat distracted."

"Of course."

He was obviously impatient to go, and Meg didn't want to detain him. "I'll discuss it with Darren," she said. "Good night, Uncle George; have a nice evening with your friend."

Cliff followed her out and closed the door. "If

you're wondering what to do with all that money, you can leave some of it to me," he suggested.

"If I were inclined to do so, which I am not, I certainly wouldn't tell you," Meg said.

He was quick—too quick, perhaps—to catch her meaning. "Have you been borrowing Kate's murder mysteries? You needn't worry about me, love; I'm far too cautious to commit a crime of that magnitude—except, of course, for the whole bundle."

"Oh, well, in that case I might leave you a small legacy. Enough to buy a mourning ring."

For once she had the last word. When she started up the stairs Cliff did not follow.

Since the lords of creation were dining out, Mary decided she and Meg would have their supper on trays in front of the TV. Meg did not comment on the incongruity of the elaborate gown and priceless lace and flashing gems in such a setting; Gran coddled and flattered men, but she dressed for herself. Watching Mary's vociferous and delighted participation in a game show, she suspected again that her grandmother wasn't as dim as she liked to let on. She was far quicker than Meg to guess the right answers.

She said as much, after Mary had snapped out the correct answer to "a country in Asia whose capital is Lhasa." Her grandmother dimpled. "You sound just like your daddy. He always teased me about pretending to be stupid."

Meg almost lost her grip on the fork she was

raising to her mouth. This was the first time in her adult memory that her grandmother had mentioned the man she had loved like her own son, and who had betrayed the traditions she held almost as sacred as her religion.

Meg could not remember exactly when she learned that she must not mention her father. The immediate result of that dreadful winter night was the loss, not of one parent, but of both. Her mother's collapse left her to the care of her grandparents; tormented and grief-stricken, they had had neither the time nor the expertise to handle Meg's frantic questions as they should have done. She didn't blame them; she didn't even blame her mother for turning to the alcohol that finally killed her. Perhaps if she had demanded more attention she would have received it, but children are much more sensitive to nuances than many adults realize, and it had not taken Meg long to realize that questions about Daddy brought tears of anger or pained withdrawal. So she had withdrawn in her turn, anxiously placating the unknown powers that controlled her life by being quiet and not causing trouble. Be a good little girl, don't bother your mother. . . . She was a good little girl. They praised her and petted her, when they had time; none of them knew that when she curled up on the window seat, holding her teddy in her lap, she was in the grip of panic that made her hands sweat and her heart thump and her stomach churn.

Over the years the panic attacks had diminished and finally disappeared, but she had never ventured to ask those dangerous questions. What she knew of that long-gone, shameful tragedy she had discovered from hints dropped by other people, and from the newspaper reports she had consulted when she was old enough to search for herself.

She hesitated, wanting to pursue the subject but uncertain as to whether, or how, she should proceed; and as she groped for the right words, her grandmother suddenly looked away from the television, but not at Meg—not at any visible object. Her eyes focused on empty air, and her head tilted in the pretty, listening pose Meg had often seen when Dan was in the middle of one of his long stories. Her smiling lips parted.

Meg's skin crawled as she waited for her grandmother to respond to the sounds only she could hear. Instead Mary gave a brisk little nod and returned her attention to the game show. "Richard Nixon!" she exclaimed.

"Richard Nixon," said the panelist a split second later.

"Ha!" Mary crowed.

They watched television for another hour, and for once Meg blessed the banalities of the tube, which prohibited sensible conversation. The appearance of Henrietta Marie, prompt upon her hour, was a further, welcomed distraction. Henrietta was far too well bred to beg for food, and far too dignified to court ignominious eviction from places where her presence was not welcome. Only when the family dined informally, in breakfast room or parlor, did she saunter in, with the casual air of someone who just happened to be passing by and who might, if the offering were made with the proper courtesies, condescend to dispose of any uneaten scraps. She had an uncanny ability to judge precisely when the appropriate moment had arrived, and an even more unnerving ability to materialize on the spot without audible or visual warning of her approach.

Gran was used to the cat's habits, but Meg started violently when she saw the fawn-and-sable form at her feet, paws primly together, feathery tail elegantly disposed. The wide blue eyes turned toward her with a look of contempt. Humbly Meg offered a scrap of lemon sole, which Henrietta disposed of without dropping a speck. She finished the fish Meg hadn't been able to eat, polished off the anchovy from Mary's salad, and waited until the maid had removed the trays before jumping onto Mary's lap and turning a sapphirine, unwinking stare toward the screen.

"She likes the catfood commercials," Mary explained, stroking the cat's thick fur. "Well, some of them. She despises Garfield—he really isn't a cat, of course, he's a rude little boy in a cat suit—and I don't believe she has a high opinion of Morris. I have seen a distinct sneer on her face sometimes when she watches Morris."

Meg could well believe it.

However, the cat's rumbling purr made a soothing background sound, and when Henrietta jumped down from Mary's lap and headed purposefully for the door, Mary rose as if responding to a signal. "Time for our beauty sleep. You'll excuse me, dear?"

"I'll go up with you." Meg turned off the TV set.

The cat led the way up the stairs. Watching her grandmother anxiously, Meg was relieved to see that her steps were slow but steady, and that she managed her long skirts skillfully. But it wasn't Mary's physical strength that worried her. They parted at the door of Mary's room, with a kiss and an affectionate exchange of good-nights.

After Meg reached her room she went immediately to the telephone. She wasn't surprised when she got Nick's answering machine instead of Nick; he often screened his calls, and if he was expecting to hear from her, as he surely must be, he would avoid tying up the phone with other callers. But after she had announced herself there was no response except an echoing silence. Meg waited for a few seconds, unwilling to believe he wasn't there. He knew how much she depended on his support and advice, especially now—especially after she had missed their usual noontime call. Before she could decide whether to leave a message, another beep told her she had waited too long. Nick had warned her about leaving personal messages—he and his wife were legally separated, he had his own apartment, but the children sometimes stayed with him. "And you know teenagers, Meg, they have no consideration for other people's privacy. . . ." Meg was tempted to call back and make vulgar, passionate noises onto the tape. Where the hell was he when she needed him?

That would have been childish, so she didn't do it. After hanging up she went restlessly to the window and pulled back the draperies, which had been drawn against the dreary night. Dreary but not dark; the security system Dan had installed, upon the insistence of his insurance company, included a battery of floodlights all around the house. Even with the security system and the strong room, Dan's insurance costs were astronomical. If he had consented to keep all the jewelry in the bank they would have been lower, but he refused to do that; he wanted his darlings close by, where he could play with them and admire them whenever the notion struck him.

It was still raining. The wet green leaves shone in the light as if newly varnished, and the flagstones of the terrace below glistened icily.

Gran also liked her jewels to be readily accessible. The ones she wore most often were supposed to be kept in the strong room, or in the small safe in her dressing room. There were as many safes in the house as there were bathrooms. Following the track of a raindrop down the pane with an idle finger, Meg wondered whether they had all been checked—or found, for that matter. Dan was skilled with tools of all kinds and childishly secretive; he himself had built the hidey-hole for the safe in Meg's closet. How many others might he have constructed?

She let the draperies fall back into place and

turned from the window. Dan wasn't that childish. He must have kept records. And the existence of Mary's safe, at least, was no secret. Meg vividly remembered Dan's fury the only time a more or less successful burglary had occurred. The thieves had hired on as painters with the local firm under contract to maintain the exterior of the house. One source of satisfaction was that the poor devils had to paint for three days, in unseasonable spring heat, before they worked their way around to Gran's window. They waited until lunch break, when the other men had retired to the shade to eat their sandwiches, and then slipped in the window and blew the safe. The few people who heard the muffled, controlled explosion paid no particular attention, assuming that it came from some infernal apparatus on the road, but the thieves beat a hasty retreat as soon as they had cleaned out the safe. They were picked up less than an hour later, after Frances had discovered the wounded safe and called the police.

Despite the fact that he lost nothing, Dan had been apoplectic, mostly at the idea that Gran might have walked in while the thieves were at work. He had rushed out and tried to buy a dozen semiautomatic rifles from the sporting-goods store in town, but he was prevented by the police chief, who knew him only too well. "Wait a couple of months, Dan. You're so damned mad right now you're apt to cut loose at anybody who comes near the place. End up blowing the mailman away or shooting some poor damned Jehovah's Witness."

Dan knew his old buddy the chief pretty well too. He hadn't argued; he had driven down the road and bought handguns for everyone in the house, including the maids, Mary and Meg, who was then seventeen. Mary placidly accepted the pretty little silver-inlaid dueling pistol Dan gave her—and "lost" it. She put her dainty foot down, however, when it came to arming the maids, and came close to one of her rare fits of temper when she learned that Dan had taken Meg into the yard and tried to teach her to fire her weapon. The lessons came to an abrupt halt and the weapon disappeared, to Meg's unspoken relief.

Why was she thinking about guns tonight? It was not a subject she cared to dwell on. There were a number of subjects she preferred not to think about. Guns, burglars, safes—and wills.

Her hand tightened on the soft fabric of the draperies, bunching it into ugly creases. She had lied to George; his question about her will had caught her off guard, and because she knew what his reaction would be, she had taken the coward's way out. She *had* made a will, three years ago, when she first became seriously involved with Nick. It had been a sentimental gesture, inspired by Nick's announcement that he had named her as the beneficiary of one of his insurance policies; at that time she had had nothing to leave except her personal jewelry, since her stock in the company and the historic gems from the Mignot Collection reverted to Dan if she predeceased him.

George wouldn't have scolded her about that

stupid will—he never scolded her—but he would not have been able to conceal his surprise and disapproval. Nor could she blame him. Sentiment was one thing, silly sentimentality was something else again. What had she been thinking of when she made that gesture? Even her personal jewelry had been gifts from Dan, and he'd come back to haunt her if he thought she would let his treasures fall into the hands of a stranger.

Meg turned abruptly from the window. "All right," she said aloud. "All right! First thing in the morning. I promise."

No one answered, of course. She realized she had been holding her head stiffly erect, neck muscles taut, to prevent herself from assuming the same listening pose Mary had taken.

Wills, guns, safes, burglars. What a grim litany. . . . Why didn't the phone ring? Meg frowned at it, but it remained dumb. Wills, safes, burglars. . . . The atmosphere of the house was affecting her. Too quiet. Too many shadows, and the soft dreary drizzle of rain at the windows. Too many problems to deal with, and the frustration of delay in dealing with them.

There was one thing she could do, though; the illusion of accomplishment might improve her mood, even if she had to do it all over again next morning. She went to her closet and turned on the lights.

It was a walk-in closet, almost as big as a dressing room, with drawers and shelves as well as rows of rods for clothing. The few garments that hung there looked lonely in the empty expanse, and Meg reminded herself again that she really must go shopping. Tomorrow, when she went to town to see Darren. What the hell, she thought, her lips twisting in a wry smile, I can buy a whole new wardrobe. I'm going to be an heiress. Lucky me. . . .

Pulling out one of the empty drawers, she pressed the panel at the back. It stuck; she had to bang it with her fist before it slid back, disclosing the face of the safe. She hadn't opened it for years. Supposedly no one else, not even her grandmother, knew of its existence, or the combination of the safe.

It was lucky she had brought so few things. The countertops were clear. She needed all the space and more, when she began unloading the safe. Once the boxes were spread out she frowned uncertainly, searching her memory. Surely there had not been so many boxes the last time she looked. Dan had mentioned he sometimes used her safe for temporary storage. . . . She went back to her desk, searched the pile of documents awaiting her study, found the ledger in which her collection was listed. She carried the ledger, and a chair, back to the closet. Might as well do it right if she was going to do it.

The rings were stored in velvet-lined boxes, with glass covers, thirty-six to a box. Except for the last box, which was only three-quarters full, there were no empty slots. Painstakingly she checked them against the entries in the ledger, though returning memory, stimulated by actual sight, assured her that nothing was missing. So much for Cliff's malicious suggestion that the memento mori ring sent to George had come from her collection. She had been certain she owned nothing of that nature.

There were additions, however—approximately a dozen new rings, which Dan must have acquired and added after she moved to New York. They checked with the entries he had added to the ledger in his firm, ageless handwriting—date of acquisition, source, price paid, description. Meg lingered over them, trying them on, inspecting them through the loupe that was always kept in the safe. Several were too small for any but her little finger, but one particularly pretty garnet-and-emerald ring slipped neatly onto the third finger of her right hand. Curved around the shank were the words "The sight of this Deserves a kiss," and she smiled when she had deciphered the ornate letters. The number of mottoes was endless, but this was particularly charming. Instead of returning it to its place she left it on her finger after she had checked the entry in the ledger—noting as she did so that Dan had gotten a bargain. The ring was early seventeenth century in style, and the emeralds were perfectly matched, a vivid deep green, and remarkably clear of flaws. Conquistadores' loot, she thought, her smile fading; stolen from the servants of the Incas, along with their lives and liberty. That was the dark side of the magic of gems, the ugly histories of the greed, theft and murder they had inspired.

She had sometimes wondered whether that was one of the reasons why Dan had been more interested in the artistry of the settings than in the stones themselves. He would have scoffed at the suggestion; he never liked admitting he had a sentimental side.

Her frown remained as she put the ring boxes back in the safe and turned her attention to the others on the countertop. They were not glass-topped, but solid storage boxes, and not one of them was even faintly familiar. Nor were they recorded in her ledger. Selecting one at random, she lifted the lid.

Nestled in crumpled paper was a flat jewel case, roughly shell-shaped, the dark blue leather stamped in gold with Dan's name. The shape of the container gave her some idea of what to expect, but when the catch yielded to the pressure of her thumb and the lid rose, she gasped aloud.

Electric light for rubies. . . . There were three of them, each as big as the end of her thumb, set in gold, with a trio of perfect pearls hanging from each setting. The sapphires, almost as large, and perfectly matched, held their glorious blue so well that they had to be the prized Kashmir gems; they were centered in heavy gold plaques that formed a necklace to which the rubies were pendant. Diamonds formed flowerlike petals around the sapphire centers. The gold work was spectacular; coils and curls of twisted metal framed the stones. The sheer opulence of the piece dazzled the eye and the mind; but when she recovered from her surprise and looked more closely she realized that the cutting of the gems was not of the same quality as the gold work. Crudely shaped though they were, their color and size were outstanding.

There were half a dozen other boxes. Each contained jewelry as important and at least as valuable as the necklace. The most remarkable was a tiara or diadem of gold so pure it could be bent with one's bare hands. The stones appeared to have been set almost at random, creating a gaudy blaze of color. Despite the brilliant yellows, rose-pinks, sea blues and the primitive cut of the stones, which failed to bring out their fires as the present-day brilliant cut could do, Meg knew that most of the faceted stones were diamonds, of unusual shades and considerable size. There were several rubies, all of superb color except for one stone that had a slightly rusty shade. . . .

Her breathing quickened as she took up the loupe and peered more closely at the off-color "ruby." It was impossible to be certain without putting the stone through a variety of tests, but its luster and brilliance told her her instincts were correct. Only zircons and demantoid garnets approach the distinctive adamantine luster of diamonds, and they reflect only about half the light. A red diamond? They were the rarest of all stones; no more than half a dozen of them were known to exist, and this was larger than any she had heard of. It must be a good ten carats in weight.

Meg closed the last box, thanking heaven for the impulse that had led her to open the safe that evening, instead of having the astonishing discovery burst upon her in the sardonic presence of her "cousin." Cliff would be as quick to jump to conclusions as she had been—quicker, he had that kind of mind—and his cynical amusement would have been hard to bear.

Meg tried to convince herself that she had also been too quick to condemn her grandfather. Perhaps the pieces were recent acquisitions; perhaps Dan had recorded them elsewhere. She tried—but she failed. There was no sensible reason why Dan should have used her little safe, except as a temporary repository for objects whose very existence he wanted to keep secret. From her grandmother, from George, from the IRS? Or from their original owners? Like love and a bad cold, such important jewels could not be disguised, they were distinctive enough to have histories of their own. Even individual stones could be traced through time, from owner to owner, and identified by means of their chemical and optical characteristics. If the odd red stone was indeed a diamond, it was absolutely unique, yet Meg was ninety-nine percent certain there was no record of it anywhere in the literature.

The pieces were all of Indian, or at least eastern, design. Wild fantasies swirled through Meg's mind. Avenging priests stalking the violators of their god; starving descendants of deposed imperial houses hunting the man who had robbed them. The tiara was of queenly quality. Where on earth—*how* on earth—had Dan acquired those objects?

With a sigh she turned her thoughts to more practical matters. Avenging priests and princes were figments of fiction. Not so the avengers of the Internal Revenue Service; she had no intention of playing dangerous illegal games with them, but before she went running off to confess she had better make certain Dan was guilty. Downstairs, in the library, were the reference books Dan had collected over many years—everything that had been published on the subject of gems and jewelry. Perhaps in one of the catalogs she could find mention, or even a photograph, of one of the pieces she had discovered.

She opened the door and started toward the stairs. Preoccupied as she was, she was halfway down them before she noticed the change in the temperature. A gust of frigid air rose to meet her; icy, invisible fingers plucked at the fabric of her robe. Shivering, she gathered its folds around her. Someone must have left a window open. But how could the temperature have dropped so dramatically? The sun had been midsummer warm earlier that day.

Holding the banister with one hand and her fluttering skirts with the other, she examined the hall below. There were no ambiguous shadows or patches of dark; the lights shone dimly but steadily, nothing moved. The chains and inner bolts on the front door were unfastened; one or both of the men must still be out. But the lock was a dead bolt, it could not be opened without a key.

Her throat was dry and her feet wanted to turn and run back up the stairs. Ridiculous, she scolded herself. If a window had been left open, all the more reason why she should investigate. No one could have entered the house without setting off the alarms, but rain coming through an open window could ruin draperies and carpets.

The brisk breeze had died by the time she reached the bottom of the stairs. Without a current of air to guide her she could not find its source; the windows in the drawing room, parlor, dining room and library were closed and locked, and nothing audibly or visually alarming occurred. But the air still felt cold.

Deciding that she had exhibited enough courage for one night, she selected a few of the large, illustrated books on historic jewels and started back to her room. The books were heavy; she had to wrap both arms around the unwieldy pile. As she climbed the steps the cold lessened, and she stopped at the top to get a better grip on her burden, feeling a little foolish. The house was old; despite the constant maintenance there must be cracks, gaps, through which air could sometimes blast. Hadn't she read about strange winds blowing through one of the Egyptian pyramids, winds whose origin no one had ever been able to find? She should have stayed in the library instead of dragging a heavy load up the stairs.

Clutching the books to her breast, she was about

to proceed when she heard a noise. It was barely audible, just over the threshold of sound—a soft, happy murmur of laughter.

Slowly, reluctantly, Meg turned away from her own room, whose open doorway spilled brightness into the dimness of the corridor. The door of her grandmother's suite wasn't far. She stopped in front of it and stood listening.

At first there was nothing but silence. No light showed under the door or through the keyhole. Then it came again, soft as a far-off ripple of water, wordless and musical. Shivering, dry lips parted, Meg pressed her ear to the cold wooden panels and heard her grandmother laughing, alone in the dark.

6

"THE FURNACE MAN says he can't come till this afternoon," Frances said dourly. She slapped a plate of bacon and eggs down in front of George. "I told him if he wasn't here by one we'd get someone else."

"There's no urgency. It's June, after all." George spoke without lowering his newspaper, but this pitiful attempt to avoid conversation was as futile as such hints usually were with Frances. Hands on her hips, arms akimbo, she said, "That's all right for you to say, Mr. George; the upstairs heating system wasn't affected, and your room was nice and toasty, but mine sure wasn't.

They said there was a cold front coming through, but they didn't say it was coming from the North Pole. It felt like a blizzard blowing through my window."

"Why didn't you close the window?" Cliff asked.

Frances glowered at him. "Dour" was the key word this morning; she had switched to role number two, the loyal family servant whose crusty exterior covers a heart of gold. In this part she was entitled to grumble as much as she liked. Cliff's question smacked of criticism; she refused to give it the dignity of a reply.

"How is Gran this morning?" Meg asked.

"She didn't sleep too good." Frances's glum face lengthened still more, but the distraction succeeded. "I told her I'd take her up a tray. If you folks are finished wasting my time, I'll get to my other duties."

"Do," Cliff said earnestly. "Oh, do, Frances. Please do.

"I wish she'd go back to being Mrs. Danvers," he added, after the door had slammed after the affronted housekeeper. "I hate the crusty old servant with the heart of gold even more than the jolly fat servant with the heart of gold. You remember that one, Meg, the one that pinched our cheeks and clasped us to her motherly bosom till we were half suffocated?"

"Now, Cliff," George murmured. Eyes still fixed on the financial page, he offered a strip of bacon to Henrietta Marie, who had jumped up on the chair next to his as soon as Frances left the room. Bacon was the only comestible that overcame Henrietta's aristocratic reserve; she had been under the table for some time, but she knew that Frances's number-two role disapproved of cats in the breakfast room. (The jolly fat housekeeper doted on pussycats.)

Meg returned her cousin's smile. She was in excellent spirits this morning; the news that her frightening experience on the stairs had been caused by a perfectly normal phenomenon had been a salutary reminder that she mustn't let her imagination run away with her. Henrietta Marie emitted a soft but peremptory mew, and George obediently offered another scrap of bacon. Meg laughed. Even if that other laughter had been real, it could be explained as rationally as the cold breeze from Frances's window. Lying wakeful and lonely in the dark, her grandmother had been chatting with Henrietta.

"It's nice to hear you laugh," Cliff said approvingly. "First time since you got here."

"Funerals don't inspire a lot of hilarity," Meg said.

Cliff refused to be offended. "That shows how much you know. I've attended some happy and hilarious wakes and at least one funeral service where the eulogy was funnier than any comedian's routine. Here, Henrietta, have one on me: a reward for making the pretty lady laugh."

Henrietta condescended to accept the strip of

bacon. She took it under the table and killed it, growling pleasurably.

George folded his newspaper and put it on the chair the cat had vacated. He looked tired, Meg thought; his closely shaved cheeks were a trifle pale and there was a suggestion of shadow under his eyes. However, he was impeccably groomed, from his thick cap of silvery hair to his three-piece suit and silk tie. He was one of the few people Meg knew who still wore shirts with French cuffs, and as he extended his arm to glance at his watch she saw a glimmer of purple at his wrist.

"What gorgeous cuff links," she said. "Are they antique?"

George offered one for inspection. It was an amethyst intaglio, showing a Medusa's head. The carving was superb; the snaky locks writhed and the mouth gaped in a silent scream. Meg ran an appreciative finger over the gem. "It's very old. Classical Greek or Roman."

"I didn't know the ancient Greeks wore shirts with French cuffs," Cliff said.

"Dan had them set for me," George said. "I believe they were originally a pair of earrings."

"The earrings probably weren't original either," Meg said. "Dan wouldn't have vandalized an ancient Greek piece, even for you, George. He was fanatical about. . . ."

George waited for her to continue. After a moment he said, "Is something wrong with the links, Meg?"

"What?" She came back to reality with a start.

"Oh—no, of course not, Uncle George. Sorry. I just thought of something I had . . . I had forgotten."

She hadn't forgotten. Dan had tirades about jewelers who failed to retain the original integrity of a piece of jewelry. He had pounded that principle into her head at an early age, but she had failed to apply it to the objects he had hidden in her safe. There was a market for such pieces. However, a collector would pay far less than the gems themselves would fetch if they were properly cut and reset. Most jewelers would have taken that course, especially if they wanted to conceal the origin of stolen jewelry. But to Daniel Mignot such an act would have been worse than vandalism. He had done it upon occasion, when the gems were sufficiently outstanding, and the design of the piece lacked originality, but even then he had mourned as over the death of a living thing.

Thanks to Dan's ledger, it did not take long for them to examine the ring collection. That was all George seemed to care about—that the entries in the ledger matched the objects themselves. Handing Meg the final box, he said with visible relief, "Everything seems to be in order. If I may make a suggestion—take the ledger to Darren and ask him to have a copy made."

"That's a good idea." Meg put the box in the dresser drawer.

"If I may make a suggestion," Cliff began.

He had spent even less time looking at the rings

than his father, but he had pored over the ledger; remembering his comment about old-fashioned methods of record-keeping, Meg was torn between amusement and resentment as he inspected the pages with her loupe. Did he really expect to find signs of erasure?

"What?" she asked, closing the drawer.

"That's not a particularly secure place to keep your valuables."

Before she went down to breakfast Meg had removed the rings from the safe. She had not been thinking clearly the night before or she would have realized she would have to do so, or disclose the existence of the hiding place. The tone of Cliff's voice, and the way his eyes moved curiously around the room, told her he already suspected there was a hidden safe somewhere. She had no intention of admitting it, though. It was none of his business.

Before she could reply to his comment her uncle said, "It's safe enough, Clifford. None of Meg's little rings is particularly valuable in itself, and the collection couldn't be marketed by a thief; it's too well known in the trade."

Does he know? Meg wondered. He suspects—but he doesn't want Cliff to know.

"I've got to run," George went on. "It's late. Meg, I took the liberty of calling Darren this morning and making an appointment for you. I knew you were too considerate to call him at home, and if you had waited till afternoon to call he might have been booked up, and. . . . I hope you don't mind?"

She did mind, but his apologetic air disarmed her. "Thank you, Uncle George. What time?"

"You've got ten minutes," her uncle said. "I'll drop you off."

"I'll meet you downstairs in five minutes," Meg agreed.

"Why rush?" Cliff hadn't moved from the sofa across which he was sprawled, as much at ease as if he were in his own room. "An important client can keep a lawyer waiting. Want me to drive you? I'm at your disposal, coz dear."

"Be at my disposal somewhere else," Meg said, opening the door.

By the time Cliff had drifted out, the five minutes were considerably less. Hastily Meg applied fresh lipstick, tied her hair back with a scarf and returned the ring boxes to the safe. When she trotted downstairs, to find her uncle waiting, Cliff was nowhere to be seen. Meg suspected he had been on the receiving end of a forceful lecture from his father, a suspicion that was confirmed when George said, "I hope Cliff isn't proving to be a nuisance, Meg. If he bothers you, tell me."

"I can handle Cliff. He's not Jack the Ripper."

Her uncle gave her a look of surprise. "I didn't mean—"

"Eyes on the road, Uncle George," Meg said, smiling.

"Of course, of course."

He was silent for the remainder of the brief drive.

The offices of Blake and Morgan were no longer in the shabby downtown building Meg remembered, but in a refurbished cottage behind the stately mansions of The Square. In a former life the row of small houses had sheltered the servants, and the horses, who had served The Square's aristocrats. Shops and offices filled them now; preoccupied as she was, Meg noticed a boutique whose window held a couple of potential additions to her limited wardrobe.

She thanked her uncle and got out of the car. "This wasn't such a bright idea," he said ruefully. "I should have let you drive the Ferrari. Call when you're ready to go home, and someone will come for you."

"Don't fuss, Uncle George." She reached back through the open window and gave his hand a squeeze, to show she was teasing. He was slow to relinquish his hold; almost, she thought, as if he were afraid she were walking into an ambush, instead of an ordinary office.

It was ordinary enough, and familiar; law books lined the walls, the rug on the floor was the same beautiful Bokhara and the woman behind the old oak desk was Mrs. Babcock, who had presided over the other office—a little grayer, a little plumper, but still unmistakably the self-appointed moral force behind Blake and Morgan. She showed no sign of surprise or pleasure when

Meg greeted her by name; she expected to be remembered.

Darren looked older and more dignified as he rose from his chair behind his father's desk; he even looked taller. The warmth in his smile and the gleam in his eyes told Meg that his pleasure in seeing her wasn't entirely professional. Mrs. Babcock lingered. "Are you sure you don't want me to take notes, Mr. Blake?"

"No, that won't be necessary." After a moment Darren added firmly, "Thank you, Mrs. Babcock."

When the door had closed, Meg said jokingly, "Is it you or me she doesn't trust?"

To her surprise a distinct blush spread over Darren's face. "She—uh—she's just curious. About you."

"Me? But she's known me all my life."

"She hasn't seen you for a long time. You've changed quite a lot, Meg."

"Not really."

But the town didn't know that, and they wouldn't have believed her if she had said so. Her prolonged absence must have aroused some degree of resentment, and a large amount of gossip. Now she was back, after years in the big city, and no matter how she behaved, some of them would see her as a spoiled sophisticate who thought she was too good for Seldon—who had neglected her poor old grandparents and returned only to rake in her share of the loot. No matter how friendly she was, some of them would find her condescending. She thought she understood Darren's blush. How many of his pals had kidded him about Dan Mignot's rich, unmarried granddaughter?

Darren began talking about her will. At her request, he explained the provisions Dan had made in the case of her predeceasing him. The bulk of the estate went to various charities, except for the store, which went outright to A. L. Riley.

"That's the way I want it, then," Meg said. "Except for one thing. I want to leave something to Uncle George. Something sizable."

Darren's head, which had been bent over the papers, came up with a jerk. "Is there some reason why I shouldn't?" Meg asked in surprise.

"No, no. You can do anything you like. In the normal course of events you will outlive your uncle, so you'll have to make alternative provisions. . . ."

After they had settled that, and decided on the amount, Darren said, "That should do it. You can make changes at any time, of course, or add codicils, but I'd like to get this drawn up and signed as soon as possible. Can you come in tomorrow at four?"

"So soon?"

"I'll bring it to the house if you prefer."

"That won't be necessary, Darren. I was just surprised that you would have it ready so quickly. New York lawyers don't move that fast."

"I usually don't either," Darren admitted. "But in this case. . . . Are you sure, now, about what you want?"

"Yes." His silence and his faint frown were as eloquent as speech. "Come on, Darren, spit it out," Meg said, remembering a favorite childhood phrase. "Something is bugging you. What?"

"Are you sure you want Riley to have the store?"

"That was going to be the next topic of conversation. What can you tell me about him?"

"Not much." Darren's frown deepened. "At first there was no reason for me to take an interest in the fellow; he was just another employee. As you know, Dan brooked no interference with the store and its management. I had no idea how much influence Riley had gained until Dan ordered me to make that last change in his will."

"Influence?" Meg repeated.

He understood what she meant, and a reluctant smile came over his face. "We wouldn't have a leg to stand on, Meg. Dan was getting a little absentminded, but he was as sharp as any man in this town—sharper than some half his age. I didn't try to argue with him, he'd have blown his stack if I had so much as implied he could be improperly influenced."

"Then he had reason—good reason—for making that arrangement."

"Well . . . I suppose so, yes." Darren leaned back in his chair, took off his glasses and rubbed the bridge of his nose. "I did suggest that before he took such a step he ought to have the man investigated. Then he did blow his stack. He said he knew all he needed to know, that it was none of my effing business, and that if I went behind his back and hired a detective he'd nail my hide to the office door."

"That sounds like Dan," Meg said, smiling. "Did you go behind his back?"

"Are you kidding?" Darren's answering grin made him look like the boy she had known. Then he sobered. "I did do something I rather hate to admit. It was unprofessional, and not my usual style, but I was so uneasy about the situation I felt it was necessary. I—er—I encouraged people to gossip."

His look of exaggerated guilt amused Meg. "Did you learn anything that would suggest Dan made an error in judgment?"

"Not really," Darren admitted. "When Riley first came to town he boarded with Sally Johnson. She told me 'he never made no trouble, and minded his own business, which was not such a bad idea even for a g——d——lawyer." I quote, of course.

"She sounds like an ideal landlady," Meg said. "Go on."

"After Dan made Riley manager, he moved to the apartment over the store. And that—Darren made a gesture of frustration—"that's about it. He isn't a member of a lodge or professional association, he doesn't attend the local churches, he doesn't borrow videotapes—"

"Oh, Darren, for heaven's sake—you didn't!"

Another, darker blush, suffused the lawyer's cheeks. "It was a last recourse. So far as I could tell the man doesn't go anywhere or associate with anybody. People don't like him—"

"Because he doesn't go anywhere or associate with anybody." Meg sniffed. "That's not a crime; in fact, it's probably a sign of good judgment. So far you've told me nothing that would explain why Dan acted as he did. I want to know, Darren. Before I can decide what to do about the store I have to know."

"Decide what to do. . . ." Darren stared at her in surprise. "But surely there's no question about that. Dan wanted you to have it—manage it."

"What Dan wanted and what I want are two different things."

"Mmmm. Yes, of course." Darren's eyes shifted. "I knew you and Dan had some—er—differences of opinion about your participation in the business. But I assumed that under the circumstances. . . ."

"They have changed, yes." Meg fought a rising tide of anger that was directed as much at herself as at Darren. "Dan is dead. Now I can run things to suit myself instead of having him on my back all the time. Naturally I'd jump at that, wouldn't I?"

"I didn't mean—"

"I know. I'm sorry. I just. . . ." She was disconcerted to find that her voice was unsteady and her eyes were swimming with tears. "This is harder than I thought it would be, Darren. Forgive me."

"I understand."

He didn't understand, though, not entirely. How could he, when she herself had not sorted out the varied emotions that pulled her first in one direction and then in another? Nice, uncomplicated, conventional Darren—how could he comprehend the mixture of love and resentment that blended with her grief for Dan?

When she had regained her composure she tried again. "Staying here in Seldon and running the store is one of my options, Darren, but it's not the only one. I had—I have another life, elsewhere. A satisfying career, friends. . . . It has pluses and minuses, but so does the alternative. Suppose I decided to sell my interest in the store?"

"To Riley?" His voice rose on the final syllable, in a squeak of pure horror.

"Why not to Riley?"

"Why—because he—because Dan. . . . You don't know anything about the man!"

"Precisely. So find out about him."

"You mean you'll let me investigate—"

"Let you, hell. I insist that you do so." His blank, uncomprehending stare fueled the anger she had tried to control; it boiled over. "God damn it, Darren, don't react to everything I say as if I were some naive little twit without a brain cell in my head! And don't make decisions for me. I'll make them for myself—but only after I have gathered the relevant data and considered it. And above all—spare me mean, petty-minded gossip. Give me facts!"

Darren's jaw was hanging. "That's what Dan

used to say," he whispered. "'Give me facts.' You sound just like him."

Before she left, Meg apologized again. She was genuinely ashamed of her outburst; Darren hadn't meant to sound condescending, it was her own self-doubt and confusion that made her supersensitive to his comments. He accepted her apology with sympathetic murmurs and a tentative pat or two, and they parted on amicable terms. No doubt he was used to grieving heirs who indulged in emotional tantrums. If hers had only been that simple. . . . It had felt good, though!

Once outside the building she took a deep breath of the clean sweet air and stood admiring the quiet charm of the street, with its pretty shops and old shade trees. She had no intention of calling for a ride home. It was an idea that would not have occurred to her if George hadn't suggested it; she had not been brought up to expect such luxuries. Despite his millions Dan had Old Country notions about Hard Work and Earning Your Way, and Getting Things Too Easily. (One could almost hear the capital letters as he lectured.) Newspaper and television stories about Rich Kids (more capitals) who were drug addicts, alcoholics and worse, were seen as confirmation of his theories. As a child Meg had had the same allowance as her friends, and she had attended local schools. Gran's needs were different, of course; she had all the servants she wanted, but Dan had never hired a valet or a chauffeur. He had driven himself until a few years earlier, when the terrified city council finally convinced Gran that they couldn't go on sounding the fire alarm to warn drivers whenever Dan Mignot took to the road.

It was a nice day for a walk, Meg decided. Besides, being on her own, for the first time since she had returned, had a certain exhilaration. She turned to look at the window of the boutique, and smiled cynically as a half-seen form quickly withdrew. If the town wanted to see what she was like, she would let them look their fill.

She was inside the shop less than half an hour. The clothes were all overpriced and badly made, and she resented the clerk's fawning assurances that everything she tried on looked "absolutely smashing, dear." Even the dress that wouldn't go down over her hips.

What she really needed were pants—not designer jeans, which had certainly not been designed for hips like hers. ("Rounded hips are back in style, madam.") Meg headed for Main Street.

She found the pants and shirts she wanted at what had been the dry-goods store when Dan Mignot first came to Seldon; it still sold fabric and clothing, but it was under new management, and Meg cut her shopping short because the stares and whispers were getting on her nerves. She needed sneakers—why hadn't she thought to bring them?—but to reach the shoe store she would have had to cross the street and pass the jewelry store. She wasn't ready for that yet, and her stomach—strengthened, perhaps, by that healthy outbreak of rage—reminded her that it was time for lunch.

There were other eating places within walking distance—a pizza parlor, the lunch counter at the five-and-dime, and a health-food restaurant—but it would have been unthinkable to go anywhere but Kate's. For one thing, Kate would hear about it and be deeply hurt. For another . . . Kate would hear about it and be deeply hurt.

Consciously or unconsciously, Meg had delayed until the conventional noon-to-one lunch hour was past. When she entered the restaurant, however, she saw that there were two people at the reserved table at the back. One was Barby. The other was A. L. Riley.

Barby saw Meg first, and stopped in the middle of what appeared to be an earnest oration. Riley turned; as Meg approached he rose in a leisurely fashion and said, "Thanks, Barby. Hello and good-bye, Ms. Venturi. I was just—"

"Sit down," Meg said, keeping her voice low and a bright smile pasted onto her face. She slid into a chair.

"I was—"

"I said sit down!"

Riley sat. "I clocked out over an hour ago, Ms. Venturi. I hope you aren't going to dock my pay; I can't afford it."

Meg laughed heartily. "Do you want the whole town to think we're feuding?"

"Oh, so that's it. I don't give a damn what the town thinks. Why should you?"

"I resent people gossiping about me. I refuse to give them grounds for doing so."

"She's right, you know," said Barby, whose head had been turning from speaker to speaker. "You're in trouble enough right now, you don't need—"

She stopped short, with a gurgle, as he turned his eyes toward her.

"Just let me know when you think enough time has elapsed to create an impression of goodwill," Riley said. "We're losing money. I had to close up."

"Where is Candy?" Meg asked.

"I fired her." He fixed an ironic gaze upon her. "I beg your pardon for failing to consult you, but if you had heard some of the things she said you'd agree with my decision."

"What things?"

"I thought you disapproved of gossip."

He had her there. And she had no reason to doubt his implication that "some of the things" Candy had said were directed at her. "You can't run the store by yourself," she said. "You'd better find—"

"I am in the process of taking the necessary steps," her partner said. "At least I was, until you arrived."

"I'll ask around," Barby said quickly. "I know a couple of kids who are looking for work, but as

I said, they don't know anything about the jewelry business."

"And as I said: thanks." He looked at Meg. "May I be excused now?"

Meg offered him her hand. "I hope the strain hasn't been too much for you."

He took her hand with all the enthusiasm of a man being offered a dead fish, but a hint of genuine amusement warmed his formal smile. "Probably harder on you than on me, Ms. Venturi."

"I've got to run, honey," Barby announced, struggling with her napkin, her chair and an oversized purse. "Wait, Riley, you can walk me back to the shop, and I'll tell you about—about somebody else I just remembered."

Riley clearly wasn't crazy about the idea, but he offered his arm and slowed his stride to match Barby's tripping steps. A waitress hurried to Meg's side. "I'm sorry, Miss Venturi, did you want to order?"

"Yes, just a minute," Meg said absently, watching the oddly assorted pair move toward the door. Barby's arthritis must be acting up, she was clinging to Riley's arm and he had put his hand over hers.

The restaurant was only half-full; the remaining diners appeared to be housewives and tourists lingering over a second cup of coffee, except for two men who had obviously lingered too long over something else. Their conversation had been loud and punctuated by guffaws of laughter, which stopped abruptly when Barby and Riley passed their table. One of them, a short, stocky man whose belly hung out over his unbuckled belt, stumbled up from his chair. His friend caught his arm and steered him back to his place, saying something Meg didn't catch.

The waitress had gone, leaving a menu. As Meg reached for it the swinging door flew open and Kate came through like a bullet from a gun. Seeing Meg, she jolted to a stop. "I didn't know you were here. Somebody should've told me."

"I haven't been here long." Meg added with a grin, "Go ahead and throw them out, Kate; that's why you came, wasn't it? Do you need any help?"

"Not with those two lily-livered creeps," Kate said, flexing her stringy arms. "They know I don't let people get sloshed in my place. Oh, well, I guess they can wait awhile. It's good to see you, honey. What have you been up to?"

Meg explained that she had been shopping, and Kate nodded approvingly. "That always perks a girl up. What'd you buy?"

Meg displayed her purchases and listened patiently to Kate's criticisms—"You don't need to buy cheap stuff like that, honey, why didn't you go out to the shopping center, there's some nice stores out there." Neither of them saw the man until he stumbled over his own feet and fell forward, catching himself in the nick of time by grabbing at the next table.

"Dammit," Kate hissed, starting up. "Rod Applegate, I told you last time—"

"Please, Kate." Applegate had smoothed his

hair and straightened his tie, but his attempt to look dignified was somewhat marred by the fact that he had forgotten to fasten his belt. He was younger than Meg had thought; his potbelly and puffy face made him look older. He went on, taking great care with his sibilants, "I jus' want to say hello to Meg. Hello, Meg."

"Hello," Meg said.

"Been a long time."

"Has it?"

"How 'bout if I buy you a drink—have a little chat?"

He pulled out one of the empty chairs. Kate, who had been vibrating like a taut bowstring, let fly. A hard shove propelled Applegate into the arms of his friend, who had come up behind him. "Get him out of here, Jim," Kate snarled. "And don't either of you come back."

Taller, heavier and less drunk than his friend, Jim managed to stay on his feet. Arms wrapped around Applegate, who stared in owlish surprise at Kate, he began, "Listen, you know why he—"

"I don't care why. Out, I said."

"But I gotta warn Meg," Applegate whined. "Tell her 'bout that sumbitch—"

"Out," Kate said.

"But I gotta—"

"Come on, Rod." Jim turned himself and his buddy around. Like an uncoordinated set of Siamese twins, they stumbled toward the door.

"Am I supposed to know him?" Meg asked.

"He was in school with you, I guess. A couple of years ahead."

The hint was enough to spark Meg's memory; stripped of excess flesh, the features were indeed those of a boy she remembered vaguely, and without fondness. He had been a bully and a loudmouthed jerk even then. "What did Mr. Riley ever do to him?"

"Hired—and fired—Candy." Kate's eagle eye was still fixed on the wavering pair, who had stopped at the cash register to pay their bill. "Rod is Candy's husband. Ex, I should say."

"What? I didn't know Candy was married!"

"It only lasted a couple of months. He's a drunk and Candy is . . . is a natural-born old maid. It was over long before Riley appeared on the scene, but Rod's the kind who has to blame somebody for his own failures. Excuse me a minute, honey, I better get up there, they're giving Ruby a hard time—"

Her approach ended the argument over the check. Jim pushed his friend toward the door, but Applegate was determined to have the last word. "Get even with that sumbitch," he bellowed over his shoulder. "Can't treat people that way an' get away with it. Gonna kill that—"

The slam of the door cut off the final epithet.

7

"OLD MAID" WAS a euphemism for words Kate would have employed if she had been speaking to a contemporary instead of someone she still thought of as an innocent little girl. But the history of Candy's romance was as clear to Meg as if Kate had spelled it out. Candy had married Rod Applegate because he was her last, perhaps her first and only, chance, and had discovered that the "intimacies of marriage," to use another euphemism, were not to her taste—particularly with a boorish clod. Poor Candy was not only a romantic, but a witless one; the contrast between her vapid fantasies and Applegate's direct approach to sex must have been brutal.

Yet she and her ex had something in common. Neither could accept reality, they saw the world not as it was but as they wanted it to be. Probably Riley had had no choice but to fire Candy, she would have been oblivious to anything less direct. All the same, and in spite of the alleged insults to herself, Meg couldn't help feeling sorry for her.

Wrapped in her thoughts, she acknowledged the greetings of passersby with no more than a smile or a nod, though several halted with the obvious desire to talk with her. Now they'll start calling me a snob, she thought. Rod and Candy were not the exceptions, but the rule. Most people went around with blinders on, seeing only what they wanted to see.

How Cliff would gloat when he heard about Candy! His idle prediction had come to pass even sooner than he might have expected. He was in for a disappointment if he thought she would participate in his scheme to persuade Candy to bear witness—false or true, she suspected Cliff didn't care—against her former boss; unfortunately there was no way she could prevent him from coming on to Candy himself. Maybe if she told him Candy's ex was jealous . . . Meg smiled wryly. Cliff had nothing to fear from a flabby slob like Rod Applegate. Come to that, neither did Riley. Either one of them could handle Applegate with one hand tied behind him.

She turned into the driveway, thinking longingly of the hammock in the rose garden. Later, perhaps. First she ought to see how Gran was doing, ask if there were any errands she could do for her. And check the mail. There might be a letter from Nick.

The shining surface of the Chippendale lowboy in the hall was bare even of dust. The mail had been sorted and delivered, then. It was one of Frances's duties, and one she never shirked, probably, Meg thought, because she was so incurably nosy. Nobody had actually caught Frances steaming a letter open, but Cliff swore he had seen her holding envelopes against a lamp and squinting to read the message inside.

Meg's room had been cleaned and her mail was

on the desk, together with several slips of paper bearing telephone messages. The letters were all notes of condolence, from local friends of the family; one had been sent by a former classmate, whose name Meg recognized with pleasure. So Jan was back in Seldon. She'd have to call, arrange a meeting. Unlike Candy, Jan had been a friend.

There had been two calls from her boss, demanding that she call him immediately if not sooner. Meg crumpled them up and threw them in the direction of the wastebasket. At the very bottom of the pile was a slip of paper in Frances's difficult handwriting, informing her that a Mr. Baggart had called and left his number.

Meg would have identified Frances's characteristic misinterpretation of the name sooner if the number had been the one she expected. There was no area code, so it had to be a local number. Curious, beginning to hope, she dialed, and discovered she was speaking to the receptionist at the Inn at Patterson's Mill, eight miles from Seldon.

An hour later Nick opened the door of his room. "What took you so long?" he asked. Meg went into his arms.

Nick decreed they would dine at the Inn. "There's no other decent restaurant near here, and I can think of better ways of spending our time than driving all over the neighborhood."

"It's okay with me. There's so much I want to talk over with you—"

"Talking wasn't what I had in mind." Nick

shaped his mobile, actor's face into an exaggerated leer. Meg laughed, but as she took his arm she felt a faint discomfort. It wasn't the first time they had met at a hotel, and this pleasant room, with its good antique reproductions, was nothing like the usual cheap motel, but still. . . .

After they had been shown to a table in the dining room and Nick had studied the wine list, she said, "I wish you didn't have to go back tomorrow."

Nick raised his glass in a smiling toast. "Darling, I shouldn't have taken this much time off. I canceled half a dozen appointments."

"I know. I do appreciate it—"

"I missed you." He glanced approvingly around the softly lit room, with its massed greenery and handsome furniture. "Quite a pleasant little place. How much longer are we going to go on meeting like this?"

"That's one of the things I wanted to talk to you about."

"We'd better order." Nick caught the eye of a tactfully hovering waiter. When they had finished and the waiter had retired, he said gently, "Now we won't be interrupted. Don't be afraid of telling me, Meg. I suspect I know what you're going to say."

"Then you're better informed than I am. I haven't made a decision. But"—her finger traced idle, meaningless designs on the white tablecloth—"but a week ago I would have said there was no decision to be made."

"You don't have to work for a living," Nick reminded her. "Especially now."

"Except for my need to accomplish something on my own, something that isn't . . ."

She didn't finish the sentence. After waiting a moment, Nick finished it for her, ". . . that isn't based on the accomplishments of your grandfather. Meg, Meg—" He captured the hand she had lifted in protest, and held it tightly. "You have to stop basing decisions on childish hurt and old resentment."

"What a neatly turned phrase. Did you compose it on the way here, or while you were kissing me?"

Nick laughed. "I adore you when you're waspish and feisty. As a matter of fact, I composed it last week, when you made that scene about the snow crystal. I didn't think you were ready to hear it then; but you can't go on brooding about the past. You are about to inherit a family business for which you are ideally suited. No, don't interrupt, let me finish. I've heard you talk about jewelry; you are very well informed, you have a trained eye and a genuine feel for the subject. You're a talented designer—"

"I don't know anything about jewelry design."

"Because you deliberately avoided studying the subject. Your success in advertising is due to your design capabilities and your business sense. Turn those talents to your own business, run the store and build it into another empire, as your grandfather did. Wouldn't that be accomplishment enough?"

"That's what Dan was going to do," Meg said.

"What, darling?"

"Build another empire." She smiled reminiscently. "Can you believe it? At sixty-five, seventy years old, he was going to do it again. He hated what the business had become—a big soulless organization that cared more about making money than creating beautiful things."

"And he wanted you to carry out his dream."

"Dan wouldn't have put it that way," Meg said dryly. "But—yes, that was the idea. He was furious when I told him that I wouldn't follow the course of studies he had planned for me. He actually cut me off, you know. Threw me out into the blizzard with my refusal clutched to my bosom like an illegitimate baby. I had to drop out of school and work as a clerk for six months."

"But he forgave you."

"Oh, yes." Meg laughed. "It wasn't that bad. Gran sent me money, secretly—she thought. Dan knew all about it, of course; he had a private detective keeping an eye on me the whole time. Finally he cracked; I guess the detective must have told him about my cold-water flat in a high-crime area, and my gay roommate. I came home one day to find Dan in the living room, drinking beer with Johnny and arguing about modern art."

"He must have been quite a guy."

"They both were," Meg said perversely. "I adored Johnny."

"So he let you go your own way," Nick said, sticking doggedly to the subject.

"Actually, I think he admired me for not giving in. He was pretty stubborn himself; perhaps that's why he realized threats weren't going to change me. He never really gave up, though. He just changed tactics."

"Like leaving you the store."

"And Gran," Meg murmured. "She's the strongest weapon in Dan's postmortem arsenal. Of course she has Uncle George, and he's been wonderful, but she's not. . . . How did you know about the store? I don't remember telling you."

Nick released her hand; the waiter was approaching the table. "It was in the paper."

"The New York papers?" Meg nodded a thank-you to the waiter as he put her plate in front of her.

"Don't look so horrified. It was just an article in the business section. I take it the tabloids haven't been after you yet?"

"Don't say 'yet.'" Meg shuddered. "Uncle George must have dealt with the press. Actually, I could almost pity the reporter who tried to force his way past Frances."

"It's bound to happen, Meg. If not now, then later, after your grandmother. . . ."

"That won't be for years. She's only . . . she's not old." Meg's appetite was gone; she studied the beautifully arranged plate of shrimp and vegetables without enthusiasm. "Anyway, I wouldn't be news, even then. We're not one of the big names, like Tiffany's or Van Cleef & Arpels or Harry Winston. Dan kept a low profile; partly for insurance reasons—Lloyds refused to insure him unless he agreed never to be photographed—and partly because he hated the whole social-business scene."

"That's the only reason you've been spared so far." Nick paused to take a bite of his steak. "This isn't bad. How's the shrimp?"

Meg forced herself to try it. Nick went on, "The media will certainly hound you when your grandmother . . . when you become a beautiful young heiress. The tabloids love beautiful young heiresses."

"I hope you're wrong. If you're not—well, I'll deal with it when the time comes. Get a reverse face-lift and gain fifty pounds."

"Start now," Nick ordered, indicating her barely touched food.

"But it's not as simple as you make it sound," she argued. "The store is only half mine, and my partner. . . ."

Her description of Riley made Nick smile. "He sounds like a misogynist Calvin Coolidge. I wouldn't worry about Mr. Riley, love. A good lawyer can get you out of that arrangement. The fellow probably doesn't have any resources of his own, and the threat of a lawsuit for undue influence—"

"I don't think there was undue influence—"

Nick's eyebrows arched. "Why would your

grandfather leave such valuable property to a man he'd known only a few years?"

Others had asked the same question. She had wondered herself. Why an answer should come to her now, in Nick's skeptical presence, she didn't know, but she responded without hesitation, as if she had always known. "Dan loved his craft—the craft I rejected. Why wouldn't he honor a talented stranger when there was no one else who cared the way he did?"

"But he had no right to saddle you with a partner you dislike and distrust. Don't let sentiment affect your decision, Meg. The partnership isn't the astonishing discovery you mentioned, is it?"

Meg told him about the treasure. Instead of sharing her concern, he was highly amused. "The tricky old devil," he said admiringly. "You're sure there is no record of those jewels?"

"I haven't found one. There are a few more sources I can check, and of course I will. But the fact that they were in my safe strongly suggests—"

"It does," Nick agreed, still smiling. "He was in the Far East during World War Two, I believe—the Burma-China theater?"

She didn't ask how he knew; they had spoken often of Dan, it might have been she who told him. "Yes. And the jewelry is definitely of Indian workmanship. I suppose Dan might have acquired it from a dispossessed rajah, or from a thief who had dispossessed the rajah." She made a sour face. "God, listen to me; I'm joking about it."

"But it has elements of humor—black humor, if you like," Nick pointed out.

"And 'acquired,' as someone has said, is such a kindly word."

"Wilkie Collins. *The Moonstone.* I hope you aren't going to be pursued by mysterious Indians, darling."

"What am I going to do with the damned things, Nick?"

"It is a bit of a problem, isn't it? Let me think about it, get some off-the-record legal advice. I can present a hypothetical case more convincingly than you could."

"That's true," Meg admitted. "Darren would know it wasn't hypothetical."

"Darren?"

"Dan's lawyer. He's an old friend, I've known him for years."

"Ha. Do I scent a rival?"

"I wish you'd take this seriously, Nick. It's not funny. Any of it."

Nick studied her downcast face for a moment and then turned to summon the waiter. "We'd better continue the discussion in private," he said.

It was almost one A.M. before Meg got home. She had spent only an hour after dinner with Nick; the rest of the time she'd sat in her locked car, in a darkened corner of the parking lot of the Inn, alternately crying and cursing, and trying to stop crying so the traces of tears wouldn't show.

She was the one who had started the quarrel,

there was no doubt of that. Everything Nick said infuriated her; the softer his voice; the louder hers became; the more rational his suggestions, the more she resented them. Most maddening of all were his attempts to get her to bed—as if she were as easily distracted as a bitch in heat, she thought angrily. Once he had been convinced she meant it, he had wrapped himself in the cold shell of disapproval that made her feel like a rebellious child facing a stern headmaster.

His suggestions had been practical and intelligent. Too damned practical, in fact. He assumed she would maneuver Riley out of his inheritance as cold-bloodedly as she would swat a wasp. Dan's wishes, her own definitions of right and wrong, were dismissed with a patronizing smile. She had felt as if she were talking with a stranger. Had he always been like this, or had she been too bemused by him to realize that they disagreed about all the things that really mattered? Nick hadn't said in so many words that she was naive and childish to worry about the legality of Dan's ownership of the Indian jewelry, but his raised eyebrows and patient voice had implied as much; the only thing that seemed to concern him was whether or not she could continue the swindle.

Those differences of opinion—to put it only too mildly—were important, but the final blow, the real eye-opener came when she realized Nick assumed that of course she would stay in Seldon, and meet him at the Inn—when he could get away.

"After all, darling, it's much more romantic than—"

"I expect that's what my father thought." The words came out of nowhere, unpremeditated and unplanned—and inevitable. The parallel had been there all along, she had simply been too blind to see it, and now recognition of it turned her stomach. "Of course in his case the ambience wasn't so elegant. Just a cheap motel. But it's the same principle, isn't it? Thanks, Nick, for helping me to see that. Live long and prosper."

Remembering her final farewell, Meg laughed with genuine if painful amusement. Nick was so sensitive about his ears. . . . She was so glad she had thought of it.

The tears had dried up, and after a few more minutes she decided it was safe to drive. However, her mind wasn't entirely on what she was doing, and she was pulled over by a state policeman for going through a stop sign without coming to a complete stop. Because she was sober, apologetic and well dressed—and possibly because the officer recognized the car—she got off with a warning, but the incident cost her another fifteen minutes. From then on she drove with pedantic attention to the traffic laws, frustrated by the throb of the powerful engine she was forced to control, and even more frustrated by the knowledge that if she made the decision circumstances were goading her into making, she would be giving up her privacy and her freedom of action. Unless Gran could admit that times and mores had changed and that

Meg was capable of running her own life, she would have to account for every move she made. Not only to sweet, unsuspicious Gran, but to Uncle George and Frances, the world's foremost busybody, who was neither sweet nor unsuspicious.

Burgeoning summer foliage hid the house until she took the final curve in the driveway. When she saw it her heart leapt and began to pound furiously. The entire facade was ablaze with lights.

The tires sent the neatly raked gravel flying as Meg brought the car to a shuddering stop. She jumped out and ran for the house. The front door opened before she reached it; her uncle's familiar silhouette loomed against the brightness within like a dark omen.

He came to meet her, and Meg threw herself at him, clutching his coat. "Gran. Is she—"

"No. No." He had to clear his throat before he could go on. "She's fine. It's you we were. . . ."

"Thank God." Meg's taut muscles sagged. George put a supporting arm around her and led her into the house.

Frances was sprawled in a chair, wringing her hands. Her face was paper-white. Cliff bent over her. I forgot about Cliff, Meg thought, the fury of relief replacing her anxiety. I'd have to account to him, too. "Damn it," she burst out. "So I'm a little late! What's the idea of waiting up for me as if I were a teenager on her first date? You scared me half to death, I thought something had happened to Gran. Why isn't she pacing the floor with the rest of you?"

"She's sound asleep and perfectly fine," George said. "She doesn't know anything about this—nor will she, unless you wake her up screaming and carrying on."

"Oh." He had hardly ever spoken to her so severely, and Meg realized that he, too, was suffering a reaction from anxiety. "About . . . this? Something has happened. What?"

"Nothing." George whisked the handkerchief from his breast pocket and mopped his forehead. "Literally nothing . . . now. Frances, why don't you go to bed? I told you there was nothing to worry about. It was just someone's idea of a joke."

"Somebody has a pretty sick sense of humor," Frances moaned. "I'm taken bad, Mr. George. I don't know if I'll get over this. My heart. . . ." She clutched her bosom.

"All you need is some rest," George said. "Give her a hand, Cliff."

Cliff heaved the housekeeper to her feet. "Trot along, Frances. A little nip of that brandy you keep in your lingerie drawer will put you right."

It was obvious that both the Wakefields wanted Frances out of the way before they explained, so Meg remained silent until the housekeeper had tottered away and her piteous groans were cut off by the closing door.

"I could do with a nip myself," Cliff announced. "How about you, coz?"

"I could do with an explanation," Meg snapped. "I'm tired, and it's late—"

"Don't we know." Cliff dropped into the chair Frances had vacated. His face was drawn and his hair stood up on end, as if he had been tugging at it. "If you'd been home by midnight, as you said—"

"For God's sake!" Meg clapped a hand to her mouth. "I'm sorry, Uncle George, but Cliff—"

"Cliff didn't mean that the way it sounded. Why don't we go into the parlor and sit down?" George took her arm. "We had a phone call a couple of hours ago, Meg. The caller said you wouldn't be coming home."

"What?" Meg dropped into the chair to which he had led her. "I don't believe it. Who was it?"

"It was a man's voice," George said. "Muffled, as if he were speaking through a handkerchief. I happened to be the one who took the call; it was a little after ten, I was working in my study."

At ten o'clock, she and Nick had been together. But that was crazy, Meg thought, shocked that the suspicion could even enter her mind. Nick was a selfish, self-centered bastard, but he would never. . . . "What exactly did he say?"

"He asked for you. I said you were out for the evening and offered to take a message. Up to that point, of course, I assumed it was an ordinary social call." Remembered shock hardened George's face as he went on, "He laughed. It was a singularly . . . unpleasant laugh. Then he said something like, 'No point in leaving a message.

She won't get it.' I thought I must have misunderstood; I assured him I would deliver the message. He laughed again, and said, 'She won't be back. She's never coming back.' "

Meg swallowed. Her throat felt dry. "And then?"

"That was all. He hung up. He was . . . laughing."

"It was a sick joke," Meg said again. "Nothing happened."

The snifter of brandy Cliff had poured for her stood untouched on the table. Of all the things Meg didn't need just then it was a substance that would cloud her thinking. Cliff had almost finished his. His concern about her had seemed genuine, and Meg would have been touched if he hadn't recovered so quickly.

Peering owlishly at her over the top of the glass, he remarked, "I have to admire your cool, coz. I wouldn't be so relaxed if I had a comedian like that after me."

"After me?" Meg glared at him. "I tell you, nothing happened. Nobody followed me, nobody tried to stop me. Nobody dropped cyanide into the soup. The man didn't even know for sure that I was out, he asked for me first, didn't he? If Uncle George had said, 'Just a minute, I'll get her,' he'd have hung up."

"Or not," Cliff murmured into his brandy.

"If you're trying to scare me," Meg began. The brave denial stuck in her throat. It turned her cold to imagine what that muffled, anonymous voice might have said to her.

"Damn right I am." Cliff slammed his glass down on the table. "First the ring, then this. I want you to be so goddamn terrified you'll start taking precautions."

"The ring wasn't sent to me."

Cliff's lip curled, in a gesture as eloquent as speech. He looked at his father, who said reluctantly, "We can't be certain of that, Meg. I talked to Frances. She couldn't remember to whom the envelope was addressed. She put it with my mail because it looked like a business communication, and you hadn't received any letters."

"I did, though," Meg said. "Sympathy cards—"

"I'm just quoting Frances." Her uncle sighed. "The way that woman's mind works is a mystery to me, always has been."

"The point is," Cliff began.

"I know what the point is." Meg put her head in her hands. "If you'll stop badgering me for a minute and give me time to think. . . ."

There was a respectful silence—respectful on George's part, at any rate. Only his father's repressive stare kept Cliff quiet. He was so charged with energy it radiated from him like a visible aura.

Finally Meg raised her head. "I appreciate your concern," she said formally, addressing both of them. "And I can understand why you were upset.

But I refuse to take extraordinary precautions against a nonexistent threat."

"What do you call extraordinary?" Cliff demanded.

"Your talent for aggravation," Meg snapped. "Let me finish, will you please? I refuse to have some sleazy private eye or bodyguard following me around. That's what you had in mind, wasn't it?"

From the glance that passed between her uncle and his son, she knew she had been right. "Furthermore," she went on, before either of them could object, "I forbid you to take such a step without my permission. If I find you have—and I will find out—I'll . . . I'll leave this house and never come back."

They spoke at the same time. George's mild remonstrance was drowned by Cliff's louder voice. "Maybe that's exactly what someone wants you to do."

"There's no indication that he wants anything, except to cause concern," Meg said firmly. "Crank calls are only too common in today's world. Dan was a well-known person and he undoubtedly had a few enemies. Don't you see—it's the vagueness of the remarks that prove how harmless they are. You interpreted them as threats—of kidnapping, or worse. But they are susceptible to other interpretations."

" 'She's running away from home.' " Cliff lowered his voice to a sinister rumble. " 'Eloping with the chauffeur.' "

"That's one possibility. Simple, dirty-minded scandalmongering. How can there be any danger? I don't threaten anyone, I don't stand in anyone's way. The only people who would gain from my death are a lot of high-minded institutions. You don't think the Metropolitan Museum hires hit men, do you?"

"Very eloquent," Cliff said, his lips twitching. "You make a good case, Meg. But you're forgetting one—no, two—little things."

"What?"

"First, this character may not have known whether you were out, but he knew one thing that's not general knowledge. The phone number." He paused, his head tilted quizzically, as if giving her a chance to reply. Meg was silent. "It's unlisted," Cliff went on. "Second point—there is one person who would definitely profit by your—let me think how to put this. . . ."

"Premature demise?" Meg suggested coldly.

"Not even that, necessarily. By your cessation of interest in a certain asset and your retreat to safer regions. Need I mention his name?"

Pleading exhaustion, Meg left them to it. That they would continue to discuss the matter she did not doubt; but she had come to the end of her rope, she couldn't take any more. Cliff's dislike of Riley had prompted his theory, but there was that business of the telephone number.

Riley wasn't the only one who knew it. Dan must have given it to his friends and business acquaintances, including Mike and Barby and Ed. Not that she thought any of them capable of such a vicious trick, but that meant the information was available to anyone who had access to their personal telephone directories—and Riley's. Candy, among others—and perhaps Candy's ex-husband. An insinuating anonymous phone call was exactly Rod Applegate's style. As a youth his sense of humor had been based on the pain or humiliation of his victims.

Tired as she was, Meg stopped to listen outside her grandmother's door. God be thanked, there was not a sound, not even a chuckle of happy laughter. Meg went to her own room and closed the door behind her with a sense of reaching a long-sought sanctuary.

Resisting the temptation to peel off her clothes and fall into bed, she went into the bathroom and proceeded grimly through her nighttime health-and-beauty routine. No more slacking off or self-pity; she couldn't afford either. "I am the captain of my soul," she told the face that glowered back at her from the mirror on the dressing table as she slapped on moisturizer with a force that gave her cheeks a spuriously healthy glow. "Also the master of my fate. Furthermore, I have miles to go before I sleep. Dan, I laughed at you and your corny old poems, but you had the right idea when you taught me to declaim them from hilltops and other high places. If you shout noble sentiments loud enough, you almost start to believe them. I have to be the master of my fate; there's nobody else now that Nick. . . . You'd be happy about that development, wouldn't you, Dan? I wonder how you'd feel about the rest of it. I wonder what you knew that you didn't tell me. Surely there was time—it happened so fast, Frances said—but surely you must have had some warning. You might have told me, Dan."

A soft rustling sound from the other room brought her to her feet and tipped over the bottle of lotion. Meg caught it in time, realizing that her pulse was a little too fast. The window was open; the breeze had moved the curtains. That was all. But perhaps she had better stop asking questions. A reply from that source would be worse than ignorance.

One final chore—unpacking the clothes she had bought, left in the bags in her rush to Nick. As she hung them in the closet, Meg realized that in a sense Dan had answered, not the question she had asked, but one that was more important. "Don't stand around asking questions, go find out!" had been one of his favorite sayings. Meg smiled as she considered her plan. Her uncle would have described it as a decidedly unpleasant smile.

8

THE CHIME OF the bells sounded slightly off-key that morning. There was no one in the store—no customers, no clerk, no manager—but the soft tinkle had scarcely died away before the workshop door opened and Riley came out. His attempt at the salesman's look of polite anticipation was so bad Meg was tempted to laugh. When he recognized her he stopped trying.

"Good morning," she said brightly.

"Good morning."

"How are things going?"

"As usual."

Meg abandoned the small talk; Riley was about as sociable as a glacier. "Have you found someone to replace Candy?"

"Not yet."

Meg put her purse on the counter with a decisive thump. "You'd better give me a quick run-through on the stock. I can't wait on customers unless I know what's here."

It pleased her to see he could display a normal human emotion. Surprise slackened his tight lips and widened his eyes. They weren't brown, as she had thought, but a clear, bright hazel.

"But—but you can't—"

"Don't ever say 'can't' to me!"

He recognized the source of the quotation, and for a moment she thought he was going to smile. Wrong again. It had been an incipient grimace, quickly controlled. "I expressed myself badly, Ms. Venturi. You can do anything you please here—and, as far as I'm concerned, anywhere else. But it isn't necessary for you to play salesclerk. I have a couple of prospects lined up, and I can manage quite well alone." The grimace reappeared as he added, "Business hasn't been exactly brisk."

"It will pick up as soon as people find out I'm here," Meg said. "They may not buy, but they'll drop in to stare and gossip." The crack about "playing" at salesclerk rankled; she added gently, "I sold socks and underwear in Filene's Basement for six months. If I can handle a Washington's Birthday sale, I should be able to handle this."

"That's. . . ." His teeth bit off the next word. She wondered what it would have been: Preposterous? Ridiculous? Something negative, no doubt.

After a moment he said, "It's up to you. I can't stop you, can I?"

You're certainly trying, Meg thought. She had not expected gratitude, but he didn't have to make it quite so obvious that he didn't want her around. "No, you can't," she said sweetly. "You can't fire me, either. But don't worry, I won't give you the sort of trouble Candy did."

"Believe me, Ms. Venturi, that possibility never entered my mind."

It wasn't a grimace. It wasn't a smile, either, but at least there was a hint that the muscles capable of producing that expression were not completely atrophied.

When they began examining the stock Meg was surprised at its quality and quantity. She knew it was becoming increasingly difficult to find good sources for antique jewelry. Riley condescended to explain: "Dan had contacts all over the world—and the best reputation in the field. Sellers knew he gave top prices." After a slight pause he added, "I'd like to continue that practice."

"Of course," Meg said absently, examining a tray of gold bracelets. "But I think we should consider raising our prices—not much, say ten to fifteen percent. Our clientele is also worldwide, they can afford to pay more. Seven-fifty for this bracelet is ridiculously underpriced."

Riley glanced at the piece, braided mesh-woven strands of gold with a clasp set with cabochon opals and small diamonds. "Dan only paid two-fifty for it. It's ten-carat—"

"In perfect condition, and a hundred years old."

"It's been repaired."

Meg raised the loupe and checked the piece more carefully. "Where? I don't see anything."

"That's what you can expect to see when I make the repairs," Riley said.

Meg gave him an incredulous look. He appeared to be quite serious, but she had begun to suspect that a sense of humor, of sorts, did exist behind that stony face. She examined the bracelet again, and then shrugged. "I'll have to take your word for it. You should know. Where did you learn how to do work like this?"

"Oh—here and there." Riley leaned against the counter, his hands in his pockets. "Didn't Dan give you my résumé?"

"Dan didn't tell me a damned thing about you," Meg said bluntly.

"Oh?" It wouldn't have been accurate to say his eyebrows rose, they tilted up at an oblique angle from the inner corners, giving his controlled face an almost comic look of surprise. "Well, you've just seen what I can do in the way of metal-work. I'm a competent gem setter—not as good with diamonds as with colored stones. I've done some designing. I have my GG—that stands for Graduate Gemologist—"

"I know what it stands for. Did you do the residency?"

"Yeah. Six months. I spent a year in Munich studying antique jewelry with a guy who used to be a curator at the Schatzkammer, and another year in New York working with Ballantyne." He paused, his eyebrows tilting even farther, this time in inquiry. Meg nodded. Josef Ballantyne had been one of Tiffany's top goldsmiths. "And for the last three years I've worked with Dan Mig-not," Riley said. "Anything else you want to know?"

He hadn't told her any of the things she really wanted to know. Who are you, where do you come from, how did you meet Dan—why did he love you, or fear you, enough to give you one of his greatest treasures? It was too soon to ask those questions. So far so good, but so far they had only talked about the business, and he seemed prepared to recognize her right to that kind of answer.

"I wasn't questioning your competence, Riley. If it was good enough for Dan, it's good enough for me. But you'd better leave the selling to me.

Even if the bracelet isn't entirely original, a collector would pay twelve-fifty for it, and not bat an eye. People are investing in antique jewelry as they are in other antiques and in fine art. You know the basic rule: a piece is worth exactly what someone will pay for it. Right now the market is hot, and very inflated."

Riley shrugged. "That suits me. Dealing with people isn't my strong point."

"Really? You amaze me."

They moved on. Meg lingered over the extensive display of earrings, passed quickly by a tray of elaborately woven hair jewelry. She was pleased and surprised at how quickly long-forgotten knowledge came back to her. Dan had been a better teacher than she had realized. Perhaps it wasn't so surprising, though; she had practically lived at the store while she was growing up, and when Dan wasn't working with gems he was talking about them. For Meg it had been total immersion as well as fascination. As a child, instead of fairy stories she had been told the legends and mysteries of the world's great jewels. Some were as exciting and even more fantastic than fiction. Captain Blood—the real Captain Blood—had stolen the Crown of England from the Tower of London itself, and been made one of the royal guard by Charles II after his capture and arrest, on the intelligent theory that a successful thief was the ideal person to catch other thieves. Then there was the incredible tale of the crown jewels of Spain, hidden behind a secret panel in one of the walls of the 360-room palace before the invasion of Napoleon. A loyal servant had kept samples of the draperies of the room so the jewels could be located afterwards, but Napoleon's upstart brother Joseph, to whom he had given the Spanish throne, had redecorated, and when the legitimate line was restored, no one could remember where the jewels were. It would have been impossible to tear down all the walls—so the jewels were still there, somewhere.

As Meg grew older, tales of hidden treasure and murder most foul were replaced by actual experience, in the store. Dan wouldn't let her handle his tools, but she developed a keen eye for style and technique. It wasn't until after she learned the truth about what had happened to her father that her love of jewels was contaminated and she turned away from anything that would remind her of his treachery.

But she hadn't forgotten. Nor had there been great changes in the field—a few more technical gadgets, some refinements of tools whose basic design hadn't changed since the ancient world, but nothing that put her knowledge out of date. Adding to her pleasure was the bemused look on Riley's face as she showed off, using her loupe with expert ease, rattling off the names of obscure gemstones (morganite, kunzite, amazonite) and identifying the date and country of origin of various pieces. She was careful not to stick her neck out too far, but if she was mistaken he didn't correct her.

Then they came to the last case.

At first glance the contents appeared to be a hodgepodge of styles, without organization or theme: a vaguely Art Nouveau silver pendant, a brooch of garnets surrounded by intricate patterns of granulation, a necklace. . . . Wide as an Egyptian beaded collar, massive as a Celtic torque, it was like nothing she had ever seen; its aggressive burst of color stunned the eye. Garnets, pale green peridots, topazes in all the golden-brown variations, aquamarines and amethysts and pink beryls (morganite) jostled one another in seemingly random confusion; but as she stared, mesmerized by the barbaric exuberance of the design, a pattern began to take shape. Just as she was on the verge of grasping it, it dissolved, leaving her to wonder whether she had only imagined it or simply failed to see what a second, closer examination would reveal. . . .

The effect was hypnotic. She had to force her eyes away, and as she started to reach inside the case she saw Riley's hands, tight-clenched and white around the knuckles, and realized that he was as rigid as the statue to which she had mentally compared him. Then she knew—and wondered only why it had taken her so long to comprehend the truth.

Without comment she took the necklace from the case. Her loupe was already in her hand; but instead of examining the piece as she had intended, she found she had hung it around her neck. It was heavy, but surprisingly comfortable;

the linked segments were joined in a manner that distributed the weight evenly across the neck and shoulders, and balanced so that each segment automatically dropped into place, giving the impression of a single rigid piece.

Meg turned to the mirror. The open neckline of her tailored white shirt didn't do the collar justice, but she could easily imagine its effect against an unbroken expanse of black silk, or bare, tanned skin. Not the milky-pale skin of an Edwardian beauty; the piece was warm and aggressive, it demanded an assurance as great as its own. The pattern was clearer now; she almost had it, it was sunset clouds, it was a swirl of giant wings. . . .

It was gone again. Meg lowered her hands; the flexible links collapsed into a shimmer of color.

"I can see why it hasn't sold," she said, returning it to the case. "It's unnerving. Mesmerizing. Did you do that on purpose?"

"It just came out that way." He didn't deny her assumption or ask how she had known.

"Did you do the rest of these too?" Carefully Meg lowered the necklace onto the black velvet display square and reached for the silver pendant. The design curving around the oval base was typical Art Nouveau, the body of a slim naked girl, her raised arms holding a spray of flowers. But there was a subtle difference in the modeling of the slender body, a suggestion of something not quite human, and the arms weren't lifting the flowery branch, they *were* the branch. The change from silvery flesh to silver wood was so gradual it was impossible to say precisely where one ended and the other began.

She didn't need Riley's mutter of assent to know he had designed and executed this piece as well. The others were more conventional, skillful copies of various antique pieces. He must have been experimenting with different techniques: the incredibly difficult process of granulation, lost for centuries; filigree and intaglio; the fine wire technique called cannetille; piqué and champlevé enameling. All the pieces bore what must be his personal mark—an open, broadened Y, stamped aggressively into the body of the piece. That wasn't necessarily vanity, it was meant to prevent a future seller from passing the pieces off as antiques. Not that any trained eye could mistake them for the genuine article; Riley was probably incapable of making a literal copy. His style was so individualistic it affected everything he touched.

It took her quite a while to inspect all of them. Riley didn't say a word. If she hadn't seen those white-knuckled fists—now thrust into his pockets—Meg would have thought him as inhuman as his silver dryad. No matter how little he valued her opinion, he must be aching to hear it. Any artist would. He probably interpreted her silence as a deliberate attempt to increase the suspense, but in fact she simply couldn't think what to say.

She rearranged the jewelry in the case, except

for the necklace, which she gathered into her hands. "You forgot to show me where you keep the boxes."

"What do you. . . ." He caught himself, on a quick intake of breath. "Under that counter."

Meg found a box of the proper size, lined it with cotton and laid the necklace in it. The silence echoed with the words neither of them was willing or able to say. Riley cracked first.

"What are you doing?"

"Buying this necklace."

"But you hate it. You said it was—"

"Unnerving. It is. It is also . . . astonishing."

She deliberately avoided words like beautiful, stunning, wonderful. Riley hadn't been aiming at those effects.

For a moment neither of them moved. Then Riley shifted position and took his hands out of his pockets. When they fell to his sides the curve of his fingers reminded Meg of the great hand in Dan's stained-glass window. "Well," he said awkwardly. "Guess I better get back to work. Unless there's something else you want to know about the stock."

Meg shook her head.

Slowly and deliberately Riley walked to the door of the shop and opened it. He didn't look at her again.

He walks like an emperor, Meg thought. Like Caesar striding to the podium in the Forum, at the head of a victory parade.

He had the right.

Her eyes returned to the necklace. Nothing Dan had said about his new designer could have prepared her for this; Dan never gushed, his idea of high praise was a grumbled "Not bad." And even if he had tried to tell her—how could he, when she herself was still groping for words? She felt shaken and overmastered by the strength of her emotions: humility in the face of a talent far beyond anything she could ever hope to achieve, triumph at having found it, excitement at the prospect of being allowed to nurture and develop it. The same emotions, beyond words, that Dan must have felt. . . .

As he had felt about her father. Meg clenched cold, sweating hands and struggled to control her breathing, as her father's betrayal came home to her for the first time in its full enormity.

It took less than an hour for the news of her presence in the store to spread. Meg had known what she was letting herself in for and she never doubted it was worth it—especially after her incredible discovery—but some of the "customers" demanded all the self-control she possessed. As she had predicted, none of them came to buy. Some made a pretense of looking at rings or stickpins, making her take out tray after tray for examination, obviously enjoying being served by Daniel Mignot's snooty heiress granddaughter. One woman, a little more inventive, brought a rhinestone necklace for appraisal and possible sale. After Meg had politely informed her they didn't buy costume jewelry, the woman settled herself more firmly on the chair and told Meg how much they would all miss Dan and how glad they were that a member of the family intended to manage the store.

She wasn't the only one to imply that "they" didn't approve of Riley; several were even more direct. One man, who introduced himself as "an old buddy of your granddad's," coolly informed her that Dan had gone soft in the head and let himself be taken in by a smooth-talking confidence man. The description was so wildly inappropriate when applied to the taciturn Riley that Meg couldn't help smiling, but her sorely tried patience snapped when another customer, who kept waving his finger under her nose, suggested that she ought to have Dan "dug up," as he gracefully put it. "I seen him a couple of days before he died and he was in the pink. Murder's been done for less than what that Riley got, and I'll give you any odds you want they'll find poor old Dan's stuffed full of arsenic."

Meg sent him on his way with a few well-chosen words. Flushed with righteous indignation, he tried to slam the door but it refused to oblige.

Meg was still seething when the door opened again, but the sight of Mike Potter turned her scowl to a smile. "Don't tell me, let me guess. You want a pinky ring, or a diamond stickpin."

He grinned and put his hands on the counter —square, competent workman's hands, unadorned except for his wife's plain gold wedding band, which he had worn on his little finger since she died. "You got it. A real big flashy diamond."

"Ten carats minimum," Meg agreed. "Come on, Mike, 'fess up—you didn't really believe I was here, did you? You came to check up on me."

"I knew you'd do it sooner or later," Mike said. "I just didn't expect it would be so soon. You've had so many other things on your mind. . . . Dan would be proud of you, honey."

Meg hadn't expected the simple grace of that tribute—or the enormity of the guilt that swamped her. Mike wouldn't be so pleased and proud if he knew she was not taking up the charge Dan had left her, but spying on her new partner. At least that had been her motive before she saw Riley's work. . . . She turned her head away, and as she hoped, Mike mistook her confusion for embarrassment, and considerately changed the subject.

"How's it going? Lots of business?"

"Well. . . ." She still felt too much anger to hold it in. After she had finished talking Mike shook his grizzled head. "Ken Masterson is the worst gossip in town, honey. Got a mind like a sewer. You didn't take him seriously, I hope."

"No, of course not." Riley, she knew, could hear every word—just as he had heard the vicious accusations. "What's the matter with this town, Mike?"

"It's not the town, honey, just a few of the people in it. They get bored, you know, and pass on everything they hear."

"Yes, but where do they hear it? Where does it start?"

"Where does any wild story start? Ever wonder who makes up the dirty jokes that get handed on?"

Mike knew about the intercom; his sidelong glance was a little too casual. Meg smiled and shrugged, accepting his dismissal of the subject; but Masterson's accusation had left a stain on her mind, like a slimy snail track. Riley's surprising legacy would be enough to set an imagination like Masterson's diving into the dirt—but Frances had talked of murder before the will was read.

"So I guess I better get back to work," Mike went on. "Just stopped by to say hello."

Meg blew him a kiss. She knew he hadn't stopped by to say hello; the only thing about which she was uncertain was whether he had come on his own or been sent by the rest of the old gang. One of these days she would have to have a heart-to-heart with Mike Potter.

She was vigorously polishing the top of the glass cases when Riley reappeared. He made no reference to the conversations he must have overheard, but Meg noticed a raw red line of burning across the back of his hand, as if the soldering iron had slipped.

"You ready to call it a day?"

Meg felt her smile congeal, like cooling gravy. It wasn't so much his curt tone as the insulting implication that she was only playing at tending store, and would walk out as soon she got bored. And after her spirited defense of him! She reminded herself that just because a man was a bloody genius didn't mean he couldn't also be an A-number-one bastard. Most geniuses were, now that she thought about it.

"I'm ready for lunch," she said, her voice as brusque as his had been. "Unless you want to go first."

"I brought a sandwich."

"I didn't." She put the bottle and cloth neatly away under the counter and reached for her purse. "Back in an hour."

He didn't say okay or right or fine or take your time. He just stood there. Meg wrenched the door open. "There's something wrong with the chimes," she snapped.

"They sound okay to me."

"Then you must be tone-deaf."

The door still wouldn't slam.

Mike hadn't gone back to work. He was having lunch. All four of them were there, even Kate —heads together, elbows on the table. Meg suspected they were talking about her, and she was sure of it when the sight of her brought a sudden end to the conversation. She pulled out a chair and waved the two men back into theirs. Ed subsided thankfully, but Mike went on unfolding his long legs.

"I just stopped by to pick up a sandwich. I'm short-handed today and business is picking up. Tourist season, you know."

"Oh, yeah? I haven't seen any of them. Just a lot of evil-minded busybodies."

She didn't bother to lower her voice. Ed looked guilty, Kate shook her head disapprovingly and Barby murmured, "Now, Meg, honey, you don't want to say things like that."

Mike Potter's long face creased into a smile. "Yes, she does. Sounds just like Dan. He never gave a hoot what people thought either."

He had not lied about the sandwich. The waitress brought it, neatly wrapped in waxed paper —one of Kate's three-inch-thick masterpieces, bulging with cheese and paper-thin slices of country ham and a dozen other ingredients.

After he had gone, and Meg had ordered a chef's salad and iced-tea, a self-conscious silence ensued. Meg studied the downcast faces with an inner amusement she managed to keep under wraps. Bless their hearts, they thought they were so sly. . . .

"Am I interrupting a private conversation?" she asked. "I'll leave if you want to go on talking about me."

Ed looked guilty—he always looked guilty when he wasn't sure what was going on; Barby looked shocked—she did it very well; but Kate leaned back in her chair and burst out laughing.

"Can't put much over on this gal, can we? Sure we were talking about you, honey. The whole town's talking about you."

"And Riley."

Kate's face didn't change. "And Riley. Hell's bells, girl, you can't blame people for wondering why Dan would do such a weird thing. And—

before you can ask—no, we don't know why he did it. We didn't even know he'd done it. It was as big a surprise to us as it was to everyone."

"We'd have warned you," Barby said softly. "So it wouldn't have come as such a shock. You believe that, don't you, Meg?"

Her faded blue eyes met Meg's. Mascara dragged the paper-thin skin of her eyelids into fragile folds. "I believe you, Barby," Meg said. "And I love you—all of you."

Kate cleared her throat. "So we're no better than the rest of the busybodies," she said gruffly. "When you went in this morning we thought maybe you'd just stopped by, the way you did the other day with Cliff; and then you stayed, and stayed, and you didn't come out, and—and so. . . ."

"So you sent Mike over to find out what was going on?" Meg couldn't control her amusement any longer. "That was a dirty trick, Kate, he hates anything that isn't open and aboveboard."

Kate returned her grin with one even broader and unashamed. "We had a bet—whether Riley would quit before you fired him."

"I couldn't fire him if I wanted to," Meg said. "I may kill him someday, but I can't fire him."

"Mike wouldn't bet," Barby chirped. "He kept insisting you were just helping out, what with Candy being gone and Riley all alone. Like Dan would have wanted you to."

The ambiguous response Meg intended to make stuck in her throat. A certain ironic gleam in

Kate's eye suggested that Kate, at least, didn't believe Mike's interpretation and wouldn't have believed it if Meg had sworn a legal oath.

Ed had been pondering, a heavy frown wrinkling his pink face. His face cleared, and he looked at Meg with a pleased smile. "I guess that's right. You couldn't fire him, could you? Since he's half-owner."

Meg patted his hand. "Absolutely right, Ed. But that's not the only reason. I saw some of Riley's work this morning. The man's brilliant. It would be like firing Cellini."

She wasn't sure Ed knew who Cellini was, but her general meaning was clear. The threesome nodded solemnly, in unison. "That's what Dan said," Ed murmured in an awed voice. "Exactly what he said. It's uncanny how you're getting to sound just like him, Meg."

It cost Meg something of an effort to keep her smile in place. She wouldn't have hurt Ed's feelings for all the jewels in the Smithsonian, but she was finding that comparison increasingly hard to take.

She didn't raise the subject of Riley again. Instead she admired the photos of Ed's grandchildren, meekly accepted Barby's affectionate criticism of her appearance—"I know you've been too rushed to bother, sweetie, but it would only take an hour for me to give you a nice shampoo and set"—and smiled at Kate's acerbic comments on the clientele and staff as she rushed from table to kitchen to cash register.

It would have been hard to determine precisely when she realized that her original intention of telling the old people about her problems could not be carried out. They would have resented the adjective, and fought to help her if they believed she needed help—and that was precisely why she couldn't ask for it. Ed's asthmatic breathing, Barby's delicate bones draped in withered skin—they were so vulnerable, so frail. Kate played tough, but she wasn't a young woman. Meg didn't doubt their goodwill. If they had known anything that could be viewed as threatening, surely they would have told her.

Yet there was something wrong, something slightly off-key, like the chimes at the store, and Meg couldn't suppress a suspicion that, despite their apparent candor, Dan's old buddies knew something she didn't know. It might be something completely harmless and irrelevant. It might be something they believed was irrelevant. Pumping them without betraying her reason for doing so would be tricky and difficult. Had she the right even to try?

After she had paid the check she started back to the store. I'll talk to them separately, she decided. And very, very carefully. Starting with Mike. He'd been Dan's best friend. Dan trusted him—as much as he trusted anyone.

Absorbed in thought, she spent several seconds rattling the doorknob before she realized the door was locked and that a sign reading "Out to Lunch" was on display. Before she could locate her keys, which had sunk to the bottom of her purse, she had time to compose several new descriptions of Riley. If he had intended all along to close up and go out to lunch, why the hell hadn't he said so? Afraid she'd suggest they go together? That, of course, would have been unendurable.

The delay gave the man who had followed her across the street his opportunity. When the warm, moist hand closed over her arm Meg whirled around, her fingers clenching over the bunch of keys.

"Scared you, huh? Sorry about that." Applegate didn't look sorry, he looked pleased as punch.

Now that he was no longer listing and buckling at the knees, he was taller than she had thought. He was also too close, crowding her against the door. Though he was neatly dressed, the effect was not so much one of good taste as of a failed attempt at it; the pink stripes in his shirt were too wide and too bright, the shoulders of the coat too heavily padded in a vain attempt to disguise the amplitude of waist and belly. Meg would not have been surprised to find that the underside of his tie sported a painting of a naked woman.

She couldn't think of any reason why she should be polite. "What do you want?" she demanded.

Her frosty tone and unfriendly stare only scratched the surface of his complacency. "I was going to apologize. For being—a little . . . uh—under the weather yesterday. I had a good reason, you know. Figured I'd explain—"

"Don't bother." Meg was more annoyed than

frightened; in fact, the strongest emotion Applegate inspired was disgusted contempt. Still, he was very large and very drunk; she kept a wary eye on him as she tried to fit the key into the lock.

Applegate leaned closer. "Hey, give a guy a chance, willya? I said I had a good reason—"

"Stuff it," Meg said, wrinkling her nose against the stench of his breath. "And get lost. You're in no condition to—dammit! Let go of me!"

She twisted, trying to free herself, but his hands held her pinned against the door. He wasn't trying to hurt her—what could he do, really, in broad daylight and on Main Street? All she had to do was yell. . . . Reluctant to make a spectacle of herself, or admit her inability to handle the situation, she didn't scream, but she did raise her voice. "Go home and sober up. I mean it, Rod—take your sweaty hands off me or I'll—"

"You'll do what? Call a cop? You better listen to me, Miss High and Mighty. You think you're better'n the rest of us, but there are a few things you might not like the cops to find out—"

The door against which Meg was leaning opened, and she stumbled back, into Riley's arms. He set her aside, as easily as if she had been a doll. "Sorry. I was in the shop, working. What can I do for you, Mr. Applegate?"

Applegate drew himself up and tried to suck in his stomach. "I'd tell you what you could do to yourself if there wasn't a lady present."

Riley glanced at Meg. "Did he hurt you?"

She brushed a loosened lock of hair from her face. "No. I'm all right."

Riley considered her for a moment, then nodded and turned his attention back to Applegate. "Excuse me," he said coolly, and started to close the door. Applegate shoved back. Riley retreated a step.

Meg approved his desire to avoid a vulgar public brawl, but she was surprised at Applegate's bravado. He had always bullied children smaller than himself, but had been quick to back off when someone his own size stood up to him. He was almost as tall as Riley and twice as broad, but most of his bulk was fat. Yet he was provoking a fight, and his anticipatory grin suggested he expected to win it.

One more step and Applegate would be inside the store; he was on the threshold now, poised, more lightly than one might have expected, on the balls of his feet. He didn't so much as glance at Meg. Riley, too, appeared to have forgotten her very existence. Typical, Meg thought with a silent snort of rage. Macho caveman mentality. . . . She had been about to reach for the telephone. She changed her mind. There was an easier, better way.

Her sudden movement took both of them by surprise and caught Applegate off balance in the middle of a step. One hard shove, powered by a healthy surge of adrenaline, was enough. In fact, it was more effective than Meg had expected. Instead of simply staggering back, Applegate stubbed the toe of one shoe on the heel of the other, swayed back and forth, arms flailing like the sails of a windmill and toppled over backwards.

For a horrible moment Meg feared he was really hurt—bones broken, head smashed against the concrete. Then a long shuddering intake of breath was followed by a stream of profanity, much of it directed at a feminine object. He started to get up. As his crimsoned face turned in her direction, Meg said clearly, "I'd rather not call the police, but I will if you don't leave immediately. If you bother me, or the store again, I'll swear out a warrant."

Several pedestrians had paused, moved more by curiosity than by concern, but there was one Good Samaritan among them. A frail little old lady, silver-haired and bespectacled, started tugging at Applegate's arm. "Poor man," she quavered. "I do hope you didn't break anything. I've always said the town council doesn't take proper care of the sidewalks. I have stumbled myself, not once but a number of times. Perhaps you ought to lie down until an ambulance can be summoned."

It may have been the ludicrous spectacle they presented—the tiny woman and the big, snorting man—rather than Meg's threat that made Applegate anxious to fade away. He had good cause to know that the undamaged victim of a pratfall provokes more amusement than sympathy. Brushing the old lady rudely aside, he pushed through the snickering crowd and disappeared, but not before he had favored Meg with a glare of pure malevolence.

Meg closed the door and flipped the sign around so that it read "Open." "He's not even limping," she said with a laugh. "I didn't want to put him in the hospital, but I hoped I might cripple him a little."

Then she turned to confront her partner.

Riley wasn't laughing. His eyes had darkened till they looked as black as hers, and his mouth was a white-lipped slit. "Thanks," he said.

"What's wrong? I just—"

"Saved the day. Defended your helpless partner. Thank you very, very much."

He turned on his heel and walked away, with that same slow arrogant stride. Recovering, Meg made a rude childish face at his retreating back; but after the door had closed behind him she shook her head and smiled ruefully. He had come riding to her rescue, sword drawn and banners flying, only to have her turn the whole episode into farce. But damn it all, she argued with herself, how could I have known his macho pride would be so delicate? He doesn't have to prove he's tougher than a fat slob like Rod Applegate, anybody would know that by looking at him. Surely he must realize that I understand why he wanted to avoid a brawl, and that I admire him for it? Maybe if I told him. . . .

No. If she had made a mistake—and obviously she had!—it was too late now. Apologies would only rub salt in the wound. Best to leave him alone till he got over it—or not, as the case might be. She had acted thoughtlessly, but he had reacted like a sulky little boy.

Riley continued to sulk, or work, or both, for the rest of the day. Meg found plenty to do; she wrote out new price tags for some of the jewelry and had the satisfaction of selling an expensive pair of early Victorian earrings to one of Dan's out-of-state customers, who had made a special trip from Rhode Island to express her sympathy and find out what was going to happen to the store. Mrs. Adamson was well bred, well informed and well intentioned; her kindness gave Meg's spirits a much-needed lift. Not only did she fail to accuse Riley of murder, rape or fraud, she didn't seem to find it at all surprising that Dan would reward such a fine, conscientious worker. Obviously unaware of the intercom, she added pleasantly, "He does excellent work. A little shy, isn't he? But I'm sure he will be an asset to the business, and I wish you the best of luck."

Riley shy? It was the funniest thing Meg had heard all day.

She sold two other pieces of jewelry and coped, politely but firmly, with more curiosity seekers. The time she spent in the office going over the records wasn't wasted in terms of learning the stock and the business, but it told her nothing she didn't already know about Riley—except that his latest raise had brought his salary to the munificent sum of eighteen thousand a year, plus the apartment over the store. As Meg remembered it, it consisted of two and a half tiny rooms plus bath, the half being a kitchen the size of a pantry. Dan might have gotten three hundred a month for it—along with the risk of having a burglar for a tenant. There was nothing between the apartment and the store except floorboards and acoustical tile. All things considered, it was a moot point as to who was doing whom a favor.

When the hands of the clock reached 5 P.M. Meg turned to the intercom. She didn't care whether the sound of her voice startled the artist into a false move; in fact she rather hoped he would singe some nonessential part of his anatomy. "It's five o'clock," she announced. "I'll lock the door when I leave. See you tomorrow at nine."

She switched off before he could reply—or not, which was more probable.

Meg had breakfasted with her grandmother, avoiding both Cliff and his father; when she returned home that evening she was surprised and relieved to learn that Cliff was gone. George gave her a hard-enough time about her latest scheme.

"I suppose Gran told you," Meg said, sneaking a watercress sandwich and rearranging the plate so Gran wouldn't notice. Tea did not properly begin until she had taken her place. In deference to Meg's new schedule, teatime had been postponed until five-thirty, and Gran wasn't down yet.

"Yes." George eyed the plate of sandwiches wistfully, but did not emulate Meg's bad example. "I'm glad you had the courtesy to tell *her* where you were going."

"Courtesy was exactly what prompted me to do so. I owe her that."

"I know you don't owe me anything," George began.

"Oh, Uncle George, of course I do. I'm sorry if that sounded rude, and I'm sorry I avoided you this morning—I did, I admit it—but I didn't want an argument with you and Cliff. Where is he, anyway?"

George smiled faintly. "I reminded him that he has a job, such as it is. I told him he could come back this weekend, but if you'd rather he didn't—"

"Oh, come on, Uncle George. You don't think I would try to kick your son out of the only home he's ever known just because he gets on my nerves sometimes! It's like having a bossy older brother; we'll work it out, Cliff and I." She hesitated, reluctant to criticize her uncle, but he and she had things to work out as well. If she was going to stay—it was the first time she had made even that much of a commitment, even in her own thoughts—her uncle would have to stop treating her like a child.

"It would be easier all around if you'd stop worrying about it," she went on. "Stop apologizing for Cliff, stop trying to protect me. I'm not—"

The sound of a door opening on the floor above heralded the approach of her grandmother. George leaned forward, speaking softly and quickly. "Fair enough. I am overprotective and

I'll try not to be. But when I see you doing something so foolhardy as you did today—"

"It wasn't foolhardy," Meg interrupted. "Supposing Cliff is right about Riley—which I don't believe—there couldn't be a safer place for me than the store. Half the population of Seldon knew I was there. Do you think Riley would be stupid enough—"

She stopped herself just in time. George's face underwent a sudden transformation, from distress to smiling welcome. He got to his feet. "Mary, dear. How lovely you look."

Yards of pale aqua chiffon floated around her and formed an Elizabethan ruffle that framed her face and soft white hair. Her jewels, of course, were aquamarines and pearls. The deep blue-green gems in her ears were the size of quarters. Posing in the doorway with innocent pleasure, she looked at Meg and allowed an almost imperceptible frown to wrinkle her forehead. "Meg, darling, have you been a bad girl?"

The gentle reproach wiped out fifteen years. Meg shifted guiltily from one foot to the other, cursing her temper and her unruly tongue. She began, "It's not what you think, Gran. . . ."

"I know you must be hungry, dear, but I've told you time and time again that it is rude to begin eating before everyone has taken his or her place."

She was looking at the plate of sandwiches. Meg burst out laughing. Her grandmother shook her silvery head. "And then to rearrange the remaining sandwiches in an effort to deceive me. . . . That is tantamount to telling a falsehood, Meg, darling."

"I'm sorry," Meg murmured.

Her grandmother floated toward her in a cloud of chiffon. "I know you are, sweetheart, and we won't say another word about it. I just want you to remember that honesty is the best policy, and ladies do not tell lies."

She enveloped Meg in a soft, sweet-scented embrace. Over her shoulder Meg saw Henrietta Marie walk regally into the room. Henrietta was definitely sneering.

9

WHAT MUST IT be like to live shielded from reality as Mary Mignot had been? Like living in a cage of glass, Meg thought. The invisible walls gave an illusion of freedom, but harsh reality never entered and the barriers muffled cries of pain from without. When ugliness came too close, someone drew a curtain, embroidered with flowers and pretty little birds.

Dan had been custodian of the cage and the curtains for almost fifty years. Now they were guarding it—Meg and Uncle George, Frances and Cliff. It's a good thing cats can't—or won't talk, Meg thought. They know what goes on outside the cage. They kill pretty little birds. Not that Henrietta Marie would ever commit the crashing faux pas of presenting such a trophy to Gran. She knew which side her kitty biscuits were buttered on.

When Meg informed her grandmother of her intention of continuing to work at the store, she was prepared for an argument, or worse, for the hurt disapproval that was Gran's method of protest. To her relief Gran took it well; in fact, she proceeded to explain the situation to George. "In my day, of course, a lady didn't tend store. But one must move with the times, mustn't one? Daniel explained it all to me, that until she finds a nice young man to manage her affairs for her, she must carry on and do her duty. He was so pleased—"

The nice young man was bad enough; when Gran started talking about Dan as if he had just stepped into the next room, Meg's amusement died a quick death. George could talk all he liked about true faith and harmless eccentricities; Gran *was* behaving erratically and her delusion might not be so harmless. What if she decided to go for a stroll with "Daniel" during a blizzard, or followed him into the path of a car? If she was seeing things that weren't there, she might fail to see dangers that did exist.

Her face must have shown some of her inner turmoil, for Mary turned a concerned, curious look upon her. Meg forced a smile.

"Gran, could I have another sandwich?"

"Certainly, my dear. Just so you don't spoil your dinner."

"We are all proud of Meg," George said, with an approving smile. "But I don't want her to sacrifice herself, even for the store. How did it go today, honey?"

Meg's mouth was full, which prevented her from replying immediately. The momentary pause gave her time to think. "It wasn't as difficult as I thought it would be," she said thoughtfully. "In fact, I rather enjoyed it."

Her uncle looked skeptical. "No, really," Meg insisted. "I've forgotten a great deal, but it started coming back to me. And Riley—George, Gran—I saw some of his work today. It's marvelous! I had no idea he was so talented."

"Daniel thinks very highly of the young man," Mary said. She covered her mouth with a dainty hand and gave the little cough that heralded a negative comment. "Rather gruff in his manners, of course. A rough diamond, so to speak."

"Don't you like him?" Meg asked.

"I've seen very little of him," Mary said coolly. "He seemed to be a trifle uncomfortable on the few occasions when he was here. Quite understandable. Artistic persons often lack the social graces. I expect Michelangelo preferred his studio to the palazzi of the Medici."

Meg choked on her sandwich. "I expect you're right, Mary," George said, his eyes twinkling. "But the comparison isn't really accurate. This young man is no Michelangelo."

"No, his manners are even worse," Meg said, recovering herself. "But oh, Uncle George, you ought to see what he's doing. There's a necklace. . . . I couldn't possibly describe it, but I'll show it to you. I bought it."

"You bought it?" George exclaimed.

"I had to have it." Meg turned to her grandmother. "You know the feeling, Gran—you're afraid that if you don't snatch it, that instant, someone is going to come along and take it away from you?"

"Oh, yes, my dear, I know exactly what you mean." Her grandmother's fingers caressed the brilliant stones of the necklace she was wearing.

"Well, I can't say I do," George admitted. "But I'm delighted that you aren't finding this duty a painful one, Meg."

"I'd rather you went on thinking of me as a martyr," Meg said with a smile. "Pity me, coddle me, sympathize with me. It isn't so much enjoying it, Uncle George; it's more than that, it's pure excitement to discover a talent like Riley's. Like Howard Carter, discovering King Tut's tomb! Of course Dan was the first to spot it, but I didn't know—I mean, I knew he thought well of Riley, but I wasn't influenced by that, I honestly wasn't. It was . . . oh, I can't explain." Embarrassed by her own enthusiasm, she looked away, in time to see Henrietta's tail disappear under the sofa. She had taken Meg's watercress sandwich with her.

Meg was early the following morning, arriving at the store before Riley had opened up. The recessed entryway was cool and shady and the morning sun had been bright in her eyes; it was not until she had inserted her key in the lock that she saw the crumpled paper bag. Recognizing the insignia of a fast-food chain, she assumed some lout had tossed his trash into the doorway, and she stooped to pick it up. It was much heavier than she had expected; before she could tighten her grasp it slipped from her fingers, spilling the contents at her feet.

Meg screamed and stumbled back. The rat was dead, most emphatically so, stiffened in a grotesque and futile posture of defense. Its gaping jaws bared yellow fangs, and its filthy fur was rank with dried blood.

The door burst open. Riley took in the situation at a glance. He kicked the rat into a corner and pulled Meg inside. "I'll take care of it," he said. "Unless you prefer to be a heroine again."

Meg was on the verge of a furious reply when she realized that she had just been given a chance to redeem her mistake of the previous day—and furthermore, that she had absolutely no desire to be heroic about rats. Without replying she retreated into the store, face averted, and left Riley to do what was necessary. When he came back, empty-handed, he brushed past her without speaking and went into the washroom. The sudden, excessive explosion of water into the sink was his only demonstration of disgust; he scrubbed his hands for several minutes before emerging.

Meg followed his example. She had touched only the paper bag, and that briefly, but she felt contaminated. When she came out, Riley was leaning against the counter. "I suggest," he said carefully, "that if you mean to continue this routine, you come in half an hour later. I didn't expect you so early."

"You mean—you mean this wasn't the first. . . ."

"It was my first rat. Or should I say your first rat?"

"What else has happened?"

"I prefer not to discuss it." Riley rose. "None of it, including the rat, was directed at you, but unless you enjoy unpleasant surprises, you had better quit being so prompt."

He headed for the workshop. His back was as unassailable as a stone wall, but Meg persisted. "Was there a tag around that creature's neck?"

"Yes."

"What was on it?"

"The message was for me. You aren't the kind that reads other people's mail, are you?"

The door closed behind him before she could reply.

Meg was tempted to kick something—the counter, the wastebasket—but the fact that she was wearing open-toed sandals made her reconsider. Who the hell did he think he was, talking to her that way? But a good deal of her anger was directed at the unknown sender of the rat, and as it cooled she realized that Riley might not have meant to be offensive. He was just being his own sweet self—arrogant, reserved, suspicious. Anyhow, he had now had the opportunity to rescue her, if only from a dead rat. Maybe that would soothe his wounded ego.

The rat strongly suggested Rod Applegate, it was just his style, and if she had to choose between Applegate and Riley, it was no contest. But there might be other people who had excellent reasons for detesting Riley. Just because a man was persecuted didn't mean he was innocent, or virtuous.

Business was brisk that morning, most of it due to sellers rather than buyers. At first Meg couldn't understand the burst of activity; as she knew from Dan's complaints, one could go for days without being offered a collection, and she had three in a row. She didn't want to consult Riley. It might have been tactful to do so, but she couldn't keep on playing ego games with him, at least not where the business was concerned. She had to build her own self-confidence, and the first two groups of jewelry offered a perfect opportunity for honing her skills; they were marketable and easily classified, and the amount of money involved was not great. The reactions of the sellers to the prices she offered assured her she had not been far off the mark. Both grumbled, argued, bargained and finally agreed.

The third seller was another matter. A spare little man with hard dark eyes, he identified himself as a collector and dealer who had often acted as picker for Dan. He had three gold-filled bracelets, several bar pins and a necklace set with green stones he claimed were emeralds. Meg put them through the usual tests and they checked out, but her newly revived instincts told her they were not natural stones. Man-made gems were not glass, but genuine crystals, grown under conditions similar to those in nature, so their optical and chemical properties were often within the same range as those of genuine stones. When she expressed her reservations the dealer dug his heels in. He knew enough about gems to tell a natural emerald from a synthetic, he insisted, implying that she did not.

By this time the truth had dawned on Meg. The news of her legacy had gotten around, and some collectors were hastening to make deals with Dan Mignot's inexperienced granddaughter. She was tempted to come down hard on Mr. MacDonald —"Just call me Jock, your granddad did"—but a check of the records indicated that he had been a useful source and it would have been stupid to antagonize him. She smiled sweetly. "There's one way to make certain, isn't there? I'll have to call my partner; the microscope is in the shop."

Mr. MacDonald's unbeautiful face fell. He had lost, and he knew it. No matter how flawless they may appear to the naked eye, gemstones contain small foreign bodies—gaseous, liquid or solid—called inclusions, which are visible under strong magnification. The wispy, veil-like inclusions characteristic of synthetic emeralds are quite different from the irregular bubble shapes found in natural stones. Before MacDonald could think of a graceful way out, Meg pressed the button and Riley emerged from the shop. He and Mac-

Donald greeted one another coolly, Meg explained, and Riley went off with the necklace. When he returned he handed it over with a brief, "Synthetic—as Ms. Venturi told you," and disappeared.

The deal was concluded, and MacDonald left, mumbling excuses. "Sure can't trust anybody these days, can you? I should've known better than to take his word, but I've dealt fair and square with him for years and I thought. . . ." He sounded no more convinced than Meg was.

The ring of the telephone echoed the jangle of the shop bells as MacDonald closed the door. The bells were still off-key. Meg reminded herself to have a look at them and reached for the phone.

"Daniel Mignot Jewelers," she said.

"You really are there," said the voice on the other end of the line. "They said you were, but I didn't believe. . . ."

"Darren?"

"Oh. Yes. Uh—I thought you were coming in yesterday to sign your will."

"I did say that, didn't I? Sorry, Darren, I forgot."

"It's quite important, Meg."

"I know. I really am sorry. I go to lunch at twelve. Why don't I run in for a minute then?"

"Well, uh—it's going to take more than a minute, Meg. Why don't you come now—it's almost eleven-thirty—and after we've finished our business we can go somewhere for lunch."

Meg glanced at the intercom. "I know those

business lunches only too well, Darren. I've only got an hour. I'll meet you at Kate's if you like; bring the will with you and we'll get Kate and one of the others to witness it."

The suggestion outraged him even more than she had expected it would. Meg let him sputter for a few minutes and then said, "All right, if you're so insistent on staying in the office, why don't I bring a couple of sandwiches from the deli?"

After a moment Darren said, "You're teasing me."

Meg sighed. "Not intentionally, Darren. I am taking one hour for lunch, no more. I am perfectly willing to give you that hour. Shall I come at twelve, or would you prefer to wait until after work?"

Darren's sigh was longer and louder. "Come. As soon as you can. We'll discuss it when you get here."

Meg hung up. She had been teasing Darren; it was hard to resist, he took things so seriously. She had been just as unreasonable—maybe more so. She was entitled to take as much time as she liked for lunch, or any other purpose; she was just leaning over backwards to prove to Riley that she was serious about the store. Not that he cared. . . .

Mrs. Babcock's greeting was several degrees frostier than usual. When Meg saw Darren's desk, with deli sandwiches and cartons of coffee laid out on a covering of newspapers, she understood why, but it was not until after the secretary had stalked out, radiating disapproval, that she realized how thoroughly she had offended. Darren spoke in a whisper: "This was a good idea after all, Meg. She was bound and determined to sit in on our next conference, but she'd think it improper to eat with her boss. In fact, she doesn't approve of my eating lunch at my desk."

Meg was absurdly touched at his efforts to adjust to her unorthodox manners. Despite his brave words he was visibly ill at ease, and when he asked her permission to remove his coat, it was with the devil-may-care air of a man who has thrown convention to the winds.

"Go for it," Meg said encouragingly. "We could spill coffee on the will; then she'd have to retype it."

Darren laughed, but glanced uneasily at the door. Mrs. Babcock had him firmly under her plump white thumb. Meg wondered, half-seriously, whether Mrs. B. had been partially responsible for the breakup of Darren's marriage. It had only lasted five years. An unusual variant of the devoted secretary problem? Any wife would resent a woman who had more influence than she over her husband, and Mrs. B. had been in control too long to give it up.

"We'll have to get her in to witness the will," Darren said. "But I'd rather she didn't know about the other matter, at least not yet."

He handed her a thin sheaf of papers. "You must have found a very efficient private detective," Meg said, glancing at the first page. "I didn't expect results so soon."

Darren had taken a bite of his sandwich. He was careful to chew and swallow before he replied. "This is just a preliminary report, using public records. An in-depth inquiry will take longer, of course."

"Mmmm." There was nothing startling about the information on the paper, but since it was all new to her, Meg read it with interest. No wonder Riley preferred to use his patronymic. His full name was Aloysius Loyola Riley—a proper little Irishman, Meg thought, with a smile. His father, who had died ten years earlier, had been a naturalized citizen,his mother was native-born. (Native-born in the truest sense, perhaps; it must have been from his mother's side of the family that Riley had acquired that distinctive hawk-nosed profile and swarthy skin. Now she was thinking like Dan, Meg realized; he had been too inclined to fit people into ethnic and national categories.) Date of birth, place of birth, education. . . .

"Service record?" Meg exclaimed. "He was in Vietnam? But surely he was too. . . ."

A glance back at the first page and a short exercise in arithmetic proved her wrong. "He was eighteen. Nineteen seventy-two—I thought it was over by then."

"Not until the end of the year. He was only there five months—"

"Long enough to be wounded," Meg cut in. "That's what a Purple Heart means, isn't it?"

"They gave Purple Hearts for mosquito bites," Darren said.

Meg was tempted to ask how he knew. Dan would have, with the wicked gleam in his eyes that turned a question into an insult. But then Darren would not have made a snide remark about his protégé to Dan Mignot.

She folded the papers and put them in her purse. "I don't see anything here to his discredit."

"Nothing yet."

"You mean to go on with this?"

Darren folded his sandwich wrappings and put them in the wastebasket. "Meg, dear, we haven't even begun. It takes some time to check possible criminal records; if he committed any crimes as a juvenile, those records will be closed. The next step is to talk to neighbors and friends, teachers—"

"Collect gossip, you mean."

"That's the way it's done, Meg. I don't blame you for disliking the idea—"

"I hate it. I despise it. Darren, Dan must have had Riley investigated. He wouldn't have risked putting an embezzler or thief in charge of the store."

"That's a point," Darren admitted. "It's up to you, Meg. You're the one who is paying the bills. If you tell me to call my man off, I will."

"I should damn well hope so," Meg muttered. "Oh, hell. I suppose he's already started the second stage of the investigation? Okay. Unless he turns up something within the next couple of days, tell him that's it. And for God's sake, don't breathe a word about this to anyone else."

"I hope you don't think I would violate a client's confidentiality," Darren said stiffly.

"I'm sure you wouldn't, but I wouldn't bet a plugged nickel on Mrs. B."

"She never opens personal letters."

"I wouldn't bet on that either. Who typed the letter to the detective, Darren?"

Darren's lips shaped a silent O of realization.

"Well, there's no harm done," Meg said, in a softer voice. "I hope. Please make sure any further communications from this guy are marked "Private and Confidential, Black Widow Spider Inside," okay? I am sufficiently ashamed of violating Riley's privacy without feeling responsible for spreading the news around town."

"I think you're being unfair, Meg."

"Just careful, Darren." Meg looked at her watch. "I've got to get back. Let's get that will signed."

Darren took it out of the folder and handed it over. As she began reading it, he said quietly, "I suppose people keep telling you how much you remind them of Dan."

"Yes."

"You're a lot prettier." Meg looked up in surprise, and he added, "Which isn't saying a great deal."

"True." Meg laughed. "I didn't mean to sound like Dan, Darren. I appreciate your help and I respect your abilities and I will always be grateful for your advice—but I have to make my own decisions."

"Of course. When I said the other day that you had changed, it was meant as a compliment. I admire decisiveness and honesty in a woman."

Meg's smile froze. He doesn't mean it that way, she told herself. Most men don't realize how demeaning that phrase sounds. "Thank you," she said.

"Could we have dinner one night, do you suppose?" Before she could answer, Darren went on, "Not only for old times' sake, but. . . . It's easier to talk things over when we're not constrained by schedules and—er—"

"Devoted secretaries? Thanks, that would be nice."

"Saturday?"

"How conventional of you, Darren. All right. Now call your witnesses and let's get this over with."

When she left the office Meg was the proud possessor of a new will disposing of her theoretical property in a way she thought Dan would have approved, though Darren obviously did not. Had she done the right thing? She paused, to stare unseeingly at the display window of the boutique and arouse false hopes in the palpitating bosom of the manager. Maybe Ms. Venturi had changed her mind about that sequined evening gown. A steady customer with her income could be a big help to the store.

Meg's mind was not on that or any other article of clothing. Her grandfather might approve the will, but only as a temporary measure. His dynastic aspirations, hanging on the frail thread of a single female descendant, would not be satisfied until she had a husband and children. The right husband, of course, and a son, by preference. It was a wonder Dan hadn't made marriage to the man of his choice a condition of her inheritance. Perhaps that sort of condition was illegal nowadays? Or perhaps Dan hadn't found a man he considered worthy. . . .

Openmouthed, Meg considered the bizarre suspicion that had entered her mind. Surely not. Such a plan would be too weird, even for Dan. Nor could she take his approval of Riley for granted. He had made plenty of mistakes in his time.

Unaware of the interested watcher, she grimaced and shook her head. However, the window display reminded her that she needed something to wear if she was going to have dinner with Darren. She knew why he had suggested it. He sensed she had not been completely candid with him, and he hoped the relaxed ambience of soft lights and good food and fond reminiscence—not to mention the effects of a few glasses of wine—would invite her confidence. If he only knew how much I've held back, Meg thought. The hoard of jewelry, the strange telephone call, the dead rat. . . . Well, why not dump the whole mixed bag onto him? She needed advice and there was no earthly reason why she shouldn't ask it of Darren, her friend and her lawyer. I'll think about it later, she decided.

The manager of the boutique watched Meg walk briskly away. "What a snob," she remarked to the saleswoman. "Did you see the way she sneered at the things in the window? I suppose she thinks she's too good for any place but Saks and Neiman Marcus."

Had she seen Meg rummaging through the racks at the local dry-goods store, she would not have changed her opinion. Reputations are shaped not by facts but by prejudices.

As Meg lingered over breakfast the following morning she wondered whether it was cowardice or courtesy that kept her in her chair. She wasn't particularly anxious to encounter another dead rat, or its equivalent, but George was so eager to please and amuse her that it would have been rude to walk out on him. Even Frances was in an amiable mood. A few days of peace and quiet had banished Mrs. Danvers. The weather was lovely, her adored mistress was in good spirits and excellent health, and Meg had settled down to do her duty as Frances and Frances's God saw it.

"Have another muffin," she urged, hovering. "You've got to keep your strength up if you're going to work all day."

Meg took the muffin. It was easier than arguing. After Frances had gone, looking smug, George resumed the conversation where she had interrupted it.

"So you're sure you don't mind if I go away for a day or two? I'll be back Sunday night at the latest."

Meg said warmly, "Uncle George, you don't have to ask my permission. You're your own boss, and as far as I'm concerned you always will be."

"That's sweet of you, child." Her uncle's face relaxed into one of his charming smiles, and he added, "But very impractical, one of these days you'll want to go over the tax and financial records for the store—"

"Don't remind me," Meg said, wincing theatrically. "I can't take on anything complicated just now. I've got my hands full with Riley. Whipping him into shape is going to take all the energy I possess, and then some."

George laughed. "If anybody can do it, you can. All the same, Meg—"

"I've got to run." Meg stood up. "The challenge awaits, and I have to tackle it while I'm fresh. See you tonight."

He didn't argue, though his expression told her he was well aware why she was beating a hasty retreat. It wasn't until she was out of the house that a possible reason for his original question finally dawned on her. He had not been asking her permission to go away; he had been asking if she was afraid to be left alone.

When Meg reached the store the door was unlocked, the shade was up and the "Open" sign was in place. Even the window glass sparkled.

Riley was behind the counter. "Morning," he said.

The greeting represented a quantum leap in affability for Riley, and Meg gave him a broad smile, like a teacher encouraging a difficult child. "Good morning. As you see, I took your advice. Did you find any little surprises when you opened up?"

She was learning to read that frozen face of his. It did express emotion, but so sparely that only someone who knew him well would notice. Meg caught the blink and the movement of his eyes, and remembered the freshly washed window. "I was kidding," she said slowly. "Don't tell me—"

"I did tell you. It's not your problem." He started toward the window, and the sight of the object he held made Meg forget what she had been about to say.

"It's Bel-shumu! I wondered what had happened to him." She held out her hands, and Riley gave her the statuette.

It was the figure of a man, bald and big-eyed, wearing only a pleated skirt and a placid smile. His hands were folded across his comfortable stomach. Meg's fingers closed over the small, eight-inch-high carving. "He was Dan's mascot," she murmured. "Patron saint was more like it. . . . How did the contract read? 'As concerns the gold ring set with an emerald. . . .' "

As she fumbled for the forgotten words, another voice took up the recitation, " '. . . we guarantee that in twenty years the emerald will not fall out of the gold ring.

" 'If the emerald should fall out of the gold ring before—before the end of twenty years, we, Bel-shumu, Bel——' Damn!

" 'Bel-ah-iddini and Hatin shall pay an indemnity of ten mina of silver.' "

"That's it. The first recorded contract between a jeweler and a client. Fifth century B.C. I always wondered why Dan named this little guy after Bel-shumu, instead of one of the other members of the firm."

"Easier to pronounce," Riley said.

"Hatin is even easier. Dan said he called him Bel-shumu because he *was* Bel-shumu." Meg laughed. "It made perfect sense to me at the time. But this character isn't even from the right time period: He's got to be a couple of thousand years older than the signer of the contract."

"He's also a fake."

"I suspected he was, but Dan would never admit he'd been taken in. Oh, well; who cares? It's the thought that counts. I'll put him back in the window. Were you cleaning him or something?"

"Repairing him. He was . . . damaged."

On closer inspection, Meg could make out the hairline fractures around the neck and one foot. "You did a good job."

"Thanks."

His face had closed down again, his eyes opaque and shadowed, his mouth clamped shut. Was he regretting those moments of relaxed, shared enjoyment, or had she asked the wrong question?

Meg suspected it had been Candy who broke

the little icon, out of sheer spite; it had occupied a central position in the show window for years, exemplifying the proud traditions of Dan's profession.

She restored it to its place, assuming that Riley would return to his; all that affability must have been a terrible strain on him. But when she turned he was still there, and she began to hope that a breakthrough had occurred.

"I have an an appointment at two o'clock," he said. "I'd like to keep it, but if it's any problem. . . ."

"Go ahead."

"You could close early."

"I could."

"Okay." He started for the workshop. "Thanks."

Meg felt ridiculously let down. For a few minutes he had been so pleasant, almost friendly. And only because he had found himself in the position of having to ask a favor.

"Have you had any luck getting a replacement for Candy?" she demanded.

"Not yet. I'm working on it."

"Maybe we ought to take her back."

That stopped him. He looked at her over his shoulder. "No. I mean—I don't recommend it. But you can do whatever you want."

"It should be a joint decision. But we need someone."

"Do whatever you want," Riley repeated. The door closed with a decisive slam.

It would serve him right if I did, Meg thought furiously. She was certain he had fired Candy not because the girl had insulted her, Meg—why should Riley care what anyone said about her?—but because Candy had backed him into an emotional corner. Amusement wiped the frown from her face as her imagination shaped a picture of the final, passionate encounter: Riley retreating, literally, into a corner, trying to fend off the fluttering hands and puckered lips of a woman half his size. What a joy it would be to see the imperturbable Riley in a situation like that—almost worth the annoyance of having Candy around.

No; tempting as the idea was, she couldn't do it. She didn't want Candy in the store either, and rehiring her would end forever any hope of establishing a rapport with her prickly partner. Really, Meg thought, it was like trying to work with an emotionally disturbed child—two steps forward, one step back. You had to watch every word, and you never knew when you were going to say the wrong thing. Yet there was that forward step . . . and the hope of finding at the end of the path something that would make the effort worthwhile. What had happened to him to make him so defensive and suspicious? Vietnam? The veterans of that non-war had suffered terribly, not only in the field but after returning home. Attitudes had changed now, but too late for some of the men who carried deep emotional scars. You couldn't batter down the defenses of a man like Riley, you could only try to win his trust. That was all she wanted—not affection or even friendship, just an acknowledgment that he could trust her to deal honorably and fairly with him, as he had trusted Dan.

And if she were able to place an equal confidence in him, she could leave the store in his hands. What a relief that would be. . . . Meg's eyes moved from the glittering contents of the showcase in front of her to the window where Belshumu had resumed his responsibilities as guardian angel, then to the case filled with Riley's astonishing creations. Would it be a relief to leave all this, or would she miss it after all? The trouble was she didn't know what she wanted. It wasn't likely that Riley could solve that dilemma for her.

Frances had packed her a lunch, so she didn't leave the store. Shortly before one Riley emerged from his lair. He was wearing a white shirt and a tie, and carried his suit coat over his arm. His funeral suit. Was it the only one he owned?

"I'm leaving now," he announced unnecessarily.

"You look very nice. Have you got a clean handkerchief?"

Riley blinked. "And cut my nails and washed behind my ears. See you later."

Meg followed him to the door. After a time she saw a rusty gray pickup emerge from the parking lot next to the store, and recognized Riley at the wheel. He didn't glance in her direction; his profile was as unyielding as one carved in stone, and she found it hard to believe he had actually responded to her feeble joke with one of his own. The words had been familiar, too—a quotation from some book or film? She couldn't remember.

She waited another fifteen minutes before she went to the door of the shop. It was locked; he must have set the latch before he left. Unthinking habit, or a conscious intent to keep her out? Give him the benefit of a doubt. He must know a locked door wouldn't stop her. She got the heavy bunch of keys from her purse. Dan's keys. Gran had handed them over, without question or comment, when she asked for them.

In Meg's youth the shop had been a place of mystery and magic. She was seldom allowed to enter it, because there were too many dangerous objects lying around. Tools were kept razor sharp, pots of Shellac bubbled over open flames, soldering irons and kilns offered potential hazards. On the rare occasions when she had been invited into the sanctum Dan had not done any serious work; he said he couldn't keep an eye on her and concentrate at the same time. But he had demonstrated many of the techniques that fascinated a child, filling cloisonné cells with powdered enamel and showing her how they changed after being fired; twisting gold wire into filigree coils fine as hair; setting pearls and turquoise into a ring for her tenth birthday. It was too small for her now, even for her little finger, but she still cherished it.

The high point of those visits was when Dan took the trays of loose stones from the safe and let her handle them. She wasn't allowed to touch the larger and more valuable gems, each of which lived in its own individual box: Burmese rubies, red as dragon's blood, cabochon sapphires holding stars drowned in their blue depths, Colombian emeralds like squares of sundrenched grass. And the diamonds. Perhaps it was from Dan that she had acquired her disinterest in the blazing blue-white stones the rest of the world prized above all other gems. The colored stones called out to her, struck a responsive chord in some part of her mind. And although she wasn't allowed to play with the expensive stones, the others gave her almost as much pleasure. Semiprecious they might be in terms of value, but they were equally beautiful—the softer, subtler blue of aquamarine and topaz, the rainbow range of garnets. Dan had taught her how to distinguish the greens of tourmaline and emerald and the rare demantoid garnets, and as a special treat he let her play the game that was not a game at all but a method of distinguishing between topazes and the less valuable citrines of identical color. As her fingers fumbled through the stones, jumbled all together in a half-closed bag, they became familiar with the distinctive oily feel of the topazes; and on the day when she found them all, with no hesitation and no mistakes, her delight was as great as Dan's.

Meg pushed the memories away. She had walked out of the shop for the last time when she was eighteen, rejecting its promise and its challenge. She had made no attempt to enter the room since she returned, telling herself it was a good tactical move to give Riley his own place, free of her presence; but there were other reasons, and she was glad now she had waited till she could be alone. It would have been hard to cope with memories and mixed emotions in his silent, critical presence.

There was no suggestion of Ali Baba's cave here. The room was strictly utilitarian, a windowless, closed box with walls and floors of reinforced concrete. The floor was carpeted, but not for comfort; an unset gemstone that slipped from the jeweler's grip might ricochet off a hard surface and end up anywhere. There were only two doors, the one through which she had entered and a back door opening onto the alley. Fire regulations required that second exit, but it was seldom used, and Dan had done everything possible to make it impregnable from without. A walled-in cubicle contained sink and toilet; the only other amenities consisted of a coffeepot and a huge ashtray, once sacred to Dan's horrible cigars, now containing a few cigarette butts. The steam-cleaning machine and the heavy gold-rolling machines, which shaped the wires of precious metal, stood off to one side, other pieces of machinery occupied space on various benches. The jeweler's workbench was of a unique design, admirably adapted to the functions it served. The work surface was sunken, so that stones that slipped from the vise mounted above it wouldn't roll off onto the floor. The most commonly used tools—calipers, files, prong pushers and so on—lay loose on the work surface; others were ranged in neat rows along or atop the ledge that ran around three sides of the bench. The all-purpose power tool, called a flexible shaft, looked like an old-fashioned dentist's drill. A variety of tools, burrs, buffers and polishers, could be plugged into its head.

As Meg approached the workbench she realized that she had her hands behind her back. Another of Dan's rules—look, but don't touch. A scattering of heavy-based bowls on the ledge to the right of the work surface held bits and pieces of gold wire and some small loose stones. Garnets. Disappointed in her hope of getting a clue as to Riley's latest project, Meg straightened up. If he was working on something, he had put the materials in the safe before he left.

It was the same heavy old iron structure Meg remembered; she frowned at it, realizing that she didn't know the combination. Perhaps George had a record of it, or Dan had hidden one somewhere. She should have asked Riley. Why not? She had every right to know.

As she wandered around the room, finding it as impersonal and uninformative as a hotel room, her indignation mounted. If she weren't such a courteous, thoughtful person, she would have demanded entry long before this, and asked Riley to show her what he was working on. He must be involved in some new project, he had hardly been out of the shop since she started coming to the store. Of course, Meg admitted to herself, her presence in the store might be the reason why he had hardly been out of the shop. For all she knew, he spent the time reading girlie magazines or snoozing or snorting coke. Well, not the last; she knew the signs too well to have missed them. The magazines on a shelf at the back all seemed to be copies of *The Journal of Gemmology* and *The Jewellers' Circular*. Perhaps Riley kept his copies of *Playboy* and *Hustler* in a desk drawer, along with a bottle of bourbon and a stash of pot.

Abandoning herself to vulgar curiosity, Meg subjected the work surface to a closer inspection. A glimmer of gold filings shone among the scattered tools; that was all, except for some clippings of thread . . . no, not thread, it was too fine, as fine as human hair. Sometimes hair had been used to make seed-pearl jewelry. Few modern jewelers would tackle the finicky process of repairing such pieces; the value of the jewelry wasn't great enough to justify the effort involved. Riley was the sort of craftsman who might, just to see if he could do it, but not with hair this color. It was too dark.

Her curiosity was now raging. Where did the man keep his personal. . . . She corrected herself: not his personal possessions, she had no right to examine those. It was his professional work that interested her—his designs and sketches. There could be no harm in looking at things like that. . . .

The desk in one corner had been Dan's—a battered oak structure as massive as a safe. The first drawer she tried resisted her attempt to open it, and she tugged again before it dawned on her that the drawer—and all the others, as she was quick to discover—were locked.

Meg no longer felt guilty. This precaution had to be aimed at her alone; there could be nothing in the desk worthy of a thief's attention, all valuable materials were supposed to be in the safe. How dare he think I'd snoop behind his back, she thought angrily and illogically, sorting through the keys on Dan's ring.

One key opened all the drawers. At first Meg couldn't understand why Riley had bothered to lock them; the contents consisted primarily of drawing and sketching materials and the miscellaneous odds and ends that accumulate in all offices. Finally she found what she told herself she was looking for: a portfolio of rough sketches for jewelry. Meg lingered over them, fascinated but still frustrated; he hadn't developed any of them, they were hardly more than jottings of ideas.

And that was it, except for several folders filled with clippings and photographs. Some were of jewelry, modern and antique, others showed a weird variety of natural and man-made objects, from flowers to computer designs. Meg went quickly through them, intrigued by the hints they offered as to Riley's sources of inspiration. She would never have seen a potential design in a broken stick, but apparently it had suggested something to the designer. She was about to return the folder to the drawer when something she had glimpsed in passing struck a delayed chord of memory. She went back through the folder.

The drawing had been reproduced from a page in a book—an old book. The copier had captured the uneven edge of the paper and curve of the inner side. From the style of the engraving Meg felt certain that it, like the black-and-white copy, had lacked color. That was why it had taken her so long to recognize it. Yet even without the glorious glow of gold and gemstones, there was no doubt in her mind that she was looking at a representation of the necklace she had found in her safe—one of the hidden treasures from Dan's cache.

10

THE CHIMES JARRED Meg out of her paralysis, and the folder slipped through her fingers, spraying papers across a wide area. That does it, she thought distractedly. I'll never be able to get them back in the same order. He'll know I was snooping. . . . Oh, God, I left the door open!

She made a dash for the door and was in time to head off the customers, who had started toward the back when they found no one behind the counter. They were a youngish, well-dressed couple in search of engagement and wedding rings. A trifle breathless Meg commended their good taste in preferring the old and unique to the modern and ubiquitous, and showed them what she had in stock. They took forever coming to a decision, and when they had finally made their choice the woman asked to look at bracelets. In the end they bought four rings and a heavy fourteen-carat band bracelet. Meg should have been pleased at the sale and at the interest they showed in other pieces, but as she smiled and chatted and explained she felt like someone entertaining unexpected visitors with a dead body under the sofa. The open door to the shop gaped like a wound, and the desk was in the direct line of sight. Riley hadn't bothered to tell her whether he would be back that afternoon. If he walked in before she could tidy the place up. . . .

"No, they aren't topazes, they are yellow garnets. No, all garnets aren't red, they come in a variety of colors. Well, there are a number of ways of distinguishing gemstones. The refractive index, for one. Of course. We guarantee everything we sell."

After a million years or so they left, and Meg dashed for the shop. She had to conceal the evidence of her snooping. Riley's files contained many examples of what he apparently considered intriguing design, but the fact that one of them was a jewel from Dan's hidden cache opened up new and frightening ramifications. She wanted time to think about them before she confronted him . . . or found herself confronted by him.

This time Meg closed the door before she got to work. She forced herself to take her time; the intercom would warn her if anyone entered the store.

After a nerve-racking ten minutes she thought she had restored the clippings to an approximation of their original order. Maybe Riley wouldn't notice the difference. She had closed the drawers and was locking them when the chimes rang again.

The ensuing sounds warned her what to expect before she opened the door. High-pitched voices and bursts of giggling—the happy widows, Dan had called them, when he wasn't calling them something more insulting. Middle-aged females, out for a day of lunch and shopping. Mostly window-shopping. They seldom bought anything, but they wanted to see everything. They leaned on the counters and got fingerprints all over the glass, and according to Dan they included a high percentage of kleptomaniacs. That accusation was probably even more unfair than the other things Dan had said about them, but it was true that it was harder to keep an eye on the stock when there were half a dozen people in the store, wandering around and asking to look at various pieces. However, it was not the prospect of a nerve-racking half hour with the happy widows that wiped the smile off Meg's face. It was Candy, standing modestly to one side, but wearing a smile that aroused Meg's deepest suspicions. Candy should not have been looking so pleased with herself.

"What can I do for you?" she asked of no one in particular. Candy's feline smile broadened. "Go ahead with these ladies, Meg. I'm in no hurry."

Neither were the ladies. After they had expressed horror at the prices and told her their grandmothers (aunts, cousins) had things much nicer than anything in the store, one of them did buy a ring set with a single pearl. Meg compromised on the price only to get them out. The door finally closed on their girlish laughter, and Meg turned to confront Candy.

"Yes?"

Candy strolled to the counter and brushed at a damp fingerprint, smearing it still further.

"I hear you haven't found anybody to take my place."

"Not yet."

"I'd be willing to come back if you made it worth my while."

Meg studied the other woman curiously. Something had given her a new confidence, verging on arrogance.

"Was your ex the one who dumped the dead rat on the doorstep?" she asked.

Candy's grin resembled that of the Cheshire cat. "Did somebody do that?"

"Somebody did, and if he keeps on doing it he's going to end up in jail."

Candy's expression indicated she didn't give a damn where Applegate ended up. She didn't want Rod, but she would be perfectly willing to use him to get what she did want.

"I wasn't the one who fired you," Meg said. "I couldn't hire you back even if I wanted to, not without consulting my partner."

"Yes, you could. You could make him take me back."

"Maybe I could. But I won't."

Meg braced herself for an argument, if not a battery of insults. To her surprise Candy shrugged and sauntered toward the door. "Think about it. Think about it real good. I could be a lot of help to you, Miss High and Mighty."

Meg let her have the last word. She had heard it and the three that preceded it, before—from Rod Applegate. What a strange coincidence!

She got out the cleaning materials and started to work on the smudged glass. As she scrubbed, her mind kept returning to Candy's odd behavior. There was a lady who thought she was sitting in the catbird seat; her final speech sounded like a quote from a sinister blackmailer in a TV soap opera. Surely she wasn't stupid enough to think that she could use the threat of harassment by her ex-husband to get her job back. Applegate was even stupider if he let Candy use him for that purpose—especially if he still loved her. Why was it so difficult to believe that two physically unattractive, mean-minded people could genuinely care for one another? In this case at least, Meg felt sure Applegate's pride rather than his heart had suffered when Candy turned to another man. He couldn't even hold on to a woman no other man wanted.

She picked at a stubborn stain with her fingernail, wondering idly why Candy had not waited until the customers left the store before she entered. The chimes had rung only once, so they must have all come in together. Had Candy been loitering, working up nerve for the confrontation and waiting for someone else to. . . .

To open the door. To account for the warning chimes. But there was no reason for her to do that unless she didn't want Meg to know she was there.

Suppose she had slipped in, not with the girls, but with the earlier customers, and gone straight to the washroom or the office. She would have had time to conceal herself—and to glance into the shop.

She must have remained in hiding until the next lot of customers entered the store. Why do that, risking discovery? The chimes would have rung if she had left the store, but she could have been out of sight before Meg reached the front door.

Meg put the cloth and bottle of ammonia away and went to the washroom. She had tidied it that morning. Now the squashed remains of a flower petal highlighted a dusty footprint. The Bradford pears were shedding petals, but none of the customers had used the washroom. . . . Tight-lipped, Meg headed for the office. The evidence of Candy's presence was unmistakable—a drawer not quite closed, a pile of papers untidily aligned. Candy had been a busy little bee. She must have gone to the washroom first, and waited until Meg closed the shop door before going to the office.

Why? What had she hoped to accomplish? It was difficult to second-guess a mind like Candy's; sneaking, prying and eavesdropping might be habitual to her. She might even have been looking for signs of what she would probably term "carrying on." She'd be only too quick to assume that was Meg's motive in coming to work at the store. Meg looked helplessly around the office. Hard to tell if anything was missing, the place was such a clutter. She opened a desk drawer, more or less at random. It was a mess, as Dan's drawers always were. Amid the jumble of papers, envelopes, pens and dust was a familiar object—a small velvet bag, tied with a gold cord.

The bag of topazes and citrines. It wasn't in the safe, then. Meg reached for it, loosened the drawstring, inserted her hand. The smooth, cool surfaces of the stones comforted her searching fingers; Dan used to say they were as soothing as worry beads. Sometimes, when he was in a bad mood, he'd keep the little bag with him so he could play with the stones.

There didn't seem to be any stones missing, but how would she know? She had forgotten how many there were; the size and bulk of the bag seemed to be as she remembered it. Meg replaced it in the drawer. She was about to give up when another memory returned. Dan's secret drawer! Many old desks had them; it wouldn't have taken an expert five minutes to find this one, and although Dan delighted in it, he had never used it for anything valuable. She pulled out the top drawer, put it on the floor and pressed the false screw-head at the back of the partition.

The compartment disclosed by the removal of the side panel was quite shallow; but it was deep enough to hold a gun. Meg recoiled. When had

Dan taken to keeping a weapon in his desk? It certainly hadn't been there during the years when she was allowed to play with the secret drawer. But times had changed; it was not a kinder, gentler world, it was a lot uglier than it had been when she was young.

There was nothing else in the compartment except dust. Meg closed the panel and replaced the drawer. It had not been locked. What about keys? Had Riley thought to ask for Candy's keys when he fired her? Even if he had retrieved them, she could have made copies. And if she had keys to the store, so might other people.

Meg reached for the telephone directory. The locksmith tried to put her off, but she cajoled him into promising he would do the job first thing in the morning. She'd have to come in early, explain to Riley—and hope he didn't notice the disturbance of his files. There was no way she could put the blame for that on Candy.

She waited on two more customers, neither of whom bought anything, rearranged some of the stock, polished two more countertops and then decided she might as well close up. The tourists from whom most of their trade derived would be starting for home now, and she was too restless to accomplish anything useful.

Before she left, she made a copy of the engraving. There was a good chance that the book from which it had come was in Dan's library. She had only checked a few of the many volumes on jewelry; at least the size and probable age of this page would give her a clue as to what to look for.

After she had locked up and set the alarm she paused for a moment to look in the display window. The complacent smile on the face of the little clay image brought an answering smile to her face. He looked as if he knew all the answers. If so, he had found them in the shadowy Sumerian hereafter, for no mortal creature lives a life free of trouble or doubt. Bel-shumu, or whatever his name may have been, had never had to worry about nuclear warfare or the depletion of the ozone layer, but it was the ordinary human tragedies that wore people down—death and loss, pain and disease. Not to mention an emerald lost from a ring. . . . That window ought to be rearranged, Meg thought. And the chimes—damn, I forgot to look at them, and they're still off-key.

She had not gone far when she saw Mike Potter cutting across the street toward her, and stopped to wait for him. "It's not closing time yet," she said with a smile. "What are you doing out of the store?"

"Come to ask you the same question," Mike said. "Everything all right?"

"Sure. I'm just not as conscientious as you. What's the point of being the boss if you can't close up when you feel like it?"

"If I didn't know you was teasing me I'd have to give you a talking-to," Mike said seriously. "You going home now?"

"Uh-huh. Unless I can buy you a cup of coffee.

You could give me that lecture about hard work and stern duty and noblesse oblige."

Mike's face cracked into one of his rare smiles. "Honey, that lecture takes a good two hours. I'll walk along with you a piece. It's a pretty day, and I need to stretch my legs."

"Seems to me they're already long enough," Meg retorted, as he fell into step with her.

Mike responded with a hearty haw-haw, and Meg thought how nice it was to be with a man who would laugh at her feeble jokes.

"Candy came by today, did she?"

"Yes, she did. Do you know," Meg said pensively, "I have a feeling that if I happened to scratch myself tonight, in my room, with the shades drawn and the lights out, tomorrow somebody would offer me a remedy for poison ivy."

"Where'd you get into poison ivy?"

"I didn't, I was kidding. Do you want to know why Candy came to see me?"

"Figured she wants her job back."

"You figure right. How did you know?"

"She's been complaining and grousing to everybody she thinks has some influence with you," Mike said. "Me and your uncle and Cliff. . . . What'd you say?"

"Nothing." She was glad Mike hadn't heard the word; he wouldn't approve of nice young women calling other young women bad names. If Candy had been present she would have called her a bitch—with several qualifying adjectives—to her face. Bad enough that she was spreading filthy stories all over town, but that she should go whining to Cliff—who now had the disaffected witness he wanted—and to Uncle George. . . . That was what he had been to all her schoolfriends—everybody's favorite adopted uncle, who presided at birthday parties and escorted the children on outings to museums and amusement parks. Playing the role her father would have played . . . or would he?

She forced herself to listen to what Mike was saying. "I told her there was no use complaining to me. Hope I didn't hurt her feelings, but doggone it, she just. . . . Well, I hate to say it, but she isn't a nice woman. Been telling lies—wild stories—"

"What kind of stories?"

"You don't want to hear such trash."

"Yes, I do. If you're trying to spare my feelings, don't bother; I'll bet I've been called worse names than any Candy could come up with."

Mike pursed his lips as if he had swallowed something sour. "She hasn't said so much about you. Except to suggest you and Riley are. . . ."

"Carrying on? Misbehaving? Doing it?" Meg laughed. "Where, I wonder? There isn't a couch in the shop."

Mike was not amused. "Nobody believes her."

"Oh, yeah? I'll bet some people do. Candy was behaving oddly, Mike. She didn't so much ask, she insisted that I could make Riley take her back."

"You wouldn't do that, would you?"

"I don't want her back. As for making Riley do anything, I can't even stir up an argument! He just grunts and shrugs and walks away."

"That must be aggravating."

"Now you're teasing me. Heavens, we're almost there. How time flies with good company. . . . Won't you come in, Mike? Gran would love to see you."

"No, thanks, honey, I got to get back. And those little bitty teacups your gramma uses make me nervous, I'm always afraid I'll squeeze one too hard and squash it."

"Please, Mike, don't run off. I haven't had a chance to chat with you, and I really want—I really need to."

He gave her a long, considering look. "Sure, honey. Anytime. I'd have suggested it before, but I figured you were too busy. Why don't you come on over to the store on Monday after you close up, and we'll have some supper and a good long talk?"

"I'd love to. See you Monday, then."

He didn't have time for a cup of coffee, but he had taken the time to walk her home; and he was still standing at the end of the driveway when Meg passed around the curve and he was lost to sight.

By the time two more people had commented on the fact that she was early, and asked why, Meg was beginning to feel like a caged laboratory animal. This, she reminded herself, was what it would be like if she lived at home. Every move she made would be observed, questioned and comnented upon. Frances's curiosity was habitual, ut it fueled Meg's irritation, and her uncle got he brunt of it.

"Yes, of course everything is all right. I just lecided to come home early. Riley didn't do any-hing, or say anything, or chase me around the tore with a butcher knife! I do wish you'd stop ussing, Uncle George. I thought you were going way for a few days."

"I wasn't planning to leave until tomorrow," ier uncle said mildly. "If I asked about your week-nd plans, would you consider the question fuss-ng or an invasion of privacy? Or could you admit he possibility that I am simply attempting to nake polite conversation?"

"Sorry, Uncle George." She reached for a bis-uit, and pulled her hand back, hearing her grand-nother approaching. "As a matter of fact, I have date tomorrow night. And another one Monday. My social life is really picking up. The fact that ne engagement is with my lawyer and the other s with a man who's old enough to be my grand-ather is irrelevant and immaterial. Both are men. That's what counts. Right, Gran?"

"I'm sure you are, dear." Mary took her place n the sofa and glanced casually at the plates of andwiches and biscuits. "What are you talking bout?"

Not until after her grandmother had trailed her lounces upstairs to bed, shepherded by Henrietta, lid Meg feel free to go about her business. The evening hadn't been a total loss; she had learned a number of useful facts about show-biz personalities, state capitals and the habits of the ring-tailed lemur, the latter topic being the subject of a "National Geographic" special. In fact, if she hadn't had so many other things on her mind she would have enjoyed herself; even the ring-tailed lemur had its points, and Gran could be very entertaining company, in her own quiet way. Her comments had been sharp and sometimes deliciously sarcastic—the sort of remark she would have made to another adult. It's as difficult for her as it is for me, Meg thought in surprise; we both have to adjust, change our viewpoints, so that we can treat one another like people instead of sticking to the old roles of child and grandparent. I've always loved her; I think I like her too! I wonder if she likes me. . . .

Getting the copy of the engraving from her purse, she went to the library. Like Riley's copy, hers consisted of two separate sheets of 9½-by-11-inch paper taped together. The book from which it had been taken was outsized, several inches taller than the average modern volume. Most of the folios were on the bottom shelves, which had been designed to accommodate their greater height, but some had been shelved sideways or laid on top of a row of books. It was going to be a long, tedious search.

Meg sat cross-legged on the floor. Her mind wasn't on her job; she was still thinking about her grandmother, and the new relationship she could envisage. It could never be as simple as friendship, the older emotional ties would always be there, and new ones would be forged as Mary became increasingly feeble, physically and mentally. Meg was ready—glad, in fact—to assume those responsibilities, but she was realistic enough to know that living in the same house with her grandmother would be too much of a strain. A strain on Gran too, perhaps. The ideal solution would be not a room of her own but a set of rooms, close but detached, separate if not equal. I suppose I could kick Riley out of the apartment, she thought. Maybe that's why he's so hostile, he's afraid he'll have to give up his luxurious quarters. He's safe from me. Dan had said something about remodeling the place not long ago, but I wouldn't live there unless the only alternative were the county jail.

Uncle George didn't seem to mind the togetherness. Of course he had his own suite of rooms on the third floor, as far away from the rest of the family as he could get. More important, he was a man. No one questioned his comings and goings, no one waited up for him.

Certainly no one wondered why he had given up the cottage on the north side of the estate, which he and his wife had occupied until that never-to-be-forgotten winter night. George had lived in the apartment over the store before he and Joyce became engaged. It was obviously impossible for Dan's petted younger daughter to live in such squalor, so Dan had built the cottage for them and Cliff, who had been four years old when Joyce became his stepmother. Dan had offered to do the same for Meg's parents, but for one reason or another the plan had never been carried out; they had occupied a separate wing of the house, an area now converted into guest rooms.

They could remain guest rooms as far as Meg was concerned. She didn't want to live anywhere in the house—especially there.

But what about the cottage? As far as she knew it was still there, abandoned and probably ramshackle, but if it could be repaired it would present an ideal solution—separate from the main house, with its own driveway opening onto Old Hammond Road, but close enough to be convenient if Gran happened to need her. Would Uncle George mind? He might not want to live there himself, but after all these years he must have come to terms with his loss and hurt. The place held no painful memories for her, except by association no more direct than many others she had had to face recently.

As she considered the idea her eyes and hands went on with the mechanical chore of checking books. Most of the folios were relatively new, big handsome coffee-table-sized books with a maximum of photographs and a minimum of text. *Three Centuries of Historic Jewels*, *Masterpieces of Jewelry from the Great Museums of Europe*, and others of that type, along with catalogs of special exhibitions, auctions and famous collections. Meg selected one at random and opened it, to be confronted with a pen-and-ink sketch of a design for a pendant. It looked like—yes, it was—Holbein. Like other famous painters he had designed jewelry for his royal patrons. Was it possible that her copy came from a modern book on the history of jewelry? If so she would have to go through dozens of books, page by page. However, a closer examination of the copied engraving reassured her. The edge of the original page had been rough and uneven, which suggested that the book was so old that the paper had started to crumble.

Concentrating on her search instead of letting her mind wander, she found the book fairly quickly. It was one of the few really old volumes on the shelf; if Dan had cared as much for books as for jewels, it would have been in a glass case or at least sealed in inert plastic instead of being jammed into a shelf so full she had to remove several other books in order to extract it. Bound in crumbling brown leather stamped with gold, it had the title *Catalogue of the Jewels and Precious Works of Art in the Collection of H.R.H. the Maharajah of Mogara*. The maharajah's title was twice the size of the other words; underneath, letters of extremely modest size read, "as depicted and described by Mr. William Cuthbert Bennett, FRAI."

Meg didn't have to open the book to know she had found what she was looking for. She paused for a moment to puzzle over the letters following the artist's name. Fellow of the Royal Academy of India? Was there such a thing? She had never heard of it, which proved nothing. Possibly it had been mere "swank" on the part of an itinerant and exiled Englishman.

Mr. Bennett had been a competent if uninspired artist. In its way the book was rather charming; some of the plates had been hand-tinted, and if the drawings lacked originality, they appeared to be almost photographically exact. The descriptions of the pieces, on pages facing the drawings, were equally pedantic. "A gold collar or necklace of fourteen square plaques, eleven linked in a chain with three pendants; the latter centred each with a ruby approximately one inch in diameter and hung with pearls; each piece in the body of the chain set with sapphires and diamonds in a frame of twisted gold. . . ." He knew more about art than he did about gems, Meg thought, and he had the descriptive powers of a plumber. The frame of twisted gold was a masterwork of intricate openwork, the sapphires and diamonds formed flower shapes. She should know, she had seen the original.

All the pieces in Dan's hidden cache were shown. There were many other objects in the book, and Meg's imagination reeled as she considered the possibilities. Was the "armband of twisted red silk cords with tassels of pearls and a large oval diamond approximately two inches by three inches" tucked away in a secret drawer somewhere in the house, along with the "breast ornament or pendant" whose most conspicuous feature was a peacock with a jeweled tail and a body formed of a single emerald?

Probably not. She thought she knew what had become of the diamond, and possibly the emerald as well. If she was right, she had found the answer to one question, only to raise a host of others that were even more disturbing. Daniel Mignot's past had come back to haunt his descendants, and it held something more dangerous than mythical priests avenging a desecrated idol.

11

IT WAS 2 A.M. before Meg finished her research in the library and put away the books she had used. She hadn't found all the information she needed, nor proof that her suspicions were correct. But she hadn't found anything that would dispel them.

Counting on Frances to awaken her next morning as usual, she was horrified to see the time when she finally opened her eyes. The housekeeper added insult to injury by waylaying her as she trotted through the hall trying to button her blouse and find her car keys at the same time.

"Where do you think you're going, missy? You get on out there and eat your breakfast before you leave this house."

"I'm late. Why didn't you wake me up?"

"It's Saturday. I was just doing you a favor letting you sleep in, since you've been working so hard—"

The housekeeper's air of injured innocence annoyed her even more. "The store is open on Saturday too, as you know very well."

"I can't read people's minds," Frances said with a sniff. "It's hard enough to do everything I'm expected to do around here without getting insulted and cursed when I try to do somebody a favor."

"I didn't. . . . Frances, I haven't got time for this. Or breakfast. Good-bye."

Because it was Saturday and still early for shoppers, she was able to park in front of the store. As she pulled into the curb she saw that the locksmith had been true to his word. He had almost finished with the front door, and he graciously accepted her apology. "It's okay, the manager was here. He said he wasn't sure what you wanted, so I went ahead like we discussed it yesterday."

Meg had expected she would have to listen to a long unnecessary explanation and admire the turning of the screws; after she had done so she went inside. Riley was standing behind the counter. His folded arms, strongly marked features and rigid pose irresistibly suggested an old-time cigar-store Indian, and when his lips parted, Meg half expected him to say "How."

"Good morning," he said.

"Sorry I'm late. I meant to tell you about the new locks."

"You didn't have to call him. I could have installed them."

"That's silly, you have more important things

to do. I would have consulted you, only. . . ." Meg glanced at the locksmith, who had abandoned all pretense of going on with his work and was listening interestedly. "Have you got any coffee made?" she asked Riley. "I came away without breakfast,and I could use a cup."

He looked as if he could too. The signs of sleeplessness were slight, but visible—heavy eyelids, a smear of sickly pallor across his high cheekbones. "In the shop," he said briefly, and gestured her toward the door.

By leaving the door open they could keep an eye on the store and still converse without being overheard. Meg perched on a stool and accepted the cup Riley handed her. The coffee was the way Dan liked it—black as sin, strong enough to melt a spoon. After she had taken a few sips and waited in vain for Riley to speak, she said, "I'm sorry I didn't consult you about the locks, but something happened yesterday that convinced me it should be done without delay.

"Oh, yeah?"

"Candy dropped in to see me."

"Oh, yeah?"

"Did you get her keys back?"

"She never had keys to the store."

"Oh, yeah?"

As humor it was on the same level as the taunts of first graders. Why it should strike Riley as funny she never knew, then or later; the effect was so dazzling she could only gape at him. His lips curved and parted, displaying even white teeth; his eyes turned from shadowed brown to brilliant hazel. Even the arrogant nose seemed to shrink into proper dimensions.

"Yeah," he said. "One of us—Dan or I—always let her in."

"Oh." Meg tried to get a grip on herself. His amusement had subsided; that helped. But what an incredible transformation! It's just the contrast, she told herself; his normal expression is so forbidding. . . .

She was saved by the locksmith demanding compliments for completing the installation on the front door. Meg sent him to the back, in spite of Riley's objection that only he and Dan had ever had keys to that door, and they moved themselves and their coffee into the store. By that time Riley had his normal poker face back, and she was able to speak coherently.

"I don't care how many people officially had keys to what," she explained. "Candy is a snoop, and Dan was notoriously careless about leaving his belongings lying around. It only costs a few bucks to have keys copied."

Riley was obviously distracted by the presence of a stranger in his private preserve; he kept his eyes fixed on the open door to the shop, but his response was, for him, almost gracious. "Having the locks changed was a good idea. I should have thought of it myself. I'm not going to say what Candy is or is not—it's my word against hers, and there's no reason why you should take mine—but for what it's worth, she hasn't got anything on me."

"Has she got anything on Dan?"

The blunt question got a reaction, but not the one she had expected. Riley's eyes narrowed to slits. "Why ask me?"

"Damned if I know," Meg said in exasperation. "Trying to extract information from you is tougher than getting classified documents from the government. Dan was no plaster saint, do you think I don't know that? He might have told you things he wouldn't tell his innocent little female grandchild. I can't protect him, or myself, unless I know what I'm up against."

"That's reasonable," Riley admitted.

"Gee, thanks."

"I can't think of anything that need concern you." He read her expression and added hastily, "For God's sake don't yell, that character will hear you. Sure, Dan pulled a few fast ones in his time, but if the IRS couldn't pin anything on the old fox, a half-wit like Candy wouldn't have a clue."

"I'm not worried about the IRS."

"Worried?"

"Strange, isn't it? I have worries, just like normal people. Candy was acting peculiarly. As if she knew something I didn't know."

"But there isn't anything. . . ." Riley paused. After a moment he said, "Not about Dan. No way. She came crying to him, asking for a job, after she left her husband; reminded him that she'd been your best friend back in grade school—"

"Best friend! She hated my guts."

"Oh, yeah?" A faint but potent repetition of the smile made Meg's senses stagger. "I sort of suspected she was exaggerating. But Dan felt sorry for her, hired her, trained her. . . . He never would have confided in her, though. Wouldn't even trust her with a set of keys."

The chimes heralded the first customer of the day and Riley retreated, cup in hand. He left Meg only slightly reassured about Candy, but giddily optimistic about her relations with him. He had never talked so freely. Or smiled.

Business was brisk. By the time Meg had dealt with the customers, the locksmith and the mailman, she was beginning to think about lunch. She was looking through a catalog of findings and materials when the door opened, and she looked up to see her uncle.

"Is there something wrong with the chimes?" he asked, squinting at the silvery shapes over the door.

"I'm glad someone else noticed," Meg said. "Riley insists they sound fine to him."

George closed the door. He was wearing a tropical wool suit of pale gray only a shade darker than his hair; the color showed off his tan and his deep blue eyes. He's a good-looking man for his age, Meg thought affectionately; what a pity he never married again.

"Before you can ask," George announced, "I'm on my way. However, I could be persuaded to take a certain beautiful young businesswoman to lunch before I leave."

"No more excuses, Uncle George. You look particularly handsome today, it would be a shame to waste it on me."

"You're looking rather sensational yourself. Is that the famous necklace?"

"Yes, isn't it gorgeous? I decided to start wearing some of the stock. This is the second pair of earrings I've had on today. Sold the first pair right off my ears."

"Is this for sale?" His fingers brushed the heavy golden coil of the necklace.

"Sorry. Not even to my favorite uncle. When customers admire it I show them some of Riley's other work. Could I interest you in a garnet brooch, sir? I predict that within a few years this designer's work will triple in value."

George smiled and shook his head. "You are a very persuasive salesperson, miss, but I'd better run along. You're not alone here, are you? Where is this brilliant designer?"

"In his lair, as usual." Meg nodded toward the shop. "Uncle George, you're starting to fuss again."

"But if someone tried to hold you up—"

"Then I quaver loudly, 'Please put that gun away,' and Riley comes rushing to the rescue. Or, if he has better sense than I give him credit for, he calls the cops." Meg grinned. "The intercom is on, he can hear every word we say. Hey, Riley,

Uncle George says the chimes are off-key. I told you you were tone deaf."

"Well, that's—that's reassuring," George said. "Uh—I must go. Have a nice time this evening with Darren."

"Thank you." Meg walked with him to the door, where he paused. "You and Mr. Riley seem to be on excellent terms."

"It's still somewhat one-sided, but I'm making progress."

"That's good. Stores have been held up, you know, even here, and a jewelry store. . . . All right, I'll stop fussing!"

"There's no need to be concerned, Uncle George. Look—I even had new locks installed."

"Excellent. I meant to suggest that. Dan was always handing out keys to people."

"That doesn't sound like Dan." Meg frowned. "Who had them?"

"I exaggerate," George admitted. "Mike Potter had one, I know that. I'm not sure about Kate and the others."

"I'm not worried about being robbed by Mike Potter," Meg said with a smile. "Run along, Uncle George. Have fun."

The discordance of the chimes as the door closed blended with a murmur from Meg's empty stomach. For some reason, though, she was no longer in the mood for a leisurely lunch at Kate's. For some reason? She knew perfectly well what it was—a growing sense that she was under constant surveillance, not only by people who were inimical toward her but by another group whose motives could only be benevolent. It had been completely out of character for Mike Potter to leave the store in order to walk her home. It was too much of a coincidence to assume he had happened to glance out the door at the moment when she had closed up. He must have been watching for her. And now Uncle George, just happening to drop by on his way out of town. His definition of a weekend, from Saturday noon to Sunday evening, was also unorthodox. Had he postponed his departure until Cliff could take over? Cliff and Uncle George at the house, and in town another group of watchers. Located as it was, right on Main Street, the jewelry store was surrounded by the old gang—Barby's beauty shop just around the corner on Motter Avenue, Ed's bakery in the next block east, the hardware store a block west and Kate's practically across the street. If she had gone east instead of west, would Ed have bustled out to find out where she was headed?

Apparently one of the few people who weren't interested in her activities was Riley. Meg turned to stare at the closed door. She had hoped he would be moved, by her good-natured baiting, if not by her compliments, to come out and act civil. Socializing Riley was obviously going to be a long, slow process. Meg was tempted to yell "Fire" just to see what, if anything, would happen.

Half an hour later she decided to try a less dramatic method. "I'm going to the carry-out for a sandwich, Riley. Can I get you anything?"

He had manners enough to reply to a direct question. He actually came to the door. "Aren't you going to Kate's?"

"I will if you want something special," Meg said agreeably.

"No. I just. . . . Well, if you don't mind—some kind of a sandwich. I don't care what."

Meg closed in on him, remorselessly pleasant. "Tuna salad? Ham? Corned beef?"

"Corned beef would be fine."

"Rye or pumpernickel? Pickle?"

"It doesn't matter."

He stood four-square in the doorway, blocking not only her forward progress but her view. Meg stood on tiptoe and leaned to one side. "Mustard? A soda?"

"Ms. Venturi, what the hell are you doing?"

"I'm trying to see over your shoulder," Meg explained. She was so close to him that her hair brushed his cheek. "I'm dying to know what you're working on."

Riley lifted his hand to his cheek. "Why don't you just ask?"

"Riley, can I see what you're doing?"

"Certainly."

Meg went to the workbench. The necklace that lay there was a beautiful old piece; sullenly glowing pyrope garnets formed a series of linked star shapes from which depended other, larger stars. She turned a disappointed face toward Riley, and he let out a brief bark of sound that might have been a laugh. No smile, though. "I'm catching up on the repairs. Pieces like that take time; it's almost impossible to match the color and the cut of old Bohemian garnets."

"Not to mention lining the socket with foil." Meg held her breath as she leaned closer to the foil scraps and the tray of small loose stones, for fear of blowing them away. "These are old stones, from pieces that were beyond repair?"

"Right. Satisfied?"

"It's fascinating, but I was hoping you were working on one of your own designs."

"Look, Ms. Venturi—"

"If you don't want me to call you Mister Riley, you'll have to find a less formal name for me. Anything but 'hey, you.' "

"Uh—yeah. I hope you don't mind, but I hate having people look at my work until I'm finished with it. Just a foible of mine."

"Oh. All right. I can understand that." Meg went to the door. "Corned beef, pickle, on rye."

If she had hoped they would enjoy a sociable lunch à deux she was doomed to disappointment. Riley opened the door just long enough to accept the food and mumble "thanks" before he closed it, practically in her face. Philosophically Meg retired to the office with her sandwich. She had never dealt with anyone quite like Riley; most men were only too eager to respond to her advances. Not that she wanted that kind of response. The game she was playing was an intriguing challenge in itself, breaking down his defenses to a point where he would admit her to his friendship but not expect anything more serious. Meg grinned and licked crumbs off her fingers. If Riley ever made a pass at her, she would probably faint from sheer surprise.

Somehow she was not surprised when Barby "just happened to drop in" a while later. "I got a cancellation," the older woman explained breezily. "Thought maybe you'd like a wash and set."

"Does my hair look that bad?"

"Oh, no, honey, I didn't mean that. You've got beautiful hair, it's so dark and thick and healthy. I'd love to try a new style on you, that one is so severe. Since you've got a date tonight—"

"It's not a date, it's a business appointment," Meg said. "How did you know about it?"

People who have face-lifts should learn not to blush, Meg thought, watching her old friend's face. "Well, it was just an idea," Barby said. "If you change your mind, let me know."

"Thanks, Barby. I appreciate the offer."

They aren't very good at this, Meg thought, after Barby had retired in visible disorder. Was Darren another of her self-appointed guardians? He wasn't the man to gossip indiscriminately, especially about a client's affairs. Barby's source might have been Mrs. Babcock. Like most of the other older inhabitants, she probably had her hair done at Barby's.

During breaks between customers Meg went on with the job she had set for herself, going through

Dan's files to see if there was any record of the maharajah's jewels. Only the past ten years of business activity had been put into the computer. A dusty, tiring search of storage boxes turned up several old ledgers, but the oldest only dated back to the late sixties. She'd have to go farther back than that, Meg thought—much farther. If she was right, Dan had acquired those remarkable pieces over forty years ago. He might not have cared to leave a record of how he acquired them, but he would have had to account in some way for his possession of certain of the pieces—the ones he had broken up in order to market the gems separately. The diamond known as the Sun of Ceylon and the Ellendorf emerald were the most famous of the great gemstones Daniel Mignot had handled; more than anything else, they had been responsible for propelling him into the front ranks of the world's famous jewelers.

Meg decided to make another foray into Riley's sanctum. He made no objection and asked no questions when she told him she needed to get into the safe—simply gave her the combination and went back to his current project. Glancing at the workbench, she saw he was repairing the clasp of a gold chain. "You shouldn't be doing hack work like that," she said. "We need to hire more people."

Riley made no comment. So what else was new, Meg thought.

For once the lure of the gemstones didn't hold her, and her search was so brief it actually prompted a question from Riley. "Are you looking for something in particular?"

Meg was about to answer when something stopped her, as emphatically as a hand clapped over her mouth. "The—uh—the bag of citrines and topazes," she said instead.

"It isn't there? Dan must have taken it. He likes . . . he liked to handle the stones. Try his desk in the office."

"Thanks."

Why hadn't she admitted she was looking for old records? Because, she told herself, she wasn't stupid enough to be seduced into unnecessary confidences by a smile and a few civil words. The drawing of the necklace had been in his file. Coincidence, perhaps; but until she was certain it was safer to keep quiet.

The chimes summoned her back to the store. The face of the young woman who stood at the counter was vaguely familiar, but Meg was more concerned about the little boy who was struggling to free himself from her hold. He was a bright-eyed, handsome child of the type merchants dread most, and Meg knew he would shortly be liberated and wreaking havoc, for the mother was distracted by a second child, who was squirming and yelling in its stroller.

The woman gave Meg a tentative smile. She looked tired and disheveled, but her faded pink shorts and wrinkled blouse had once had a certain touch of style and she had taken the trouble to cover the hole in her sneaker with a Band-Aid.

She was twenty pounds overweight, but she must have been pretty once. . . .

Good God. Mercifully, Meg caught herself before she said it aloud. The woman had been pretty once; she had been Homecoming Queen of Meg's high school class, second runner-up in the state beauty contest. Dottie—Darlene. . . .

"Debbie! How nice to see you."

The tentative smile strengthened. "I wasn't sure you'd remember me."

"Of course I remember you. It's so nice. . . ." I said that, Meg told herself. "Uh—what beautiful children."

Maternal pride beamed from Debbie's eyes. "Thank you. This is Tommie. Say hello to the lady, Tommie."

The three-year-old stopped struggling and gave Meg a cold, appraising stare. "I want a lollipop," he stated.

"Tommie, you mustn't ask! Dan always gave him one," Debbie explained apologetically. "He was so fond of children. He used to keep a box of lollipops under the counter."

"It's still there." Meg went in search of the treat. Tommie rejected the first one she offered, demanding a red one instead, and Meg handed it over.

"Let's go now," Tommie said.

"Mama wants to talk to the lady, honey."

"I wanna go. I don't wanna see the bad man."

"Oh, Tommie, he isn't bad. He's a nice man."

"I hate him. He said he was gonna smack me. I told my daddy and my daddy said he was a—"

"Tommie!"

"The bad man isn't here," Meg said, with a malicious smile. "Don't you want that lollipop, Tommie?"

Tommie plugged his mouth with the object in question, and Debbie looked at him fondly. "He's named after his daddy. You know I married Tom Gentry."

She spoke as if the name were one any idiot would know—Elvis Presley, Clark Gable, Tom Gentry. Oddly enough, Meg did know. Tom had been the quarterback of the football team, the class president, the handsomest boy in the class. A fitting mate for the class beauty. . . . She shivered involuntarily.

Debbie introduced the occupant of the stroller. Warned by the ominous scowl on Cheryl Jean's juvenile countenance, Meg hastily produced a second lollipop while Debbie told her about Julie, nine, and Liz, seven.

Tommie created a diversion by trying to climb onto one of the showcases. In less than thirty seconds he had managed to smear essence of cherry lollipop all over both hands and the lower part of his face. By the time he had been pried loose and reprimanded, a good deal of it had been transferred to Meg.

"I guess I better not stay," Debbie said. "He's kind of restless, he really should have a nap in the afternoon, but he gave it up a while ago, and he. . . . Now, Tommie, don't wipe your hands on the lady's pretty skirt. I'm sorry, Meg."

"No problem," Meg said.

"It would be nice if we could get together sometime," Debbie went on. "The old gang—you know?"

"That would be fun." Even Gran would forgive her that lie, Meg thought wryly. If Debbie was representative of what had become of that old gang of hers, an evening with them would be more depressing than amusing. A sense of self-preservation made her add, "I'm pretty busy right now—you understand how it is."

"Oh, sure." But Debbie lingered, and Meg began to realize that she had something other than reminiscences on her mind. Tommie was whining and demanding ice cream, the baby had begun to whimper. Why didn't Debbie come to the point?

"How's Tom?" Meg asked, groping.

"Fine. Just fine. He's selling used cars, you know. I . . . I used to work too. At the new restaurant at the shopping center. My mom was real good about taking the kids, and . . . and the money sure helped—you know how it is, trying to raise kids on one salary these days. And Tom . . . the used-car business isn't too good right now."

So that was it, Meg thought. The past tense made it clear. Debbie had lost her job and was looking for another—a job she obviously needed. A job for which she had no qualifications and no aptitude; she had barely scraped through high school, and the existence of Julie, nine, strongly suggested that she had had no further education.

Meg didn't know what to say. Again Tommie saved her, snatching the lollipop from his little sister and sending the deprived infant into a screaming fit. Meg was so grateful she produced seconds for both children. "See you soon," she said, opening the door.

It was probably the wrong thing to say. Debbie's face brightened. "We're in the book. Call any time. Or I'll call you."

"Right."

As Meg got to work on the sticky showcase she wondered why no manufacturer had ever explored the adhesive qualities of lollipop syrup. Already it had dried to a consistency resembling that of cement. If Tommie had pulled a similar stunt before, she didn't blame Riley for offering to smack him. She was sorry, though, that Debbie had cut Tommie off before he could repeat his father's epithet.

It was silly of her to feel sorry for Debbie. The ex-beauty queen was probably blissfully happy. At least she thought she was, which was the same thing. She had what every woman was supposed to want—a husband who had been voted best looking, most likely to succeed and class hunk, and four beautiful children. So they were short on money. Most young couples were. What was money, Debbie would undoubtedly claim, compared to Love and Family Values and Maternal Bliss? You couldn't hire people just because they had holes in their sneakers. Debbie hadn't even been a close friend. The girls who had been closest to Meg were no longer in Seldon; they had married and moved away, or were pursuing successful careers in cities that offered more opportunity than the sleepy little town.

Saturday was early closing day. At four o'clock Meg buzzed her invisible partner and informed him she was leaving. "Have a nice weekend, you child-beater," she added.

"Thanks," said Riley. The distortion of the intercom robbed his voice of inflection. She could only hope he knew she was kidding him.

Meg had driven to work that morning because she planned a quick trip to the shopping center outside town. She still hadn't found a dress suitable for the sort of place to which Darren would probably take her. One did not wine and dine one's best client at Friendly's.

She was still wearing Riley's necklace. The very touch of it against her skin was seductive; it seemed to mold itself to the contours of her neck and breast. It was also an arrogant creation that demanded exactly the right setting. After trying on half a dozen dresses, Meg finally found one it would accept—plain, natural raw silk with a full skirt and a neckline that repeated and framed the curve of the necklace. It was of a style and color she never wore, and although she felt a faint resentment at being dominated, she knew she looked terrific.

Like many simple, plain dresses, this one cost

the earth. It was strange that as Meg handed over her credit card she should find herself remembering the Band-Aid on Debbie's sneaker. Annoyed at her sentimentality, she proceeded to buy half a dozen outfits suitable for work at the store, and several pairs of shoes. She needed them, and depriving herself wouldn't supply Debbie with what she needed—whatever that might be. It was probably something more difficult to provide than a new pair of shoes or even a job.

Though she drove a trifle faster than she should have on the way home, her grandmother was already in the parlor when she ran in. In her crisp lavender-and-old-lace gown Mary looked like a porcelain doll; instead of embracing that fragile perfection Meg blew her a kiss and backed toward the door. "Darling, I can't touch you until I've bathed and changed. I'm sorry I'm late, I went shopping and it took longer than I expected."

"It always does," her grandmother said wisely. "What did you get? You are going to show me, aren't you?"

"Of course. I'll just run upstairs—"

"There isn't time for you to change now, dear. Just wash your hands like a good girl. Germs, you know."

"Yes, ma'am."

Mary gave her a fond smile. "Goodness, you sound more and more like Daniel every day. He's always late coming home when he works at the shop, and sometimes his hands are absolutely filthy. All those chemicals and things, I sup-poke. . . . 'Wash your hands,' I tell him. 'You don't want to eat germs.' And he says, 'Yes, ma'am,' just the way you did. Jokingly."

"I'll be right back," Meg mumbled.

When she returned Cliff was there, looking as if he had just stepped out of the male equivalent of a bandbox—not a spot, not a crease, not a hair out of place except for the one carefully careless lock that dropped artistically across his tanned brow. He rose, threw his arm around her and drew her into a close embrace. His kiss would have landed on her mouth if she hadn't turned her head at the last second. The warm lips traced a tingling path across her cheek and brushed her earlobe before he loosened his grasp and guided her into a chair.

"It's nice to see you children so affectionate," Mary said fondly.

Meg swallowed the comment she had been about to make and Cliff's grin faded when he saw the spot on his hitherto spotless designer T-shirt. "What's that?"

"Cherry lollipop, I expect," Meg said, her good humor restored.

It was impossible to put Cliff down. He cocked his head and studied her thoughtfully. "I do like a woman who keeps surprising me. I would never have suspected you of a secret passion for lollipops, much less cherry lollipops. Don't you know the green ones are the best?"

Meg didn't know whether to laugh, explain or throw a cookie at him. The last idea was extremely tempting; Gran would scold, but she wouldn't be surprised at such behavior from "one of the children," and Henrietta would dispose of the broken bits.

Before she could succumb, her grandmother distracted her, reaching for the plastic shopping bag she had left on the floor. "Now, Meg. Show."

Her eyes sparkled with delight as Meg drew the dress out of the bag and held it up. "If you hate it, I'll take it back," she said, smiling.

"Let me see." Her grandmother sobered; clothes were the joy of her life, second only to jewels, and they were not to be taken lightly. "Very pretty, dear. But isn't it just a teeny bit low at the neck?"

"No," Cliff said promptly.

Meg scowled at him. "Well, perhaps I'm old-fashioned," Mary admitted. "You shouldn't have let them put the dress into a bag, though, it's all wrinkled. I'll have Frances press it for you. I think it's a trifle too informal for the rubies, don't you?"

"Just a trifle," Meg said, picturing the reaction if she walked into a local restaurant wearing the Maria Theresa rubies—including the tiara.

"Pearls, I think," her grandmother mused. "But we'll decide after tea; we mustn't bore Clifford."

"I'm not bored," Cliff assured her. "What could be more fascinating than the adornments used by beautiful women to make themselves even more desirable?" He took Mary's delicate, wrinkled hand and raised it to his lips.

She smiled at him, head tilted, eyelids lowered—flirting with him, Meg thought, in gestures as mannered as the steps of a formal dance. How had Cliff learned to play that old-fashioned game so expertly? Few men of his generation would know, or would bother. It must be love, Meg told herself—and hoped she was right.

"So what's the occasion?" Cliff asked, restoring Mary's hand to her knee with a last little pat. "Of course I know you ladies don't need an excuse to shop."

"Bad boy." Mary shook a playful finger at him. "Meg is going out this evening. With a gentleman."

"Oh, yeah? Who?"

"With Mr. Blake," Mary said. "Isn't that nice?"

"Darren?" Cliff frowned. "The neck is too low."

"Do you really think. . . ." Mary peered at him. She was a trifle nearsighted,but would have rather risked falling and breaking her neck than wear glasses. She broke into lovely laughter. "Oh, you're just being naughty. Meg, you had better run along if Mr. Blake is calling for you at seven. I'll come shortly and help you select your jewelry."

"I'm going to wear this, Gran. I bought the dress to go with it."

"Oh." Mary blinked at the necklace as if she were noticing it for the first time. Meg knew that was a pretense; her grandmother's eye for gems was twenty-twenty, and this piece would have been hard to miss. "It's just a touch—large—isn't it?"

" 'Garish' would be more like it," Cliff said.

Meg couldn't comment on his lack of taste without implicitly criticizing her grandmother's, so she bared her teeth at him, and left the room. Cliff followed, catching up with her at the foot of the stairs.

"Wait a minute."

"What do you want?"

"For one thing, another look at that object you're wearing."

"Why?" Meg's hand went to her throat in an involuntarily defensive movement.

"That's my question, why? Is it one of Riley's?"

"Yes."

"You like it?"

"Why else would I wear it?"

"I can think of other reasons."

"Go to hell, Cliff." Meg started up the stairs.

One of these days, she promised herself, she would buy the biggest, gummiest, greenest lollipop to be found and stick it right between those full, sensuous, smiling lips.

Darren arrived on the dot of seven, to find Meg waiting at the door in order to avoid Cliff, who was lurking in the parlor like a spider in its web. Deprived of the entertainment he had expected, he followed them to the door doing an exaggerated imitation of a nervous father. "Have a good time.

Not too good a time, though, old boy, ha ha, if you know what I mean. . . .”

Smiling and oblivious, Darren pretended not to hear. It was an effective technique, born of past experience. As he handed Meg into his BMW, a voice bellowed, “Have her home by midnight. She turns into a. . . .”

The last word blew away on the wind as Darren pulled away. Meg laughed and shook her head. “I’m almost sorry I didn’t hear. Do you defend murderers, Darren?”

Darren gave her a startled look. “Murderers! What made you. . . . Oh. Oh, I get it.” He laughed heartily. “Old Cliff’s not so bad, you know. Just ignore him.”

“That’s easy for you to say. You don’t have to live with him.”

“Neither do you.”

Cliff’s teasing and Darren’s placid response had taken Meg back to the old days, when the three of them had played the same roles of victim, villain and defender. She spoke without thinking. “Why, Darren, this is so sudden.”

“It may seem so to you. Not to me. I’ve been in love with you for years.”

They had gone almost a mile before Meg recovered. “I don’t know what to say, Darren.”

“You don’t have to say anything. I knew you were kidding. I was going to wait till we had spent some time together, gone on a few dates. . . . I even had my speech all worked out. It was a very eloquent speech, if I do say so. And then I blurt it out like some dumb teenager while we're barreling along at sixty miles an hour! I know it's too soon for you to give me an answer, but you will think about it, won't you?"

Meg felt like Eliza crossing the ice with the bloodhounds baying at her heels. She didn't want to shatter the thin ice of Darren's sensitivity, but neither did she want the dogs on her trail. What she wanted—what she needed. . . . For a second she thought she knew, but the knowledge faded before she could catch hold of it, leaving her filled with frustration and resentment. She reminded herself that Darren had no idea his was the second proposal of marriage she had received in less than a week—and that it wasn't a hell of a lot more romantic than Cliff's offhand suggestion had been.

Nor could he possibly know that marriage, to any man, was the last thing she wanted.

She realized that he had been waiting too long for an answer, and selected her words with the delicacy of a goldsmith shaping a setting. "Darren, it would be unfair to both of us for me to raise false hopes. Right now . . . right now I need a friend and adviser, not a lover. Can't we just leave things as they are and wait to see what, if anything, develops?"

Darren nodded. "Fair enough. We'll pretend I never said what I said. But I'm not sorry I said it."

Meg did not reply. His faint smile warned her she had not got the hounds off her trail, and she found herself more frustrated than flattered. Why did men assume that a declaration of love was the most desirable offering they could make to a woman? Like having the plumber offer to take a customer to bed instead of fixing the leak that was flooding the basement. What made it even worse was feeling that you had to apologize to the plumber for preferring a dry basement to his unsought embraces.

Darren roused himself occasionally to point out landmarks and make "do you remember" comments, to which Meg replied with a minimum of speech. She knew the road, and she was beginning to get a nasty premonition of what their destination would be.

She should have known. It was the best restaurant in the area, and the ambience was drenchingly romantic. No less an authority (on both subjects) than Nick had determined that.

Darren was obviously a regular customer. The maître d' greeted him by name, and led them to the same table where she and Nick had sat only a few days ago. Meg told herself it was coincidence; the secluded location must make this a particularly favored table. All the same, she braced herself for disclosure. Sooner or later someone was going to make a reference to her earlier visit, even to the fact that it had not been confined to the dining room. If it had not been for Darren's declaration on the way, she wouldn't have minded. Gran was the only person she wanted to keep in the dark, and even to protect Gran she would not submit to blackmail.

Blackmail made her think of Candy, and the possibility that Candy had learned of her evening with Nick. Small towns were more prudish than cities, but surely even Candy realized that Meg was more likely to laugh than cower if Candy threatened to spread her indiscretions around Seldon.

She realized that a menu was being waved under her nose and that she hadn't heard the question Darren had asked. After the waiter had taken their orders for drinks and departed, Darren said casually, "Nice young chap. Do you know him?"

Damn, Meg thought. The boy must have said something while she was wrapped in thought. "Nice to see you again," or "Glad to see you back."

"I had dinner here with a friend a few days ago," she said.

"Oh, I'm sorry. If you had told me we could have gone somewhere else."

"It's a nice place, and the food is excellent," Meg reassured him. "I'm perfectly happy to be here."

"Well, okay, if you say so."

The service was almost too good, at least for Meg's purposes; it was not until the entrée had been served and wine steward, maître d' and assorted waiters had departed that she got down to business.

"I suppose it's too soon to expect another report from your investigator."

"As a matter of fact, I had a call today." Darren took a bite of swordfish and chewed it thoroughly.

Meg started to speak, stopped, counted ten and tried again. "A direct call, Darren? Or did it come through Mrs. Babcock—as usual?"

"She wouldn't listen in. And even if she did," Darren went on, blandly negating what he had just said, "she's completely discreet."

"I asked you . . ." This time Meg had to count to twenty. There was no use arguing, Mrs. Babcock had Darren brainwashed. But that he could disregard her expressed request so casually. . . . "Well? What did the gumshoe say?"

Darren looked at her reproachfully. "I didn't bring my notes with me. I meant this to be a pleasant social evening, without—"

"I am having a very pleasant time, thank you." Hadn't he heard a word she had said? "And I apologize if I seem to be forcing unseemly duties upon you, but my life is getting a little complicated. In the next few days I have to make some serious decisions. I have only a few more days of leave. My boss has been raising cain about my taking so much time, he won't give me any more. It's fish or cut bait—go back, or give notice."

"I thought you had decided." Darren put his fork down and gave her his undivided attention. "When you took over the management of the store—"

"I haven't taken over."

"But, everyone assumed. . . . You certainly aren't an employee!"

"You seem to have forgotten the terms of Dan's will," Meg said. "I'm not an employee, or the boss. Neither is Riley." She leaned forward, pushing her plate away and planting both elbows firmly on the table in defiance of etiquette, so intent was she on making him understand. "The ideal arrangement could very well be the partnership Dan envisioned. Riley is the most talented designer I've ever encountered. He's also a fine craftsman. I lack both those talents, but I have some assets he lacks—especially money. He couldn't take over the store without borrowing heavily and risking bankruptcy; I doubt that finance is his strong point. But if I bought him out, I could never replace him. Together we could make Mignot and Riley a name like Van Cleef and Arpels. One of the reasons why I went to work was to find out whether I could get along with Riley. I can. He's a pain in the ass, but I can work with him—providing people leave us alone. Why do I get the feeling that the whole damned town is rubbing its collective hands and waiting gleefully for the fight to begin? I don't want a fight. I don't want a war either, but by God, if people don't get off my back and keep their long noses out of my affairs, I'll start one!"

Darren had tried several times to interrupt; finally he sat back, composed and patient, and waited for Meg to run out of breath. "Are you finished?" he asked.

"No. Don't tell me I sound just like Dan!"

"I wasn't going to. I was going to say that it sounds to me as if you have already reached a decision."

Meg thought it over. "It does sound that way, doesn't it?" She cupped her chin in her hands and smiled at him. "Now it's your turn. Talk me out of it."

"Fat chance," Darren muttered.

"No, really. This was just what I needed—a chance to talk, without being interrupted—"

"I couldn't get a word in edgewise."

Meg laughed. She felt as if she had been drinking champagne, relaxed and happy and a little giddy. "I was arguing with myself, not with you. I've been going back and forth on this so long, unable to make up my mind—but I had, really, I just didn't know I had until you let me spill it out. That doesn't mean I don't value your advice, Darren. What did the detective find out?"

"Nothing." Darren's voice cracked. He cleared his throat. "Sorry. Nothing of importance. So far."

If Meg had been a little less pleased with herself she would have noticed that Darren seemed subdued and preoccupied. However, he perked up when she told him about Candy's peculiar performance that afternoon. "That is strange. You say she asked for her job back? I was under the impression she quit because Riley had—uh—"

"Forced his attentions upon her? If anything, it was the other way around."

Darren smiled. "I admit I found her version a trifle unbelievable. Let me add, in all fairness to the woman, that I got the story second- or third-hand. It may have been distorted by the time it reached me."

"That's not the point, Darren. She didn't just ask for her job back. . . ." But Meg found it difficult to convey in words the impression Candy had left her with. Darren listened patiently, but he kept shaking his head. The dead rat and Applegate's attempt to pick a fight with Riley also failed to impress him. "I told you Riley isn't popular. I shouldn't have to tell you that Rod Applegate is a jerk. Always was, always will be. Keep me informed, and if he does or says anything actionable, I'll deal with him."

"Thank you."

"That's what I'm here for. More coffee?"

Meg declined. If Darren had set out deliberately to deflate her he couldn't have done it more effectively. At the beginning of the evening she had almost convinced herself that she ought to tell him about everything that worried her—the ring, the telephone call, the cache of hidden jewelry. The slow, gradual erosion of her confidence in his understanding left her feeling more alone than ever—and her suspicion that anything she told Darren would eventually be known to Mrs. Babcock was another concern. Cliff was a better audience than Darren; at least he took her seriously.

As they crossed the parking lot toward his car Darren said, "I guess I won't find out what peculiar object you turn into at midnight. Unless you'd like to stop someplace for a nightcap?"

"Thanks, but I'd better not. Gran will expect me to go to church with her tomorrow, and I'm tired, after working all day."

Traffic on the interstate was moderately heavy, but Darren drove easily and skillfully, the speedometer hovering close to the legal speed limit. Meg leaned back, enjoying the smooth ride and the cool night air.

It happened so suddenly she didn't have time to react until it was over—a brilliant burst of light in the rearview mirror, a wordless yell of rage and warning from Darren as he twisted the wheel violently to the right. The headlights swung in a dizzying arc; the car jerked and skidded as the wheels hit the grassy shoulder, and the seat belt squeezed her ribs like an iron hand. She closed her eyes and waited for the crash.

12

THE SCREAM OF tortured metal and rubber died, and Meg heard Darren cursing with an inventiveness worthy of Dan at his best. He broke off in the middle of a vivid description of some unknown male individual and turned anxiously to Meg. "Are you all right? Are you hurt?"

"No," Meg said vaguely. "What did we hit?"

"Nothing. Thank God for good brakes and dry weather. If the grass had been wet. . . . Meg, are you sure you're all right?"

"Don't—don't." Feebly Meg pushed him away. "The seat belt practically cut me in two; if you touch me I'll scream."

"If it hadn't been for the seat belt. . . ." Darren bowed his head over the wheel. His breathing was harsh and uneven.

"Are you okay?" Meg asked.

"Not a scratch. But you could have been. . . . Goddamn drunk drivers,they ought to lock 'em up and throw away the key."

"Drunk," Meg repeated. She took a deep experimental breath and rubbed her sore rib cage.

"They hit the roads like a tidal wave on weekends," Darren said bitterly. "We'll go straight to the emergency room, dear. I apologize for my language, but that was such a near miss. . . ."

He touched the starter and the engine throbbed into life. "I have to go home," Meg said. "Right now."

"You could have cracked a rib." Darren eased the BMW back onto the road.

"No, I don't think so."

"Really, Meg—"

"You don't understand. The last time I went out. . . ."

Darren's hands tightened on the wheel as he listened. "Why didn't you tell me this before?"

"You dismissed the other things I told you

about—Candy and Applegate's behavior, and the rat—"

"There is a big difference between a harmless if disgusting dead animal, and an anonymous telephone call. I wish you'd let me be the judge of what is important and what is not."

Neither of them spoke for a short time; Darren was deep in thought and Meg was trying to overcome her resentment of his autocratic manner. When she thought she had succeeded, she said, "You said the driver who forced us off the road was drunk. It could have been an accident."

"I made a logical assumption, based on the prevalence of such occurrences. I didn't know about the telephone call. That alters the situation. You've been out at night twice this week, and both times something unusual has happened. I don't suppose you happened to see the license plate?"

"Are you kidding? It all happened so fast I couldn't even tell you what make of car it was."

"It wasn't a car," Darren said. "It was a truck. A rusty, dark gray pickup."

Without further argument Darren drove her straight to the house. From the outside everything looked perfectly normal. Still, Meg's hands were unsteady as she inserted her key in the lock. The hall sconces burned dimly, the house was dark and still, and no one awaited her.

Or so she thought. Something moved in the shadowy recess under the stairs, and a sound like the screech of rusty hinges brought Darren quickly to her side. “What on earth—”

“It’s only Henrietta Marie,” Meg said. “That’s odd; she usually spends the night with Gran.”

With a soft thud the cat jumped down off the chair on which she had been resting. As she sauntered toward them, reflected light made her eyes glow like miniature taillights. Meg said uneasily, “Wait here, Darren. I just want to. . . .”

Dropping her purse, she ran up the stairs. Henrietta Marie followed, at her own leisurely pace.

Gran’s door was closed. Meg reached for the knob. Foolish though her fears might be, she would not rest easy until she had made certain her grandmother was peacefully asleep. Before she could turn the knob, however, she heard a soft murmur from within.

She’s talking in her sleep, Meg told herself. Everybody makes noises in their sleep—groans, sighs, sometimes words. Do people laugh in their sleep? Please, Gran, don’t laugh. I am going to assume you are asleep, I am going to turn the knob slowly, quietly. . . .

Henrietta, behind her, let out a raucous squawl. It was part of her heritage from a Siamese ancestor, and it sounded like the mating call of a miniature werewolf. Meg turned on the cat, hissing a demand for silence. Henrietta sneered back at her and applied a claw-studded paw to the door.

The damage was done; that yowl would have wakened the heaviest of sleepers. Meg called the cat a vulgar but accurate name and opened the door. Henrietta slithered through the gap and disappeared.

"Thank you, Frances," said a soft voice. "I do hope Henrietta didn't wake you. If she's going to keep this up, we had better see about having a swinging panel installed."

"It's not Frances, it's me," Meg said."I'm sorry, Gran, I tried to keep her quiet, but she was determined to get in."

"That's quite all right, darling, I wasn't asleep." Thump, went Henrietta, onto the bed, and Gran cooed, "There she is, my baby. Of course she wanted in, didn't she? Was that why she wouldn't stay with me this evening? She was waiting for Meg to come home. What a sweet, thoughtful kitty she is."

Concealed behind the half-closed door, Meg stuck out her tongue at the thoughtful kitty. Life in the old homestead was going to be hard if even the cat rode herd on her.

"Good night, Gran," she said.

"Good night, darling."

From the darkness came a sound like that of a giant bumblebee. Henrietta was purring.

Darren was waiting at the foot of the stairs when Meg came down. "Everything all right?" he asked.

"Yes, fine." Meg rubbed her bare arms. "I've got goose bumps, as we used to say. That cat gives me the creeps."

Darren laughed. "I can't say she appeals to me either, but then I prefer dogs. I guess we can assume there was no telephone call tonight. Unless you think the cat took the call."

"I wouldn't put it past her," Meg muttered. "What about a nightcap, Darren? Or would you prefer coffee?"

"I would like a little chat with you. But please don't go to any trouble."

They settled themselves in the parlor, where Darren was persuaded to help himself to Dan's excellent brandy. Returning to his chair, he said, "From the way you galloped up those stairs I gather your injuries are minimal, but I still think you ought to have those ribs checked by a doctor."

"It's not necessary," Meg said shortly. She wished Darren would finish his drink and go home. What more was there to say? She was so tired. She almost wished someone would fire a shot or throw a rock or send a threatening letter. One could then take action, to defend and to strike back, instead of floundering in a sea of uncertainties. One might then convince one's lawyer that one was not a neurotic female.

Despite her poorly concealed yawns and brief responses, Darren stayed on, sipping his Napoleon brandy and talking about subjects that would have held little interest for Meg under any circumstances. About the handsome house he had built a few years earlier, its location, its furnishings and how its value had increased. About general real estate values in Seldon. About the way the town had grown. About business investments in the area.

They had been sitting for over an hour when Meg heard a car coming up the driveway. It had to be Cliff; and when she saw the alert turn of Darren's head she realized that this was what he had been waiting for.

Cliff showed no surprise at finding them there; of course, Meg thought, he had seen Darren's car. "So, did you have fun?" he asked, beaming at them. "So nice of you to wait up for me. Tell me all about it. What are you drinking, Darren?"

Darren accepted a refill; Meg refused, biting off the words. Cliff looked as fresh as he had when they left. His hair was becomingly tousled (by wind or fond fingers? she wondered) and his collar was a little limp, but he seemed prepared to go on for hours. She was about to excuse herself and leave them to it when Darren said, "Meg, dear, if you want to go to bed, don't feel you have to entertain me. I want to have a little chat with Cliff anyway. A nice long soak in a hot bath would probably be the best thing for those sore ribs."

Meg couldn't have said what annoyed her more—the unnecessary endearment, the proprietorial tone or the so-subtle way in which he had introduced the subject of the accident. She was also getting fed up with the phrase "little chat."

Cliff was prompt to pick up his cue. "Sore ribs, is it? What have you been doing to the woman, Darren?"

"Why don't you run along to bed, dear?" Darren repeated.

Wild horses couldn't have dragged Meg away now. "Because I don't want to run along to bed."

"Oh, good, a lovers' quarrel," Cliff said, grinning. "Don't expect me to be tactful and excuse myself. I adore arguments."

"You're quite mistaken, Cliff," Darren said. "There isn't going to be a quarrel. I was only thinking of your comfort, Meg. If you want to stay, by all means do so. But I intend to tell Cliff what happened tonight, and ask his advice."

"I also adore giving advice." Cliff was still smiling, but his eyes had narrowed. "Tell me all, children."

Meg let Darren tell the story, since he had every intention of doing so anyway. He was clear and concise, including every relevant detail. "Apparently no telephone call was received tonight," he finished. "Which leaves some doubt as to whether this incident was related to the earlier call, or was only the accident it appeared to be. However, I thought you should be informed of it."

Cliff slid slowly down in the easy chair until he was resting on his spine,the balloon glass balanced lightly between his fingers. "Mmm-hmmm," he murmured lazily. "I appreciate that, Darren. And to show how much I appreciate it, I'm going to inform you of a few things I suspect Meg hasn't mentioned. The day after the funeral. . . ."

The "morbid memento mori ring," as Cliff called it, failed to impress Darren. "That sounds like pulp fiction," he said skeptically. "It's probable that the ring was returned by someone who had taken it on approval—Dan did that for good customers—or was sent for appraisal."

Cliff peered owlishly at Darren over the rim of the glass. "I'll show you the damned thing. If it doesn't raise your hackles, you have no more imagination than a slug."

He was up and on his way out before Darren could reply. The errand took him longer than Meg had expected, assuming, as his confidence had implied, that he knew where his father had put the ring; and when he came back his steps were slow and deliberate. They stopped outside the door, and there was a pause of several seconds before he came in. The expression on his face made Meg sit up. "Couldn't you find it?" she asked.

"I found it." Cliff leaned over the table and opened his clenched hand, spilling not one but two rings onto the shining mahogany. "Apparently it spawned."

"You mean this was with it?" Meg picked up the second ring.

Seed pearls formed a circle around a glass dome. Under the glass lay an intricate coil of intertwined black and shining silver-gilt. "It's hair work," Meg said.

Darren, who had been examining the other ring with an expression of mild distaste, leaned closer to see the one she held. "I believe I've heard of such things. Weren't they—er—tokens of affection? People still clip babies' curls to put in lockets or in baby books."

"They could be love tokens," Meg said. "But just as often—perhaps more often—they were memorial rings. Mourning rings. Not only rings, bracelets, pendants, you name it. The hair was cut from the head of the dead."

"Ah. I believe I understand what you are suggesting." Darren looked again at the delicate little skeleton, turned the ring to read the motto. " '*Hier lieg ich, Und wart' auf dich.*' I grant you that the message has a certain—er—morbid tone. And it is certainly possible to see a pattern in these apparently disparate events. First the delivery of the message ring. Then the telephone call. To term it threatening would be an exaggeration, but certainly it was worrisome, designed to cause alarm and/or embarrassment. Tonight's occurrence on the road may or may not be part of the pattern. This second ring seems to me ambiguous, but I am willing to defer to your considered judgment that it may be another reminder of death. You didn't mention this one, Cliff, so I presume I am safe in assuming you didn't know about it. It's strange that your father didn't mention it."

"No," Cliff said.

"He didn't mention the first one, either," Meg said. "It was pure accident that I happened to see it, and I was the one who suggested it might be interpreted as a threat. I had a hard time convincing him."

"I'm not entirely convinced myself," Darren said. "However, I am willing to admit that the delivery of a second ring, under what we may tentatively assume to be similar circumstances, does tend to strengthen your theory, although the specific meaning—"

"Oh, for God's sake," Cliff exclaimed. "Are you blind? Look at this filthy thing." He snatched the ring from Meg's hand and shoved it under Darren's nose. "Look at the color of the hair. It's an unusual shade—pure jet-black. The same shade as Meg's. It's her hair, dammit! How specific can a threat be?"

Darren was the first to break the silence. "That's rather farfetched, Cliff, don't you think? Millions of people have black hair, and there are two different shades in this ring. Hair from two different people. Unless you think Meg is a natural blonde who dyes her hair."

"Check my roots," Meg said. "That's a good point, Darren."

"It would be if we didn't know someone whose hair is—or was—silver-blond," Cliff said.

"Are you enjoying this?" Meg demanded angrily and unjustly. Cliff obviously wasn't enjoying any of it. He was actually pale under his tan. If Darren had too little imagination, Cliff had too much. And he adored Gran.

Darren also knew to whom Cliff referred. Mary Morgan had been famous for her beautiful silver-gilt hair. There were photographs of her all over the house, and a portrait in the drawing room.

For a time no one spoke. Then Darren said, "Any debater knows that it is possible to arrange a set of random facts to prove almost anything. The connection between the events we've mentioned is purely theoretical; so far there is absolutely no proof that they are connected at all."

"Right," Cliff said surprisingly. "If you were lowbrow enough to read mystery novels, Darren, you would know that the same principle applies there. The writer takes a set of unrelated facts and supplies a connection. However. . . ."

"I knew there would be a 'however,'" Meg muttered.

"However, don't you think it's interesting that so far—"

"And a 'so far.'"

"Quiet, please. If these events are related, the perp, as I believe he is called in the trade, is being damned careful to avoid any act that would justify official intervention. In other words, so far we've no excuse for calling the cops."

"Precisely." Darren appeared depressed. "I can see myself trying to explain this—what did you call it?—memento mori ring to Sheriff Buchhandler."

"Sounds like fun, all right. Let me know if you decide to try." Cliff went to the liquor cabinet and poured more brandy. "How about you, coz? A little cognac is great for relieving fluttery nerves."

"My nerves aren't fluttering," Meg snapped.

"No? Mine are." Cliff wandered back to his chair. "But I am beginning to think we don't have to worry about actual physical danger to . . . anyone. This looks to me more like a campaign of intimidation."

"Mmmm." Darren accepted the glass Cliff handed him. "Yes, I think you're right, Cliff. It would be extremely foolish for a would-be attacker to warn his victim, not once but several times."

"Gee, thanks, guys," Meg said. "That really cheers me up. As a friend of mine used to say, I'd just as soon they'd shoot me as scare me to death."

Both men made deprecatory noises. "Anyway," Meg went on, "you still haven't convinced me this is aimed at me. Are you forgetting the dead rat?"

"I haven't forgotten it," Darren said coolly. "But I doubt it is part of the pattern."

"You think it was aimed at Riley." Meg remembered what Riley had said, or rather, not said. The rat had not been the first demonstration of hostility against him. "Well, maybe you're right. But I. . . . Wait a minute. Let me see that ring again."

She snatched up the hair ring. "Darren, will you hand me my purse? I need my loupe."

But a glance at the inside of the bezel of the ring told her the loupe would probably be of no use. The surface had been crudely scraped away, leaving a rough hollow.

"What?" Cliff asked.

"Mourning rings often had the initials or name of the deceased, and the date of death," Meg explained. "This one did. At least it had something inscribed inside. It's been filed off. And recently."

She squinted through the loupe, then shook her head. "Not a trace."

Darren frowned. "Let me get this straight. Aren't these rings fairly old, Meg?"

"Most of them are nineteenth century."

"Then it can't be your hair," Darren said triumphantly.

"That's right, Darren," Meg said.

Cliff was less tactful. "You're missing the point, Darren. If this ring is an antique, it was selected because the hair is the same color as Meg's. You yourself pointed out that millions of people have black hair, and there are hundreds, maybe thousands, of these cheerful little mementos in existence. The initials were filed off because they weren't hers."

"Because they weren't. . . . Oh. Then why didn't the—er—perp add her initials after he had scratched off the others?"

"How the hell should I know? Maybe he didn't have the tools or the. . . ."

Cliff broke off, looking chagrined, and Meg laughed humorlessly. "You just backed yourself into a corner, Cliff. You've been trying to prove that Riley sent these rings. Believe me, he has the tools and the know-how. If he had wanted to add my initials, or a copy of the Gettysburg Address, he could have done it."

She rose to her feet, yawning. Cliff said, "Wait a minute. You haven't heard my alternative theory."

"I don't want to hear it. This is a waste of time,

we're playing guessing games. When Uncle George comes home we'll ask him when and how he got this. Not that I think that will add anything to our store of information. Good night, Darren. Thank you for a delightful evening."

As she dragged her aching body up the stairs she heard the discussion resume. What Darren hoped to accomplish she could not imagine; he had been the first to admit their theories were no more than idle speculation. She knew what Cliff hoped to accomplish. If he could convince her that Riley was capable of an underhanded, cruel campaign of mental terror, she would move heaven and earth to rid herself of Riley. Meg didn't doubt she could do it. She had all the advantages Riley lacked—money, power, position, reputation.

And though the evidence was not enough to convince a judge and jury, it was piling up—the pickup that had run them off the road, the jewelry. The hair might be her own. The rings need not be antique. Riley was skilled enough to have made them himself.

Sunlight sifting through the stained glass gave the minister's head an inappropriate crimson aureole. The church was less than half full. Meg shifted position, regretting the impulse that had led her to remove her aching body from bed in order to accompany her grandmother to church. Despite the hot soak Darren had recommended she was stiff as a poker this morning, and bands of handsome bruises ornamented her midriff and chest.

Her martyrdom hadn't even been necessary. Gran had been pleased, of course, but obviously hadn't expected Meg to make the effort. Dan only went to church when he felt like it, which wasn't often, and in this as in so many other areas Meg was his designated successor. That was one advantage of an otherwise uncomfortable position, Meg thought, as she rose, wincing, for the final prayer.

The sight of the congregation did nothing to cheer her; the only faces she recognized were those she didn't want to see: Candy, looking so sickeningly pious it was enough to turn one to atheism; Debbie, decked out in Sears' Sunday best. She was alone; presumably the children were at Sunday school or at home with Daddy, and Meg imagined that Debbie's main reason for attending church was to get an hour of peace and quiet.

After the service Gran lingered to greet friends and accept delayed condolences. It would have been unfair to say she enjoyed the routine, but she certainly didn't seem to be in any hurry to leave. The pastor hovered over her like a guardian angel, and in her immaculate white gloves and flower-bedecked bonnet she was as pretty and as antique as a daguerreotype.

Meg smiled and shook hands and accepted kisses from a number of elderly persons of both sexes who claimed to have known her since she was "this high." To her relief Candy didn't stop to speak to her, and Debbie lingered only long enough to repeat her suggestion that they get together with the old gang. Her grandmother accepted several invitations to tea and luncheon, all of them prefaced by phrases like "Just a small quiet affair, dear, you mustn't brood, you know, Dan would have wanted you to carry on. . . ."

No doubt Dan would have, Meg thought. He had expected the same of her, and had done everything he could to force her to do it.

Sunday dinner was always a prolonged, formal meal, and this Sunday, Gran—carrying on—did not omit a single course, though only three of them were present. Cliff was on his best behavior, flattering and flirting with Gran and treating Meg with affectionate courtesy.

After dinner Gran went up for her meditation time—a long nap with an open Bible resting on her stomach—and Meg followed her upstairs. She waited in her room until she thought Cliff had taken himself out of the way. George would be back that evening, and she would undoubtedly be dragged into another long debate. She had no intention of spending the entire afternoon arguing with Cliff about the same subject.

The soft green lawns were cool and peaceful in the lengthening shadows. Bathed in sunlight, the roses glowed like gems: ruby and garnet, coral and ivory, amethyst and rose-quartz, with leaves of jade. Meg passed through a gate behind a weeping willow and entered a wilderness.

She had changed into jeans and shirt and sneakers, and as she forced her way through the weeds she was grateful for the fabric covering her legs and arms. Brambles tore at her sleeves. She was hot and perspiring before she came to a break in the green wall and saw the cottage before her.

Forlorn and abandoned though it was, it was still a charming house. Little dormer windows broke the peaked roofline. There was a round tower on one corner, with a roof like a witch's cap, and a wide porch swung in a graceful curve across the front and one side. One of the green shutters had lost a hinge and hung at a drunken angle. The doors and windows had been boarded up, and overgrown shrubbery enclosed it in a brambly wall.

What broke Meg down into a sudden, startling flood of tears was none of these things. It was the rambler rose embracing one of the porch pillars, defiantly asserting rebirth in a curtain of crimson blooms.

As she stood swabbing her wet face with her shirt sleeve and cursing herself for sentimentality, someone put a handkerchief into her hand. "Blow your nose," Cliff said. "I promise I won't tell Mary you came out without a hankie."

The words were joking but the tone was not. Meg buried her face in the handkerchief, and when Cliff offered a supporting arm and a shoulder to cry on, she took full advantage of both. When her sobs had subsided into hiccups Cliff held her out at arm's length and studied her thoughtfully. "You are not beautiful when you cry," he said. "Your nose looks like a cherry lollipop. Come on over here and sit down."

He led her to the porch and they sat down on

the steps side by side. “By rights I should be crying on your shoulder,” Cliff said. “You never lived here. She was my mother.”

“He was my father. And she wasn’t your mother, she was your stepmother.”

“If love and caring make a mother, she was mine,” Cliff said quietly. “If she felt the difference she never let me feel it.”

Meg leaned her head against his shoulder. “Forgive me, Cliff. I never knew how you felt about her. I never cared to know. Why haven’t we talked about this before?”

“I’ve been wanting to talk about it ever since you came home. That particular talk is way overdue. It would have been impossible when we were kids, we were both too raw with hurt, and too bewildered by loss. And too young to understand.”

“I’m still too young to understand,” Meg said. “I know, it was the era of sexual freedom and to hell with tired old moral standards. But this wasn’t just a case of double adultery. Your . . . mother was my aunt, my mother’s sister. My father was Dan’s protégé as well as his son-in-law. Call me priggish and old-fashioned if you like—I think what they did was vile. There was no excuse for it. It was treacherous and contemptible!”

The echoes flung her passionate voice back at her, and she clapped her hand to her mouth. “I’m sorry. I didn’t realize I was so angry. It wasn’t grief and loss that tormented me all these years, it was anger. At him. At my father.”

Cliff put his arm around her shoulders. "Of course. Did you just now realize that?"

"I'm a little slow," Meg said wryly.

"You never got help?"

"Psychiatric help, you mean? I tried—once. I had to do it behind Dan's back, he'd have hit the ceiling if I had proposed spending hard-earned money on a shrink. He despised psychiatrists—and the self-indulgent weaklings who went to them. . . ."

Her voice trailed off; the memories hurt more than she had expected. After a moment Cliff said gently, "What happened?"

Meg shrugged. "It didn't work. I guess I went to the wrong person, that's not uncommon. He made me feel even more inadequate and guilty, I started having panic attacks again, I'd cry for hours after every session. . . . Finally I just got mad—told him off and stormed out of his office. I suppose I should have tried someone else, but. . . . It wasn't easy to save the money out of my allowance, Dan kept pretty close tabs on my expenditures, and I was feeling a lot better by then. Or so I thought. I can admit now that I didn't really want to face the facts. They never told me, you know—Dan or Gran or Uncle George. I found out for myself, when I was old enough to look through the back newspaper files—and do a lot of reading between the lines. Dan had enough influence to arrange a pretty neat cover-up."

"What did you know?" Cliff asked.

"Right after it happened?" Meg thought. "It's so long ago, and so overshadowed by later discoveries. . . . I guess all I *knew* was that Daddy and Aunt Joyce were dead. That was bad enough; but I sensed, as children do, that something else was wrong, something even worse. And my mother. . . . She went downhill so fast, Cliff. It was only a few months before she went away—for a rest, they told me—and never came back. I knew that story about her needing a rest was a lie, she was getting plenty of rest. She spent most of her time in bed and everyone waited on her hand and foot." Meg picked absently at a stain on her jeans. "So that was another thing I could add to my father's account. He killed her."

Cliff said nothing. His silence and his closeness were the greatest comfort he could have offered.

"What about you?" Meg asked after a while.

"I was a couple of years older," Cliff said. "But I was no more up on adultery than you were. It was the same sense of wrongness, I guess—and the way my father would turn away and leave the room when I tried to ask questions."

"Poor Uncle George. He had more guts than my mother, though."

"I think what kept him going was the fact that everyone depended on him," Cliff said. "He had to fill a lot of shoes."

"I know. Cliff, do you think he'd mind if I had the cottage renovated and moved in? Or would it be too painful for him?"

"So you have decided to stay in Seldon?" He

didn't sound surprised. Darren must have told him, Meg thought.

"Yes. At least I want to give it a try. But I have to have my independence. I could find an apartment, or a house in town, but. . . ."

"But you could exorcise your ghosts by living here? I don't know, Meg. It could be the best possible thing. It could be a disaster. The ghosts may not want to leave."

"You sure know how to encourage a lady," Meg said. "I don't want to hear that, Cliff."

"Well, hell, what do you expect from me? I'm not Dr. Freud. Half the time he didn't know his id from his ego either. If you want a guarantee, buy a refrigerator."

"I expect I'll have to," Meg said with a wry smile. "And a whole set of new appliances. I wonder what the cottage is like inside."

She swiveled around to look speculatively at the boarded-up windows, and Cliff said, "Don't ask me to flex my muscles by wrenching those boards off. I'm not dressed for it. I'll talk to Dad, if you like; it would be politic, not to say polite, to get his approval first."

"Of course. I'll ask him myself. Tonight."

"Okay." He stood up, in one smooth motion, and offered a hand to help her to her feet. "Ready to go back?"

"Yes." But Meg lingered to lift a branch heavy with crimson blossoms. She had a half-formed wish to pluck a few of the flowers; but the wiry stem resisted, and the thorns pricked her fingers.

When she looked at her hand she saw a bright drop of blood on her thumb, perfect as a tiny cabochon ruby.

13

WHEN MEG SHOWERED and changed she found more scratches, and a glance in the mirror justified Cliff's critical comment about her appearance. Her nose was still red, her eyes were puffy and her hair hung in gypsy dishevelment. Physically she was a mess. In other, more important, ways she felt better than she had for days. The "little chat" with Cliff had been astonishingly therapeutic.

She smiled at her reflection, remembering what Cliff had said when she thanked him for the little chat. "Just do me one favor, coz—don't marry Darren Blake. He's a nice, steady, dependable nerd, and he talks in clichés."

Meg had snapped back at him as she would have done before that cathartic conversation. On the surface their relationship hadn't changed, but Cliff was probably the only person who could help her exorcise her ghosts, and he had offered a strength and compassion she had never expected to find in him.

She twisted her hair into a coil and tucked a few pins into it to hold it at the nape of her neck. She needed a haircut; the thick mass resisted her efforts, and a shining jet-black coil fell across her bare shoulder. Meg paused, hands raised, struck by the contrast of ebony against ivory—like a curve of niello enamel on a silver ground. Would she ever look at her hair again without remembering the silver-gilt and jet-black curls under glass? She had always hated hair jewelry. Now she had a stronger reason for disliking it. The motive of the sender of the ring was obscure, but she doubted it had been kindly.

Sunday's high tea was another long-standing custom. It took the place of the evening meal, and there was always enough food on the table to feed a small army—cold ham and pâté, molded salads and hot breads. When Meg came down she was startled to find her uncle in the parlor.

"If this is your idea of a long weekend—" she began.

He interrupted her, rising quickly and taking her by the shoulders. "Cliff told me what happened last night. Are you all right? Darren should have taken you to the hospital. I can't believe he would be so negligent. I knew I shouldn't have gone away, I had a feeling—"

"Uncle George, please!" Meg freed herself; she appreciated his concern,but his hard grip was painful. "What could you have done if you had been here? It was an accident, there was no harm done."

The appearance of the others ended George's attempt to resume the discussion. Gran was wearing one of her most elegant tea gowns, a confection of pale coral ruffles and extravagant lace. When George commented on how pretty she looked she said cheerfully, "It has been a delightful day, George. The sermon was one of dear Mr. Black's best, and many friends were there. And then this afternoon I had such a lovely chat with Daniel. He suggested I wear this gown, it was one of his favorites.

"He sent his love, of course," Mary went on, "and he said I was to tell Meg to keep her wits about her and to watch the store. I'm not quite sure what he meant by that, but I expect you do, don't you, darling?"

"Uh—yes, Gran."

"That's a beautiful set of cameos, Mary," Cliff said. "I don't think I've seen them before."

Mary allowed a tiny wrinkle to furrow her brow as she studied the bracelet on her arm. "I wasn't certain about them, Clifford dear. They are a trifle heavy for this gown, but the color is perfect—and they were, I believe, extremely expensive."

Meg thanked her courteous cousin for the change of subject with a sidelong smile. She was able to talk knowledgeably about coral cameos and the origin of this particular parure, which had once belonged to a daughter of Queen Victoria. Thanks primarily to Cliff the conversation remained safely neutral throughout most of the meal.

They were finishing a trifle rich with cream and custard and the first fresh strawberries, and one of the maids had served coffee when Cliff asked, "Where's Frances? She usually serves tea, doesn't she?"

"Oh, my dear!" Gran put a spoonful of cream

onto a Chelsea plate and offered it to Henrietta. "Poor Frances is not at all well. I insisted she stay in bed today. She had one of her seizures last night, and didn't sleep a wink."

"Seizures!" Cliff carefully avoided Meg's eyes. "Since when has Frances been subject to fits?"

"They aren't fits, darling. She doesn't throw herself around or foam at the mouth, or anything vulgar." Henrietta let out a hoarse mew and Mary added more cream to her plate. "Frances has always been sensitive, you know. Occasionally she has—spells, I should have said. Or perhaps 'trance' is a more appropriate word."

Cliff was having a hard time controlling his mouth. "Good old Frances. I don't know why I didn't anticipate this one. So Frances is mediumistic, is she?"

"She is the seventh daughter of a seventh daughter," Mary said. "She sees things."

George cleared his throat. "What did she see last night?"

"She wasn't too clear about that, George. One doesn't get distinct images,you know, only impressions. It was more a feeling of impending doom— Oh, Clifford, dear, do be careful. Pat him gently on the back, Meg."

Cliff sputtered into his napkin. "No—don't—it's. . . ." He recovered himself. "Something went down the wrong way."

"Eat more slowly, dear. What was I saying? Oh, yes,the feeling of impending doom. And lights. Bright, blinding lights." Gran shook her shining silver head. "It must have been a terrifying experience for poor Frances, seeing those lights."

"Yes," Meg said. "Terrifying."

They had to wait until Mary went upstairs. It would have been unthinkable to retreat to the library and leave her alone. Finally Henrietta indicated it was time for bed, and mistress and cat (or was it the other way around?) took their departure. The others retired to George's study. George settled himself behind his desk with a ponderous severity that carried its own message: somebody was in for it.

Cliff took off his jacket, loosened his tie and arranged himself in a boneless sprawl across the sofa. "How do you like that damnable woman? Now she's a seer. I hope she has sense enough to—"

"Never mind Frances's fantasies," his father said in freezing tones. "You pried into my drawers, Clifford. How dare you do such a thing?"

Apparently neither of them had noted the uncanny accuracy of Frances's vision. But neither of them had been in the car as Meg had, and seen the lights burst into blinding brilliance as the following vehicle swung out to attack. It had to be a coincidence, Meg thought. There was no way Frances could have known.

During her moment of distraction the argument had blossomed into a quarrel. Cliff went on the attack. "Who the hell do you think you are, the autocratic paterfamilias? Why didn't you tell Meg?

She's the head of the family; you're just a hired employee."

It was a cruel thing to say and it made George so furious that for a moment he was incapable of speech. Meg turned on her cousin, eyes blazing. "That's a damned lie, Cliff, and you know it. Apologize to your father this instant."

Cliff chortled. "Ha! See what I mean?"

"For two cents I'd slap your silly face!"

"Children, children," George said mildly. "Don't be rude."

It was a more effective put-down than any scolding, and the combatants looked as foolish as they felt. "Sorry, Dad," Cliff muttered. "I know why you didn't say anything, and it does you credit. I just don't agree with you."

"You might have expressed your opinion more courteously," his father remarked. "Meg, thank you for that warmhearted defense. It touches me all the more because I know you're really on Cliff's side in this."

"I just don't want any more arguments about who's boss," Meg said, with a final glare at her recumbent cousin. Cliff had shown her a new and lovable aspect of his personality that afternoon, but he could still be a pain in the butt at times. She went on, "What I want is cooperation among equals. Isn't that fair?"

"More than fair," George said warmly. "I was wrong, and I swear I'll never do it again. This time the package was addressed to you, Meg; it gave me something of a shock, I admit, and I wanted to think about the situation for a while before I told you."

Cliff sat up. "You kept the envelope, I hope."

"Yes." George unlocked a drawer and took out the two rings and a padded brown mailing envelope.

As Meg took the envelope from him she found herself in sympathy with his reaction. To see her own name, written in heavy black block letters, was as direct as a blow. She could understand why the people of some cultures kept their true names secret, and believed that an enemy could strike at them through that extension of their personality.

"No return address," she murmured. "And no postmark."

George nodded."It was in the box with the rest of the mail. Obviously delivered in person."

Cliff subsided again. "Nothing new there, then."

"Except that we now know for certain that this campaign is directed at me," Meg said. "But why? What does this person want from me?"

"There are none so blind as those who will not see," Cliff recited. "Why are you so reluctant to admit the obvious, Meg? Have you fallen for the guy, or what? Is he the reason you decided to stay in Seldon?"

The suggestion was so outrageously off the mark, Meg wasn't even angry. Before she had time to compose a properly contemptuous reply, George exclaimed, "Stay in Seldon! When did you decide this, Meg? Why didn't you tell me?"

"I was going to tell you. I didn't actually make up my mind until last night. Uncle George, don't look so horrified. I thought you wanted me to stay."

"I do. I did. . . ." George took his handkerchief from his pocket and wiped his forehead. "I'd be absolutely delighted if it weren't for this. . . ." His outstretched finger indicated the rings, which lay on the blotter in front of him. "Meg, are you sure it's not a touch of the famous Mignot stubbornness that has influenced your decision?"

"Oho," said Cliff. "A new and provocative theory. Someone wants Meg to stay, so they try to frighten her away."

"It's not funny, Clifford. I don't like this business. What makes it even more alarming is that we can't take any action against it."

"I don't like it either, Uncle George." Meg realized her hands were tightly clenched, and forced them to relax. "But I'll be damned if I will be frightened away from doing what I want to do by a series of nasty tricks. If that's stubbornness, I'm stuck with it. But I really do want to try my hand at running the store. The last few days at the store have been so. . . . It's hard to find the right words. Fulfilling, satisfying. As for Riley, I admit I haven't made much headway with him. But I have made some, and he's the biggest challenge I've ever encountered. Helping to develop that talent—oh, you can't imagine and I can't explain, but it's an incredibly exciting prospect."

"Hmph," said Cliff. He rolled over, presenting his back to them.

"And it's not because I have the faintest interest in the man personally," Meg said, directing a critical stare at Cliff's tousled head. "I'm even willing to admit he may be the one who is trying to force me to leave town. But I think I can win him over. If I can convince him I really want to work with him, that I respect his abilities and his dignity. . . ."

"Hmph," said her uncle. "Well, Meg, I see you have made up your mind. I won't argue with you. Just tell me what I can do to help."

It was a perfect opening, and Meg hesitated only for a moment. If she didn't introduce the subject Cliff would, and he would do it less tactfully than she. "Thank you, Uncle George, I knew I could rely on you. I always have, and I probably haven't told you often enough how much love and gratitude I feel for you. The thing is, I really don't think I can live in this house. I'm used to being independent, and staying here would be falling back into the old patterns. I need a place to stay."

"That's understandable," her uncle said. His eyes were shining suspiciously; he had been visibly moved by her praise. "I'm sure we could find a nice apartment or house—"

"She wants the cottage," said a voice from the sofa.

It wasn't as bad as Meg had feared. George did drop the pen with which he was playing, but his objections were the ones any overprotective parent or guardian might have raised: the isolation of the cottage, its run-down condition—and finally, hesitantly, the unhappy memories it would arouse.

"Less so for me than for you," Meg said. "That's why I was reluctant to ask you."

Cliff stirred uneasily, as if he could feel the look she aimed at him, but he did not speak, and Meg went on, "If you'd rather I didn't, I'll find someplace else. But I wouldn't be as isolated from all of you there as I would be elsewhere in town."

"That's true," George admitted. "You seem to have made up your mind about this as well, Meg."

"I'd like to do it. But I won't if you object."

Cliff rolled over and sat up. "Stop being so polite and settle the matter, so we can get on to the next subject."

"There isn't any next subject," Meg said. "We've discussed the other thing until I'm sick of it. I'm going to bed. Think about the cottage, Uncle George, and let me know."

"I don't have to think about it, honey. It's fine with me. Perhaps it's the best possible solution."

Meg leaned over the desk to give him an affectionate kiss. The rings lay on the desk, gleaming in the lamplight. She picked them up and put them in her pocket.

"What are you doing?" George asked.

"Taking them with me," Meg said. "They're mine, aren't they?"

The sky was overcast and the air was muggy when Meg left the house next morning, but she decided to walk anyway. She hadn't slept well; fresh air, however oppressive, might dispel her headache.

She knew why she felt depressed, and it had nothing to do with the rings or the accident or her suspicion of Riley. She had dreamed about Nick and awakened to find she had kicked all the blankets off and twisted the sheet around her body like a variety of straitjacket. It wouldn't have bothered her so much if she could have remembered her dream, but nothing remained except an indefinable sense of danger and malaise.

A voice hailed her, and she was so grateful for the distraction that without thinking she stopped and waved. It was old Mrs. Henderson, yelling from her front porch, and beckoning with such vigor she appeared to be in danger of hurling herself over the railing. It was impossible to ignore such urgency, but as Meg started up the walk she cursed herself for her lapse of attention. Their mutual loathing of Mrs. Henderson had been one of the few subjects on which she and Cliff had agreed during their childhood. She had wooed them with cookies and kisses when they were too young to refuse her attentions; her cookies had been rock hard, studded with raisins so petrified they might have come out of an Egyptian tomb, and her kisses were the reverse—sloppy, soft and wet. She had used these repellent bribes for one purpose only—to pump the children about their parents and the family scandal. She hadn't gotten much out of them, only mumbles and embarrassed silence. But oh, the horror of those visits with dear old Mrs. Henderson!

She stopped by the steps. "Good morning. Did you want me for something?"

"Come up and set awhile," Mrs. Henderson said, baring her dentures.

I'd just as soon "set awhile" with Jack the Ripper, Meg thought. And, thank God, I'm old enough to know how to refuse your invitations more or less gracefully. "I'm afraid I can't," she said. "I'm late as it is."

"That's the way of it," Mrs. Henderson informed the world at large. "Kids grow up and get snotty, forget the people that was good to them. Guess you're too above it all to waste time with the common folks."

Age had certainly not mellowed Mrs. Henderson. Meg clung to her manners. "I certainly haven't forgotten you, Mrs. Henderson. But I'm very busy with the store these days."

"I heard about that." Mrs. Henderson leaned over the railing. Her nose jutted out like a jagged, broken branch,and every feature quivered with malice. "You must be crazy, shutting yourself up with a man like that Riley. He'd just as soon rape you as look at you."

"Do you really think so?"

Meg's frosty tone was wasted on Mrs. Henderson. "I don't think, I know. Ask that other poor girl that worked for him. He practically tore her clothes off her, right there on the counter. And he's a embolizer too. You better check them books."

"After he rapes me, or before?" Meg inquired.

"Why, after . . . I mean, before. . . . Are you smart-mouthing me, young lady?"

"I wouldn't dream of it. Good-bye, Mrs. Henderson. Have a nice day."

Mrs. Henderson's quavering voice followed her as she strode away; Meg caught the words "uppity" and "too smart for your own good."

Nothing like a flood of adrenaline to cure a headache, she thought—and nothing so satisfying as settling an old score. She realized she was humming softly, and smiled as she recognized the tune: "Here's to you, Mrs. Henderson. . . ."

Riley might be capable of embezzlement, but Meg seriously doubted that he had assaulted Candy, on or off the counter. It wasn't funny, though. Mrs. Henderson had a mind like a sewer and a mouth like a rattlesnake, but so did other people. If hers was the common belief, Riley was in trouble—and so, Meg realized, was she. By the time Mrs. Henderson got through embroidering and spreading the report of their conversation, half the town would think she and Riley were doing it on the counter.

The first raindrops spattered down as she passed the hardware store and she broke into a trot, arriving at the store breathless and damp around the shoulders and head. Nothing nasty on the threshold; she paused to check, though the lights inside were on and the "Open" sign was displayed. Riley was nowhere to be seen, but the office door was ajar, and she heard his voice, accompanied by an odd, whining sound like a lathe cutting through metal.

"How often do I have to say it, Debbie? I can't do it."

"You could if you wanted to. You're in charge now—"

"No, I'm not. And if I were, I still wouldn't do it. Tom is already suspicious. . . . Damn it, can't you shut that kid up?"

Tommie's whine took on words. "I wanna go. I wanna lollipop. I wanna—" The unmistakable sound of a slap cut off the noun, and the child's voice rose to a scream.

Meg had been holding the door open. Now she let it close. Glancing up, she saw that the chimes were missing. Bad luck for Riley, she thought, advancing toward the office. He must not have expected Debbie or he wouldn't have removed the warning signal.

Debbie was trying to calm her writhing, shrieking son. The baby had added her voice to the uproar, forming a soprano obbligato. Riley had retreated behind the desk. His face was as cold as a plaster death mask. It didn't change when he saw Meg.

It would have been impossible to make herself heard, so Meg didn't try. Instead she went back to the register, got a couple of lollipops, and shoved one under Tommie's nose. The screams stopped instantly, and Debbie, avoiding Meg's eyes, began to wipe her son's scarlet face with a tissue. Not that it was needed; Tommie hadn't shed a tear. He couldn't have been hurt much, Meg decided. And he is a thoroughly detestable brat. Even so, Riley had no business hitting him.

Debbie's cheeks were as red as Tommie's. "I guess I better go," she muttered. "I'm sorry."

"You're out early," Meg said.

"Yes, well, Tommie has a dentist's appointment, so I thought I'd stop and talk to you, but you weren't here, so I—uh—I asked Mr. Riley about a job."

"And he turned you down." Might as well let them know she had overheard part of the conversation—let them guess how much.

"Well. . . ."

"It wouldn't work, Debbie," Meg said. She was still furious with both of them, but the other woman's woebegone countenance—and that damned pathetic patched hole in her shoe—made her add, "We need someone with experience. Selling antique jewelry isn't like selling oranges and carrots, you have to know something about the subject so you can answer questions intelligently."

Debbie didn't argue. She seemed to be more concerned with getting herself and the children out of the store as quickly as possible. Meg accompanied her to the door and then turned to Riley, who had followed them out of the office.

"What happened to the chimes?"

He had been braced for another question. It

took him a few seconds to make the mental switch. "Uh—you kept saying they sounded funny, so I decided to have a look at them. One of the bells was dented, so the clapper didn't swing freely. I fixed it. Thought I'd let you listen to them before I put them back up."

"How did it get dented?"

"Somebody threw something at it."

Candy or Debbie, or some other infuriated female admirer? Meg didn't ask. "Let's hear them," she said shortly.

The chimes were antiques, a set of silver bells that had once adorned the collar of a sacred cow in India. At least that had been Dan's story. Riley lifted them with his big scarred hand and swung them back and forth. "That's much better," Meg said.

"Better? If they're not right—"

"They're perfect."

"I'll put them back up then."

"Need any help?"

"I got them down all by myself, didn't I?"

"All right, all right. Don't be so grouchy!"

Returning to the office, Meg sat down at the desk and reached for the telephone. Thanks to Riley she was now in the proper mood to deal with her soon-to-be former boss.

His reaction was exactly what she had expected—a howl of rage and a torrent of reproaches—but instead of feeling apologetic and defensive Meg focused her anger and waited for a chance to let fly.

From the shop came a muted jingle of bells and Riley's heavy footsteps. From the receiver at her ear came a torrent of profane reproach. How could she do this to him? She couldn't do this to him. Quitting without notice was unprofessional. And ungrateful. After all he had done for her. . . .

"Finished?" she inquired, when the curses faltered.

"Hell, no. The least you can do is get your ass back here for a month while I train your successor."

"My ass is fine where it is, thank you." There was a loud, startled peal of the bells, and Meg grinned. She went on, "You've been training my darling assistant Kimberley for weeks, on the couch in your office. Don't tell me my job wasn't part of the payoff. Tit for tat, if you'll excuse a bad pun. As for giving notice, I'm giving you the same you gave Danny Bernstein and Joe DeMerritte and half a dozen other people since I've had the dubious pleasure of working for you. I don't owe—what was that? Why, Jack. That's no way to talk to a lady."

A thud and a crash from the room beyond gave her an additional reason to hang up the phone. She went to the door. The ladder lay on its side. Riley, his back to her, was in the act of righting it.

"Are you sure you don't want me to hold the ladder?" she asked sweetly.

Riley swung around to face her. "I didn't hit the kid."

"Oh? I mean. . . . Oh."

"He's a spoiled brat, but I don't hit children. Or little old ladies."

She didn't understand why it mattered so much to him. He must know he had been accused of worse things than slapping a naughty child. "Or women?" she inquired.

"Not unless they hit me first."

"Or offer to help you."

"Yeah. I'm sorry if I was rude. I don't—I'm not very good at accepting favors."

"Oh, yeah?"

This time it didn't work. Riley's eyes shifted; he scooped the ladder up, one-handed, and backed away. "There's something wrong with this thing, it wobbles. I'll put the chimes up later."

Meg hesitated for a moment,but she didn't feel capable of continuing that peculiar conversation, so she let him go and returned to the office.

He had overheard everything she had said on the phone, as she had meant him to, and he was too intelligent to have failed to comprehend how her decision would affect him. Why hadn't he asked her point-blank about her intentions regarding the store, instead of bringing up the inconsequential issue of whether or not he had slapped Tommie? If he cared that much about her opinion of him, he should be just as concerned about her reaction to his relationship with Tommie's mother. His personal life was none of her business, but if he couldn't keep his women out of the store it *became* her business.

He had some cause for resentment, though. She had told almost everyone about her decision except the person it most concerned. Since their first exchange on the subject of the store she and Riley had avoided the subject. Her own feelings had changed, but there was no reason to suppose he felt any differently, nor would it have been fair to expect him to read her mind, as her friends and family had done, anticipating her decision before she acknowledged it herself. She had better have it out with him, man-to-man and face-to-face. And the sooner the better. Touchy as he was, he might think she had allowed him to overhear the phone call as a subtle and insulting method of breaking the news.

It took her some time to work out her strategy. The arrival of the mailman was a welcome distraction; after filing the bills, receipts and checks that had arrived, she went to the intercom. "I've got a couple of errands to do," she announced. "Back in half an hour."

The response was not encouraging. A grunt.

It was raining hard. Meg had to borrow an umbrella. There was always a random assortment of them in a Chinese vase behind the door. Some had been forgotten by customers, others acquired by Dan in his forays around town; he had a habit of borrowing things like pens, umbrellas and books, and never returning them. The one Meg selected was a woman's, pale pink nylon with printed pansies. She wondered to whom it had belonged. It looked like Candy's style, but Candy wasn't likely to have left anything behind.

When she got back she carried her parcels into the office and then buzzed Riley. "Let's do lunch."

Another grunt. This one had a rising inflection, so she interpreted it as a question.

"I said, let's do lunch."

"I brought mine."

"So did I."

A long pause. "Are you suggesting we eat our sandwiches in the same room?"

Meg rolled her eyes heavenward. "The phrase 'do lunch' has certain connotations, Riley. I'd like to talk with you."

Another pause. "It's not time for lunch."

"At your convenience," Meg said.

"Twenty minutes."

"Thank you."

There was no reply, not even a grunt.

Meg went to the case in which Riley's jewelry reposed and took out the silver pendant. It's worth it, she told herself, running a reverent finger over the sensuous silver curves. I hope.

Exactly nineteen minutes and thirty-five seconds later Riley emerged, and in spite of her exasperation Meg was amused at the wariness of his expression, which suggested he would have felt safer holding a chair and a whip. His hair was damp; he must have slicked it down with his hands. They had been scrubbed until they looked raw, especially across the knuckles.

His eyes went to the door. "You closed up?"

"It's Monday and it's raining. There hasn't been a customer all morning. Besides, I don't want to be interrupted."

At her gesture he followed her into the office. Meg had taken some pains with the arrangements; both chairs faced the desk, which was covered with newspapers and spread with the food she had picked up that morning. The tall, slim wine bottle stood like a sentinel in the midst of the waxed-paper wrappings. Riley stared at it as if it had been a cobra raised to strike. "What are you celebrating?"

Meg took a deep breath. She felt ridiculously nervous. She seized the back of the chair to hide the fact that her hands were shaking. "I hope we'll both be celebrating, Riley. Our partnership."

Riley transferred his horrified stare from the wine to her face. "Don't look at me as if I had suggested we rob a bank," Meg said. Now that she had taken the plunge her nervousness was gone. She sat down, arranging her skirts gracefully, and gestured at the other chair. "It might not be so bad, you know."

Riley didn't so much sit as fall into the chair. "I don't understand."

"No? Then I'll spell it out. Dan always wanted me to become involved in the business. I turned him down because . . . well, I had my reasons. I should have known he wouldn't give up that easily—that he would use any means,even his own death, to force me to do what he wanted. And the worst of it is . . ." Meg had to stop and clear her throat. She had almost lost sight of the fact that Riley was there; he was as silent and rigid as a piece of furniture. "The worst of it is, Dan was right. This is where I belong. This is what I want to do. Damn the old devil anyhow—wherever he is, I'll bet he's gloating."

Riley shifted position. "You really mean it."

"Yes, I really mean it. Have a sandwich." Meg reached for one at random and bit into it.

"Okay." He wasn't accepting her offer of a sandwich, he was acknowledging her sincerity. "Dan always said you were fighting him out of pure bullheadedness, but I figured maybe he was indulging in wishful thinking. I guess he wasn't. You can buy me out."

Meg felt as if her jaw had come unhinged. "What. . . . What are you. . . . You still don't get it, Riley. Seeing your work was my catharsis, my moment of truth." She put her sandwich down and leaned forward, holding his eyes with hers. "You have an extraordinary talent. The fact that I can see it, thrill to it, doesn't give me the right to buy it, or you. You can walk off into the night with your nose in the air. But you'd be a damned fool to do it. I'm offering you. . . . No. I'm asking you to let our partnership stand. I'll run the store and market your work. You do your own thing your own way. Maybe do some of the repairs, until we find another goldsmith to help you. We can work out the details. We can talk about it. What do you say?"

"We." The word came slowly and with difficulty. "Riley and Mignot?"

"Oh, no. Mignot and Riley."

It was a good thing she was sitting down. Not a smile this time, a full-fledged, spontaneous grin that curved his cheeks and brightened his eyes to topaz. "Yeah, right. You're crazy, you know that? For all you know, I could be a serial killer."

Meg felt light-headed. "Mrs. Henderson says you're an embolizer."

"An. . . . Oh. As in embolizing money?" The grin faded. "That's one thing I haven't done. But it's probably the least of the crimes this town thinks I've committed."

"I don't care what the town thinks. Well?"

Riley's heavy eyebrows lowered. "I'll think about it."

"That's damned condescending of you," Meg said.

The deep mellow sound was so unfamiliar she looked around the room seeking its origin before she realized what it was. Riley was laughing. "Give me the wine," he ordered. "Most people can't open wine bottles without breaking the cork."

14

AFTER RILEY HAD gone back to the shop Meg tidied up the desk, crumpling crumbs, uneaten food and miscellaneous wrappings into the newspaper tablecloth and putting the wine bottle aside. They had each had one small ceremonial glassful. He didn't drink to excess, at least not on the job. . . .

Mignot and Riley. Most people can't open wine. . . . He hadn't said "Women can't." He could laugh. He had offered to walk away, without a fight, and leave her in control. . . .

In the "Oh, my God, what have I done?" reaction that follows the burning of bridges, Meg was counting Riley's virtues, such as they were, in an attempt to reassure herself. She didn't need to count the entries on the negative side of the ledger; she was only too well aware of them. So he didn't hit children. Good for him. Apparently his reputation as a Don Juan was based on something more than idle rumor, though at first glance he seemed an unlikely candidate for the role. No doubt some women found his dour manner a challenge, and there was no denying the appeal of that unexpected smile. Even those big hands of his, so clumsy-looking but capable of the most delicate touch. . . .

Watch it, lady, she told herself, stuffing the newspapers into the wastebasket. Relationships of that kind were fatal in business, especially for the woman, who got screwed in every sense of the word. There was nothing wrong with an erotic fantasy or two, but she didn't want Riley's hands on her—she wanted them on the tools of his trade, turning out masterpieces to make the name and fame of Mignot and Riley.

The name tasted good, as smooth as chocolate melting in the mouth. She'd be trading to some extent on Dan's reputation, but it couldn't carry her all the way; if she failed it would be her failure, if she succeeded, her own triumph.

And Riley's. But he needed her, or someone like her; he didn't know how to sell himself, he was too prickly, too suspicious, too innocent to survive in the dog-eat-dog world of business. Meg settled herself behind the desk and stared at the papers in front of her. Innocent. . . . It was a strange word to associate with Riley. More likely she was the innocent one, hoping to win his loyalty simply by playing fair. It was not a recommended technique for survival, much less success, in the ordinary world.

So why did she think it would work with Riley? He was the most obvious suspect in the matter of the rings. If he had sent them it could only be because he was trying to drive her away. Yet just now he had said she could buy him out. It might have been a lie designed to disarm her, but it had been unnecessary and oddly without guile—too good to be true, too noble not to arouse suspicion. Meg shook her head despairingly. None of it made sense. The anonymous phone call and the attack of the deadly pickup truck didn't mesh with the affair of the rings. She had a sense of two different minds at work, one direct and threatening, the other more subtle. And neither of them fit Riley.

The day dragged on, dreary with rain, inactivity and a sense of letdown. Waiting for customers who never came, Meg kept glancing at the closed door of the shop. Was he sitting idle, staring at nothingness as she had done most of the day? She hadn't expected him to fall down and kiss her feet, babbling with gratitude, but some demonstration of increased goodwill would have been welcome.

Late in the afternoon Darren called to ask if she wanted a ride home. "It's still raining, and I noticed you didn't drive to work. You should get in the habit, Meg, that's a rather lonely stretch of road between the edge of town and the estate."

"How do you know I didn't drive?" Meg asked.

"Your car wasn't in the lot or in front of the store. Why don't I come by in, say, half an hour?"

"Because I'm not going home tonight. I have an engagement for dinner."

"Oh?"

Shame on you, Meg told herself. "With Mike Potter."

"Oh! That's nice!"

She asked him how the probate was proceeding and got the conventional noncommittal answer; he asked her if she would care to see *The Mousetrap* at the local dinner theater on Saturday. He sounded so confident of an acceptance Meg took pleasure in declining, but when he persisted, she finally agreed to Friday.

The hardware store didn't close till five-thirty and Mike would as soon walk out on a sick friend as leave early, but as the hands of the clock approached five, Meg decided she would rather hang around that store than this one. At least there would be signs of human life and the sound of voices. She buzzed Riley and announced her imminent departure, to which he replied with a mumble that might have been interpreted as "Good night." Tight-lipped, Meg collected her belongings and locked up. She borrowed a big black umbrella. The pink one might not belong to Candy, but its color suggested a confection and even that reminder was too close.

There weren't many customers at the hardware store either, but the lights were bright and people said "Hello" and "Hi, there" and "Lousy weather, isn't it?" Mike was trying to explain the difference between Molly bolts and toggle bolts to a bewildered matron. Meg waved at him and went on back to the decorating section, where she amused herself with wallpaper books and paint samples, becoming so engrossed she didn't notice the passage of time until Mike joined her.

"I'm about ready to close up, honey. Sorry you had to wait."

"That's okay. Can I borrow some of these, or rent them, or whatever the custom is?"

"In your case, I'll waive the usual deposit," Mike said with a smile. "What are you going to wallpaper, your room?"

"The cottage. Or I may paint, I haven't decided."

Mike's long face went blank. Thinking he had not understood, Meg elaborated. "You know the cottage—the one where Uncle George used to live. I'm planning to renovate it and move in."

"I know it." He ruminated for a moment. "You want to take them books now?"

"I guess I'd better wait. I haven't even seen the interior, or lined up a contractor. I thought maybe you could suggest someone."

"Yeah, I guess I could. You ready to go?"

He made her wait in the shelter of the doorway till he got his car, and insisted on escorting her to it under his own big black umbrella. Meg had barely fastened her seat belt before he stopped again, in front of the beauty shop.

"Is Barby joining us?" she asked.

"Yep. Hope you don't mind."

"Of course not." She did, but she couldn't say so.

Mike got himself and the umbrella out of the car and plodded up the walk to where Barby was waiting, attired in a raincoat and matching hat of a lilac so brilliant it glowed through the gloom. Meg unfastened the seat belt and "scootched over," smiling wryly. She might have known Mike would provide a chaperone. Or was this a conference? After she had greeted Barby she asked, "Are Ed and Kate joining us?"

"No, Kate has a silver-anniversary dinner tonight, and Ed's sister and her husband are visiting." Barby beamed at her from under the hat; it was a trifle too big and made her look like a cute drunk playing lamp-shade games at a party. "It will be cozier with just us three, don't you think?"

"It would have been even cozier with just the two of you," Meg said.

Barby giggled madly. People had been teasing Mike for years about his girlfriends; he didn't seem to mind, though he never responded. Kate, the other "girlfriend," usually reacted with a snort and a sneer, but Barby enjoyed the jokes. Meg didn't believe for a moment that there was anything between them. They had something that, if not better, was more enduring.

Mike drove at a careful thirty miles an hour while Barby chatted about the weather, her customers and other topics of negligible interest. It took twenty minutes to reach the house where he had lived all his adult life. It had been a ramshackle ruin of Victorian gingerbread when Mike bought it for his bride, getting it cheap because it was a genuine handyman's delight—or curse. Now it gleamed whitely through the gathering dusk like a mammoth wedding cake, every curl and curlicue in place.

A chorus of barks greeted them as they stepped onto the porch. Mike always had dogs, in the plural; at least two, sometimes more, if he couldn't find homes for the strays he picked up. Meg identified this chorus as a trio. The shrill soprano yapping belonged to a featureless brindled mop, too big for a Yorkie, too small for a sheepdog. It was followed out the door by a black Labrador and a middle-sized canine mixture with floppy ears and Dalmatian-style spots. After careening around the humans a few times the animals rushed out into the yard to relieve themselves and rushed back to further express their delight at having company.

Barby batted at them with her umbrella, yelling "Shoo," and Mike led the whole procession down the hall to the kitchen. He had anticipated the country look before it became fashionable, when braided rugs and solid well-made furniture could be bought for pennies at local auctions. The room was big enough to hold it all, pie safes and rocking chairs, an enormous sofa and a cupboard that contained books as well as dishes. Since the death of his wife Mike practically lived there. Sometimes, after reading half the night, he slept on the sofa.

Meg sank into its softness with a sigh of content and kicked off her wet sandals while Mike fed the dogs and Barby bustled to the table and began unloading her carry-all. "I wish you hadn't gone to all that trouble," Mike said over his shoulder.

"It was no trouble, I like to cook and I don't get much chance." Barby took the foil off a casserole and put it in the oven. "Anyhow, I wasn't going to eat your cooking, Mike Potter—or that awful potato salad and frizzled chicken from the carry-out. No, I don't need any help; just fix us a drink and then set yourself down and keep out of my way. You too, Meg."

It was a pity they didn't get married, Meg thought, just for the comfort of it. Mike didn't have to ask what Barby wanted, he poured her a shot of bourbon as generous as his own. Meg watched in amusement as he got out a cola and started to open it; then he caught himself and gave her an apologetic smile. "Guess you don't drink this stuff anymore, now you're a grown-up woman. I've got a bottle of wine somewhere, or there's some beer I keep on hand for the boys."

Meg accepted the beer, wondering which "boys" Mike meant. Surely not his sons; they lived hundreds of miles away, and both were in their late forties. He was active in the Big Brothers movement, but she doubted he would serve alcohol to young people many of whose problems stemmed from its overuse, by their parents or themselves.

"I love this house," she said. "I don't suppose I could talk you into taking a few months off and renovating the cottage for me?"

A clatter and a curse drew her attention to Barby, who managed to catch her pie tin of biscuits before they fell to the floor. "What cottage?" she demanded. "You don't mean that old—"

"The one on Dan's propitty," Mike said. "Meg's figuring to live there. Makes sense, when you come to think about it."

His attempt to head her off was evident, but she refused the hint. "Makes sense? You don't mean it, Meg! Why, I wouldn't live there for a million bucks."

"Is it haunted?" Meg asked solemnly.

"Well . . . I guess not. Least I never heard of anything going on." Barby put the pie tin in the oven and straightened. Her face was flushed. "We figured you'd probably want a place of your own, so we've been kind of keeping an eye out for a nice piece of propitty. The old Barlow place—"

"Never mind the old Barlow place," Meg interrupted. "Honestly, you guys are the most. . . . Are you mind readers, or what? I didn't make up my mind until the day before yesterday."

The two exchanged glances. "We just figured you you would," Mike said.

"You're smarter than I am, then." Meg relaxed against the soft cushions. "Which is a left-handed compliment if ever there was one."

"You're not mad, are you?" Barby asked anxiously.

"Of course not. Why should I be mad?"

"Because we're a bunch of nosy old coots," Barby said, sitting down at the table with her bourbon. "And—well—we sort of promised Dan we'd keep an eye on you. You don't want to live in that gloomy place, honey. Whether or not you believe in actual ghosts, there was a lot of unhappiness in that house. Some folks think feelings, of joy or misery, kind of soak into the walls. Why live with that? The old Barlow place—"

"Has probably seen its share of misery and joy," Meg said. "Barby, Mike—don't think I don't appreciate the way you and the others want to protect me. But I'm a grown woman now, and what I really need is the truth. Dan never talked to me. Nobody ever told me what really happened to my parents. I couldn't ask him, couldn't hurt Gran by reminding her. . . . The biggest favor you could do me is to let me ask questions, and answer them honestly, without trying to spare my feelings."

Mike had been setting the table. He put the last

fork neatly in place and looked at Meg. "Want another beer?"

She felt absurdly like crying. "Yes, Mike. Please."

Barby got up and took the biscuits out of the oven. After she had put the food on the table she resumed her seat and reached for the bourbon. "I'm not driving," she explained to Meg.

"You got a head like a rock anyhow," Mike said admiringly. He handed Meg her beer and sat down.

"Yeah, sometimes it's as hard as a rock," Barby muttered. "Okay, Meg, you got the floor. Go ahead."

It was hard to know where to begin. The question came into her mind unbidden, and yet strangely important. "What was she like? Aunt Joyce?"

Barby thought.

"She looked a lot like your gramma. A tiny little bit of a woman. Your ma was taller, heavier. Not that she wasn't just as pretty in her own way. It wasn't that."

"What, then? What was there about her that made my father gamble on losing everything that mattered to him? He must have known Dan would never forgive him, even if Mother did. He risked his job, his family—"

"He was crazy about you," Mike said. "Don't ever doubt that."

"Honey, every man, or woman, who fools around takes the same chance," Barby said. "For what? If I knew the answer I could make a fortune writing books and doing talk shows."

Meg said steadily, "He was supposed to be in Washington, on business. She said she was going to Boston on a shopping trip and would stay overnight with a friend. Neither of them was where they were supposed to be. They were in a motel less than fifty miles from here. Together. In bed together. They were drinking and smoking, and a cigarette ignited the bedclothes, which may have been saturated with alcohol. The fused remains of a bottle of vodka were found next to the bodies."

The others sat staring dumbly at the untouched food on their plates. Meg's throat was dry. She took a sip of her beer. "Luckily, or unluckily, the units on either side were empty. It was winter, after all, and midweek; no tourist business at that time of year. The fire was well under way before it was discovered. It was over twelve hours before the police made a tentative identification. She wasn't registered at all, and he was registered under a false name—the same one he had used half a dozen times before. The affair had been going on for months. If they hadn't been so careless, it might have continued indefinitely."

"Nobody had any idea," Barby murmured. "They all seemed so happy. . . ."

Mike shook his head. "That's easy to say, Barby. But nobody knows what goes on inside families."

"For years I hoped there was some mistake,"

Meg said softly. "But there wasn't, was there? It really happened. There's nothing you haven't told me?"

"No," Mike said, and Barby echoed, "Nothing you don't already know. So now you see why you shouldn't live in that house. The old Barlow place. . . ." She caught Meg's eye, and stopped with a sheepish grin. "Hell, there I go again. Just like a mother hen."

Meg grinned back at her. "Eat up, mother hen. The food is getting cold and it's too good to waste."

Barby sighed. "Damn right. Took me two hours to put this casserole together. . . . You had the right idea, Meg. I feel better myself, now that's over and done with."

"Not exactly, Barby. I have a few more questions."

Barby put her fork down. "Oh, Lord. Now what?"

Meg helped herself to another serving of the casserole while she debated what to say. Barby's presence had forced her to alter her original strategy, but even that had not been well defined; she kept vacillating between an almost irresistible urge to lean on Mike's rocklike strength and integrity, and the fear that she might endanger him by involving him. Not—she had argued with herself—that she had firm evidence of a deadly threat, to herself or anyone else. That was just the trouble.

There was one area, though, she felt fairly safe in discussing. "Some peculiar things have happened to me since Dan died," she began, choosing her words carefully. "I wasn't going to tell you about them, but I have a feeling you already know. Don't you?"

Mike gave her an odd, sidelong look; he understood why she had not gone into detail, but Barby promptly provided part of the information she had hoped to elicit. "That time you got run off the road was nothing but a drunk driver, honey. We all agreed—"

"Well, now, that's not exactly right," Mike interrupted. "You and Kate agreed. I wasn't so sure, and neither was Ed."

"Oh, Ed. He doesn't know what he thinks." Barby's cheeks were pink. "Anyhow, we agreed it couldn't have been Riley."

Meg leaned forward, forgetting to eat. Now that they had let down the protective barriers, they were being candid with a vengeance. "Why not, Barby?"

Barby's blush deepened, and she avoided Mike's eyes. "He just wouldn't do anything like that. And don't you grunt at me, Mike Potter. I said it before and I'll say it again—my feelings about people are just as important as your damned evidence!"

"I didn't say they weren't important. I just said—"

"You did too. As for those silly rings, a lot of people could've taken them from Dan's stock at the store. That sniveling sneak Candy, and her rotten ex, and—and—uh. . . ."

"Don't get so upset," Meg exclaimed, genuinely distressed by the acrimony she had aroused. "I hate to see you two fighting."

Mike let out a gruff bark of laughter and after a moment Barby echoed it with one of her shrill giggles. "We fight all the time, honey. It keeps the juices flowing, as Dan used to say. You don't believe Riley's behind all those stupid tricks, do you? Kate is afraid you do; she thought maybe you went to work at the store so you could keep an eye on him."

Meg decided to avoid answering that question. "I won't ask you how you learned about this. Cliff, Darren, Uncle George. . . . You've all been hovering like a bunch of self-appointed guardian angels. What I'd like to know is whether the harassment is directed at me personally, or at the firm. Dan had enemies. Have I inherited one of them?"

"We asked ourselves that too," Mike said. "I don't know . . . but I doubt it, Meg. Sure, Dan had people who didn't like him, even here in Seldon. Rod Applegate was one of 'em. Dan had him put in jail one time after he beat Candy up pretty bad. There was other cases like that; he didn't have much sympathy for wife-beaters and swindlers."

"What about the people Dan swindled?" Meg asked. "You're trying to make him sound like a sweet old saint, Mike. He wasn't a saint."

"Well, no. But no such things ever happened while Dan was alive. We'd have known."

He spoke slowly and reluctantly. Barby nodded, avoiding Meg's eyes. They saw the implications as clearly as she did.

After Mike had dropped Barby off and they were on the way home Meg tried once more. "Mike, are you sure Dan never dropped a hint about pulling a fast one on some client or business rival? Even if the deal wasn't actually illegal, someone might harbor a grudge."

"Dan was always bragging about the deals he made," Mike answered. "I wish that was the answer, but I don't think it is." He took one big hand from the wheel and patted her knee. "Don't you worry, we'll figure it out."

He brought the car to a stop in front of the house. Meg leaned over and kissed his leathery cheek. "I'm sorry if I spoiled our date, Mike. But I feel a lot better. Thanks. No, don't get out; it's stopped raining, and there's Cliff, ready to take over the bodyguard job."

She slammed the car door and trotted up the stairs to where Cliff stood waiting. "Working your wiles on Mike, I see," he remarked. "Get anything out of him?"

"You have an absolute genius for impertinence," Meg informed him. "And for the good life. Don't you ever work?"

Cliff locked the door and barred it, then tripped the unobtrusive switch that turned on the alarm system. "If you think I'm hanging around on your account, don't flatter yourself. Mary's the one I'm worried about. There is such as thing as delayed reaction, and her heart isn't strong."

And one strand of hair in the ring had been pale silver-gold. Guilt and alarm gripped Meg. "Has something happened?"

"No." Cliff's face relaxed. "I didn't mean to scare you. But I'm here to make damn good and sure nothing does happen. To either of you."

He took her face between his hands and tilted her head back, looking deep into her eyes. Then he gave her a brotherly kiss on the forehead and stepped back, grinning. "Good night, good night; parting is such sweet sorrow. . . . Or, as another famous poet has put it, Sleep tight and don't let the bedbugs bite."

He went off up the stairs, whistling softly under his breath. After a brief interval Meg followed him, and stood in the hall listening to his retreating footsteps. When she heard the far-off slam of a door she went into her room and opened her safe. Cliff appeared to have retired for the night and it would be easier to take Dan's jewels downstairs to the library rather than bring the necessary reference books to her room. Until she started working with them she couldn't be certain which ones she might need.

She was certain Mike had told the truth when he denied knowledge of any specific act of skulduggery on Dan's part. If he had known about the jewelry hoard he would have betrayed himself when Meg questioned him about Dan's army record. Mike had served in the European theater in

World War II, Dan in the Far East, but like all old soldiers they had swapped war stories, and Mike confirmed some of Meg's hunches. Dan had been in India part of the time, in some sort of liaison position with the British. "He did brag about what great bargains he got over there," Mike had explained. "I guess you know lots of jewels come from that part of the world. But other guys brought back precious stones, there was nothing illegal about it."

Maybe not about rough stones, Meg thought. The gem gravels of Ceylon, the island off the coast of India, were among the richest in the world. Ratnapura, the City of Gems, had for centuries supplied the world not only with fine rubies and sapphires but with an astonishing variety of semiprecious stones—tourmaline and topaz, moonstone and garnet and zircon. Kashmir, in northern India, was the source of the exquisite cornflower-blue sapphires, the most prized of that variety of corundum. The best rubies came not from Ceylon but from the mines of Mogok in Burma. Like those of Ceylon, the Burmese deposits contained a variety of stones, including sapphires and peridots.

For Dan, being stationed in that part of the world must have been like turning a child loose in a candy store in the middle of a hurricane. The upheaval of war sent whole populations fleeing for their lives. The Japanese had swept through southeast Asia with the same blitzkrieg speed their German allies had shown in Europe, driving ahead of them a ragtag army of refugees who carried with them their most valuable and portable treasures.

From desperate people and in a market flooded with gems Dan could have acquired cut and uncut stones legally, and still made a killing. Meg didn't doubt that he had "forgotten" to declare some of them on his return; authorities couldn't have searched the duffel bags of hundreds of thousands of returning heroes.

The treasure trove must have been more difficult to smuggle into the country. How he had done it Meg didn't know, but that he had done it she could not doubt. Like many other small kingdoms and principalities, Mogera had been taken over by the British in the nineteenth century. Though it had lost its independence it had preserved royal dignities—including, obviously, the royal treasury. Mogera was shown on no modern map, but she knew it must have been high in the mountains, in upper Burma. That was where the resistance to the Japanese invaders had centered.

Searching through other books, she found no further reference to the princes of Mogera, but she ran across a story that suggested a possible parallel. It was one of the legends Dan had told her years before, the mysterious disappearance of the crown jewels of Austria. The larger part of them, including the Empress's diamond-and-pearl crown, had vanished without a trace after the revolution of 1918. According to one version, the Emperor had entrusted them to a friend, who was supposed to sell them in order to finance a counterrevolution. The friend had fled to South America instead; but if he had taken the jewels, what had he done with them? None of them had ever been heard of again. Were they sunk in the sands of the ocean or buried in a forgotten grave—or in the secret strong room of a private collector?

Had the Maharajah's treasure also been entrusted to a friend who betrayed his master? There would have been much less risk in that theft than in the case of the Austrian crown jewels, which had been photographed and inventoried in painstaking detail. So far as Meg had been able to ascertain, the crown jewels of Mogera were mentioned only in the rare publication she had discovered. She understood why the rulers of that small beleaguered principality had kept quiet about their riches; the world was full of predators, and precious stones attracted the most deadly of them.

With the tattered volume in front of her, she spread the jewels out across the table. Comparing them to the illustrations in the book, she saw that they represented only a fraction of the original collection. Some might have been dispersed during the century that had passed since the book's publication, but several, she knew, Dan must have possessed, even though they were not among the ones she had found: the armlet with the immense pink diamond, the emerald peacock and a sword hilt set with crudely cut stones, the largest of which was a pigeon's-blood ruby. Meg opened another of the books she had taken from the shelf, and found the photograph she wanted.

The diamond in the photograph hung from a heavy platinum chain studded with smaller blue-white stones. It was considerably smaller than the rough chunk of rose-pink ice in the armlet, but precious stones always lost some of their bulk when they were recut in the modern, brilliant style. According to the text, it had been purchased from "a dealer" in 1949 and sold to "a private collector." No help there; but naturally Dan wouldn't admit the truth if he had come by the stone dishonestly. Diamonds had individual characteristics by which they could be identified even after drastic recutting; at least some experts claimed to be able to do so. But in this case the original stone had never been inspected by an expert. Dan would have been willing to sacrifice the diamond. He didn't like diamonds anyway, and the setting of this one appeared to be undistinguished. A few stones of that quality would have been enough to lift him into the ranks of the world's foremost jewelers—especially if he got them for nothing.

As for the ruby. . . . Meg went back to the shelves and selected another book. She had good cause to remember that ruby, for Dan had often talked of it, bemoaning its loss and berating himself for succumbing to an offer even he couldn't resist. After selling it to a Denver businessman who fell on hard times, he had bought it back in 1960 and had it reset. Meg stared at the photograph with a painful constriction of her throat. The ring was one of the first pieces her father had made. Most modern designers would have surrounded a colored stone of that size and quality with diamonds. Instead, Simon Venturi had cupped the central stone in a frame of smaller rubies and carved emerald leaves. He was good, Meg thought. Not as good as Riley, but who knows what he might have become? How could he. . . .

The creak of the door rang through the silence with such startling effect that she dropped the book. Her uncle looked in. "Oh—it's you, my dear. I saw the light and wondered who. . . . Good lord!"

He stood frozen, staring at the table with its opulent covering. Meg picked up the book and smoothed its crumpled pages. "The cat is definitely out of the bag," she said with forced lightness. "Come in, Uncle George. I take it you didn't know about Dan's private hoard?"

The explanation took quite some time; Meg had to explain her theory and show him the sources she had used. His reaction took her by surprise. "Well, I'll be damned! Imagine squirreling these things away all these years. But that would be just like Dan. I'm only amazed he could bring himself to part with a portion of them, he sulked like a spoiled child when he had to sell one of his pet stones."

"But, Uncle George, you don't understand. Dan stole these, he must have. He smuggled them into the country, he hid them. . . . What am I supposed to do, put them back where I found them and leave them there?"

"Hmmm. I see what you mean." Her uncle replaced a jeweled belt on the table. "It is a problem. Have you told anyone else about this?"

This time, instead of telling him a direct lie, Meg lied by implication. "I was going to consult Darren—"

"Don't do that."

"Why not?"

"Let me put it this way. Do you want to hand these jewels over to the government? Because that may happen if you report them to the proper authorities. You might successfully argue that they qualify as antiques and were therefore exempt from ordinary customs duties, but there is still a matter of failing to declare them. However, I suspect the main problem will be with the Internal Revenue Service. Obviously Dan never paid taxes of any kind on these objects, and whether they are considered a capital investment or a part of his estate—"

"Stop." Meg raised her hands in protest. "Let's not go into that, Uncle George, talking taxes always makes me dizzy."

"No need for you to worry about it, my dear; that's my job. If you'll take my advice, you'll hold off talking to Darren until I can make a few discreet inquiries. There must be parallel cases, but I'm not familiar with them. I wonder if the laws regarding treasure trove and antiquities would apply? It's an intriguing little problem."

"Intriguing? How about dangerous? Or deadly?"

George studied her quizzically. "You've been watching too many TV thrillers, my dear. There can't be any connection between this hoard of Dan's and the harassment we've experienced. The rings certainly didn't come from this collection, they are European."

Meg leaned forward, intent on convincing him. She could see the way his thoughts were tending, and they were completely at variance with her own. "Uncle George, stories of crime and violence connected with jewels aren't all fictional. I could tell you tales that would make your hair stand on end, all of them true. Oh, I'm not suggesting that the heirs of the Maharajah have finally tracked us down, that really would be stretching probability after so many years. But consider this. Dan got these jewels from someone—maybe a thief, maybe an agent of the owners. He may even have paid for them. But suppose he didn't. Suppose he pulled a swindle of some kind. Isn't it possible that one of the other people involved in the deal still holds a grudge?"

"For almost fifty years?" George laughed. "He'd be an old man, honey. Old and decrepit."

"Not necessarily. Not if he was only a boy when it happened. Oh, hell, Uncle George, I don't care whether he's seventy or ninety-nine, whether he's real or imaginary. If Dan stole these things, I want them to go back to the rightful owners. If he swindled somebody, I want to make—"

The noise sounded like a buzz saw, harsh, shrill, penetrating. It came in short bursts, three in all, and then stopped. Before it died away George was on his feet. Then he was gone. Meg had never imagined he could move so fast.

Assuming that something had set off the alarm system, she followed her uncle as quickly as she could, arriving in the hall in time to see him taking the stairs two at a time. As she started up after him she heard the howling—not a mechanical cry like the first, but a desolate, high-pitched wail reminiscent of the old Irish tales of banshees. Meg knew what it was, and the realization terrified her more than any supernatural manifestation. She was younger than George and in better condition, and now she was equally frightened; she caught up with him outside her grandmother's door.

Light overcame the darkness within when George hit the switch and Henrietta Marie's outcries stopped. The cat was pacing back and forth across the bed. The covers had been thrown back. Mary lay in a twisted turmoil of silk and lace, arms outflung. Her face was a sickly blue-white.

Meg had only one flashing, dreadful glimpse of her grandmother before George threw himself at the bed. "Call," he shouted. "Rescue squad, 911. Hurry!"

Meg snatched up the telephone. Stammering out the information the dispatcher requested, she saw Henrietta Marie go flying as George shoved her out of his way and bent over the still body. He paused in his efforts only long enough to gasp, "Go down, let 'em in."

In the doorway Meg collided with Cliff. He was wearing pajama bottoms and his hair was wildly on end. There was no time and no need for talk; Cliff sent her on her way with a sharp shove and ran into the room.

A century later the ambulance arrived.

"She's going to be all right," George said. "Why don't you go to bed, honey? You must be exhausted."

"Let her unwind first." Cliff went to the liquor cabinet and took out a glass. "We're all too keyed up to sleep. What would you like, Meg? I've got some sleeping pills, if you'd prefer them."

"No." Meg slumped into a chair. The doctor had insisted they go home. Mary was sedated and sleeping, there was no immediate danger.

"She's going to be fine," George insisted.

"Thanks to you," Meg said. "If you hadn't acted immediately, known just what to do. . . ."

"Oh, well." George shrugged and looked uncomfortable. "I'll have my usual, Cliff, if you're playing bartender. My throat feels dry. Nerves, I guess."

Henrietta Marie sauntered in, considered the options and jumped onto Meg's lap. Meg stroked her ruffled fur and was rewarded by a faint purr. "She's upset, too. It's going to be all right, Henrietta. She'll be home soon. Oh, Uncle George—did Henrietta do that?"

The bloody scratches on his hand were only too apparent when he reached for the glass Cliff offered him. "I wasn't the only one," he said wryly. "She bit one of the rescue squad on the ankle."

"I thought Frances was going to bite me," Cliff said, dropping onto the sofa. "Dad, couldn't you talk Frances into early retirement? She's too old and too loony to take proper care of Mary. That was quite a scene she made at the hospital."

"I'll try to convince Mary," his father said, sighing. "But I've tried before, without success. The relationship between those two baffles me, but it's strong. And nobody could be more devoted than Frances."

Meg had to agree. After her initial outburst Frances had proved more than competent. Refused a place in the ambulance, she had turned up at the hospital fifteen minutes later, fully dressed and carrying an overnight bag, and announced she was staying. "I don't care whether there's a bed available, I'll just sit here till there is. I won't get in nobody's way nor cause trouble unless you try to make me leave her."

There was no doubt that she meant it, and no one was in the mood to argue with her. Cliff expressed Meg's sentiments fairly accurately when he added, "On the other hand, I'd rather she were there than here. Now the only neurotic we have to cope with is Henrietta. I refuse to have her sleep with me, Meg. Looks as if you're elected."

"Like certain other people, Henrietta sleeps where she likes," Meg said, tickling the cat under her chin. "But I promise I'll keep her away from you, Uncle George; I only wish I could begin to tell you how much I appreciate. . . ."

"Oh, now, honey, don't cry. She's had a couple of minor heart attacks before—"

"I didn't know that. Why didn't you tell me?"

"She didn't want to worry you. The fact is, we couldn't get her to take it seriously. What she needs is a pacemaker; that's almost a routine operation these days, and it would solve the problem, but she raised holy cain when the doctor suggested it. Said she didn't want an ugly scar."

"Oh, no." Meg exclaimed. "I knew she was vain, but that's ridiculous."

"Not at all," Cliff said. "For Mary it was a logical decision. If God had meant us to have artificial devices installed in our bodies, he'd have equipped us with zippers."

George was not amused. "I had a hard-enough time persuading her to install that buzzer."

"Thank God you did," Meg said.

"It could be improved, though," Cliff said. "For one thing, it sounds too much like the burglar alarm. Another problem is that we're too far from her room. What if she doesn't have enough warning to reach the buzzer? I don't know how she did it last night, it had fallen to the floor, out of her reach."

There was a brief, uncomfortable silence. Then George said, "It dropped from her hand when she lost consciousness. It must have happened that way. There was nobody else in the room."

Meg looked at Henrietta Marie. Henrietta Marie bit her.

15

THE HOUSEMAID WHO found the jewels on the library table the next morning was young and excitable. She fled the room screaming incoherently about burglars, and the ensuing uproar woke everyone in the house, including Meg and Henrietta, neither of whom appreciated being wakened. Henrietta expressed her feelings vigorously before stalking out of the room with her tail lashing.

The maid, who had prudently gotten herself out of the cat's way, reappeared in the open doorway and Meg wiped beads of blood off her calf. "There aren't any burglars, Linda. It's my fault, I forgot to put the damn things away last night. Tell everybody to go back to bed. I'll take care of it."

By the time she had bundled up the treasure and carried it to the safe, she was wide awake and so were the others. George was at the breakfast table when she came down; Cliff soon joined them. George brushed her apologies aside. "I forgot too. Small wonder! No damage was done, my dear."

Except that the secret hoard was no longer a secret. The staff had been warned not to discuss the incident with outsiders, but Meg had no illusions about how much heed they would give to that warning. However, most people, including the staff, would assume the jewelry was part of Dan's regular collection. Perhaps the damage was minimal after all.

They had all called the hospital, and agreed that the reports were encouraging. "I'm going over there after breakfast," Cliff said. "Want a ride, Meg?"

"I'll try to see her later today. They said no visitors."

"That doesn't apply to us."

"I bet they won't let you in. If they do, and if she's awake, for God's sake don't say anything to upset her."

"What do you think I am, an idiot?"

"You're no idiot, but you have an overactive imagination." Meg reached for the coffeepot. Her appetite was nonexistent, but she needed a large jolt of caffeine if she was going to make it through the day. "I know what you're thinking, because. . . . Because I've been wondering the same thing."

"I don't know what you're talking about," George said in bewilderment. "Am I missing something?"

"No, we're the ones who are missing something. A couple of bricks off the load,maybe. You said she'd had attacks before, Uncle George. There's no reason to suppose something happened last night to send her into another one?"

George looked from Meg's anxious eyes to his

son's downcast face. "I never thought. . . . Surely not. She was asleep. The room was dark."

Cliff looked up. "The phone didn't ring?"

"No. Now, I'm absolutely certain of that; we'd have heard the one in the library." He patted Meg's hand. "Forget it, child. Nothing could have happened. And I'm sure Cliff has better sense than to ask questions of a sick woman."

Cliff threw his napkin onto the table and stood up. "Cliff is humbly grateful for the confidence you have in him. So maybe I am missing a few bricks off the load. I'd rather be overly cautious than criminally careless. At least while she's in the hospital she's safe."

He strode out of the room, giving his chair a kick as he passed it.

"He didn't mean to be rude," George said. "He's just upset."

"I know." Not just upset about the illness of someone he loved; distressed because he was afraid he had failed her. In some ways he's more devoted to her than I am, Meg thought remorsefully. Or is he simply less able to accept reality? Nothing any of us can do will make her immortal.

"Where are you off to?" her uncle asked, as she rose from her chair.

"The store, of course. I'll take a car, so I can run over and see Gran later."

George opened his mouth and then closed it. Meg smiled at him. He was learning.

Riley was behind the counter when she went in.

He looked up in surprise. "What are you doing here so early?"

"You heard?"

"Several people have called already. I'm sorry about Mrs. Mignot," he added awkwardly.

"She's going to be all right."

"That's good. She's always been nice to me." Amusement brightened his dark eyes, and he added, "Even though she thinks I'm a lout."

"That," said Meg gravely, "is the sign of a real lady."

"Yeah. Look, you don't have to hang around here if you'd rather be at the hospital. I can handle things."

"Thanks, but I'd rather be working. The doctor assured us there's no cause for alarm, and that what she needs most today is rest."

"Suit yourself."

"I always do, don't I?"

"Do you?"

At first Meg didn't understand the question, or the penetrating look that accompanied it. "I haven't changed my tiny mind, if that's what you mean. My offer yesterday was not a whim, or a sentimental tribute to Dan's memory."

"Okay." After a moment he added, "We got some answers to our ad for a clerk."

"Oh, good. Any likely possibilities?"

"One sounds promising." Riley took a handful of letters from his pocket and passed them to her. "She worked for Murdock and Sons, the jewelry store in Augusta, for ten years."

"I'll give her a call, shall I?"

"Yeah, you better. I'd probably scare her off." The telephone rang before Meg could reply, and Riley went into the shop.

The caller, like others who followed, was a friend inquiring about Mary. Later that morning, however, Meg got a call of another kind. After she had hung up she let out a whoop that brought Riley plunging out of the shop. "What the hell—"

"Guess what?"

"What?"

"That was Mrs. Randolph Bacon Mercer's secretary!"

"Oh, yeah?"

"You know who she is?"

"You just told me," Riley said.

"She's selling her collection!"

"The secretary?"

"No, Mrs. Randolph. . . . Riley, you definitely need practice in the humor department. This is a serious matter. Don't you understand—she called us first! She's giving us a chance to make an offer before she notifies other buyers."

"Oh,yeah?"

"Riley!"

"Oh—sorry. That is interesting. Could be she needs cash in a hurry and wants to keep it quiet. Yeah. If she wants us to reset the stones and market them without bringing her name into it, we could get the lot cheap."

"Oh, Jesus."

"What's the matter?"

"I'm scared. Cheap, he says. We're talking millions, Riley. I don't think I can do it. I don't know enough."

"You can learn."

"In a week?"

"Sure. Dan sold her most of her important pieces. We've got the receipts and the descriptions."

"You'll have to go with me."

Riley looked at her as if she had suggested he join her in a visit to a leper colony. "To her house? Not me."

"A week," Meg mumbled, pacing. "I can't, Riley. What if I make a horrible mistake? If the bid is too low, we'll lose the collection. If it's too high, I could bankrupt us before we get off the ground."

"She's a millionaire," Riley muttered. "She's probably got a butler."

The raw horror in his voice penetrated Meg's nervousness. She stopped, facing him, and saw the reflection of her own consternation in eyes as candid as a schoolboy's.

Meg had no intention of laughing. It was rude, it was inappropriate, it was tactless. She couldn't help herself. To see Riley the imperturbable thrown into a panic at the idea of meeting a real-live butler was too much for her. She tried to stop; then she realized that he was laughing too, laughing at her and with her and at himself. They came together in a movement as spontaneous as water flowing, and clung to one another, shaken by their shared laughter, the very rhythm of their bodies matching. Under her hands the hard muscles of his back rose and fell, and his uneven breath stirred the loosened strands of her hair. Uneven now, not with laughter, but with something else; the arms that held her tightened and he bent his head. . . .

Neither of them heard the soft tinkle of the chimes. Riley was facing the door, but Meg had no warning, and the violence of his recoil was as intimate and shocking as a blow. His hands moved to push her away; then another pair of hands seized her and sent her reeling back against the counter.

The impact brought tears of pain to her eyes, but the blurred image she saw was alarming enough to move her to action. She caught Cliff's raised arm. "Don't! It's not what you think. Stop it, Cliff!"

Cliff's fists were clenched and his face was mottled and distorted by rage. "Let go, Meg. You don't know what this bastard has done or you wouldn't defend him. Or are you so hot for him you don't mind if he almost killed Mary?"

"What?" Shock loosened her hold and Cliff shook himself free. Riley had retreated as far as he could go, which wasn't far; his back was against the closed shop door, with the counter on one side and Cliff closing in on him. His features had hardened into the familiar impassive mask.

Cliff opened his right hand and tossed something onto the counter. Riley recognized it before

Meg did; a flash of surprise—and guilt?—passed across his face. "It was on the floor beside Mary's bed," Cliff said. "Do you wonder she had a heart attack when she saw it?"

Meg picked up the ring. It was not one of the ones she had seen before. The setting enclosed a small, heart-shaped ruby. The motto running around the hoop read, "I thee await."

"It's a fede ring," she said. "A love token."

"A love token from a dead man," Cliff said. "It's not just this one, it's the cumulative effect. You sent this to her, didn't you, Riley?"

Riley shook his head. "No. I never saw it before."

Cliff's sudden move caught him, and Meg, by surprise. The blow was clumsy and relatively ineffectual; it was Riley's attempt to avoid it that did the damage. Pivoting, he slipped and lost his balance; in the confined space he had nowhere to fall, and his face smashed into the reinforced metal of the doorframe. He hit the floor in an awkward tangle of limbs and crumpled clothing and lay still.

"Oh, my God," Cliff whispered. He was staring, not at Riley's bloody face but at his ankle and lower calf, where the leg of his jeans had been pulled up by his fall. Strips of plastic and metal failed to hide the raised ribbons of scar tissue.

"Get out of the way," Meg said, in a voice that echoed oddly inside her skull. She squeezed herself into the narrow space behind the counter.

"Is he—"

"Get some water."

Riley's head was twisted at a painful angle between the wall and his bent arm. Meg used her skirt to wipe away the blood; it was flowing freely, which was a good sign, but she didn't draw a full breath until her careful fingers assured her there was no hollow of fractured bone under the gash on his temple. Drops of water falling on her hair made her look up to see Cliff leaning across the counter, offering a wet, wadded-up bundle of paper towels. Meg snatched them from him. "Call the rescue squad," she said curtly.

"No. Don't call." The voice sounded as eerie and far away as a voice from the tomb. "Knocked myself out. . . ."

"He's not dead," Cliff said.

"Sorry about that," Riley muttered. He kept his eyes firmly closed, but when Meg repeated, "Cliff, call the rescue squad," Riley's free hand fumbled for her wrist. "No, I said. Just leave me alone for a minute. And quit slopping water all over me."

That sounded like the old Riley. Meg stood up. Cliff was still leaning across the counter; their eyes met.

"Hero," Meg said softly. "Big, macho hero."

"I didn't know about. . . . Hell, I didn't know! You don't suppose I'm stupid enough to swing at a cripple, do you? Now you're mad at me and sympathizing with him. He's still a murderous swine, but women always—"

"Get out of here, Cliff."

"Look, I'll drive him to the hospital. You don't

need to worry, I'll never touch him again, he's perfectly safe from me."

Riley reacted to this generous offer as he might have to a deadly insult. Despite Meg's efforts to restrain him he pulled himself to his feet.

"Oh, yeah? Well, don't do me any favors, buddy, because you sure as hell aren't. . . . Damn it, Meg, will you please—"

Meg pushed him against the wall and held him there. "You both make me sick!" she shouted. "*You* get out and *you* sit down and both of you shut up!"

Riley winced and covered his eyes with his hand. Cliff backed away. "Okay, I'm going. I'm sorry I made a scene, but I'm not sorry I said what I did, it was the truth, and I'm going to prove it and then maybe you'll. . . . Oops."

He turned and fled as Meg reached blindly for the first object she could find and fired it after him. It was a mirror, and it hit the floor with a satisfying smash. She swung on Riley, who had lowered himself cautiously onto a chair. "Don't sit down!"

Riley took the bloody wad of paper towels from his face. "But you just told me to—"

The phone rang. Meg snatched it up. "What?" she shouted. "Oh. . . . Oh, I'm sorry, Mr. Casey. Yes, Mike told me about you, I was going to call you. . . . Today? Well, if that's the case, I suppose. . . . All right. Why don't you meet me here at four and I'll take you to the cottage. . . . No, you can't meet me there; it's difficult to find the place without a guide and I'll have to locate the keys, it's been boarded up for years. . . . Mr. Casey, I have to go now, we'll discuss it later, okay?"

She hung up without waiting for an answer and turned back to Riley. "We're going to the hospital. I'll be damned if I'm going to have you wobbling around here all day with a possible concussion. Come on."

Looking more than ever like an Aztec idol, Riley came.

There were advantages to being the descendant of the town philanthropist. The emergency-room staff jumped to attention when Meg marched in with her silent hostage in tow. She explained about the accident, with due deference to Riley's sensitivities—"He slipped in some water I spilled on the floor—"and was about to abandon him to their tender mercies when one of the nurses said hesitantly, "Miss Venturi, if you're going to see your gramma, maybe you should wash up first."

Meg looked from her bloodstained hands to the red-brown stains on her skirt. "Oh. I guess you're right. Thanks. I'll be back in about half an hour."

She directed the last statement at Riley but got no response, not even a nod. She was reminded of a prisoner of war stoically awaiting interrogation. Name, rank and serial number. . . .

Alone in the washroom, with the door locked, she found she was shaking so violently that the water splashed all over her when she put her hands into the flow. There was blood on her face, too. Riley's blood.

She leaned against the wall, wet hands tightly clasped, until the tremors subsided. The necessity of showing her grandmother a smiling, untroubled face finally drove her back to the washbasin and the makeup in her purse. She applied it piece by piece—eyelids, lips, cheekbones—carefully avoiding an overall view, but the confrontation couldn't be avoided indefinitely, and when the eyes in the mirror caught and held hers, she cringed away from the knowledge they held.

When she got back to the emergency room, Riley was gone. With a twist of the lips that expressed her opinion of her erstwhile patient more clearly than words, the nurse directed Meg to the waiting room. Riley was seated on a bench reading a month-old copy of *Newsweek*. He had tried to arrange his hair over the patch of bandage on his forehead; instead of appearing unwounded, he looked like a wounded drunk. Meg's fingers itched, but she managed to keep them away from him.

They were well away from the hospital before he spoke. "How is Mrs. Mignot?"

"They're moving her out of intensive care this afternoon." Meg could only hope the hospital staff had not been driven to this move by Frances, who had planted a chair outside the cubicle in which Gran lay like a pathetic little robot plugged full of tubes and wires. She had smiled at Meg, hough, and whispered something about Henrietta Marie. Thankful for such a harmless topic of conversation, Meg had reassured her about the cat, and was rewarded by another, stronger smile. She had tripped over Frances's feet on her way out.

Having made the proper gesture, Riley relapsed nto brooding silence, which Meg chose not to break. She tried to concentrate on her driving, but every sense, every inch of her skin, was acutely aware of the man at her side. His breathing sounded as loud as a windstorm; the beating of he small blue vein in his wrist set her own blood pounding in matching rhythm. She had had a similar reaction during a single youthful experiment with peyote—a feeling that her nerve endings were raw and exposed, unendurably magnifying he slightest sensation.

He had his keys ready when they reached the tore; she stood back, careful not to brush against him, while he unlocked the door. The telephone was ringing. Meg went to answer it, thankful for further respite. She had herself under tighter control now, but she still hadn't decided what to ay to him.

Darren's voice rasped along her nerves like a ingernail on a blackboard. "Of course I'm all ight," she snapped. "Why shouldn't I be?"

"You haven't been answering the phone. I was just about to run over there and make sure you were—"

Meg blurted out a word that cut him short and made Riley give her a curious stare. After a brief silence Darren said, "Are you free for lunch? We need to talk."

"Yes, we do," Meg said. "We definitely do. I'll meet you at Kate's at. . . . Good lord, I had no idea it was so late. How time flies when one is enjoying oneself."

Riley had turned and was heading toward the shop. His shoulders twitched as if he had been stung on the back of the neck, but he didn't look at Meg.

"Not Kate's," Darren said. "I'll be out in front in five minutes."

The door to the shop closed, gently but with an air of finality. Meg hung up. Darren was useful for one thing, at any rate; he was so annoying he took her mind off other things.

Her skirt was still damp and wrinkled, but there was nothing she could do about that, and, to be honest, nothing she cared to do. When his car pulled up to the curb Meg was waiting; she got in before he could come around to open her door for her, and slammed it as hard as she could. "Cliff came to your office, didn't he? As soon as he left the store."

"Fasten your seat belt," Darren said.

"Answer me, dammit! What did Cliff tell you? He was the aggressor, nobody was hurt except Riley."

Darren brought the car to a gliding stop at a red light. Leaning across Meg, he reached for the seat belt and plugged it in. "Why don't we wait to discuss it until we're comfortably settled down with a drink and a—"

"Because I'd rather not make a scene in public. I'm going to make one, Darren. Who gave you and Cliff and God-knows-who else the right to run my life? Plotting and scheming, behind my back —goddammit, Darren, I authorized that investigation and I'm paying for it. How dare you presume to edit the information you're getting from your tame private eye? Why didn't you tell me about Riley's injury? It was Vietnam, wasn't it? That's how he got his Purple Heart. And you said they give those things for mosquito bites! Jesus Christ, Darren! Have you seen his scars?"

She stopped talking only because she had run out of breath. Darren had gone white around the mouth and his hands were clenched on the wheel. "You've just answered your own questions," he said.

"What are you talking about?"

Darren put on his turn signal and swung into a parking lot. "I did know about Riley's war record. It was in the second report I received."

"Then why didn't you tell me?"

Cruising slowly along the line of parked cars, Darren found an empty space and pulled into it. He switched off the engine before he turned to Meg. "Because I knew how you'd react. Women always. . . ."

Driven beyond endurance, Meg swung at him. The blow glanced off his chin and hurt her a good deal more than it hurt Darren. She regretted it even before it landed; but before she could apologize, Darren grabbed her by the shoulders and shook her till her head spun. "You see? You see? So he was wounded. So what the hell does that prove? It proves he was dumb enough or unlucky enough to step on a land mine. Period! It doesn't make him a saint or a martyr. Meg—Meg, darling. . . ."

"If you try to kiss me I'll hit you again," Meg said.

Darren let her go so abruptly the back of her head banged against the window. Meg yelped, and the angry color drained from Darren's face. "Darling, I'm sorry. I didn't mean—"

"Oh, shut up," Meg said.

They sat in mutual, resentful silence for a few moments, facing forward like two dummies in a crash test. Meg's much-tried sense of humor finally struggled back to life. "Darren," she said.

"What?"

"Two things. Don't ever say, 'Women always . . .' And don't call me darling. Until further notice you are my lawyer. Lawyers don't call their clients 'darling.' "

"I'm sorry."

"You don't sound sorry. You sound sulky. I apologize for slapping you. Now are we going to start again, with you treating me as you would any other client, or do I find a new shyster?"

Darren rubbed his jaw. "I'll stop calling you darling if you refrain from calling me a shyster."

"I only did it to annoy you. Well?"

"Deal." Darren held out his hand. "You may not like the new arrangement," he added, giving her a firm, businesslike shake and immediately releasing his grasp. "I'm going to give it to you straight."

"I can take it."

"No more hitting, okay?"

Meg laughed. "Okay."

Darren glanced wistfully at the door of the restaurant, but evidently he wasn't confident enough of Meg's self-control to suggest they go in. "Riley was in an army hospital for six months. Apparently he was lucky not to lose his leg; he ended up with permanent nerve damage and considerable loss of muscle tissue, but he insisted he'd rather wear a brace than a prosthesis. He's had several operations and a lot of physical therapy. Recently they developed a new technique for dealing with injuries like his, and he has been going to Boston for weekly treatments. My man wasn't able to find out what the chances for improvement are. Doctors don't discuss their patients with nosy strangers."

"I see."

Darren glanced at her. "I'm not sure you do. I refrained from telling you about this in part because—well, because I allowed my personal feelings to affect my professional judgment. I felt, rightly or wrongly, that you were beginning to think more favorably of him. I was reluctant. . . . I didn't want to encourage. . . ."

"You were jealous."

"Er. . . . In a word, yes."

"Jealous of a man because I expressed admiration for his talent? That's a helluva poor prospect for a successful marriage, Darren."

He had been right, though. Probably for the wrong reasons—but he had seen it coming long before she did.

"That's now irrelevant," Darren said. "I had another reason for keeping the information to myself, until I could decide what to do about it. You may not believe this, but I was trying to be fair. Hasn't it occurred to you that Riley's experiences in Vietnam may explain his present actions? Call it shell shock, call it post-whatever-the-current-fad-is syndrome—many of those men came back with permanent psychological damage. For years after he got back, Riley was little more than a bum. He worked as a laborer, a bartender, a janitor; he never held a job for more than a year. He was arrested several times for vagrancy. Eventually he landed in another army hospital, where they kept him for eighteen months. It wasn't his leg this time. He was being treated for drug abuse and mental illness."

They had their lunch. It was not the friendly, comfortable tête-à-tête Darren had envisioned, but he appeared to enjoy it. Meg found his sympathy even more infuriating than his jealousy. "The poor devil doesn't need pity, he needs help," Darren kept insisting. "You're not doing him any favor by denying the evidence against him, Meg. He seems to have been stable for a long time—"

"Yes, what about that?" Meg looked up from the slice of avocado she had been mashing into a pulp. "The rumors about his behavior here in Seldon—"

"Are no more than rumors," Darren admitted. "I suspect it was the shock of Dan's death that made him lose control. He needs treatment, Meg. Heaven only knows what wild fantasies he's harboring."

Meg put her fork down. She couldn't eat; the sight of food made her sick. "It always goes back to Dan, doesn't it? He might at least have had the decency to leave me one of those long rambling letters exposing his dirty secrets and tying up the loose ends. What's the connection between him and Riley? There must be a connection, a strong one, somewhere in the past; they couldn't have developed such a tight relationship in only three years. Couldn't your tame 'tec dig it out?"

Darren adjusted his glasses. He looks just like a stupid Jersey cow, Meg thought bitterly, with those big brown eyes of his beaming placid satisfaction. "Dan was the one who paid for his college and technical training."

"Another little item you chose not to tell me. Why?"

"I was wrong," Darren admitted magnanimously. "From now on I won't hold anything back. But surely you can see why I feared you might be distressed. Think it through, Meg. How did Dan happen to find a designer of Riley's quality? What did he see in a mental patient, a bum, that would lead him to go to such expense and trouble?"

Meg stared, aghast, and Darren gently administered the coup de grace. "He's Dan's bastard son, Meg. He must be. There is no other logical explanation."

Only the stiff-necked pride she had learned from both grandparents kept Meg from bursting into hot denials. Darren would think she was objecting because she didn't want Riley to be a blood relative—and maybe Darren would be right. However, that wasn't the only logical explanation. It was a possible explanation, and the one Darren wanted to believe. Meg didn't believe it. (Because she didn't want to believe it?)

"How old is Riley?" she asked.

"Thirty-six. Dan was fifty-three when he was born. That's an age when many men go off the rails, even men as devoted to their wives as Dan."

"The midlife crisis in males seems to run from thirty to eighty," Meg said caustically. "Never mind the soothing psychology, Darren. Have you any concrete evidence that Dan knew Riley's mother, or are you suggesting she was just a common whore?"

Darren winced. "Meg, dear, your language—"

"What would you prefer—prostitute, tart, easy lay? Oh, the hell with it, Darren. You may be right, you may be wrong. Tell your boy to keep digging. And from now on I want to see those reports with my own eyes."

It was not a happy note on which to end the discussion, but Meg was in no mood to be conciliatory. She had not had a good day—and the preceding night had been nothing to brag about either.

Darren was studiously polite during the return drive, but whenever he stopped talking his lower lip protruded like that of a sulky child. Meg decided this was not the time to tell him about the partnership. She had a lot of things to settle in her own mind before she came to grips with that matter, not the least of which was the question of the cottage. Mr. Casey would be arriving shortly. Why hadn't she put him off? Just because it happened to suit his schedule and good contractors were hard to find—but she was in no state to cope with the physical and emotional trauma of renovation. Her eyelids felt grainy from lack of sleep.

When she got back to the store she stole like a thief into the office and closed the door. After she had seated herself at the desk she sat for a few moments with her shoulders bowed and her hands over her eyes. Then she straightened and reached for the phone.

Nick sounded even warier than usual when his secretary finally put her through to him. He probably thinks I'm going to make a scene, Meg thought dispassionately. "I need a discreet private inquiry firm," she said, without wasting time on apologies or explanations. "Can you recommend one?"

"Why, uh—yes, I do know of one." He gave her the name. Meg thanked him and was about to hang up when he said, "I find I'll be able to make that business meeting after all. Is Friday still okay with you?"

It took her a few seconds to understand what he meant. "No. It isn't okay with me."

"Saturday, then. I have a new set of figures I'd like to present."

I'll just bet you do, Meg thought, marveling at her own detachment. A few days ago—a few hours ago—she might have responded, given him a chance to repair their relationship. Now she could only marvel at his smug assumption that theirs had been a standard lovers' quarrel rather than a final break.

"Sorry," she said, and hung up before he could answer.

She dialed the number he had given her. As she described what she wanted done, her voice got gradually softer. After he had asked her for the second time to repeat a name, she said, "Just a minute," and hurried to the door.

There was no one in the store. It had been her guilty conscience that imagined the click of the extension being lifted. She went back to the telephone and forced herself to finish the call. "It's extremely urgent. I want it done as quickly as possible."

After she had hung up she crept back to the

door and peeked out. To think that only a few days earlier she had made that smug self-righteous speech to Darren about invading someone's privacy. . . . But it had to be done. She didn't trust Darren; she didn't trust anyone, except possibly Mike, and even he. . . . They were all keeping things from her, editing the facts, sometimes deliberately, sometimes unconsciously, telling her what she wanted to hear or what they thought she ought to hear. She found herself remembering another of Dan's favorite sayings. "Don't take anybody's word for anything. Find out for yourself." Well, that was what she was going to do.

The chimes tinkled, heralding a customer. Riley emerged from the shop, saw Meg and retreated without speaking. She advanced, smiling stiffly, to do her job.

The customer, a balding, heavyset man with eyes like gimlets, wanted a present for his wife. After discovering they had nothing in his price range—under fifteen dollars—he left, muttering discontentedly. "Cheapskate," Meg said, as the door closed after him. Now what? Mr. Casey would be there in twenty minutes, and she had no idea where to find the keys to the cottage. They were not among the neatly labeled keys on Dan's ring. There must be a set somewhere. George might know, but she hated to ask him, it might be tantamount to rubbing salt in his wounds. Perhaps Riley. . . . No. He was the least likely person. She was just looking for an excuse to see him, hear his voice, win back the ground she had lost. . . . He had told her he didn't accept help gracefully. But it wasn't fair, it wasn't her fault that she had been witness to his weakness, as he obviously considered it. How many other people knew about it? He had gone to great lengths to conceal it; even that slow, arrogant stride was probably the only alternative to a betraying limp. When he took off work Friday afternoon he must have gone for one of the treatments Darren had mentioned. He had looked exhausted the following morning; probably the procedure was painful. . . .

I've got to stop this, she thought. He doesn't want pity. That's not what I feel. How can I make him understand? It wasn't his physical handicap that opened my eyes, it was what happened before I found out—that moment of mutual dependence and confidence, when he trusted me enough to admit his vulnerability and lend his strength to mine. . . . If Cliff hadn't come in just then. . . . I'd like to kill him. I'd like to kill Riley, for being so bullheaded and stiff-necked and unresponsive. . . . With a muttered curse she snatched up the telephone and dialed the number of the hardware store.

The sound of Mike's slow, deep drawl failed to have its usual calming effect, and his deliberate answers annoyed her inordinately. No, he was sorry, but he had no idea where the keys to the cottage might be. He couldn't get anybody out there on such short notice. Anyhow, what she needed was a locksmith.

"Mike, please stop telling me what I can't do," Meg said. "I'm getting into that cottage today if I have to break down the door. I had hoped you might suggest a better alternative."

"Now just calm down, honey. What's the rush? You sound upset. You better wait a day or two, take time to figure things out."

"Thanks, Mike." Meg hung up. After hesitating for a moment she dialed the house.

It was such a pleasant change to have someone acquiesce unquestioningly to her orders that she began to relax—until, having settled the arrangements, she turned to see Riley standing in the door of the shop.

16

AS SHE WAITED for him to speak, Meg was aware of a disconcerting sensation of upheaval, as if all her internal organs were changing place. The chaos of shifting viewpoints, from "Uncle Aloysius" through "drug addict" and "psychotic," finally stabilized and she found herself able to see him as she had before Darren dumped his load of news onto her—complex, enigmatic, troubled and, she hoped, salvageable. Even her new awareness of him as a man who could arouse her physically and emotionally subsided into something controllable; it was still there, but instead of roaring through her veins like rapids it had become a background murmur—but a murmur as steady and necessary as her heartbeat.

"I heard," Riley said, indicating the intercom.

"That's okay. It wasn't a private conversation." She thought of the very private conversations she had conducted earlier and was glad she had forgotten how to blush.

"Are you leaving now?"

"As soon as Mr. Casey gets here. Why don't you close up?"

I shouldn't have said that, she thought. Damn the man, why can't he wallow in female sympathy, like some of the guys I know?

"It's not necessary," Riley said. "I'm all right. Do you mind if I ask you a personal question? You don't have to answer."

"Ask," Meg said. Her heart, or some equally inconvenient organ, beat an unsteady tattoo against her rib cage.

"The cottage you were talking about. . . . Is that the one on the estate, that's been closed up all these years?"

"Yes." The inconvenient organ sank into her shoes. "Is that your idea of a personal question?"

"I haven't asked that one yet. Are you. . . . Why are you so anxious to get in the place?"

"I'm planning to live there."

"Why?"

"I want a place of my own. The cottage is ideal—close to Gran, in case she needs me, and yet offering the privacy I want."

"It's private enough," Riley muttered. "That's the only reason?"

"What other reason could there be?"

"If that's how you feel," Riley said slowly. "There isn't any other reason."

The chimes rang an accompaniment to the last words. Mr. Casey had arrived.

As Meg had requested, one of the gardeners was waiting for them when they reached the estate. He was loaded with tools and wearing an anticipatory grin. At his age—he looked no more than eighteen—the prospect of being allowed to break into a house, violently and legally, must have been appealing. Meg had forgotten his name, so she let the two men introduce themselves, and led the way.

"Dunno how I'm gonna get a crew in here," Casey said doubtfully, beating a path through the weeds.

"There used to be a back gate and driveway," Meg said. "The drive was gravel, I think; it must be completely overgrown. Dennis, will you check that out first thing tomorrow? Clear the drive, find out what has to be done to open the gate; it may be rusted shut. I want these weeds cut down too."

"Yes, ma'am."

She listened patiently to Casey's grumbling as they circled the house looking for a way in. If she had taken him seriously she might have concluded it made more sense to tear the place down and start all over. Chimneys, walls, shutters, foundation, all were in "turrible shape, it was gonna cost a mint of money—and that was just the outside." However, she had done some minor remodeling of her apartment, so she was familiar with the mind-set of men who fix things, be they painters, plumbers, electricians or humble handymen. "I'm sure you can do it," she said firmly. "Dennis, let's tackle the back door. It will have to be replaced anyway, the boards are rotting."

"Termites," groaned Mr. Casey.

Splinters flew as Dennis hurled himself and his crowbar joyously into the fray, but when the door finally yielded and he faced darkness thick with the stench of sour air, he stepped back, his grin fading.

"Geez, Miz Meg, I wouldn't go in there if I was you. Smells like something died."

A lot of things had died—mice, birds and at least one larger mammal,whose bones had been picked clean by smaller predators. With the help of the flashlight Dennis had brought, Meg picked her way across the dusty, squeaking floor while Dennis began removing the boards from the windows. As sunlight replaced the darkness she beheld a scene of desolation that almost converted her to Casey's pessimistic view of the task ahead.

It wouldn't have been quite so bad if the house had been empty. Some of the contents must have been removed—trinkets, personal possessions, favorite chairs or pictures—but most of the furniture remained, shrouded in tattered dust covers. The fabric had been fouled and chewed by animals. Broken glass had fallen from several panes, and only the breeze coming through the openings made the air breathable.

Her handkerchief to her nose, Meg was in the hall, heading for the dining room, when she heard voices outside. One was that of Dennis. The other was Cliff's.

Meg hurried to the back, hoping to head him off. The wreckage distressed her, and she had never lived here. It had been Cliff's home. Seeing it as it was now would be like viewing the rotting corpse of a friend.

She was too late. He was standing in the open doorway when she entered the kitchen. He didn't look at her; his eyes wandered from the open cupboard doors to the scarred surface of the kitchen table, and she knew he was seeing the past: shining chrome, gleaming floors, a table spread with food. Not knowing what to say, she followed him into the living room, where he stopped short, swaying as if from a physical blow.

"I'm so sorry, Cliff." She moved to his side, put her arm around him. "I had no idea it would be this bad."

"What are you apologizing for? Serves me right for butting in where I wasn't invited." But his voice was remote, without its usual bite, and his eyes remained focused on memory. "We used to sit there, on the couch in front of the fireplace, after supper. She always read me a story before I went to bed. Dad built a fire on winter nights. I remember. . . ."

A shudder rippled through his body. When he spoke again his voice was normal. "So much for the joys of nostalgia. I don't remember all that much, to be honest. How old was I—seven?—when they sent me to boarding school? I blamed you for that, you know."

"You picked on me," Meg said. Casey had joined them; conscious of his curious stare, she moved away from Cliff. "I don't remember much either, but I remember how you used to bully me. A poor helpless little four-year-old girl."

"Yeah, I was a rotten kid." He turned to Casey and held out his hand. "I'm Cliff Wakefield, Ms. Venturi's cousin. Think you can do anything with this ruin, Mr.—"

"Casey, Joe Casey. It's not so bad, Cliff. Basic structure's still sound."

Reduced to her proper inferior status, Meg followed the two from room to room while they discussed the repairs man-to-man. In the presence of another male, Casey waxed positively garrulous, and Cliff nodded and looked wise as the contractor talked learnedly about joists and vents and subflooring. Meg suspected he knew no more about them than she did. What it came down to, she decided, was that she would have to install new wiring and plumbing, buy a new furnace and new appliances, have the chimneys repaired, repair the windows and frames and replace floorboards, molding and steps eaten by termites . . . gut the house, in other words. So why couldn't Casey just say so?

She remained discreetly quiet until Casey informed her he'd try to get his crew out a week from Thursday. When she protested, he looked hurt. "I'm backed up six weeks already, Miz Venturi. Only reason I'd put you in ahead of the others is as a favor to Mike, and your grampa."

"She appreciates that very much," Cliff said, taking Meg by the arm and leading her out.

After waving a fond farewell to Mr. Casey, Meg dropped onto a bench. "He won't be here next Thursday."

"Of course not." Cliff hesitated, then ventured to take a seat next to her. "He'll be here when he's damned good and ready. The more you complain, the longer it will be."

"Dan wouldn't agree with that." A giant yawn interrupted her.

"Dan didn't complain. He screamed. And threatened."

"Sounds good to me."

"Maybe. It's not my style. Now just a minute," he added quickly, edging away from her as she fixed him with a frigid stare. "Today doesn't count. I already apologized for that. Mary doesn't seem to remember what—"

"For Christ's sake, Cliff, you didn't ask her about that damned ring, did you? You promised!"

"I didn't say anything to upset her. She asked *me* what happened. She doesn't remember a thing."

Meg planted her elbows on her knees and rested

her aching head on her hands. "All right. I don't want to talk about it, Cliff. I'm too tired."

"Why don't you hit the sack?"

"I can't, not yet. I've got to shower and change and go to see Gran. Oh, hell. I left my car at the store."

"I'll drive you."

"All right." Meg pulled herself to her feet. "I have a lot to say to you, Cliff, but I'm too far gone to say it now. I feel as if I were covered in cobwebs like an Egyptian mummy."

Cliff trailed along behind her, hands in his pockets. "We could get started on the cottage before Casey comes. There's a lot of cleaning and clearing that could be done by unskilled labor."

"Like you?"

She had meant it as a joke, and was taken by surprise when Cliff said readily, "Like me. And Dennis, and anybody we can hire on a temporary basis. I don't suppose you want to keep the furniture. . . ."

"God, no." Meg shivered. "It'll have to be hauled to the dump. There's nothing worth saving."

"So why pay Casey's crew two hundred an hour to do it? I'll find a couple of guys, and we'll clean the place out, cut down the weeds and so on."

"But, Cliff—"

"I'd like to do it."

"Would you?" She stopped and turned to face him, softened, against her better judgment, by his effort to please her. "It's a good idea, and I'll follow through on it, but you don't have to be involved. I could see how painful it was for you to be there."

"Painful? Why should it be, when the few memories I have are happy ones? For a minute I felt like Rip Van Winkle, losing twenty years in one night's sleep, but that's over and done with. I really want to do it, Meg." He straightened, and smiled at her with all his old insouciance. "It'll keep me busy and out of your hair. If that isn't a compelling argument I don't know what is."

"Sold," Meg said, smiling back at him.

When they went on, he walked beside her.

Cliff was as good as his word. When Meg came down to breakfast, after ten solid hours' sleep, he was already at the table, shoveling down food as if he didn't expect to eat again for weeks. He was wearing faded jeans and a shirt that had seen better days, but somehow, despite the wrinkles, he managed to look like a model for a beer or cigarette advertisement—manly, sexy and perfectly groomed.

"Excuse me for not waiting," he greeted her. "Got to run, my crew's coming at eight."

Punctilious as always, George put down his newspaper and held a chair for Meg. He still looked tired, his eyes darkly circled, but he had raised no objection the night before when the plans for the cottage had been discussed.

Meg thanked him with a smile and looked at

Cliff. "You've got a crew already? How did you accomplish that?"

Cliff's mouth was full. His father said dryly, "Clifford's social, professional and business contacts in Seldon are centered in the same place—that roadhouse on Route Four. If you picked up your crew there, Clifford, I suggest you frisk them before you let them onto the grounds."

"You've got the wrong impression of the Golden Calf," Cliff said breezily. He was in such a good mood that his father's inevitable criticism didn't seem to bother him. "I'll bet you've never even been in the place."

"No, and I don't intend to."

"You know what your trouble is, Dad? You're an effete intellectual snob." Cliff tipped his head back to get the last drops of coffee from his cup, and jumped to his feet. "Don't worry about my crew, Meg; they're good dudes. See you later."

Meg had never visited the Golden Calf either, but she had heard about it; it was one of the places the local cops staked out on Saturday nights, when they needed to fill their quota of DWI arrests. A popular hangout for what her grandmother would call "the rougher element," it was probably harmless enough—but if that was where Cliff picked up gossip, it was not surprising that he was up-to-date on the ripest of Seldon scandal. She wished he hadn't been in such a hurry to leave. She hadn't expected he would act so promptly, and she would have preferred to discuss their plans in more detail.

However, considering the state the cottage was in, there was little chance that even an unskilled crew could do much damage, and she didn't want to worry her uncle by expressing her nebulous reservations. "Go ahead and read your paper," she said, seeing he was casting sidelong glances at the folded page beside him. "You don't have to make conversation."

"That's all right, I've finished. Did you call the hospital?"

"Mmm-hmmm. The doctor hadn't been in yet, but she had a good night."

"She's an amazing woman," George said fondly. "I thought she was looking much better last night, didn't you?"

"She looked wonderful. Having Frances with her seems to perk her up."

George lowered his voice to a conspiratorial whisper. "Having Frances out of the house perks me up. Have you noticed how smoothly things run without her? I wish we could persuade her to retire. Annie is managing very nicely."

"Frances will never leave Gran. Not that I don't agree with you, Uncle George. Why do you think I'm so anxious. . . ." She stopped, reaching for the coffeepot to cover her confusion. Despite George's apparent indifference to her plans for the cottage she still didn't feel comfortable discussing the subject with him.

"You've definitely made up your mind, then," George said.

"Yes. It disheartened me to see how much work

needs to be done, but it will take less time than building a new structure. I want to be close to Gran."

"What about the store? Darren tells me probate is proceeding on schedule and before long you'll have to make up your mind what to do about Mr. Riley."

"I have made up my mind. I'm not going to sell, and if Riley wants to stay he's welcome to. That decision isn't irrevocable; if the partnership doesn't work, we can find a way out. But I'm going to give it my best shot, and I think he means to do the same."

"I see. You're becoming . . . fond of him, aren't you?"

The word was innocuous enough; a casual, amused rejoinder was on Meg's lips when to her horror she felt her cheeks grow hot and realized she had not, after all, forgotten how to blush.

"I see," George said again, in quite a different voice.

"No, you don't. I'm not sixteen years old, and I'm not . . . I've never. . . ." She stammered to a stop. "I'm not *fond* of Riley. It would be like being fond of a—a tornado. He's too talented to lose, he's worth any effort and he . . . well, I just don't believe he's the sort of person who would try to frighten and harass people."

Oh, great, she thought in disgust. First you blush, then you babble and finally you fall back on good old feminine intuition. Next you'll be spray-painting his initials on walls.

"I hope you're right," her uncle said. "The least I can do is trust your judgment; Dan would be proud of you, my dear, taking charge the way you've done."

After he had excused himself and gone, Meg lingered over her second cup of coffee. She was trying to take charge of her life, but every time she got a grip on something it slipped through her fingers—or was pulled. How much did being a woman have to do with the failure of others to trust her? The answer was obvious; it had everything to do with it. Mike, George, Cliff, Darren—none of them would have dared to treat Dan that way. Even when he was nearing ninety he'd have blasted them out of the water if they had tried to protect him or condescend to him.

Meg's lips set. She couldn't change her sex, nor did she wish to; she'd simply have to show them that a woman could yell as loud and accomplish as much as a tough old man.

The cottage seemed like a good place to start. Cliff meant well, no doubt—they all meant well, damn them—but she intended to make it clear that he was the foreman, not the boss. She was the boss.

It didn't surprise her to find Dennis, Cliff and two other men sprawled on the porch steps eating doughnuts and drinking coffee instead of working. What did surprise her was the fact that one of the newcomers was Debbie's husband. She recognized him instantly, despite the puffiness of a face that had once been voted handsomest in the class.

As he and the others scrambled to their feet, Meg saw that he was still massively built, though the muscle was softened by sagging flesh. The used-car business must not be going well, if Tom was willing to accept a temporary job doing manual labor. It was nice of Cliff to give an old friend a helping hand—but if Tom and Debbie were so hard up, what was he doing hanging around the Golden Calf?

Tom greeted her with a mixture of embarrassment and swagger. Crisply she explained what she wanted done. Cliff kept grinning like a clown; he knew quite well why she had come,and he paid her a deference that verged on caricature. The others took her seriously, or seemed to; when she left, they were starting work.

On her way to the store Meg saw a wizened, malevolent face peering out from behind the roses that bedecked Mrs. Henderson's porch, but this morning the old lady didn't hail her. Chalk up another point for rudeness, Meg thought smugly. And now for Riley. Had Dan yelled at him, and bullied him into submission? No matter; what had worked for Dan wouldn't work for her. Not in this case.

She had no opportunity to speak privately with Riley that morning. The tourist season was in full bloom and the fine weather brought customers out in droves. At one point there were so many people in the store Riley actually emerged to help out—the risk of shoplifting was directly related to the proportion of customers to clerks—but after a motherly woman cooed over his bandaged brow and asked a series of sympathetic questions, he retired in haste and did not reappear.

Between the customers, the telephone and the mail, Meg managed to examine the folder Riley had put on her desk. It contained the receipts and records of the transactions between Dan and Mrs. Mercer.

The records included color photographs and detailed descriptions of the jewelry Dan had sold Mrs. Mercer. Sorting through them, Meg fought a mounting sense of inadequacy. How much could she afford to pay for such pieces and still hope to make a profit when she resold them? Which pieces should be kept intact and which ones should be broken up? That would have to be taken into account when she made her bid. . . . Her lips curled in a humorless smile as she came to a photograph of an ornate necklace whose central stone was a magnificent emerald. She suspected this wasn't the first time that emerald had passed through the hands of Daniel Mignot.

She was still staring at the photograph when the chimes sounded; laying it aside, she went into the store. Her fixed professional smile faded when she saw her courtesy cousin bending over the counter, apparently intent on a display of pearls.

"I thought you were supposed to be working."

Cliff gave her a seraphic smile. He had changed into tan slacks so crisp they might never have been worn before and a short-sleeved shirt in a shade of blue that made him look as innocent as a young saint. "Lunch break. How about joining me?"

Mindful of the intercom and the possibility of being caught by a customer in the middle of a tantrum, Meg confined herself to a shake of the head, though her frown would have daunted anyone less certain of his charm than Cliff. "Riley, too," he said cheerfully. "We'll bury the hatchet in a loaf of Kate's fresh-baked sourdough."

Meg wished—how she wished!—that she could believe in his sincerity. While she was debating what to say, the shop door opened and Riley came out. Meg groaned silently. Cliff knew about the intercom; he had also known Riley's masculine pride wouldn't allow him to skulk in the back after such a challenge.

He was stiffly civil, but he refused Cliff's invitation. "We're pretty busy today. You two go ahead."

"If you say so. Hey—no hard feelings?" Cliff approached him as if to shake hands, then looked in surprise at the parcel he was holding. "Forgot about this. I brought it to show Meg. How about this for nostalgia, coz?"

From a bag that had once held doughnuts he extracted an object and put it on the counter, along with a shower of dirt that wrung a cry of disgust from Meg. "I just polished the glass! What is that revolting thing?"

Cliff stood back, grinning, as she edged closer. The ragged bundle was so coated with filth, she could not identify it until she saw a dim gleam of reflected light and realized it was an eye, staring at her with melancholy reproach. "Oh, my God," she exclaimed. "It can't be—it is—it's Pooh! My poor darling Pooh—where have you been all these years?"

"Under the floorboards in my former room," Cliff said. "I found him this morning." Turning to Riley, he explained, "She used to sleep with him. When he disappeared she carried on like a juvenile Medea; the whole family searched the house and grounds for days."

"Under the floor. . . ." Meg's voice rose. "You stole him! You son of a bitch!"

Cliff's eyes widened. "I was a seven-year-old son of a bitch. Jesus, Meg, I didn't know you'd get so upset. I thought it was kind of funny."

"Kind of funny? Oh, God—I remember now, I cried for a week. Look at him—poor old bear, rotting away in the dark all this time. . . ."

Cliff caught her hand as she reached for the toy. "Don't touch it, it's crawling with germs. I swear, I'd forgotten all about that secret hiding place of mine until this morning. I was checking the floors upstairs, and one of the boards was loose. . . ."

Riley cleared his throat. He was staring at them as if he thought they had both lost their minds. No wonder, Meg thought; they made quite a picture, holding hands over the decayed body of a stuffed bear. Cliff's voice was unsteady and her eyes had filled with tears.

"Let's give him a decent burial," Riley said. He went into the office and came back with a cardboard carton. After glancing at Meg, he took a handful of tissue paper from under the counter and lined the box. Meg freed her hand and brushed at the tears trickling down her cheeks. "Excuse me," she said in a stifled voice.

When she came back from the washroom, the body was encoffined, and Cliff was tying a red ribbon around the box, looking as sober as if he were preparing to conduct the funeral of a friend. Riley's expression indicated that he thought the red ribbon was a touch too much.

"Sorry about that," Meg said. "You were right, Cliff; it is funny—now. I got lost in time for a while."

"Yeah." Cliff finished the elaborate bow. "It happens, doesn't it?"

Dismissing the incident, Meg asked, "What kind of shape is the second floor in?"

"Not bad at all, compared to the downstairs. We're making progress," Cliff added. "I think you'll be pleased when you see it, Meg. This afternoon I want to get rid of the rest of the furniture. Actually, I had an ulterior motive in asking you to lunch, Riley; I was hoping we could borrow your pickup. Tom's radiator sprang a leak this morning and nobody else has one to rent on such short notice."

Riley hesitated.

"Just for the afternoon," Cliff urged. "I'll bring it back by five."

"Okay." Riley fished in his pocket and handed over a set of keys.

"Thanks, I really appreciate it. Sure I can't talk you into joining us?"

As she and Cliff left the store, Meg said, "I don't know how you do it."

"Do what?"

"Get your own way without appearing to do so. You didn't want Riley to join us. I didn't intend to have lunch with you. He's back there, and I'm here, and I'll be damned if I can figure out why."

"It's my overpowering charm and sincerity." He took her arm to guide her across the street.

This time the old gang consisted of Mike and Ed, and the topic of conversation immediately became technical as the two questioned Cliff about the work on the cottage. Meg had long since stopped wondering how the news spread so rapidly; she listened with a smile while Ed spouted misinformation and Mike placidly corrected him. "No, Ed, that little rider mower of yours won't make a dent in them weeds. Anyhow, Dan's got two or three of the things. You'd be better off using a scythe, Cliff, the good Lord only knows what's lying hid that could wreck a piece of machinery."

"The gate's my worst problem," Cliff said. "I cut the chain off, but the lock's rusted solid."

Ed's eyes lit up. "Sulfuric acid—"

Kate materialized in a cloud of steam from the kitchen, like a genie in a chef's hat. "Ed, you damn fool, you don't know your ass from your elbow when it comes to that kind of thing. Sulfuric acid! Next thing you'll be suggesting dynamite."

Cliff shoveled the last of his pie into his mouth, stood up, set Kate's hat straight, kissed her on the ear and announced, "Back to work. Put it on my tab, Kate. And for God's sake, get a new hat."

Mike got up. "Hold on a second, Cliff. If you'll come by the store I'll sell you something should take care of that rust."

After they had gone, Kate dashed back into the kitchen and reappeared with two pieces of pie, which she slapped down in front of Meg and Ed. "Strawberry-rhubarb. Made it myself. New recipe. Tell me what you think."

Meg took a bite. "Mmmm. It's wonderful." Ed, his mouth stuffed, nodded in enthusiastic agreement. Kate planted her elbows on the table. "So what's this about the cottage?"

Meg explained, though she suspected she was not telling Kate anything she didn't already know. At least Kate didn't give her any guff about ghosts. "Good idea. Always hated to think of that place falling apart. It was such a pretty little house."

"I thought you'd be out looking for property for me, like the others," Meg said.

Kate gave Ed a look of disgust. "I told 'em that was stupid. You already own half the town—or you will, when your gramma passes on."

"That won't be for a long time."

"It's all in the hands of the Lord," said Ed. "He giveth and he taketh away—"

"He isn't gonna take Mary Mignot till she's damn good and ready to go," Kate said. "That sweet-little-lady act of hers fools all you men, but underneath she's tough as nails."

"Do you really think so, Kate? I've been worried about her."

"They say at the hospital she's doing just fine, honey."

"Physically, yes. It's not her heart. . . . I mean, that's a concern, of course, but she's also been saying some of the most peculiar things—"

"She misses Dan something terrible," Ed said, shaking his head mournfully. "And she knows he's waiting for her on the other side. That there ring must've been one he gave her—ow!"

He looked reproachfully at Kate. "Just stop that dismal talk," she ordered. "I swear to God, there's nobody so depressing to be around as you religious types. Don't you give Meg any more of that crap about the other side, you hear? And Meg, you quit worrying. There's nothing wrong with your gramma's mind. Bet you never heard her say anything sillier than what just came out of Ed's big mouth."

"I'd better get back to the store," Meg said quickly. "Riley's alone."

"You haven't found anybody yet?" Kate asked.

"Not yet. There's a woman we might hire; I've got to call her and set up an interview."

"Hold on a minute. . . ." Kate vanished into the kitchen.

"Don't run off," Ed said, looking at her with round, sad eyes. "I didn't mean to make you feel bad, Meg; seemed to me it should be a comfort to you, knowing your gramma was safe in the hands of Jesus."

Meg patted his plump pink hand. "You didn't make me feel bad, Ed."

The swinging doors parted and Kate came out with a parcel that she thrust at Meg. "Take some pie to Riley. That boy never eats right."

"You knew, didn't you?" Meg said. "All of you knew about his injury. Why didn't you tell me?"

"He gets real mad when you tell people," Ed said innocently. "I don't want him mad at me. They said he knocked Tom Gentry clean across the bar at the Golden Calf the night after—ow!"

"Never mind, Kate," Meg said with a smile. "It's no news to me that Riley is at odds with half the husbands in town. I'm sure he'll appreciate the pie."

If I don't ram it down his throat, paper and all, she thought as she headed for the door.

The man must have some good qualities, though—aside from the ones that had made her a victim, along with Candy, Debbie and God only knew how many others. Meg made a sour face; it stung her pride to put herself in the same category as those two. Well, anyhow, Mike and Ed liked him, and they weren't susceptible to sex appeal. And Ed's casual suggestion about the fede ring made as much sense as any other theory. The ring might well have been one Dan had given his wife to commemorate some private anniversary or moment of tenderness. Compared to his other magnificent gifts it appeared insignificant, but it might have a special meaning to Mary.

Meg arrived at the store in time to rescue Riley from a customer who was berating him because her locket wasn't ready. A few well-chosen references to the recent tragedy reduced Mrs. Flockey to silence, if not apologies; Riley promised to have the locket ready in an hour, and the woman grumbled her way out.

"It wasn't supposed to be finished till Thursday," Riley said after the door had closed.

"She's an unreasonable old bitch," Meg said. "Dan was always complaining about her. Here."

"What's this?" Riley eyed the package suspiciously. It was oozing red juice; Meg had unconsciously vented on the gift some of her frustration with the recipient.

"Strawberry-rhubarb pie. Kate sent it."

"Oh. Thanks. I guess I'd better get to work on that locket."

"Riley. . . ."

"Yes?" The juice had stained his fingers. Without warning or conscious intent, Meg pictured her lips and tongue tasting the sweetness of the syrup and the texture of his skin. She turned scarlet. Riley couldn't have known what she was thinking, but neither could he mistake the change in her expression. His lips parted. Meg didn't hear what he said; something odd seemed to have happened to her hearing.

She heard the telephone, though. It was practically at her elbow, and it shrilled like a siren.

Riley turned and headed for the shop, clutching his pie. Meg took a deep breath, picked up the phone and dealt, not too coherently, with a woman who was interested in selling her mother's jewelry and who insisted on describing it, rhinestone by rhinestone.

I've got to stop this, she thought, as the dreary catalog of costume jewelry droned on. It's ridiculous. I haven't blushed since I was fourteen. What's the matter with me? I never felt like this about Nick. . . .

A flurry of customers and telephone calls kept her busy for a while and gave her time to regain her composure. She placed a call to their prospective clerk and set up a time for an interview, wiped strawberry juice and moldy sawdust off the counter and searched, vainly, for the box containing the bear's remains. Riley must have taken it into the shop. Sparing her tender feelings, no doubt. What an ass she had made of herself over that stuffed toy. But no more of an ass than she had made of herself in another, more demoralizing way.

The telephone rang again. When she heard the voice on the other end she was suddenly, coldly herself again. He identified himself only by name, as she had requested, and asked if she wanted to call him back.

"Yes—I mean, no," Meg said, glancing at the closed door at the back of the store. If she watched what she said, there was no way Riley could tell to whom she was speaking. "Go ahead."

He didn't explain how he had gotten the information so quickly. Meg didn't have to ask; she knew only too well that computer technology had made private records an oxymoron. Legally or illegally, there were ways of tapping into almost every system, from credit ratings to FBI files.

The early records were scanty. There wasn't much one could say about a child, after all—birth date, place of birth, school attendance. Meg listened impatiently, her fingernails tapping a soft tattoo on the glass of the counter. She was beginning to wonder why she had asked the detective to go so far back in time. Mrs. Riley had been only twelve years old when Dan returned from the war, only twenty when she married.

Her husband was ten years older than she. British-born, he had come to the States in 1948 after serving. . . .

Meg straightened. "What? Say that again."

He repeated the information. "Is that what you wanted? Shall I go on?"

"Yes. . . . No, never mind. I'll have to . . . I'll have to let you know. Later."

She had a feeling she wouldn't need the firm's services any longer. They had found the connection between Dan and Riley, though it wasn't the one Meg had expected. Not his mother; his father, who had served in the Burma-India theater during World War II. The words she had spoken to George came back to her with damning force. 'Suppose he pulled a swindle of some kind. Isn't it possible that one of the other people involved in the deal still holds a grudge?"

Or had passed it on—to his son.

17

WAS THIS ONE of the pieces of information Darren had chosen not to pass on? Meg would have been delighted to find another omission for which to blame him. He had not known about the jewelry, but if he had an ounce of imagination he ought to have realized that the relationship between the families might be based on a friendship that had been forged in the fires of war, instead of being so quick to cast aspersions on Dan and an innocent woman.

Darren didn't have an ounce of imagination. That was one of his problems.

Meg pressed her hands to her head. If she accused Darren of leaping to conclusions he would politely point out that the original relationship between Dan and Riley Senior didn't eliminate the possibility of a later, stronger relationship between Dan and Mrs. Riley. In fact, it would explain how he happened to meet her. Thank God she hadn't told Darren about the jewelry; he would dive on that like an owl on a mouse. It was a much stronger motive for harassment than some hypothetical psychosis.

Meg's eyes went to the clock. It was getting late—but not late enough to offer an excuse fo further delay. She was torn between a cowardly fear of confronting Riley, and an equally pervasive need to know the truth. She stood biting her lip in a frenzy of indecision until something quite outside herself took control of her limbs and moved her toward the back of the store.

"Riley. I need to talk to you."

"Come on in, then."

The door wasn't locked. He was sitting at the workbench, his back to her. Without turning, he said, "If it's Mrs. Flockey, tell her I'll be finished with this in a minute."

"It's not Mrs. Flockey."

To Meg her voice sounded perfectly normal, but Riley dropped the locket and spun around. "What's the matter? Is your grandmother—"

"No." Meg took a deep breath. "Your father and Dan were both in India in World War Two."

"That's right." His eyes narrowed. "Didn't you know?"

"Which one of them swindled the prince out of his jewelry? Or did they just steal it?"

Every muscle in his face stiffened, freezing mouth and eyes into parallel slits. "You didn't know," he said softly. "He didn't tell you a damn thing, did he?"

He got up and started toward her. Meg shrank back, but despite his bad leg he was too quick for her. Reaching around her, he caught hold of the door and slammed it. "Sit down," he ordered, nodding toward the chair he had vacated.

"I don't want—"

"Sit down. Please."

The "please," hurled at her as an afterthought didn't move her so much as her awareness tha she had very little choice. She had never been sc conscious of the fact that the room was as secur as any prison cell—windowless, banded in metal bolted and barred except for the single doo blocked by Riley's body. She edged toward th chair, never taking her eyes off him, and sat down

"You found the jewelry," Riley said.

Meg nodded.

"He must have told you where it came from Otherwise—"

"I figured it out," Meg said. She met his eye defiantly. "I searched your desk one day whe you weren't here."

"Ah." He looked—pleased? It hardly seeme likely, unless her admission had confirmed hi suspicions. "You recognized the sketch and re alized it came from a book. . . . Smart work." H leaned back against the door, his arms folded "Must have come as quite a shock to you, findin that hoard. I suppose you went running to te your uncle and your lawyer all about it."

"I suppose I did."

"And neither of them. . . . But they wouldn' know either, would they? If Dan didn't te you. . . ."

He raised his eyebrows inquiringly, but Me remained stubbornly silent. "All right," Riley sai after a moment. "It was my old man who foun the stuff."

"Found it?" Meg repeated ironically.

"That was how he described it. He was among the British troops who retreated to India when the Japs took the Burma Road in early 1942. The Brits began organizing a Burmese resistance movement not long afterwards; my father was one of the people who went back and forth between India and the Karen tribesmen who were fighting the invaders. A couple of years later, in '44. . . . Am I boring you?"

Meg gave herself a little shake. She felt dazed by the sudden switch from melodrama to pedantry. "I don't want a history lecture," she snapped. "Get to the point."

"As you like. It was while he was scrounging around the countryside with one of these guerrilla groups that he ran across a guy who claimed to have escaped from Karenni, which is . . . Okay, okay; no history, no geography. Dad said he saved this guy's life, risking, of course, his own in the process. The guy had been wounded, though, and they had no medical facilities; when gangrene set in, and the man realized he wasn't going to make it, he told Dad where he had hidden the treasure. His version was that he had been a court official, and that the prince had entrusted him with the family jewels when the Japanese came their way. He managed to get out, disguised as a beggar, but the whole royal family was massacred."

He paused, waiting with tilted eyebrows for her response. "How sad," Meg said. "And how very convenient."

"Yeah. Dad thought the guy was raving, but he figured it was worth a look. Imagine how surprised and touched he was when he found the loot. He managed, with considerable difficulty, to get it back to India, where he showed it to Dan. They had gotten acquainted because of their mutual interest in gemstones. My grandfather was a gem setter—not a very good one, but Dad grew up around precious stones and knew enough to tell a zircon from a diamond, if not much more.

"I never did know the exact details of the dea they made," Riley went on. "Dad was vague about that; he could invent all the lies he wanted about the rest of it, there was no one alive who could contradict his story; but it was a little hard to explain why he didn't turn the treasure over to the British authorities until the legitimate heirs, if any, could be located. It's a reasonable assumption, however, that Dan took full advantage of my old man's dubious legal position. How much of the help Dan gave him in later years was due to Dan's conscience, and how much to some discreet blackmail from Dad, I don't know; but Dan sponsored him when he came over here and found various jobs for him—and subsidized him after he started hitting the bottle.

"You have to understand—I didn't know anything about this until shortly before my father died, and I didn't think much about it then—figured it was just another one of his boozy fantasies. After the funeral Dan took me aside and offered—no, he *told* me he was sending me to college. I'd only met Dan a few times, and I didn't know Dad had shown him some of my sketches; but I wasn't having any of that college crap or anything to do with the jewelry business. I told Dan to take his offer and stuff it, and a few months later I got drafted, so that took care of that. After . . . after I got back from 'Nam. . . . Well, never mind. Dan finally tracked me down and that time I was in a more receptive mood. I'd been working for him for almost a year before he showed me the jewelry and told me his version of how he acquired it. It never occurred to me that you didn't know."

He had moved from the door to the desk as he talked; now he sat on the corner of it, absently rubbing his leg.

"No wonder you hated him," Meg said.

"Hated Dan? Why—"

She cut him short. "Did I hear the chimes?"

"I didn't hear anything."

Meg ran to the door and looked out. "I don't see anyone. Riley, for God's sake tell me the truth. I can understand why you'd resent Dan. He robbed your father. That's what it amounted to. He became rich and successful, in large part because of what he stole—"

"Hey, wait a minute." Riley got to his feet, his eyes a brilliant topaz brown, "You've got it all wrong. My father was the one who. . . . I've wondered for years whether he murdered that poor devil to get the jewels. Why in God's name should

I resent Dan? He probably saved my life. I loved the sneaky old bastard!"

She had never seen his face so unguarded—the barriers lowered, not for her, but for Dan. "I loved him too," she said in a choked voice. "Damn him."

"Hey! Anybody home?" The voice shattered the silence. It came from the intercom. Meg started. "That's Cliff. It must be. . . ."

"Five o'clock and all's well," Cliff called. "What's going on? Here I come, ready or not."

Meg wrenched the door open and found herself nose-to-nose with her cousin. "Ah, there you are," Cliff said. "Am I interrupting something?"

"I didn't hear you come in," Meg said.

"No? You must have been absorbed in . . . conversation." Cliff peered over her shoulder, his eyes bright with curiosity. Meg stood firm; for reasons she could not precisely define, she didn't want Cliff in the shop. Cliff waved at Riley. "Hi, there. I brought your truck back."

"Thanks," Riley said shortly. He came forward to take the keys.

"Thank you. You know, you shouldn't huddle back here and leave the store unwatched. Lucky for you I'm so honest; I could have robbed you blind."

How much had he overheard? Meg decided to ignore his comment; the verb might have been used innocently.

"I had no idea it was so late," she said.

"Time does fly when one is having fun. Can I

bum a ride home, coz? Unless you were planning to work late."

Meg didn't find his heavy-handed innuendos embarrassing, only tiresome. Before she could compose a proper put-down the shop door opened, and the tight little group in the doorway dissolved. Riley turned to the workbench and Meg advanced to placate Mrs. Flockey, closing the door firmly behind her.

It took Riley more than a minute, but less than two, to finish the job; when he came out Meg was looking at pictures of Mrs. Flockey's grandchildren and mentally kicking herself for choosing that method of distraction. Mrs. Flockey refused to take possession of the locket until all three of them had admired every snapshot. Cliff entered into the game with enthusiasm; anyone other than a doting grandmother would have noticed he was overdoing it, for the children were conspicuously homely. Sated at last, Mrs. Flockey collected her snapshots, inspected her locket, paid her bill and waddled out.

Cliff was the first to speak. "All that for twelve-fifty? She kept you half an hour overtime, and then had the gall to complain about the price."

"If you hadn't cooed over those grisly grandchildren of hers she wouldn't have stayed so long," Meg said.

"For all I knew she was planning to buy a diamond necklace." Cliff flipped the sign over, from "Open" to "Closed." "Ready, Meg?"

"I . . . yes, I guess so." Cliff was obviously

prepared to hang around until she was ready. Perhaps it was just as well; she needed time to think over what Riley had told her, away from the distraction of his presence. If he ever looked at her —for her—the way he had looked when he spoke of Dan, she wouldn't be able to think at all.

"Go ahead," Riley said. "I'll lock up."

"Thanks. I'll be in early."

It was as close as she dared come to a request that they continue their interrupted discussion. She couldn't even give him a meaningful look; Cliff was watching her with the bright-eyed interest of a squirrel (or some other rodent) and to turn her back on him would only pique his curiosity.

Riley was slow to reply. "Yeah," he said at last. "That would be a good idea. We could finish the—the inventory before we open up."

Cliff gave a snort of laughter and Meg turned on him, knowing she would blow up if he made another of his stupid jokes. At least Riley had gotten the point. "Come on, Cliff. Let's go."

As they walked to her car Cliff said, "Congratulations. You seem to be taming the lion."

"What makes you think so?"

"Hey, don't go defensive on me. All I meant was that he seems less prickly. You were right and I was wrong, and I'm man enough to admit it. Didn't you notice that I've adopted your method?"

"You're spreading the honey a little too thick," Meg said.

"We'll see. Want me to drive?"

"No."

Cliff didn't argue; he got into the passenger seat and let himself slump. "I'm beat. We put in a hard day's work this afternoon. Have you asked Riley about the rings?"

Meg's foot hit the brake harder than she intended. "Fasten your seat belt. No, I haven't asked him."

"Look, I'm willing to admit that he may not be responsible for the other incidents. But the rings point directly to Riley. It could be that we've misinterpreted his meaning—that we're condemning him without giving him a chance to defend himself."

"It could be. What's come over you, Cliff? You're awfully tolerant and high-minded all of a sudden."

"Seems out of character, does it?" Cliff smiled lazily. "I'm a much more complex person than you realize, coz. The truth is, I've been talking to some of the guys about Riley—"

"The good old boys at the Golden Calf, you mean?"

"What other guys are there? Turns out there is a certain diversity of opinion. He even has a few defenders. They say he's surly and unsociable—though not, I admit, in those words—but they don't know anything to his discredit."

"Some defenders," Meg murmured. She signaled for a turn and swung into the driveway.

"The ones who dislike him have personal reasons for doing so," Cliff went on. "Like our buddy Tom. He made some crack about Debbie hanging around the store all the time, and Riley took offense. My informants agreed that Tom had no business insulting his wife in public, and that Riley had every right to punch him out. He—Riley—said she was only looking for a job and a few kind words."

"Riley hangs out at the Golden Calf?" Meg asked. His explanation could be the simple truth, she supposed. Or was that wishful thinking?

"He never was one of the regulars, just dropped in occasionally. He hasn't been back since he decked Tom."

Darren hadn't mentioned the guys at the Golden Calf. Was that because some of them had a kind word for Riley, or because Darren wouldn't have been caught dead in such a place?

Meg brought the car to a stop. "I'll never understand men," she said. "Hearing that story seems to have changed your opinion of Riley, and yet you went ahead and hired Tom."

"What does that have to do with it? He's a good worker, and he needs the job."

Meg shook her head. "Men."

"You don't have to understand us; just adore, admire and respect us." Cliff reached for her. She eluded his hands and got out of the car. Cliff followed suit, grinning his infuriating grin. "Come on back and inspect the work, why don't you?"

"Well—maybe I will." Meg glanced at her watch. By tacit consent the tea ritual had been abandoned while Mary was in the hospital. It wouldn't have been the same without her. In fact, Meg thought regretfully, the charming old custom had no place in the modern world; people were too conscious of calories and cholesterol to indulge in an extra meal.

Cliff expanded at length about his arduous labors as they walked toward the cottage. "Getting that back gate open was one hell of a job. It will have to be replaced; the lock was rusted solid, and both hinges had broken. At least Casey can get his equipment in that way, which will save wear and tear on the landscaping. Oh, and you'd better have a talk with Jeb McComber, he's pissed because you co-opted Dennis without asking him first. He's been in charge of the outdoor staff so long he thinks he owns the place."

"I knew I should have consulted him," Meg admitted. "I just wasn't in the mood for an argument. Gran has a battle with him every year when they discuss the planting schedule. She says he has a fixation on foxglove. He. . . . Why, Cliff! You really did get a lot done today."

From where she stood at the gate the cottage was still hidden by trees and overgrown shrubbery, but a wide swath had been cut through the weeds, exposing the remains of a graveled drive. The difference was as much psychological as physical; it exposed the once isolated house, opened it to the present day. As they approached, Meg heard voices. "Who's there?" she asked.

"The guys were still working when I left. I thought they'd have gone by now, but I guess. . . ."

The other workers had gone, leaving only Tom, but he was not alone. The truck parked by the side of the cottage was not a heavy-duty pickup, but a sleek little Camaro. Meg didn't recognize it, but there was no mistaking the identity of the man who was hastily getting into the driver's seat. Rod Applegate. Tom stood by the open door on the passenger side, waiting for the third person to get in. The third person was Candy.

Tom had followed Candy into the truck and closed the door by the time Meg reached it. "What are you doing here?" she demanded, confronting Rod.

He hadn't quite the nerve to start the engine and drive off. His hand dropped from the keys. "Hello, Meg. How've you been?"

"I asked you what you're doing here."

Candy leaned across her ex-husband and glared at Meg. "No call to be rude, is there? We came out to get Tom. His truck's in the shop."

She was dressed as if for a party, in a low-cut blouse whose neckline bared bony shoulders and a patch of reddened skin at the base of her throat. Her lipstick had been applied with a lavish hand; it glistened like fresh paint and some of it had transferred to her teeth, which she bared at Meg in what might have been meant as a smile.

"Yeah, that's right," Rod mumbled. "Came to get Tom. Well—see you around." The engine roared as he applied a heavy foot to the gas.

The truck bounced forward and disappeared behind the cottage, following the now-open route toward the back road. Meg turned to Cliff.

"I want a barricade across that gate," she said.

Cliff shrugged. "I guess I could rig something. Not much sense in it, though; there's nothing here worth stealing."

He walked toward the house. Meg started to follow, and then saw something she had failed to notice in her concentration on the intruders. Her soft cry of distress brought Cliff back to her side. "What's the matter?"

"The rose. Why did you cut it down?"

The leaves had already begun to wilt. Amid the tangle of stems, dying blossoms lay like rusty bloodstains.

"What rose? Oh—that. We chopped down all the vines, the woodwork underneath had rotted. It wasn't worth saving, Meg, it had gone wild."

He was right on both counts. The rose would have had to go. The demise of a flower was a minor loss, in comparison to the others the cottage had suffered. I'm just in a sour mood because of that bitch Candy, Meg thought, climbing the porch steps. They didn't have to come for Tom, he could have gotten a ride home with the other man. It was just an excuse to pry. I'll bet she went through the whole house. And she and Rod seem to be back together again. They deserve each other.

"Found the keys," Cliff announced, displaying them.

"Where were they? I looked all over."

"Dad had a set. You know him, he never loses track of anything."

There was no need to unlock the front door; it was already open. Cliff ushered her in with obvious pride. "What do you think? Looks a hundred percent better already, doesn't it?"

It did look better; without the furniture the house was just an empty house, not an abandoned home. The floor was inches deep in dead leaves and plaster dust and scraps of paper, but the improvement, if not one hundred percent, was considerable. Meg gave Cliff the praise he deserved, and he expanded visibly. "Come on upstairs. No, it's safe; the steps are solid. This is a well-built house."

Besides the landing there were three bedrooms and two baths on the second floor. Cliff sounded like a realtor with a prospective client as he showed her around. "Lots of closet space, you see. Nice view from this window in the master bedroom. You'll want to install a new bathroom. With sauna and hot tub, naturally."

"I don't know about the sauna." His enthusiasm had infected her, she was beginning to have visions of flowered wallpaper and Victorian draperies. Country Victorian—it would suit the demure look of the cottage. "One of those old claw-footed tubs, and matching fixtures?"

"Not old, it's more trouble than it's worth to have them reporcelained and repaired." Cliff pursed his lips and studied the room thoughtfully. "They make excellent reproductions these days, including the classic john with the overhead tank and pull chain."

He had a lot of good ideas. They were deep in a discussion of lace curtains versus blinds when they heard a voice from below. "Meg? Are you there?"

"It's Uncle George." Meg's voice dropped to a whisper. She and Cliff stared at one another like disobedient children caught in the act. "How did he know. . . ."

"He saw your car, I suppose. Stop looking so guilty, you're infecting me. We haven't done anything. Dad! Hey, Dad, we're up here."

Meg went to the landing. George was at the foot of the stairs, looking up. "Oh, Cliff is with you," he said, smiling. "I was afraid you were here alone, and I was a trifle concerned."

"Come on up," Cliff said.

"No, thanks. I don't trust those stairs."

"We'll come down," Meg said. "The stairs are fine—see?—but we were about to leave anyway. Cliff's been giving me some ideas about decorating. Hasn't he gotten a lot done?"

She was talking too much and too fast, in an attempt to cover her lingering sense of discomfort. George appeared to be more at ease than she.

Glancing into the living room he said, "Yes, he has. I expected it would take more than a day just to get rid of the furniture. This is certainly an improvement."

Meg went to him and slipped her arm through his. "Do you really feel okay about this, Uncle George? You needn't come out here if it brings back unhappy memories."

"I've been here a number of times, honey. Once or twice a year, to check for damage." Glancing at his son, who stood at the foot of the stairs with one hand absently stroking the carved newel post, he added, "Cliff was the one who refused to come near the place. I'm glad he's gotten over that. Once you face things you find they aren't as bad as you thought. Right, son?"

Cliff made a sour face. "Right, Dad. Sometimes they're even worse."

"You volunteered for this, buster," Meg said.

"I wasn't referring to this little job. It's turning out to be rather satisfying. Bringing order out of chaos, so to speak."

"Just be careful," George said anxiously. "There are a lot of potential hazards in a job like this. The wiring must be defective—"

"I'm not stupid enough to mess with the wiring," Cliff answered. "That's a job for Casey and his crowd." His voice softened. "Don't worry, Dad. I know what I'm doing and I don't take chances."

"Of course. Well, are you two ready to go? I

thought we'd have an early dinner so we can go to the hospital."

They followed him out the door, which Cliff carefully locked. Meg teased him, pointing out that the back door had no lock, and reminding him of his promise to put a chain or barricade across the bar gate. "For the psychological effect," she added. "I know there's nothing you could do tonight that would constitute a permanent barrier."

"There's nothing I can do tomorrow or the next day," Cliff said. "I told you, you're going to need a new gate."

"And a new porch and a new kitchen. And a new teddy bear."

Cliff groaned and raised his hand to cover his eyes. "I was hoping you wouldn't bring that up. When's the funeral?"

"I don't get it," George said with a bemused smile. "Is it a private joke?"

Meg explained. She could see the humor of it now. "I called poor Cliff a very vulgar name," she said, laughing.

George didn't laugh. "So that's what happened! I'll never forget that damned bear, we tore the place apart looking for it. I distinctly remember searching your room, Clifford; in spite of your protestations of innocence I suspected you had something to do with the case. What possessed you to do such a thing? And to tear up the floor—"

"Oh, for God's sake!" Hands in his pockets, head down, Cliff kicked furiously at a loose stone.

"All I did was pull out a few nails. It made a perfect hiding place. You always blamed me for everything. She wasn't so perfect, you know."

His voice had risen to a near falsetto—the high-pitched sexless tones of a young boy. "Cliff," Meg said in alarm.

"She used to do things and then I'd get blamed," Cliff whined. He turned his head and gave Meg a broad, mocking smile. "Come on, admit it, coz. Remember the time you dug up all the bulbs McComber planted and let me take the rap?"

"I remember," Meg admitted. "I was searching for treasure, I think. Okay, Cliff, we'll call it square. Neither one of us was a perfect kid. You were a tease and a bully, and I was a smug, spoiled brat. Isn't it amazing we turned out so well?"

She smiled at her uncle, inviting him to join in the cessation of hostilities. His answering smile was perfunctory; the glance he gave his son was more critical than amused. Once again Meg found her sympathies veering toward Cliff. Perhaps he had not lived up to his father's expectations, but a perpetual air of disapproval was no way to encourage a child, or a man, to greater accomplishments.

The same thought seemed to have occurred to George. During dinner, he joined in the discussion about the renovations, commending Cliff's ideas and adding a few of his own. He even made a mild joke about the deceased teddy bear. "Let me know when the services are to be held. Pots of honey in lieu of flowers, I presume?"

After dinner they went straight to the hospital. The room to which Mary had been moved was in reality a luxurious suite, its specifications having been drawn up by Dan when he gave the money for the new hospital wing. He had been characteristically blunt about his motives. "It's for me and my family. I don't give a damn if the President of the United States is in there, if one of us needs a hospital room, you kick him out."

Mary was still being carefully monitored, but the equipment didn't seem so obtrusive amid the flounces and finery. Her own lace-trimmed muslin sheets had been brought from home and she lay against the embroidered pillows like a porcelain doll, her face carefully painted by Frances, her silk bed jacket as elaborate as a wedding gown. A lacy cap covered her hair; the doctor had stood firm and refused her demand for a shampoo and set.

Frances was sitting by the bed reading aloud. She raised her hand in a demand for silence, and went on reading. Gran's eyes were closed; her hands were folded on her flat little stomach. She looked like a particularly elegant effigy on a tombstone by Della Robbia.

Frances's voice was a slow drone, encouraging sleep. It was several seconds before the content of what she was reading struck Meg. "A phosphorescent figure, like a mummy, was growing out of the door in low relief. It drew out and grew slowly, and rounded. . . ."

"Frances!" Meg exclaimed.

Gran's eyes popped open. "Hello, darlings. You must have crept in like little mice. How nice to see you."

"You were asleep," Frances said in an accusing voice. The accusation was directed at Meg, who scowled back at her. "What kind of a bedtime story was that? Ghosts and mummies—"

"Oh, it's a lovely book," Gran said cheerfully. "*The Uninvited*, by Dorothy Macardle. A brother and sister buy an old house on the coast of Cornwall. It is haunted, of course. But I won't tell you any more, you must read it for yourself, and anyway I want to chat with you. That silly old doctor says you can only stay for fifteen minutes."

Meg pulled up a chair. "Does the silly old doctor know Frances is regaling you with horror stories?"

"Oh, darling, it's not a horror story, it has a happy, romantic ending, just the kind I like. Now tell me all about what you've been doing."

It was a little difficult to comply with the request. They had agreed Mary wasn't to know about the work on the cottage; it might not bother her, but there was no point in taking chances. In fact, none of the subjects that really interested Meg were safe topics of conversation. "I've just been working," she said lamely. "Everything is fine."

"Except for Mrs. Flockey." Cliff came to lean

on the back of Meg's chair. "I was in the store this afternoon, Mary, when she came in to pick up some tacky piece of jewelry, and I had to look at five thousand pictures of her grandchildren. They all look like guppies." He made a face to illustrate his point—mouth pursed, eyes popping.

Mary giggled delightedly. "They aren't very attractive children. I'm afraid. They take after their father."

Cliff carried the burden of the conversation, regaling Mary with the tidbits of local gossip she loved. When the nurse put her head in to warn them their time was up, Cliff said teasingly, "I'll tell you the rest of the dirt tomorrow, Mary. There's a rumor running around town that the Bells are splitting up."

"Again? Well, darling, I do appreciate your keeping me up-to-date. Frances is no help at all, she refuses to leave the hospital." She raised her hand to hide a yawn.

"I'll not be leaving this place until you come with me," Frances said. Meg deduced that there was an Irish housekeeper in the current book.

"So sleepy all the time," Gran said peevishly. "I think they are giving me dope, Meg."

"I expect they are, darling." Meg bent to kiss her on the forehead. The lace border of the cap tickled her nose. "You're supposed to rest, you know."

"Mmmm." Her eyelids, crumpled as tissue paper, drooped. "There was something Dan wanted me to tell you. . . ."

"Tell me tomorrow," Meg said. She glanced at Frances, who rolled her eyes and produced her version of a Gaelic shrug.

Amid a chorus of soft good-nights they started toward the door, where the nurse was making gestures. "No, wait." The voice was as faint and chirping as a bird's, but it stopped Meg in her tracks. "I remember," Mary said. "It was about Henrietta. Watch out for Henrietta, he says."

"I'm taking good care of her, Gran. She misses you, but she's fine."

"So irritating." Gran's eyes had closed. "They never tell you things. Even Dan. . . . He means well, but I wish. . . ." The sibilant trailed off into an unmistakable snore. Frances shooed the visitors out.

"How are you holding up, Frances?" George asked solicitously. "You don't have to stay here twenty-four hours a day, you know. We'll find someone to relieve you if you like."

Behind Frances's back Cliff made horrible faces at Meg, who tightened the corners of her mouth to keep from laughing. It was a safe offer, though, as George undoubtedly knew. Frances shook her head.

"Sure an' I'll not be leaving the dear soul to the tender mercies of those nurses. They'd be after thinking she's lost her mind if they heard her talking away to Mr. Dan. I have to admit it gives me a bit of a chill, when I wake up in the night and hear that soft little voice of hers; I swear, there are times when it seems as if I can almost hear him answering her."

The brogue had vanished by the time she finished, and she appeared genuinely troubled. George patted her shoulder. "It's a harmless habit, Frances, and it comforts her. But if it really bothers you—"

"Better me than those nurses," Frances said. "I'll be all right, Mr. George." She smiled bravely.

There was little conversation during the drive home. When they reached the house Meg went directly to her room, refusing Cliff's invitation to join him for a drink at the Golden Calf. As she climbed the stairs she heard him make the same offer to his father, who reacted predictably; Cliff laughed, and the two went off together, presumably to George's study. Their relationship was an odd mixture of resentment and deep affection, but, Meg supposed, not much different from most parent-child relationships. She wondered, wistfully, how it would have been for her and her father. Suddenly she missed him so desperately that her whole body ached with emptiness—missed him not as the doting daddy of a young child, but as the loving, supportive friend he might have become. If he had lived. . . .

What would her father have thought of Riley? A skilled designer himself, he would surely have appreciated Riley's talent. Or would he have been jealous of it? Would he have been able to break through the reserve that protected Riley like a crustacean's shell? Silly, irrelevant questions.

How could she know? Everything would have been different. . . .

A sound from without jerked her back to wakefulness; she had been drooping over the desk, half asleep. It came again, and Meg swore under her breath. Brooding over insoluble problems, she had ignored one that was immediate and imperative—and after being reminded by Gran only a few hours earlier. Henrietta. She hadn't even noticed the cat's absence. Henrietta came and went as she pleased, and she was not particularly pleased with Meg. Now she was outside.

One firm rule of Mary's was that Henrietta should not be allowed out at night. It was an issue on which the two violently disagreed; despite her effete appearance Henrietta was a mighty hunter and as all predators know, the best time to hunt is after dark. Mary disapproved of this custom for two reasons: first because no one appreciated the unsavory trophies Henrietta left on the doorstep and second because at night Henrietta was not only predator but potential prey, to wild dogs foxes and other larger animals.

A louder, more penetrating yowl brought Meg to her feet. That wasn't Henrietta's cry of triumph; it was a challenge, rippling with rage and frustration. Damn the damn cat, she though furiously, already on her way to the door. If anything happens to her, Gran will never forgive me

Searching for a flashlight, she resolutely refused to acknowledge the strange coincidence of Gran' warning. A superstitious person might wonde how Mary—or Dan?—had known Henrietta would be in peril that night.

It was later than she had realized. Everyone seemed to be in bed, or out. Cliff must have gone to the Golden Calf; the alarm had not been switched on and the inner bolts were unfastened. Meg opened the front door and ran out, calling.

At first she didn't need the flashlight, the outside lights blazed and the moon was almost full. Finally she heard a response to her calls. It sounded just as furious, and even farther away, somewhere in the garden. Meg started in that direction. Before long she had to use the flashlight. From the sound, Henrietta appeared to be moving, retreating farther back into the grounds. Stumbling over a stone, Meg swore and hopped, nursing a bruised toe. She should have changed to sneakers instead of the sandals she had worn that day. The bright hunters' moon might have told her Henrietta would be in no mood to be tamely captured.

A rustle in the shrubbery to her left caught her attention, but when she shone the flashlight around she saw nothing. It wasn't the first time she had pursued Henrietta through the darkness, and she knew the search was an exercise in frustration; no one can capture a cat, he can only persuade the cat that it wants to come to him. "Henrietta," she called. "Nice kitty, adorable kitty, come to Meg. . . ." It was hard to keep her voice sweet and affectionate when what she really wanted to do was scream threats.

Henrietta suffered from no such inhibition. If a cat could be said to swear, Henrietta's next comment was unquestionably profane. It sounded close at hand, however, and it drew Meg onward. It was not until she saw the light ahead that she realized where she was and how far she had come.

The area Cliff and his crew had cut that afternoon gave a clear view, not of the cottage itself but of its immediate surroundings. The light seemed to be that of a torch or lantern, and it was moving, flickering bright and dim as foliage intercepted its rays. Meg stopped short, forgetting Henrietta as she debated her options.

The temptation to go on and catch the intruders red-handed was strong. If she went back for help they might get away. However, there was really no choice; she'd be crazy to confront—whoever it was—alone. She started to turn.

The blow skimmed the side of her head instead of connecting squarely, but it was hard enough to fog her eyes and make her knees buckle. She was dimly aware of sharp-edged stones biting into her arm and hip as she fell; then her vision was blotted out altogether by a stifling, evil-smelling fabric that covered her face. Struggling, not even to free herself, but simply to breathe, she felt rough hands pull the fabric farther down, over shoulders and arms. Pain pierced her skull as her head hit the ground and sent her spiraling into unconsciousness.

18

THE ROUGH HANDS belonged to Riley. She still couldn't see, but she knew the feel of them, the feel of him. How? He had seldom touched her, and never so violently—pushing her, pulling at her, slapping her face. Never mind how. She knew. Under the impact of his open palm her head rolled to one side and rolled back, and he slapped her again. Meg opened her eyes. That was why she hadn't been able to see anything. Her eyes had been closed. He had removed the sack, or whatever it was. . . . That was nice of him.

"But you better not hit me again," she said clearly. "Because as soon as I feel better I'm going to. . . . Oh. Oh, God, my head. . . ."

His face looked like a satanic mask, all dark shadows and flame-red highlights. It blurred and dissolved, like melting wax. Horrible. . . . Far away in the closing dark someone was screaming.

When Meg opened her eyes again she was alone, lying flat on a hard, lumpy surface. The scream had risen to a pitch that pierced her aching head like a needle. It cut off in midshriek, to be replaced by a dull, insistent roaring. Dawn was breaking —a strange, brilliant sunrise, crimson and hot and flickering.

She rolled over onto her side and sneezed violently as a thistle pricked her nose. She lay under a tree, among the uncut weeds, not far from the cottage. The scream had not come from a living throat, but from a siren, and the light was not that of sunrise. The cottage was burning.

She pulled herself to her feet with the help of the tree trunk.

Her aching head and bruised limbs were forgotten in the spectacle before her.

Hoses had been trained onto the fire, but the firemen might as well have been spitting on it; the flames soared toward the sky as if laughing at the feeble efforts of men. It's gone, Meg thought dispassionately. All that rotten wood and dried plaster . . . flammable as kindling. The volunteer fire department had certainly responded quickly though. It was like Old Home Week, so many familiar faces—Tom, and Rod Applegate, Mike Potter, Cliff and George.

The last three stood close together. George had both arms around his son, as if restraining or supporting him. She could see every detail, the fire made it bright as day. But—she realized, as her head slowly cleared—they probably hadn't seen her. She had been hidden by the weeds earlier, and now the fire held all their attention.

She started walking toward them, and still they didn't seem to see her. An odd, sick fancy struck her: maybe they couldn't see her. Maybe she was dead. She actually stopped and turned to see if her body was lying there on the flattened weeds.

No body. Stop it, Meg told herself. When you pass to the Other Side the first person you'll see won't be Riley, it will be Dan Mignot, and he'll be cussing you out for being damned fool enough to ignore his warning. He told you to watch out for the cat, didn't he? A pity that sentence could be interpreted in two different ways. Not that you'd have paid any attention to it anyhow.

I must be slightly concussed, she thought in mild surprise. Such crazy ideas. And it doesn't feel as if I'm moving, but they're getting closer and closer, as if they were gliding toward me. How very strange. She was close enough to reach out and touch George. She was afraid to do it. What if her hand went right through his arm?

"Hello," she said. "Hi, everybody."

For one long, unendurable second she thought they had not heard her. What if. . . . Cliff was the first to turn, then George and finally, slowly, Mike. They looked—what was the phrase? They looked as if they had seen a ghost. Cliff made a weird gurgling sound, deep in his throat, and collapsed onto the ground at her feet.

Everybody was drinking brandy, even George. An hour later, after the fire had subsided into smoldering ruin and the volunteer firemen had gone, his hands were still unsteady. He said very little but his eyes kept moving restlessly from Meg to Cliff, as if he couldn't believe they were both there.

Cliff was furious—at himself, for passing out. "What was I supposed to think?" he demanded. "When I got home the front door was open and you were nowhere to be found, in or out of the house. While I was foraging around in the shrubbery yelling for you, I saw the glow of the fire. I got there just as the porch roof fell in, but before it fell I saw . . . I saw a little . . . a woman's shoe, on the steps."

Meg looked at her bare foot. She hadn't noticed one of her sandals was missing until they started back to the house.

"He tried to go in the cottage," George said, in a dull monotone. "I had to wrestle with him to hold him back."

Meg couldn't think of anything to say except "Were you the one who called the fire department, Cliff?"

"No. I was too busy trying to immolate myself."

Mike cleared his throat. At Meg's insistence he had come back to the house with them. He had left his boots and the rest of the uniform in the hall, but Mary would have had a fit if she had seen him, overalls pulled over his pajamas, smeared with soot and dripping with water. But then none of them was looking his or her best, Meg thought.

"The call came in at eleven-ten," Mike said in his slow drawl. "Didn't give a name."

Meg looked at her uncle. He shook his head wearily. "I was in bed reading when Cliff burst in asking why the front door was open. We searched . . . after that everything happened so fast. . . ."

Cliff stopped pacing and went to his father, resting one hand on his bowed shoulder. "What he hell were you doing outside, Meg? Did you see the flames? And if so, why didn't you call the fire department?"

"I was looking for Henrietta." Meg glanced at he cat, curled up next to her and purring with nsufferable satisfaction.

"She was in the hall when I came in," Cliff said. "Yelling her fool head off."

"I can't help that, she was outside earlier—yelling her fool head off. She must have sneaked back in while I was. . . ." She wasn't sure how o finish the sentence—or how much to tell them. A painful lump on the side of her head indicated hat her memory of falling was accurate, but it wasn't severe enough to account for such a long period of unconsciousness. The bag or gunnysack hat had half-smothered her had had a peculiar smell, something more pungent than mold and dirt. Chloroform? Dan used to keep a bottle of he stuff around, to use on fatally injured animals. . . .

"What happened, honey?" Mike asked.

"I heard Henrietta outside and went to look for her," Meg began. "She kept retreating—you know how she is—and I followed her all the way back through the gardens. Then I saw a light near he cottage. It wasn't fire. More like a flashlight or an electric lantern."

Cliff was pacing again. He stopped and pointed an accusing finger. "So you thought you'd play hero and catch the intruders red-handed?"

"I'm not that stupid," Meg snapped. "I was

about to go back and call the police when someone pulled a sack over my head. I fell and . . . and that's all I remember, until I woke up and found myself lying in the weeds, and saw the cottage ablaze."

Three pairs of eyes focused on her with varying degrees of concern and skepticism. "What do you mean, that's all you remember?" Cliff demanded. "What do you mean, someone? You must have seen him. Who was it?"

"Now, Clifford, just calm down," Mike said. "If she knew who it was she would have said so. It was dark, and I expect he was taking considerable pains not to be seen. You sure that's all you can remember, honey?"

Meg nodded. She had made her decision. That brief, vivid vision of Riley might have been a dream, or a hallucination. Her hand went to her cheek, where his palm had struck with stinging force. It still stung. Some hallucination. . . .

Her uncle's face had regained its color. "Bad as this is, it's not as bad as I feared. He—they—didn't mean to harm Meg; she was only an innocent bystander who happened to be in the wrong place at the wrong time."

"Looks that way," Mike agreed. "Kids, fooling around in an empty house, accidentally starting a fire. Don't they cook that dope of theirs?"

"Some of it—some combinations of it," Cliff answered vaguely. He threw himself onto the sofa. "That's not the point, there are a number of ways in which carelessness could start a blaze in an abandoned house. Hell, they could have been holding a wienie roast. The point is, was it care-essness or was it deliberate?"

"They'll be investigating the cause of the fire omorrow," Mike said. "If it was arson, the ex-perts will find traces. But arson doesn't make sense. Why would anyone want to burn the place down?" He paused, his mild gaze moving from one o another, inviting a reply. The silence echoed with answers no one wanted to voice aloud. Mike shook his head. "It doesn't make sense neither that the purpose was to hurt Meg. First, nobody could have known she'd leave the house. Second, she wasn't in the cottage, she was outside, at a safe distance from the fire. One way to figure it s, she accidentally interrupted a little private pot party. One of 'em saw her nosing around, lost his head and grabbed her. He carried her into the cottage—that would explain why her shoe was on he porch—and then, when the fire started, dragged her out to safety before they all ran for t. Well? Anybody got any smarter ideas?"

George let out a long, sighing breath. "I'd like o believe it, Mike. If it weren't for the other hings that have happened. . . ."

"This is just like the others," Cliff interrupted. "The same ambiguity, the same apparent lack of motive—the same impossibility of proving any-thing one way or the other. If they left any evi-dence in the house, it's ashes now, and the fire ngines will have obliterated tire tracks or foot-prints. It's like trying to grab a handful of fog!"

"We'll have a look around tomorrow, in daylight," Mike said. "They must've been pretty scared, and in a hurry. Maybe one of them dropped something."

"Or scratched his name on a tree, for our convenience," Cliff said sarcastically.

"Well, there was sure as heck somebody there," Mike said. "Meg didn't walk up to the cottage, toss her shoe on the porch, light a match and then go lay down in the grass."

Cliff sat up with a jerk. "Yes, by God, there was somebody! I saw him—I saw something, anyhow. It didn't register at the time, I was focusing on that little shoe, and the flames reaching out for it. . . . Dad, you were right behind me. Did you. . . ."

"Among the trees at the back of the lot?" George nodded. "I had only a glimpse before you distracted my attention by bolting toward the fire. If I hadn't tackled you. . . ."

"It's all over and done with, George," Mike said quietly. "I can see why you might not have paid close attention at the time, but this could be important. Try to remember. Anything at all that could help identify him?"

"I can't even be sure it was a man," George answered. "Though I had the impression of someone tall, moving slowly and stealthily." His eyes went to Meg's face. She realized she was sitting bolt upright, her hands clasped tightly in her lap as she waited for her uncle's reply. He let her wait, it seemed, interminably. Then he shook his head.

"I'm afraid that's it. A shadow, tall and dark, gliding through the grass. I couldn't identify anyone."

He knows, Meg thought.

Meg wasn't the only one who suspected George was holding something back. Cliff kept badgering him until finally he lost his temper. "I'll be damned if I am going to be cross-examined like a hostile witness by my own son! What possible reason would I have for lying?"

"Hey, Dad, I'm sorry. Just calm down, okay?"

"We're all of us too tired and upset to think straight," Mike said. "Better get some sleep."

If he was tired and upset he didn't show it. Unfolding his long legs, he stood up and smiled at Meg. "You must be beat, honey. Sure you're all right?"

Meg nodded. She had too many things on her mind to worry about a few aches and pains. "Why don't you sleep here, Mike? It's getting late, and your car is—where? At home, or at the fire station?"

"I'll drive Mike home," Cliff said quickly. "He's welcome to stay, of course."

Mike shook his head. "I've never yet failed to open up at eight sharp and I can't hardly go to work looking like this. Besides, the dogs will need to be let out. I'll take you up on the offer of a ride, Cliff, if you don't mind. Just to the fire station."

On general principles Meg kissed everybody good night, including Cliff, who looked surprised.

Henrietta followed her up the stairs and into her room. "I wish you could talk," Meg murmured, watching the cat jump onto the bed and turn in circles, clawing the sheet into a comfortable nest.

Henrietta rolled herself into a ball and covered her eyes with her paw. A muted grumble got her point across, clear as speech: it was long past the time when decent people should be in bed.

Meg overslept next morning. It had taken her a long time to fall asleep, and apparently the staff had been warned not to wake her. Even Henrietta demonstrated unusual courtesy; she was pacing back and forth in front of the door when Meg focused bleary eyes on the morning, but she hadn't uttered a sound.

As she hurried to shower and dress, Meg found scrapes and bruises she hadn't felt the night before, and a hiss of pain escaped her lips when she started to comb her hair. The bumps were no worse than several she had acquired from open cupboard doors, but they would be tender for a while. She braided her hair and wound it around her head in a coronet, avoiding the sore spots when she stuck the pins in. Her wardrobe was in a pitiable state; the laundry hadn't come back and she had to wear a light wool suit that wasn't quite light enough for the summer weather. At least it was loose-fitting; nothing fretted her varied bruises and the pockets were deep enough to hold her wallet and keys and a few other things, eliminating the necessity of carrying a purse. The shoulde strap of the only one she had brought with her rested right over the most painful spot of all, where the first blow that skimmed her head had landed.

Cliff was at the breakfast table when she came down, and so, she observed without surprise, was Darren. They presented quite a contrast—Cliff in his rumpled work clothes, cheeks sallow with sleeplessness, and Darren looking like a *Business Week* ad, tie precisely knotted, glasses freshly polished.

He got up and started toward her. Meg ducked away from his outstretched arms. "Don't touch me, I know exactly how I'll feel when I'm eighty and riddled with arthritis. You shouldn't have come, Darren. I haven't time to talk now, I'm late."

Darren adjusted his glasses. "You can hardly expect me to be indifferent to this latest outrage, Meg. This has to stop. We must take action."

"What do you propose?" Meg asked, accepting the coffee Cliff handed her.

"Why—uh—obviously the first thing is to investigate the scene of the crime. Cliff and I are going out there as soon as he finishes breakfast."

Meg turned to her cousin. "You called Darren?"

"I didn't call anybody, damn it. You know the way the grapevine works in this town." Cliff's sleepy eyes brightened as he studied Darren's impeccable attire, and he added maliciously, "He isn't going to look so pretty when he gets through. Want to borrow a pair of jeans, Darren?"

He rose, stretching, in a flagrant display of his narrow hips and flat stomach. Darren flushed. "No, thanks. Are you ready?"

"Wait a minute, I'm coming with you." Meg said, swallowing the last of her coffee. "Where's Uncle George?"

"I made him go back to bed," Cliff answered. "I'm worried about him. He's got high blood pressure, you know—"

"I didn't know," Meg said.

"Well, now you do. I accused him of not taking his medicine, and he admitted he forgets sometimes. See if you can't get him to take it easier, Meg. He won't listen to me."

He didn't wait for her to answer, but led the way out, with Darren close on his heels. Anxious as she was to get to the store, Meg felt she had no choice but to accompany them. Neither man was an impartial observer. One or both of them might be . . . something worse.

She had to give Darren points for dogged persistence, though. A lesser man might have retreated in dismay when he saw the messy mixture of weeds and brambles, water and ashes; Darren plunged straight into it and kept on looking till his pants were soaked to the knee and his once polished shoes were clumps of mud. Meg stuck to Cliff like a burr. He was even more thorough than Darren, crawling on hands and knees through the patch of weeds where Meg had been lying when she came to. The only "clue" anywhere in the vicinity was an empty beer can, whose unrusted state indicated it had not been there long.

"Isn't that the brand your friend Tom drinks?" Meg asked.

"Half the guys in town drink it." Cliff tossed the can away. "He brought a six-pack with him yesterday. I had one myself."

He could have competed in a wet T-shirt contest; the thin fabric clung to his shoulders and back, displaying an impressive set of muscles. The hands that had been so smooth and well tended now showed the signs of hard manual labor, including a network of scratches.

Meg glanced at Darren, who was poking the sodden ruins of the cottage with a stick. "This is a waste of time," she said. "Didn't Mike say they were sending an arson team? Why don't we leave it to the experts?"

Cliff shrugged. "Maybe you're right. Any luck, Darren?"

"I shouldn't have let you talk me into this," Darren muttered."We're interfering with an official investigation. Destroying evidence—"

"What evidence?" Cliff demanded. He clapped Darren on the back, with more force than friendliness. "Stop being such a stuffed shirt. This ground was trampled over by a couple of dozen flat-footed firefighters last night, there's not a hope in hell of finding footprints."

Darren grunted and went on poking the ashes. A sour, foul stench rose from the wet and blackened mass, and Meg realized they were all breathing through their mouths. It was Darren who voiced the thought that weighed on all of them. "You don't think there was anyone inside?"

"If there was, it will take more guts than I've got to look for him," Cliff said, wrinkling his nose.

They trudged back toward the house. Darren refused Cliff's unenthusiastic offer of coffee and drove off, while Meg ran upstairs to clean up, and place a call to the hospital, which she had neglected to do earlier—a shocking omission, but one for which there was some excuse, she thought grimly. Gran's survival was in the hands of the doctors and the good Lord, if you believed in Him; Meg didn't feel she could count on either to intervene on her behalf.

Frances flatly refused to put Mary on the phone. "She's still asleep. She had a bad night. No"—grudgingly—"nothing like that. They say she's coming along fine. Only she was tossing and turning half the night, and muttering in her sleep, all about that damned cat, and you being in some kind of trouble. What have you been up to?"

Apparently the grapevine stopped at the door of Gran's hospital room. Thank God and the nursing staff for that. Meg said, "I'm fine. Tell her I called, and that I'll be in later."

She hung up before Frances could ask any more questions and slipped her feet into dry shoes. Should she call on the other invalid, see how he was feeling? She decided against it. George would be resting in his room or he wouldn't be resting in his room, there was nothing she could do in either case. Suddenly she was overcome by a desperate, irrational need to hurry. She tried to tell herself that five minutes more or less didn't matter, but her mind could not convince her body; her fingers fumbled with the buttons of her blouse, she dropped an earring and had to crawl under the bed to retrieve it. When she ran down the stairs she made herself hold tightly to the banister. That was how traditions of bad luck and ill omen started—when fear distracted people and haste made them careless.

Gran hadn't passed on any warnings about the car, but Meg drove like a timid little old lady, testing the brake before she left the estate. Once she had thought she would never get used to Gran's conversations with Dan. Now she was not only accepting them, but wishing he would be a little more specific. Make that a lot more specific.

The clock at the bank read a quarter to ten when she pulled into a parking spot. She hurried toward the store. It was not until the knob resisted her efforts to turn it that she saw that the "Closed" sign was up, and then the mindless panic she had been fighting took full possession of her. Her fingers felt as thick and soft as raw sausages when she fumbled for her keys.

Faintly, from within, she heard the telephone ring. It increased her panic and made her more clumsy; by the time she got the door open it had stopped. Meg slammed the door and leaned against it, gasping for breath. He wasn't there. No one was there.

She had known this might happen—but not so soon, not before she could take steps to prevent it. As she fought to control her ragged breathing the doorknob rattled and she sprang away from it, eyeing it as if it had been a snake. Riley? He had his own key, but if he had seen her come in just ahead of him. . . . She flung the door open.

Following upon renewed hope, the sight of Candy brought the terror back, worse than before—cold, damp hands, queasy stomach, dry mouth. She stared, unable to speak.

"Good morning," Candy said. "You're a little late, aren't you?" She shifted her weight, peering past Meg into the shadowy interior of the store. "I guess you're entitled, after last night. Riley's late too, I see."

Meg moistened her lips. "Did you. . . . Have you seen him this morning?"

Candy's smile looked like a bloody gash across her cheeks, rimmed with the blurred bright crimson of lipstick. She spoke slowly, drawing out the words, savoring Meg's anxiety. "Not this morning. No. Not this morning. You don't suppose I hang around here watching for him, do you?"

"What do you mean, not this morning?"

"It all depends on how you define morning, doesn't it?"

Meg's fingers itched to slap the grin off Candy's face. She clenched her hands till her nails bit into her palms and forced herself to speak coolly. "How do you define it?"

"Oh. . . . After the sun comes up, I guess. I

just got here, you know. I don't stand on street corners waiting for the great man to show up."

"Oh, really?" Meg produced what she hoped was a fair imitation of a knowing smile. "Well, Candy, much as I'm enjoying this conversation, I'm afraid I must tear myself away. Goodbye for now."

"Wait a minute. I haven't told you about Riley."

"Tell me, then." Meg managed not to let her relief show. If necessary she would have shaken the information out of Candy, but pretended indifference seemed to work better.

"I saw him last night. Late last night. You could say it was morning, it was after midnight."

"Oh?"

"Don't you want to know where I saw him?"

"Not particularly."

She's really not very good at this, Meg thought, watching the struggle on Candy's face. She knows she's being manipulated, but she can't handle it. She's dying to tell me. It must be something damning.

"It was at the Golden Calf," Candy said suddenly. "Some of us went back there after the fire."

"After the fire," Meg repeated.

The implication was not lost on Candy. Her cheeks turned an ugly shade of magenta. "I said 'after.' You can't pin that one on me. Or on any of my friends. We were all together at the Golden Calf. Some of the guys are on the volunteer fire squad, so when the alarm went off, we all went along. After the fire was out we went back, like I said. Riley was there. He was drinking like somebody else was paying."

"So?" Meg managed to sound bored, but her palms were slick with sweat.

"So I went over to him to say hello. Rod didn't want me to, but I did anyhow."

"Did you succeed in starting a fight?" Meg inquired.

"What the hell do you mean by that? I didn't. . . . I was trying to be nice."

"Get to the point," Meg snapped. "If there is one."

"There's a point, all right." Candy's eyes narrowed. "It was pretty dark in the Golden Calf. I was the only one that got close to Riley. I was the only one that saw the burns on his hands and smelled the gasoline. Nobody else noticed. Just me."

It was damning, no question about that. Whether or not it was true hardly mattered, so long as Candy was willing to swear to it.

"What time did he leave?" Meg asked.

"Around one, one-thirty."

"And that was the last you saw of him?"

"It was the last I saw of him. Rod followed him out."

"Did they. . . ." Meg stopped. The gloating look on Candy's face was more than she could take. "Never mind."

"Hey—what are you doing?"

"Closing the door. Move your foot or lose it, I'm in a hurry."

"No—wait—I wanted to ask you. . . ."

"Well?"

"I wondered . . . I thought maybe you'd changed your mind. About giving me my job back."

In her eagerness she had edged closer; her face was pink with expectation, and with another emotion so raw that Meg almost pitied her. She wanted Riley so badly she was willing to use blackmail as a means of being near him. Sisters under the skin, Meg thought, wincing.

But the sheer naive stupidity of the demand cleared away any lingering doubts Meg may have had as to Candy's complicity. She was only a dupe, a pawn; it would be a waste of valuable time to question her further.

"No," Meg said.

"What?"

"No, I haven't changed my mind." She slammed the door and locked it. Candy's yelp was, she thought, one of outrage rather than pain, but she didn't really care. The telephone rang and she ran to answer it. Maybe he was still in bed, too hung over to move. Or in the drunk tank at the county jail. Or. . . . She snatched up the phone. "Hello?"

"Meg, is that you?" It was Darren's voice.

"Who else would it be?" Dashed hopes harshened her voice.

"Is Riley there?"

"No."

"I thought not." Even the mechanical distortion of the telephone couldn't conceal the satisfaction in Darren's voice. "He wasn't there when I drove past, shortly after nine, and I've been calling every ten minutes."

"Why?"

"Darling, I know how you feel, but it's time you faced facts. He's bolted. He went too far last night, and he knows it. Once they find evidence of arson—"

"Even if they do, it won't prove Riley did it." But her voice betrayed her lack of conviction and Darren was quick to catch it.

"Meg, dear, flight is a tacit admission of guilt. All the same, I'm not happy about you being there alone. He could be hiding somewhere in the area. I'm coming by to pick you up—"

"You're fired, Darren."

"I. . . . What?"

"I said you're fired. I'm not your client. You have no right, legal or moral or otherwise, to interfere with me. Leave me alone."

She hung up. Almost immediately the phone rang again. It went on ringing. Meg ignored it. The glass of the countertop felt cold against her palms as she leaned forward, her head bowed in an unconscious pose of prayer. Dan—Dan, you tricky old bastard—talk to me, for a change. You got me into this, show me how to get out of it in one piece. Tell me what to do. Just a hint, Dan. . . .

Apparently she wasn't on his wavelength. The only thing that came to her was one of his infuriating old maxims: Keep your head, and use your brains. Easy for you to say, Dan.

Meg realized that the phone had stopped ringing. Good for Darren; it had only taken him sixty seconds to figure out she wasn't going to answer it.

Perhaps she shouldn't have cut him off so abruptly. Darren was impervious to gentle hints, though; you had to drop a piano on him just to get his attention. There was no way she could explain to him what she intended to do; he'd try to stop her, by one means or another—for one reason or another—and in her present state of mind, delay or interference would be unendurable. This way was better, safer, for everyone concerned.

He could be right, though. Riley might have gone to ground somewhere nearby, waiting to see what would come of the investigation of the fire. His pickup was in its usual place. That fact surely argued against flight, but she knew how Darren would explain it; an intelligent fugitive would prefer to use a vehicle that couldn't be as easily traced as his own. It would take the police a while to locate a driver who had picked up a hitchhiker, or hear about a stolen car.

When she straightened up, she saw that her hands had left damp prints on the countertop. She wiped them on her skirt and then reached for her keys. Maybe Dan had gotten through to her after all. Her brain might not be functioning at top capacity, but at least something was happening up there, and she no longer felt as if she might throw up.

The stairway leading to the apartment was narrow and gloomy, wedged between the masonry walls of the adjoining stores. A dusty skylight on the second-floor landing admitted a ray of feeble sunshine that illumined only the topmost steps. Both of the fixtures on the wall were dark; they remained so even after she pressed the light switch. She groped her way up, trying not to hurry and risk a stumble.

The key, labeled in Dan's minuscule handwriting, turned easily in the lock. Meg gave the door a shove. It hit the wall with a reassuring thud. No one behind the door. . . . Yet as she stood on the threshold she could feel her skin crawling. It was a sensation she had read about but never experienced; the description was in fact quite accurate.

The door opened directly into the living room. It too was poorly lit, since the building next door was four stories high and the windows opened onto an airshaft. However, there was enough light for her to see the signs she had hoped not to see—signs of frantic, furious haste. Drawers stood open, cushions had been tumbled onto the floor and books from the shelves lining one wall littered the floor. A stab of déjà vu pierced Meg as she remembered how she had rushed around her apartment after hearing of Dan's death. She had left it in a mess too.

Meg turned on the lights and closed the door. A dull, fatalistic calm had replaced her feeling of panic, and she went about her business without bothering to move quietly. Logic, as well as an instinctive consciousness of human presence, told her the apartment was empty of life.

Only the floor plan was as she remembered it. Dan's recent remodeling had improved the apartment almost beyond recognition, so much so that she wondered how much of its look of quiet comfort was Dan's contribution. His taste was strictly limited to jewelry; left to himself, he was inclined to go for baroque, favoring garish colors and an overabundance of ornaments. Pale ivory paint had replaced the faded wallpaper of the living room, brightening it and forming a fitting backdrop for prints and a few unusual but attractive pieces of three-dimensional art. The kitchen had new appliances and countertops; the cabinets were finished in smooth unvarnished walnut. It had not suffered the same violence as the living room; only a plate, cup and saucer and some pieces of silverware, washed and left to drain, were out of place.

However, the bedroom was a second, minor shock—minor only because she had seen the living room first. The bed was unmade, the sheet thrown back. There was no indication as to whether he had slept in it the night before; he might be of the school that considered daily bedmaking a waste of valuable time. The bureau drawers were all open, clothing had been dragged out and left where it fell.

Kneeling, she picked up the books that lay tumbled on the floor, smoothing the crumpled pages, reading the titles as she returned them to the shelves. Bookshelves here and in the living room, even a few paperbacks in the bathroom—they showed a side of Riley she had never suspected, and the titles were even more enlightening in their wide range: hard-boiled detective stories rubbed shoulders with Dorothy Sayers; Rebecca West and Loren Eiseley shared a shelf with Dave Barry and Henry James. Dorothy Sayers . . . that was the source of the quote she had failed to identify when she asked Riley if he had a clean handkerchief. . . .

After she had replaced the books she returned to the living room. There was nothing more to be done here. Picking up the mess would take time she didn't have, looking through his clothes would tell her nothing—she wasn't sufficiently familiar with his wardrobe to know whether anything was missing.

Most of it was clear in her mind now. She had known for some time who must be responsible. Only the motive still eluded her. The motive, and Riley himself. Where could he be? Was there a chance that, like Darren, she had jumped to conclusions—that there was another explanation for his absence besides the worst-case scenario she envisioned? But she had eliminated most of the remaining possibilities. He hadn't had an accident on the road, or been picked up for DWI; the truck, parked with its usual precision, proved that he had made it safely home.

There was one last chance. If he had left a message for her, it wouldn't be here, it would be somewhere in the store.

There was no one waiting outside, and no indication that anyone had come to the store during her absence. Not even a dead rat on the doorstep. Nevertheless, she hesitated before entering, feeling the now-familiar prickle of tightened nerves as her eyes probed the shadowy silence of the store. He had keys, he knew the exits and entrances, the working of the security system, as well as she did. But—she assured herself—he wouldn't risk coming here. Not in broad daylight, with people on the street.

The logic failed to convince her completely, but she forced herself to go in. After she had looked into the washroom and behind the counters, she ventured into the office, finding it equally empty of life.

She pulled out one of the file drawers, glanced into it and then slammed it shut. It would take days to go through every folder, and what would be the point of such a search? She wasn't even sure what she was looking for. If Riley had left her a note it would be on the desk or on the counter. Unless. . . .

She pulled out the center desk drawer and pressed the false screw-head that opened the so-called secret compartment. No note. Nothing except the ugly, deadly weapon.

Meg fully intended to close the drawer. She watched with remote interest as her hand moved to the butt of the gun. It was astonishingly heavy. She examined it curiously, wondering if it was loaded, looking for the safety catch. This wasn't the weapon she had used so briefly so many years ago—but it didn't matter, she couldn't remember how to use that one either.

When she opened the door of the shop a rustle in the dark made her heart jump and her fingers fumble on the light switch. The glare of the overhead lights showed nothing alarming. The rush of air into what was essentially a sealed room must have stirred a loose piece of paper.

The workbench was bare except for tools and a scattering of scraps. Despite her efforts at control, it took her three tries to open the safe. Teeth sunk in her lower lip, she inspected each tray and each box. Nothing was missing, but there was one tray whose contents were unfamiliar. It must be Riley's current project, still unfinished. The jumble of shimmering color took shape as she moved it with a careful finger. Earrings, one almost finished, the other only a promise of loose stones and gold wire. They matched her necklace.

A stab of pain in her lip and the salty taste of blood brought her back to her senses. She replaced the tray. That was everything, except for a box of discarded gold findings and the little velvet bag of mixed citrines and topazes. What was it doing in the safe? She had left it in Dan's desk drawer.

Meg loosened the drawstring and put her hand in the bag. The smooth, cool surfaces of the stones, Dan's worry beads, slid through her fingers. When her fingers touched the alien object, she knew at once what it was.

The slender gold hoop had been shaped by a master craftsman, its design combining delicacy and strength in a variation of the old gimmel rings—two separate circles that joined to form clasped hands. This was no antique, nor a copy of an older ring, but a brilliant modern variation on the theme. It was not one of Riley's pieces; she had good reason to be certain of that. Yet it must have been Riley who put it in the bag and returned the bag to the safe.

With the ease of remembered habit her fingers found the hidden catch and pulled the golden circles apart. She needed a loupe to read the letters engraved on the miniature open palms: Letters and numbers, four of each, two on either side. EM 19, SV 60.

Meg slipped the ring on her finger. It was still too big, but not grossly oversized as it had been all those years ago, on the small hand of a child. Playing with the ring had been a special treat allowed by an indulgent parent to a beloved, spoiled little girl. How often had she tried to see the message entire, always failing because it became whole only when the ring was closed, reserving its message for the eyes of the heart? The initials were those of Simon Venturi and Elissa Mignot, the date was the year of their marriage. The ring was her mother's wedding ring, which should have been resting in the eternal darkness of her grave, its gold untarnished by the corruption that would by now have reduced the finger it encircled to bare white bone.

19

WHEN MEG CAME out of the store, sunlight dazzled her eyes. It was later than she had realized. The sun rode high above the buildings across the street. Half-blinded and uncertain as to her next move, she didn't see the tall lanky figure approaching until he called her name.

"Meg! Did you just get here? Where's Riley?"

Trust Mike to come straight to the point. She answered the last question first. "I don't know. He's not in the apartment, I looked."

"So did I." The bright sunlight brought out every line and wrinkle in Mike's face, including a few she had never noticed before.

"You have a key to the apartment?"

The question surprised him. "Why, no. I just knocked. He didn't answer, so I figured he wasn't there."

"Why were you looking for him?"

Mike took his time about answering, studying her face with a shrewd, unblinking scrutiny that made her feel like a bug under a microscope

'Something the matter, honey? You seem kind of ıpset."

"It's not like him to be late," Meg said. "And .fter last night. . . ."

"Uh-huh. There's some ugly talk going around own."

"About Riley?"

Mike nodded. "Somebody claims to have seen ıis pickup near the back gate on Old Hammond Road last night."

So the net was closing. Meg wasn't disturbed y the information; she wasn't even particularly nterested. The case against Riley had become a natter of minor importance.

"I'm worried about that boy," Mike went on houghtfully. "He could be in bad trouble."

He didn't know the half of it. Meg bit her lip, ut didn't quite succeed in repressing a gasp of ysterical laughter. Mike gave her a reproachful ɔok, and she explained disingenuously, "I was— : was you calling him a boy. He wouldn't appre- iate that."

"I don't suppose he'd mind." Mike's forehead esembled a patch of crumpled leather, all creases nd cracks. "I don't like this, Meg. I wanted to ılk to him—that's why I was watching for him ıis morning."

He looked and sounded so concerned that Meg as seized with an almost overpowering urge to our out her anxieties and dump them, in one nothering load, onto the broad shoulders of her ld friend. Her fingers clenched over the cardboard box in the pocket of her skirt. She couldn't do it. Couldn't take the risk.

"I'll let you know if I find—if I hear from him,' she said.

"Where're you off to? How about some lunch?'

"No." The thought of food was nauseating "No, thanks. I've got to—I've got some errands See you, Mike."

He was still standing in front of the store scratching his head, when she pulled out of th parking lot. She waved with forced cheerfulness

Now where? Someplace quiet and isolated away from people, where she could get he thoughts organized and decide what to do. Sh drove almost at random, heading out of town, an away from the Manor. It wasn't until she foun herself approaching the ornate iron gates of th cemetery that she realized she had meant to g there all along.

It was quiet enough. There was no funeral tha day; the only people she saw as she drove alon the winding road were a handyman mowing th grass and a woman arranging flowers at one of th graves. She pulled to the side and stopped whe she saw the marble angel on Dan's monumen lifting white wings over the soft green ground.

Dan's last joke, that sweet-faced alabaster ange . . . He had had no expectation of ending up in conventional Presbyterian Heaven, and the ide of flapping around in a long white robe lugging harp would have moved him to ribald laughte He had accepted the design partly because pleased his wife and partly because he enjoyed its irony. Mary would lie beside him one day, under the shadow of those wings. Now they hovered over the graves of his two daughters. There was a plot reserved for George,too, but Meg's father was not there. He had been buried in Akron, Ohio, with his kin. She had read that in the newspaper. She had never visited his grave.

She took the cardboard box from her pocket and opened it. One last look at the ring; then she wrapped it carefully in tissues and returned it to the box, which she taped closed. She had already typed the statement she meant to enclose with it. She inserted box and statement into the mailing envelope and sealed it.

Just in case.

Her courage failed her then, for a moment, and she bowed her head over the steering wheel, fighting the panic that was her enemy within. She couldn't let it conquer her now. If the tenuous chain of evidence she had woven was right, she had several more hours before the situation became critical. But there were so many factors she couldn't control; her actions from now on would resemble those of a player in a computer game, trying to shoot down the bright, darting shapes of the enemy while at the same time avoiding their shots at her. What made it even more difficult was that she didn't know how many darting shapes were involved. Nor did she have the faintest idea where to look.

Think. Use your brains. There weren't that

many possibilities. Not a hotel or motel; too public. An abandoned house? Possible; but she had been away too long, she didn't know the town as well as he did. How about going to a realtor? She had a good excuse, especially now that the cottage was destroyed; people knew she had been looking for a place to live. The old Barlow place—Barby had mentioned it. . . . But an empty house, one that was on the market, was risky. A realtor might choose that day to show the place.

It was no use, she couldn't force herself to sit quietly. Her foot was tapping, her hands twitching. The need to take action, to be moving—doing something, anything—was stronger than the need to plan her strategy. An idea was just as likely to come to her while she was driving, she told herself.

With one last look at the marble angel and a half-formed prayer to the cynical old pagan who had erected it, she drove away.

After a stop at the post office to dispose of her parcel, she forced herself to take the time for one additional precaution—renting a car. The bright red Ferrari was too well known. Leaving it in the parking lot of the supermarket, she walked to the rental agency and selected a modest blue Ford Escort. He could trace that transaction, she had had to use her own name and credit card; but no matter how numerous his allies, he suffered from constraints similar to hers—time running out, the need for concealment.

With dark glasses hiding her eyes and a scarf covering her conspicuous black hair, she felt se ure enough to risk a drive down Main Street, .oping against hope even now that she had been vrong. But the store was closed and dark, the ·ickup was still in the parking lot. Passing the ·akery, she turned her head away; Ed stood sun-ing himself in the doorway, his round pink face ixed in its habitual smile. The hardware store was oing a thriving business, but there was traffic ehind her, she couldn't stop to see whether Mike vas there. He always was, though. . . . Lights hone from the windows of Barby's Beauty hoppe, and Kate's Kafe was open for business. he drove on through town, catching a glimpse f Mrs. Henderson peering out from behind the oses—did the dreadful old woman ever go inside? he was like a vampire, deriving her life energy rom the unhappiness of others. Meg pictured her anging like a great black bat from the trellis, vatching through the night with malevolent yes. . . . She passed the gates of the Manor—no gn of unusual activity there.

A quarter of a mile farther on was a small shop-ing center, boasting the usual conveniences—rocery store, cleaners, drugstore, liquor store, ısurance office . . . realtor. Meg went first to the hone booth outside the drugstore.

Frances answered the phone. Before Meg could ay more than "hello," the housekeeper started erating her. "Where've you been? They've all een here except you. Clifford called twice, look-ıg for you. He wouldn't say so, but I could see e was worried about you. What are you—"

"Clifford had no damn business worryin Gran," Meg cut in. "I've been—I've been ver busy, Frances. I just wanted to check in and mak sure she was all right."

"She's all right," Frances said, with heavy em phasis on the pronoun. "Nobody is gonna worr her, not while I'm around. You're the one wh should be—"

"Is she listening?"

"I took the phone in the bathroom. It was di turbing her. Like I said, they keep calling her and asking about you. You want to talk to her?

"No! I mean—not now. Later."

"When?"

"Later. Don't let her worry, Frances. Tell he everything is all right. And, Frances—watch ove her. Don't leave her."

"As if I would." The housekeeper's voice shar ened. "What are you trying to say? Does some body want to hurt her?"

Again Meg had to fight the urge to seek suppo and comfort by telling all she knew. If she couldn trust Frances to defend her mistress with her lif she couldn't believe in anything; yet for all he wiry strength Frances was an old woman, wit too much imagination and too little commo sense. Gran's best security now was ignorance.

Inspiration came to her from out of nowher as it sometimes does when it is desperately neede She even summoned up a laugh. "Who woul want to harm Gran? But she's still not out of th woods, and worry could set her back. I'll tell you the truth, Frances—"

"High time." A sniff emphasized the criticism.

"I have to go to New York. I left everything in such a mess, there are bills to pay, and food rotting in the fridge and—and I need more clothes, Gran knows I've hardly a stitch to wear. Explain it to her—she'll understand about the clothes, at any rate!"

"Oh. Well, why didn't you say so in the first place, instead of scaring me half to death? You can tell her yourself, I think she just woke up—"

"I haven't time to talk, I'm at the train station now; but I'll be back tomorrow night, I promise. Give her my love."

She hung the phone up before Frances could reply.

Seldon's small-town status was in no way more clearly demonstrated than by the fact that there was a telephone book in the booth, and that most of the pages were intact. Meg looked up several addresses and wrote them down. Then she put in another quarter and dialed.

The phone rang for some time before it was answered. That in itself told Meg one of the things she wanted to know, before her assumption was confirmed by Annie. "Sorry to be so slow, Miss Meg, but things are in a terrible mess around here. People running in and out, the police. . . . What? Oh, it's something about the fire. I don't rightly understand it, but your uncle's been looking all over for you, and Mr. Cliff—"

"Where are they now?"

"Well, I figure they aren't here, or one of 'em would have answered the phone," Annie said wearily. "I'll go look if you want."

"No. Tell them. . . ." She repeated the story she had given Frances.

"Then you'll be at your apartment in New York tonight? Mr. George, he'll want to know."

"Yes, that's right. He has the number. I have to run, Annie, they're calling my train."

No time for the realtor now. The new idea that had come to her might eliminate the need for that expedient, which had been a last-ditch hope at best, time-consuming and probably unproductive. She needed one more thing, though. She found it at the drugstore, in a rack next to the checkout counter—a local map.

As she headed back toward the center of town she realized the dark glasses were no longer necessary, except as a disguise. (Some disguise. . . .) Clouds were piling up and the sun was gone. Meg's heart jerked painfully. Early darkness might bring the crisis sooner than she had expected. Unless her stratagem had gained her an extra day. . . . The delay might backfire on her, though. What could he do with an additional twenty-four hours? She put a clamp on her imagination, denying the unthinkable pictures it showed her.

She turned into the alley behind the store. After her years in New York it looked unreal, cleaner than most Manhattan streets, even with trash cans and dumpsters lining it. Ignoring the "No Park ing" signs, she pulled in close to the back door. It had been stupid of her to leave it bolted and chained, she should have known she might want to come and go unseen. At least this way the car was out of sight.

She hurried through the narrow private parking lot, emerging onto Main Street, and taped the sign she had prepared to the front door. As she started back she thought she heard someone call her name, and she began to run. Jumping into the Escort she gunned the engine and took off. There was no one in sight when she risked a glance behind her.

With the aid of the map she found the first of the addresses she had copied from the phone book. It was in one of the new subdivisions west of town—a modern split-level, or whatever they were calling the little crackerboxes these days, on a street tightly lined with identical houses. There were no sidewalks, no alleys, no fences—no privacy at all. The small structures stood so close together, a resident could call to a neighbor without even raising his voice. Meg stopped across the street from the Applegate house. Rod wasn't much of a gardener. The hedge was untrimmed, the lawn needed mowing. A short driveway led to an attached garage. Its door was raised and the interior was empty.

It didn't look promising, but Meg got out of the car and walked boldly to the front door. She didn't ring the bell, but occupied the time that might reasonably have been employed in waiting for a response to a ring in peering through the picture window at the right. Either Candy hadn't come back to her ex, or she was a lousy housekeeper; the living room was a mess, dusty and littered. A pair of crumpled socks rested on the coffee table, together with several stained glasses.

The first drops of rain spattered on the sidewalk as Meg turned away from the door, but it wasn't fear of getting wet that quickened her steps, nor was it fear of Rod Applegate. It was the dismal little house that was not, and probably never had been, a home—disheveled, neglected, gloomy. No Gothic ruin or abandoned manor house could have conveyed such an air of hopelessness.

The next address on her list was an apartment house. Candy's tan Ford was in the parking lot Meg didn't stop. There was only one other Applegate in the book. He, whoever he might be lived in a trailer park. A sudden downpour, brief as it was heavy, encouraged her to pull to the side of the road and consider her next move. Not to the trailer; she wasn't even sure the owner was related to Rod, and it certainly wasn't a suitable hiding place.

The rain slackened, but the clouds were thicker and blacker. Like her mood. She lowered her aching head onto her folded arms. I ought to eat something, she thought vaguely. Keep up my strength. I may need it. They all know by now that I'm supposed to be in New York. Will it work? There's an outside chance. But I can't go there yet, it's too early. If I wait too long, it could

e too late. . . . Don't think that, don't think of
ailure. Act. Get something to eat? I'll throw up
f I do.

Barby lived over the beauty shop. It was con-
eniently close to the store, a handy bolt hole for
hunted man. Kate's apartment was over the res-
aurant. Ed had a house—and a cheerful friendly
vife and dozens of relatives. Mike. . . .

Meg sat upright, so abruptly that her head
napped back. Why hadn't she thought of it be-
ore?

She drove too fast on rain-slicked roads. The
ands of the clock on the dashboard seemed to
pin in double-quick time. It was almost five and
ark as night, with ever-increasing rain to aid con-
ealment. Mike would be leaving the store in
lightly more than half an hour, he'd be home
efore six. Hurry.

In the rainy dusk the house no longer looked
harming and welcoming; blacker than the dark-
ess, it loomed among the dripping trees. He
adn't left lights burning; normally he would have
een home before dark, he must not have expected
he storm. As Meg ran for the front porch a ca-
ophony of barking greeted her, and she heard
he thud of heavy paws against the door.

Nice, trusting Mike always left a key under the
nat. Not so trusting, perhaps, Meg thought, as
he door shook under the impact of a heavy body
nd the barking rose to a frenzy. It would take a
rave burglar to risk such an encounter. She
vasn't keen on it herself. Would the dogs remem-

ber her, or did they only admit people who ac
companied their owner?

She flung the door open and stepped aside. I
she hadn't taken that precaution she would hav
been knocked flat; one of the dogs paused to snif
her shoes, but the others swept past her into th
yard, howling with delight. Meg didn't stop t
close the door. Turning on lights as she went, sh
hurried through the house.

Riley wasn't there. But he had been there. Sh
found the evidence in the basement, in the furn
ace room—a small windowless cubicle hung wit
cobwebs and littered with mouse droppings. Th
dust on the floor had been disturbed, and in on
corner, near an overturned packing case where
tired man might have sat to rest, was an empt
cigarette packet. It was Riley's brand, and th
crumpled cellophane was so fresh it crackled whe
she picked it up.

On the way back to town she saw Mike hastenin
home. She recognized his truck, even though
contrary to his usual custom, the cap was on th
bed of the truck. Though there were no othe
vehicles on the narrow back road, he paid no at
tention to hers, and Meg congratulated herself fo
having replaced the Ferrari. It was too early t
know whether her other brilliant ideas would pa
off—or whether she had overlooked some vita
point that would bring everything crashing dow
in failure.

The trees writhed in the grip of the wind.

sudden violent gust rocked the little car. Meg raised her foot from the gas. The storm was gathering force. Surely it couldn't be a hurricane; it was the wrong time of year and there had been no warnings. Just a bad storm. Bad enough to keep people at home, off the streets.

Main Street was indeed deserted. Kate's Kafe was the only business establishment on the block that was still open. Its carved wooden sign swung back and forth, and the fringed awning flapped violently. At least there was no problem parking. Meg stopped across the street from the jewelry store.

In the glow of the streetlight she could see the white square of her note fastened to the door. Someone had been there since she left it. The show window was illumined and the night-lights had been turned on. Yes, of course, Meg thought; he knew that any deviation from the normal routine might attract attention. Dan had paid for, and received, excellent service from the Seldon police force. They checked the store several times during the night. She doubted they would be as alert tonight, though. The bad weather would produce traffic accidents and other emergencies to keep them busy.

From where she sat she could see the small parking lot next to the store. Riley's pickup was still there; it was the only vehicle in the lot. Cars passed along the street, their headlights blazing through the dark, their tires hissing on the wet pavement. A pedestrian hurried by, looking like an animated mushroom under the black hemisphere of his umbrella. No one seemed to be paying any attention to her, but when she reached for the door handle she found she couldn't make herself get out of the car. The idea of crossing the patch of light from the street lamp, in full view of a hidden watcher, made her cringe. She'd have to turn her back on the street in order to unlock the door, which was enclosed on three sides—a nice dark private niche, made for muggers.

Was there something else she should have done—some other precaution she might have taken, might still take—before she nerved herself to act? The lights from the café, down the street, beckoned like an invitation to an oasis of warmth and safety. The telephone booth on the corner offered another excuse for delay. She could call Nick, tell him what she intended to do, warn him of the package that would arrive on his desk the following day. But she had already considered that option and rejected it, knowing what his reaction would be. Poor paranoid Meg, she's been under a strain, no wonder she's finally flipped. By the time he got the ring and her explanatory note it would be too late for him to remonstrate, soothe or interfere—and if the worst did happen, if all her plans failed, the news of her death or disappearance would substantiate her story.

That she should have chosen Nick as the recipient was not a sign of renewed trust, but rather of an almost shameful indifference. None of her friends could be asked to bear such a burden; if t didn't place them in actual, physical danger, it vould certainly cause them enormous distress and lifficulty. Nick would be distressed if something happened to her, but the wound would not be nortal. He was powerful enough to protect himelf and important enough to force the authorities o take action. Anyway, it was the best she could lo, and with any luck—please, God; please, Dan—it would be unnecessary.

She had done all she could to protect Gran and he others. The best she could do for them was tay far away from them, make it clear she had not communicated directly with them.

She couldn't think of anything else. She was lmost past thinking or hoping or praying—cerainly past praying. The Lord helps those that help hemselves, and Dan didn't seem to be in the nood to help anyone. Damn him, she thought. This is all his fault. He got me into this and then leserted me.

When she reached again for the handle the same llogical reluctance stopped her—only this time he realized why she was hesitating. Cursing her tupidity, she returned her hand to the wheel and ook her foot off the brake. She had been about o neglect the most obvious precaution of all. Even xhaustion was no excuse.

The alley was well lit by fixtures on the walls f the stores and offices that backed onto it. Dan ad mounted no less than three, so that if one ulb burned out there would be ample backups. Meg's foot barely tapped the gas; the car crawled

along, sometimes stopping and turning, so tha
the headlights could illumine dark corners an
spaces behind dumpsters. A small dark shap
scuttled between the trash cans, its eyes reflectin
the headlights in an unnerving flash of red. Tha
was the only sign of life; the only vehicles in sigh
were small delivery vans, one behind the floris
shop, the other belonging to the cleaners at th
end of the alley.

After traversing the entire length of the alle
Meg returned to the back of the store and parked
This time she got out without hesitating, he
keys in her hand. It was worth a try, at any rate
Surely he had come—and gone—by the bac
door, and there was no way he could fasten th
bars and chains from outside.

The old familiar symptoms of panic thicken
her throat and made her damp fingers fumble wit
the keys, but this time she flung them away a
she would have kicked off heavy shoes to kee
herself afloat in deep water, obeying an instinc
tive, primitive need that overpowered every othe
sensation. By the time she inserted the second ke
her hands were dead steady, and she moved wit
the speed and assurance of a trained burglar
When she turned the knob the silence remaine
unbroken. He had not reset the alarm. Her min
noted this and assessed its meaning even as he
body reacted with unconscious agility, slippin
through the opening, reaching for the light switc
and closing the door, in smooth successive mo
tions.

She had time to die twice over while the over-
ıead fluorescents flickered into brightness. Not un-
il she was certain there was no one waiting for her
lid she shoot the bolt on the back door, but sick
lisappointment warred with relief. She had been so
ure he would take the bait, it had seemed eminently
ogical that he would. . . . And he had been here.
The signs of his presence were clear, not only in
he unbarred door, but in the overturned chair
ınd spilled coffee. . . .

Not coffee. The stains were too dark, too thick.

Meg knocked over another chair in her mad
ush for the washroom. That door could only be
ocked from the inside. The knob turned freely
n her hand.

His feet had been pressed against the door.
When she opened it they slid out, causing her to
tumble. The room was so small his body was
queezed in between the sink and the toilet, half-
itting, half-lying. His hands were behind him;
he assumed that, like his ankles, his wrists were
ound. The pad of cloth covering the lower half
f his face was stained with red, and his eyes were
losed.

The blood was fresh; a thin trickle still flowed
rom his nose. Dead men don't bleed. A thriller
itle if there ever was one. . . . Meg tried to
queeze past his long legs, but there wasn't room;
he had to lower the toilet seat and lie across it in
rder to reach him, and part of her mind roared
vith slightly hysterical laughter at the absurdity
f the position.

"Riley!" His head rolled to one side when he fingers tore off the gag. The bruises on his fac were hours old; dried blood from the gash on hi temple had traced bizarre dark brown pattern across the swollen flesh. The bandage was gone torn off, accidentally or deliberately, during th day. "Riley—talk to me! Say something, dam it!"

One eye appeared to be swollen shut. The othe one opened, focused and brightened. He contem plated her for a moment with vague satisfaction "Meg. Mignot. . . . Little Mignon."

Dan's pet word for her. Riley's voice was hars with dryness, his bruised mouth had trouble shap ing the word, but it sounded sweeter than an music she had ever heard. She grabbed his shir in both fists. "Stand up. Hurry!"

"Mignon. . . . What a way to go." His ey closed. The distortion of his mouth was an attem at a smile. "They say you see a bright white light This is . . . better. Kiss me?"

She wanted to laugh, she wanted to cry, sh wanted to scream with relief and terror. " can't. . . ."

She could, though. Despite the fact that sh was sick with fear and knew that every secon counted, her lips found his torn mouth, and h met them with a hard thrust that denied pain an weakness, with the urgency of a man dying c thirst who has found water at last. For a timeles moment she forgot everything but the fulfillmer of her own need, too long denied and unrecog nized; and it was Riley who finally broke away, his one functional eye widening in horrified awareness.

"Jesus," he gasped. "My God—it really is you. I thought I was. . . . Get the hell out of here! You don't—"

Meg took his face in her hands. "I've been going crazy all day looking for you, Riley. We go together or neither of us goes."

"You don't understand," Riley croaked. "This is what he wants—he set this up. The two of us together—"

"I know. Stop talking and move, for God's sake." He was trying to move, but so feebly that she exclaimed in renewed alarm, "What's wrong? How badly are you hurt?"

Riley subsided with a grunt, his head against the toilet tank. Sweat streaked his face, blurring blood and bruises into an unholy mask. "I'm not hurt. Not much. I'm drunk."

"What?" Meg stared at him.

"Drunk," Riley repeated firmly. "He's been pouring bourbon into me off and on all day. Can't you smell it? Quite a bit got spilled."

"Now that you mention it. . . ." Meg wrinkled her nose. "I must have been too preoccupied to notice before. That was smart of him. Drugs leave traces in the bloodstream, but you were seen drinking last night. . . . Riley, I don't give a damn whether you're drunk or sick or *dead*, you've got to stand up! We've got to get away from here.

Wait a minute—I'll cut the ropes on your ankles, that will make it easier."

"No, it won't. He took my leg brace, too. I don't think I can . . . Meg, please. Go for help."

Meg slid off the toilet seat and went to the workbench. "Can't risk it. He has another option, and I'm sure it's occurred to him." She selected a knife and went back to him. "He thought of everything, didn't he? Padded the ropes so they wouldn't leave marks. There—that does it. Come on, Riley. I swear to God if you don't help me I'll grab you by the ankles and pull you out."

His first effort to get his feet under him made him slip sideways and brought his head into painful contact with the washbasin. "I'm sorry," he gasped. "If I could use my hands—"

"Oh, shut up, Riley. I admire a man who can say he's sorry, but you're carrying it too far." She forced his knees up and braced herself against them, twisting her hands in his shirtfront. "Try it again."

"I was in love with you before I even met you." Riley squeezed the words out between grunts of pain and effort. "Dan talked about you all the time. I knew I didn't have a chance, you were young and beautiful and loaded—with money, I mean—ouch!"

"You are drunk," Meg said critically.

"And hung over. I don't think I've ever felt worse in my life. And then when I saw you, at the church, and you looked just the way I felt—angry, not resigned—ready to fight the whole lamned world—oh, Jesus, Meg, that hurts. Give ne a minute—"

"We don't have a minute. Push against the wall."

He came upright with a sudden rush, swayed iolently and would have fallen if she hadn't raced all her weight to hold him. His chin resting n the top of her head, Riley murmured, "Too lamned beautiful for the likes of me. But that vasn't what finished me off, Meg—Mignon . . . ou being beautiful. If you hadn't also been tough nd kind and funny and smart and a fighter. . . . Why'd you kiss me? You did kiss me, didn't you? Geez, my head feels like a tornado hit it. I thought was starting to sober up."

"You've had a hard day," Meg said, fighting o keep her voice steady. "Sit down for a minute. No, with your back to me, so I can untie your ands. How did you get those bruises on your ace?"

Riley subsided onto the toilet seat and rested is head against the wall. "He was waiting for me vhen I came home last night. Caught me off uard. I'd had a few beers, and I wasn't expecting im to move so soon. I guess he figured I'd be asier to handle if. . . . He was right, too."

"And the burns on your hands? They didn't ome from the fire."

"No, I got you out of the cottage before either f us was singed."

"You mean he. . . ."

"Cigarette lighter."

"But he doesn't smoke."

"My cigarette lighter. That sort of added insul
to injury," Riley said thoughtfully.

In a voice choked by tears, laughter and out
rage, Meg said, "Oh, Riley, I do love you," anc
slid her arms around him. "Come on. My car'
out back."

He came obediently to his feet when she pullec
at him. His one functional eye looked dazed
whether by her confession or by the potent com
bination of pain, alcohol and cramped limbs sh
couldn't tell. He had to lean heavily on her—th
injured leg wouldn't support his weight at all—
and they had only taken a few difficult steps whe
it happened. She had been watching the bac
door. It hadn't occurred to her he would dare ente
through the store.

"That's far enough, I think," he said in hi
calm, pleasant voice.

Meg whirled around, letting go of Riley, wh
fell to his knees and then slumped forward, brac
ing himself on his hands. Involuntarily Me
stooped to help him, but the same calm voic
stopped her. "No. Get away from him. Ove
there."

The gun in his hand was aimed, not at her, bu
at Riley's bowed head. Meg backed away, step b
step, until a smiling nod told her she had gone fa
enough.

She had been almost certain, but actually to se
him was as great a shock to her sensibilities a
surprise would have been. It didn't seem possib
that the same gentle, quiet man who had console

. grieving child and tended an aging woman could)e responsible for a twenty-year-long campaign of)etrayal and crime—that he could be holding her .t gunpoint, with every intention of using that veapon.

Then she saw his eyes, and shuddered and ooked away.

She had known he had a gun, and a license for t, but this wasn't his gun. It was one of the ones)an had bought after the burglary—a classic Colt evolver, sleek and gleaming, its grip inlaid with nother-of-pearl. She remembered it well, for she ιad been impressed by its deadly beauty, though he hadn't seen it for years. Dan must have con-'inced the sheriff it was a collector's item—which t was—and been allowed to keep it. Or else it ιad more or less got lost in the shuffle—there had •een so many guns. . . .

His face sickly gray under the bruises, Riley •ulled himself to his feet. "Don't be foolish," ȝeorge said. "You'll only fall and hurt yourself. Vhy suffer unnecessary pain? I'll make it quick."

"Uncle George. . . ."

"Yes, my dear?" He glanced at her, but the •arrel of the gun didn't move.

"You won't—you won't hurt Gran, will you?"

He had expected her to plead for her life and Riley's. The question surprised and amused him. Certainly not. I'm very fond of the old darling, nd she won't live much longer. Long enough, hough, to make a new will. She's always had a soft spot for Cliff, and with you out of the picture. . . ."

"That's not my gun," Riley said suddenly. "They'll never trace it to me. How are you going to make people believe—"

"They'll trace it to Dan," George said. "The assumption will be that he kept it here, in the store. Many merchants do."

He had closed the door behind him, but remained near it, at a safe distance from both his prospective victims. When the voice boomed out apparently from thin air, he started violently.

"Dad! Dad, are you there?"

George's gloved hand flashed out and hit the intercom switch. "He must have seen me come in," he muttered, frowning. "I wonder what. . . ." Fists beat a fusillade on the door behind him and Cliff's voice came again, faint and far away now that the intercom was off. "Dad! Answer me! Is anybody there?"

George moved slowly away from the door, toward the safe. "He'll leave in a minute." His voice was barely audible. "But he may be back. Open the safe, Riley."

Riley's lips set in an expression Meg knew well. "Don't be a hero, Riley," she said. "Do what he says. Open it."

He caught her meaning as quickly as she had hoped, but his lurching progress, from one supporting piece of furniture to the next, wasn't quick enough for George. "Don't stall, Riley. I don't really need that safe opened, it will just help o set the scene. If you want me to kill you ıow—"

"I'll do it." Riley caught the edge of the safe .nd lowered himself to one knee.

Cliff was more persistent than his father had :xpected. He began to kick the door. "Open up! know somebody's there, I heard voices. Meg, is hat you?"

"Scream if you like," George said softly. "It vill only precipitate matters."

Meg moistened her dry lips and put her shaking ıands in her pockets. "Then Cliff isn't in this with 'ou?"

"He doesn't know anything about it. He nustn't know. I'm doing this for him."

Meg felt an illogical lift of relief. The fact of 'liff's innocence changed nothing for her; he'd ıever be able to get help in time, even if she could lert him to her danger. Yet she was glad her xasperated affection for him had not been mis-laced. "For him," she repeated.

George didn't miss the irony in her voice. "It's our own fault, Meg. This needn't have hap-ened. If you had loved him and turned to him, ıstead of believing this—this intruder. . . ."

"You're wrong." Still on his knees, Riley urned, slowly and painfully. "I told her nothing. 'ou don't have to do this, Wakefield. You're still ı the clear, there's no proof. Let her go. It would e your word against hers."

"That would be enough to hang me. What kind f fool do you take me for, Riley? She's like him—like Dan. She'd hunt me down if it took the rest of her life and every penny she possessed. Get on with it! I know what you're trying to do, but it won't work."

With a shrug and a betraying glance at Meg, Riley turned back to the safe. He had managed a few more seconds' delay, but George was right, it didn't matter. Yet she felt the same need to delay the inevitable; a few more seconds, a few more breaths of air. . . .

"Cliff didn't want me, George," she said. "Except as a friend."

"That's a lie! He'd have loved you if you had given him the slightest encouragement. I didn't want to do this, Meg. You forced me into it. If you hadn't started work on the cottage . . . I wasn't worried at first, I didn't think he'd remember—and I didn't know about that hiding place he had in the floor of his room. He must have heard Joyce and me quarreling. Heard me. . . . What the hell is the matter with you, Riley?"

"Almost there," Riley whispered.

"What if he does remember?" Meg forced the words through stiff lips. "Will you kill him too?"

"He won't remember. There's nothing left now to waken forgotten memories. Those memories aren't damaging in themselves, all he heard were a few fights; he was away at school when I. . . . Why the hell couldn't you have left well enough alone?"

He was quite sincere; the anger in his voice was

;enuine, and directed at her. But if he was insane, hen half the world was crazy too—all the people vho wanted to pass the buck, refuse to accept 'esponsibility for their own actions, blame someone else. The lines in his forehead smoothed out ıs he accepted his own facile excuses, and his voice vas almost gentle when he said, "Ten seconds, Riley."

"It's not there," Meg said. "I mailed it today —to someone who'll know what to do with it if ınything happens to me."

Her uncle smiled. "I'm afraid that remark ather weakens Mr. Riley's claim that you are unvitting, my dear. So it was in the safe after all. I uspected it might be, but that was the one place couldn't search since my—er—informant was n no condition to respond to questions earlier. It loesn't matter. Without your testimony and his, here is really no case against me. Riley, I still vant that safe opened."

"Got it." The safe door swung open. George tarted toward it. Riley edged back, but he was oo slow; without breaking stride George swung ıis foot, and the tip of his polished shoe caught Riley on the side of the head, toppling him over. The worst thing about the blow was its cool alculation—not hard enough to do lasting damge, just hard enough to stun Riley momentarily. Meg's hands clenched. George kept his eyes fixed n her as he reached into the safe and scooped ıandfuls of loose gems onto the floor. A neat finshing touch, that one—the fugitive financing his

flight by stealing easily convertible gems, caugh
red-handed by the rightful owner, whom he hac
already threatened and tried to murder. And a fev
extra goodies for George? Yes; he was putting th
best, the biggest, in his pocket.

The pounding on the door had stopped. Soon
He had to do it soon. If Cliff did go to the polic
it wouldn't be long before someone tried the bacl
door, and that would cut off George's means o
escape—the unmarked van in which he had bee
hiding, waiting for her to come—and in which h
had probably kept Riley prisoner part of the time
She had thought she was so clever, renting a car
why hadn't it occurred to her he was equall
clever? That big Mercedes of his was as conspic
uous as the Ferrari.

Riley groaned and rolled over onto his back
The merciless eyes of the killer, cold as ice, tol
Meg that the final moment was upon her. He ha
to come out from behind the open door of the saf
to get a clear shot at Riley, and he had to do i
before Riley was fully conscious, because the fata
bullet must appear as if it had been fired by hi
own hand. The angle, the powder burns, all ha
to be right to substantiate a verdict of suicide. A
stupid, irrational verdict—but that was what Rile
was supposed to be, irrational. Drunk and des
perate and crazy—seized by remorse after mur
dering the woman he both loved and hated. . .
She could almost hear George's sad, controlle
voice explaining. They would believe it becaus
there was no other possible explanation, and i

vouldn't matter if Riley died a few seconds before he did, they couldn't tell the exact time of death o closely. George knew all about those things.

It took three shots. The first one went wild, as he had intended; in fact it came closer than she neant it to, the heavy gun jerking in her hands. t brought George upright and staring, safely disant from the man who lay on the floor. The second shot missed him by a foot. He could have illed her then, while she steadied the weapon, ighting not only her shaking hands but her loathng of what she had to do. He hesitated for a noment that seemed to last a decade and then urned, with the same unnatural slowness, away rom Meg, toward Riley, who was struggling to nove.

She had all the time in the world. Through the inging in her ears a distant voice murmured intructions. "Closer. Brace your wrists on something—the chair, the bench. Don't pull, squeeze. 'hat's it."

She aimed for his thigh, and missed. The bullet ore through his side and sent him spinning in a alf-circle before he fell.

It hadn't been fondness, or a last, belated attack f conscience, that made him turn from her to Riley. It had been contempt. He hadn't believed he would do it—could do it.

George was screaming and squirming, hands lawing his side. She hadn't killed him. He was armless though, his gun lay on the floor where e had dropped it, and pain had wiped everything

else from his mind. Meg took the precaution o
kicking the weapon under the bench before sh
went to unlock the door. Not a bad shot, sh
thought, wondering at her own coolness. Shock
she supposed; she'd be a blubbering wreck whe
it wore off, so she had better go for help whil
she was still coherent.

Not a bad shot at all, considering the circum
stances. And it had not been the ghostly hand o
Dan Mignot that steadied hers. He had never bee
able to hit the side of a barn.

20

"I FOUND THE ring when the apartment was bein
remodeled," Riley said. His bruises had starte
to fade; they stood out like patches of greenis
lichen on a granite head. "It had fallen down be
hind the baseboard in the bedroom. I couldn'
imagine how it had gotten there, or who it be
longed to, but it was obviously valuable. So
showed it to Dan, told him where I'd found it.'

He paused, shifting position uncomfortably. Th
chair he had chosen, ignoring Meg's gesture at th
place next to her on the sofa, was a stiffly elegan
construction of mahogany and petit point. Me
didn't suggest he change seats. She had pushed he
luck far enough getting him to the house.

It was the first time they had been alone. Sh
had visited him once in the hospital, bearing th
conventional gifts of flowers and candy—whic

she knew Riley would despise as much as she did. Conversation of the sort that was desperately necessary would have been impossible in the constant bustle of the hospital and the presence of his roommate, a bored, garrulous old man recovering from prostate surgery. Finding he was to be released that afternoon, she had effectively kidnapped him, sending the car and chauffeur to pick him up. When she greeted him in the hall he had accepted her excuses and explanations quite graciously—for Riley. "Yeah, I know. There are still reporters camping in the hospital lobby. And I figured you'd want to talk."

She hadn't summoned enough courage to tell him what else she had done. Even in the small parlor, which she had chosen for their tête-à-tête because it was the least pretentious of the reception rooms, he was visibly ill at ease.

Of course he had good reason to dread the conversation. He had plunged into his story with the air of a man determined to face the worst and get it over with.

Riley abandoned his efforts to find a comfortable position. Stiff as a statue, he went on. "I thought he was going to have a stroke. Maybe it was a stroke, a minor one; his face turned purple and he kept clawing at his throat like he couldn't breathe. Scared me half to death. I tried to get him to go to the hospital, but you know how he was. . . . After he calmed down some, he started talking. We'd gotten to be good friends, but I don't think he would have spoken so freely if he

hadn't been so shaken. It was like he was talkin
to himself—in broken phrases, and with a lot o
cussing.

"I knew some of the story. If I hadn't, I migh
not have been able to make sense of what he said
But one thing was clear: the ring couldn't hav
gotten where it was unless she'd been there, i
the bedroom."

"And on the bed."

"That's what Dan said. He made me describ
exactly where I found it."

"But she had another ring," Meg said. "A
exact copy. What did she do, tell my father sh
had lost the first one and ask him to make another
She'd have to invent some story, he'd be boun
to notice."

Riley shook his head. "Not your father—Dan
She came to him, crying and hysterical, said you
dad would be hurt if he found out she'd been s
careless. Your dad was out of town on business
so Dan was able to get the copy made before h
came back. Dan was no designer, but he was
damned fine goldsmith, and he had the origina
sketches. Your father never knew. And Da
didn't give it a second thought until the origina
ring turned up."

"George was living in the apartment then," Me
murmured. "So the affair must have begun befor
he and Joyce were married. But it didn't sto
then."

"That's what Dan figured. He . . ." Riley'
eyes darkened with memory. "I was afraid th

seizure had affected his mind, the way he sputtered and swore and jumped from one unsupported statement to another—but his reasoning wasn't as illogical as it sounded. He'd been brooding about the facts of that old tragedy for more than twenty years. He really loved your dad. Don't get me wrong, he loved her too, but she was his little girl, and Simon was the son, the successor, the strong right arm he'd always wanted. It's hard to explain; I have trouble understanding that viewpoint, much less sympathizing with it—but in a funny sort of way he wasn't as hurt by her guilt as he had been by Simon's."

"She was only a woman, after all," Meg said. "A poor weak sinful female."

"Uh—yeah. I guess you could put it that way. That stained-glass window in the church was his design, you know. Your father's. Dan had it installed a few years after he died."

It wasn't a non sequitur, though it might have sounded like one to an outsider. Meg turned her face into the pillow. "I never knew that."

He might have come to her then; short of dissolving into tears and asking aloud for comfort she could hardly have expressed her need for it more directly. The chair creaked as he shifted his weight, but he didn't get up.

"Now, after all those years, Dan had a single feeble fragment of evidence that let him believe he might have been right about Simon after all. He fell on it like a starving man on a scrap of bread, and proceeded to build a whole new struc-

ture of theory. There were a few odd incident
that could be said to substantiate it. Joyce's and
George's marriage wasn't as great as people be
lieved. Once or twice Dan had seen bruises on he
arms and body. She claimed she'd fallen—th
usual thing. Suppose she found out he was als
cheating on her, with her own sister. If she con
fronted him, accused him, threatened to divorc
him. . . . George had a nice cushy job, practicall
a member of the family. He wouldn't want to los
that. Dan would not only have fired him, he'
have made sure he left without a character, as the
say. Dan could be pretty vindictive."

"Dan would have spent the rest of his life trackin
George down," Meg agreed. She shivered involun
tarily, remembering George's own words—abou
her. He had been right, and so had the others
when they said she was more like Dan than sh
wanted to admit. Like Dan, and perhaps for th
same reasons, her understanding of the meanin
of the wedding ring had been more intuitive tha
logical. "Seeing that ring had the same effect o
me as it did on Dan," she went on, half to herself
"I knew she had another one, I used to—I use
to play with it. So the one I found had to be
duplicate, and you had to be the one who hid i
in the bag of citrines. You were living in the apart
ment, George had lived there before you did. . .
But I don't think I would have grasped the im
plications so quickly if I hadn't already realize
that George must be the one who had planned tha
campaign of harassment—with or without Cliff'

ıssistance. It wasn't until George actually said so hat I could be certain Cliff wasn't an active partıer in the conspiracy. The fede ring that was found n Gran's room after her heart attack—either it vas one of hers and had nothing to do with the ›ther incidents, or it was planted by a member of he household. No outsider could have put it here. And the threatening telephone call—Ӡeorge took it, or so he claimed. People who play ıgly games like that don't usually stop with one :all, but no one else received such a call. George vas away the night the truck tried to run us off he road. He could have rented one that looked ike yours. The fire at the cottage was the final hing that convinced me of George's guilt. The :ottage had to be destroyed, not because of any ›hysical evidence of what had occurred there—ıe'd had more than twenty years to remove that —but because Cliff was starting to remember. Vhen Cliff confessed about the hiding place under he floor of his room George realized he might ıave overheard—quarrels, accusations, even ›hysical violence. Cliff had blotted out those nemories, but they were coming back, and he ntended to spend a lot of time in the cottage. 'oyce was killed there, wasn't she? George virually admitted as much. But I still don't underıtand how he arranged . . . how he arranged the 'est of it."

"Dan had a theory about that." For all the emoion in Riley's voice he might have been discussing he prospect of rain. "In the light of what has

happened since, it makes perfectly good sense
Dan thought Joyce's death was probably no
premeditated—they were arguing, George hac
been drinking—"

"God, yes—I was so stupid, I missed all the
signs of George's alcoholism. Even the amethys
cuff links—that stone is an old, an ancient charm
against drunkenness. A typical Dan Mignot touch
that gift—George was unaware of its meaning, I
suppose. He was careful never to touch alcohol—'

"Except on his occasional weekend binges," Riley said. "Dan knew about them. He knew everything. He never confronted George, he said wha
a man did in his off-hours was his own business
so long as it didn't interfere with his work."

Meg shivered again, and pulled her feet up under her, huddling to keep warm. The robe she
wore was a sensational concoction of crimson silk
and silver thread that molded itself to her body
when she sat still and flowed gracefully when she
moved. She had bought it that afternoon. I should
have gone for a sensible wool bathrobe, she
thought, hugging herself in an attempt to ward
off the cold. This is harder than I thought—and
the effect is certainly wasted on the Aztec idol
Can't he see. . . . "Go on," she said curtly.

"You're sure you—"

"Go on."

"What precipitated the final, fatal quarrel, Dan
believed, was Joyce telling George she was leaving
him. She had her suitcase packed—the remains
of it were found in the motel room, if you re-

member. She also told him that she was going to blow the whistle on him and her sister. She had already told Simon—but he didn't believe her. So, to prove her case, she demanded he meet her at the motel that George and Elissa had been using. She must have followed them, and bribed the clerk to show her the registration card. She knew the name George had used. Photographs would identify him, and possibly Elissa as well.

"She threw all that at George, and he struck out. When he realized she was dead he had to think fast. He's good at improvising," Riley said. "The motel was only an hour's drive away. He put her in the car and took off. When Simon arrived he was waiting. He had all night to . . . arrange the rest of it, and still get home before daybreak. The fire was necessary. Even if he'd tried to set up a murder-suicide, an autopsy might have shown Joyce died several hours before Simon."

"Makes sense," Meg mumbled. It didn't matter how tightly she curled herself; she was still freezing.

"Yeah. But as Dan admitted, once he'd calmed down, there was no chance of proving it, not after all this time. So he decided to break George down by playing on his nerves."

"The rings."

"Yeah. I thought it was kind of a crazy idea, but Dan was set on it; he insisted that if George was guilty he'd get the point—not only the implicit threat, but the reminder of the lost wedding ring."

Meg blew on her icy hands. "That wasn't the real reason. Dan would have done something like that even if he'd had absolute proof. He wanted George to sweat and suffer."

Riley looked at her uneasily. "Maybe so. After Dan died . . . well, it seemed like the least I could do was carry out his plan for him."

"I thought the rings were meant for me."

"Uh—yeah. That finally dawned on me, and I just about. . . . But I couldn't explain without telling you the whole thing, and I was beginning to realize that Dan's scheme had succeeded only too well. George had gotten the point, all right, and he started hitting back. Initially the attacks on you were designed to incriminate me, rather than harm you; he knew I was the one responsible for sending the rings. But how you could have supposed they were directed at you. . . . The packages were addressed to him, the hair ring had Simon's and Joyce's initials on it—"

"Not when I saw it. He'd filed them off. My hair is the same color as my father's, and Joyce had her mother's silver-gilt hair. He destroyed the first mailing envelope, and replaced the second one with a fake. That was another thing that gave him away—after the first ring arrived, he made a point of collecting the mail before I could get to it, even postponing a weekend trip until after the Saturday delivery. But you were the only one who could have made the rings. The first one might have come from Dan's collection, but to find one that contained hair the exact color of mine. . . ." She had to stop talking, her teeth had begun to chatter. She clamped her mouth shut.

"You're shivering," Riley said, "Can I get a blanket or something to—"

Meg swung her feet onto the floor and sat up. "I don't want a goddamn blanket! What's the matter with you? You are the most insensitive, cold-blooded, uncaring bastard I have ever met. I want someone to hold me. I want *you* to hold me. Maybe I should pour bourbon into you. You were a hell of a lot nicer when you were drunk!"

"Don't do that," Riley said. He sounded as if he were choking.

"Do what? Shiver? Talk? Crawl to you begging for affection like all your other women—"

"God damn it!" Riley erupted from the chair and crossed the room in a few long, stumbling strides. Meg had no time to react even if she had been wrongheaded enough to try to help him; he collapsed onto the couch, and onto her, with a thud that shook the whole room. He was clumsier than she had imagined. Even with her active co-operation it took his lips several unendurable seconds to find hers. That impact felt as monumental as the first, and it went on longer, like the after-shocks of an earthquake.

"You're not wearing anything under that dress," Riley muttered after a while. "I knew you weren't," he added accusingly. "Stop that. Stop

it right now. We can't. . . . Not here. What woul
the butler think?"

"I fired him," Meg said, fighting the hands tha
tried to keep her fingers from the buttons of hi
shirt. "Anyway, I would have, if we had ha
one. . . . Oh, all right, if you're going to be suc
a cold fish, we can go upstairs."

"No." He ended the argument by wrappin
both arms around her in a grip that was half em
brace and half restraint. "I wasn't going to let thi
happen. Not till you'd had time to think. Yo
can't be sure how you feel—"

"Watch it." At least she could move her head
Turning it, she kissed him on the side of the neck
"You're on the verge of making one of the mos
infuriating statements a man can make to
woman: 'You don't really mean it.'"

"I am not." Except for the warmth of his ski
it was like kissing a piece of wood. Petrified wood
Meg's tongue traced a path to his earlobe. Rile
jumped. "Cut it out. We haven't finished talking
I can't think when you. . . . Oh, shit."

The long, lingering gentleness of his mouth o
hers was more dizzying than the first violent de
mand. When he let her go she lay in the circle c
his arms, her eyes closed, feeling warm and re
laxed for the first time in days. . . . No. In years

"Now that you've got that out of your system,
Riley began.

"I haven't. I won't. Ever."

"It wasn't bad," Riley said.

Meg's eyes popped open. "Riley, one of these days—"

"I hope so." His smile faded. "Meg, please lay off—if I kiss you one more time I won't stop. It isn't that easy."

"You aren't that easy," Meg murmured. "You told me that once. Surely you can't believe that this is nothing more than pity or guilt—"

"It's more complicated than that," Riley insisted. "You saved my life. I can only begin to imagine what you went through that day—I've heard some hints of it, from Mike and the others—it wasn't just a single impulsive gesture, like jumping in to save a dog that was being beaten, you had to use every ounce of intelligence and dogged determination you possessed to pull it off. I was barely conscious at the end but I'll never forget the look on your face when you fired that gun. It will come back to you, and you'll think, I did it because of him, he was the one who forced me—"

"I won't buy that one, Riley. You didn't force me to use the gun. If I hadn't had it with me, if I hadn't unconsciously depended on it, I wouldn't have been so careless. There were a number of precautions I could have taken—calling for help, making certain the doors were bolted from the inside—something as simple as setting off the burglar alarm. That would have taken only a few seconds, and the police would have responded immediately. Talk about saving your life—I came close to getting both of us killed, thanks to that damned gun. You saved mine, if it comes to that the night the cottage burned. What were you doing there?"

"He sent me a note. Only it was supposed to be from you."

"Summoning you to a rendezvous?"

"You're shivering again," Riley said, holding her closer.

"No, I'm—I'm trying not to laugh. It's such a tired old cliché in romantic novels—"

"You wouldn't have been dumb enough to fall for it," Riley mumbled. "But we'd been interrupted that afternoon, just when I was starting to tell you—"

"Darling, it's all right. I don't blame you."

"I couldn't very well call and ask if you—"

"No, of course not."

"Then quit laughing."

"It wasn't very funny, was it? If you hadn't been there—"

"Not only was I there, I was early," Riley said reluctantly. "That was what frustrated his neat little scheme."

"He underestimated the ardor of a lover."

"Meg, if you don't stop that. . . ." Riley's voice deepened. "You're right, of course. I couldn't wait—Ihad so much I wanted to tell you, ask you if you could possibly forgive me for acting like such a stupid ass. . . . I was hiding in the trees when he carried you into the cottage. One of your shoes fell off on the porch. . . . The place went up like a bomb, he must have dumped gallons of gas around before he waylaid you. I didn't have ı chance to grab him, I knew if I didn't get you out right away. . . . After I made sure you were okay I knew I'd better get the hell away from here. That was what he wanted, for someone to find me on the spot. I waited till I heard the fire engines before I left."

"That was his only mistake, though." Meg no longer felt like laughing. "He went straight to your apartment after the rest of us went to bed. He had duplicate keys to everything—"

"Except the store. You'd had those locks changed. I had a set of the new ones, though. He. . . ."

"Tell me," Meg insisted.

"When I came to, he'd searched me, taken my keys. In between working on me, he searched the apartment looking for the ring. I wouldn't—I didn't tell him where I'd put it. He was . . . pretty uptight. Time was running out, he had to get me out of the apartment and hidden before daybreak."

"Where were you before he took you to Mike's?"

"In the trunk of his car," Riley said briefly.

"But, my God—he was back at the house early that morning. Cliff was worried about him, he looked ill. . . . No wonder! And you were there, not a hundred feet from me. . . ."

"I was there in body, but not in spirit," Riley said. "Between the liquor and—and the other stuff—and a dose of carbon monoxide from the

exhaust, I didn't come to until he dragged me out
and hauled me into Mike's basement. He poured
some more booze into me and left me. When he
came back, he had a van—must have rented it
someplace. We spent part of the day just driving
around, I think. It was dark when he went back
to the store."

"He must have had a nerve-racking day," Meg
said vindictively. "He had to keep showing up at
the house from time to time, and he must have
talked with Candy—heard her lies about your
burned hands. I hope he did sweat. Damn him!"

"I can't say I'm wasting a lot of sympathy on
him," Riley agreed. "When I think of how scared
you must have been—I should have told you abou
the rings. I underestimated the bastard. How he
could have turned them around, made you
think. . . ."

"Where did you get the hair, Riley? Did you
rape one of my locks while I wasn't looking?"

"Uh—no."

"That's right, you couldn't have. You mus
have finished the ring before I. . . . Riley, you
devil—don't tell me you got it from a horse's tail?"

She twisted around to see his face, and burs
out laughing at his stricken expression. "Oh
Riley—you didn't."

"No, not a horse. It was—well, hell. It was tha
dog of Mike's. Are you laughing? How can you
laugh? It isn't funny!"

"Yes, it is. I have to laugh when I can, it's the
only thing that keeps me sane. That and . . . Ri

ey, you do love me, don't you? I know you do. Stop being such a bullheaded selfish pig and admit t. Can you say the words? Say them, Riley. Please."

"Of course I do."

"Say them."

"I love you."

"There, that wasn't so bad, was it?"

"But that's irrelevant," Riley insisted. "How could I help loving you? That doesn't mean—"

"We don't have a butler."

"Yes, but—"

"We won't live with Gran. We can stay in the apartment until we find a house."

"Yes, but . . . I mean, no. But—"

"I love you, Riley."

"I don't know," Riley said gloomily.

"Come upstairs and I'll prove it."

He captured her hands and held them. "I wanted you to have time to think. It isn't . . . believe it or not, what's holding me back is not my damned male pride. We could form a pretty good partnership, and I don't just mean the store. I have to be sure. . . . Oh, hell, I'm not much good with words. But you are like Dan in some ways—the best ways—you're stubborn, you hate to admit you could be wrong. And you've invested so much in me—"

"I plan to invest a lot more. You've got it backwards, Riley." She let her hands rest quietly in his; the physical need that blazed between them was, just now, less important than honesty and

mutual trust. That could not be attained in a moment or an hour, but they could make a beginning
"If I were moved by stubbornness and a desire to
have my own way, I'd be running as fast I could
Don't you realize that this was Dan's idea? He se
us up. He set me up. You're the man he woulc
have chosen for me if he could have arranged my
marriage in the good old-fashioned way. The store
is my dowry, in case you had to be bribed to take
me."

Riley's jaw dropped. "You're kidding. Dan
wouldn't—"

"Oh yes, he would. He did. And it worked, a
his schemes always did unless some malevolen
force intervened. He's still. . . ." She stopped
biting her lip. It would be some time before sh
could admit to herself, much less to Riley, tha
she had felt Dan's invisible presence pulling th
strings that guided her actions. Mary's innocen
reports from the Other Side could be dismisse
as coincidence, but that last dreadful day whe
inspiration had seemed to come from some sourc
outside her mind. . . . No, she certainly didn'
want to put that idea into Riley's head; it woul
inhibit any man's ardor to visualize a guardia
spirit hovering over the nuptial couch like a ce
lestial Peeping Tom. Dan in a white nightgow
flapping his wings and grinning with smug ap
proval. . . .

"What are you laughing at now?" Riley askec

"Nothing. Riley, there aren't any guarantees—

xcept for refrigerators. Why not take a chance nd—"

"Okay."

"I mean, after all, we have a fairly good foun- ation in our. . . . What?"

"I said okay. I may be stubborn, but I'm not tupid." His hands brushed the hair away from er cheeks and tilted her head back, and his face as open and unguarded, as she had seen it once efore—but warmer, softer, infinitely more lov- ng. "I'm so crazy about you it scares me. I want ou so much—"

"Come on, then."

"Woman, you have no shame." Smiling, he let er pull him to his feet. "Your room or mine?"

"Mine, I. . . . Oh, damn it, Riley, how did you now?"

"That you'd moved my things here, without so uch as the courtesy of asking me? I figured it as the sort of thing you'd do."

They climbed the stairs together. Riley's arm as around her shoulder, in an unashamed de- and for support; he was moving quickly enough ow so that his limp was perceptible.

"After all," he continued, "you're the senior artner. You run the show. Mignot and Riley, ou said—"

"I've decided to change the name."

He lifted his arm. "I didn't mean to lean on ou. You're out of breath."

"That's not why I'm out of breath."

"Oh. What do you mean, you're changing the

name? Don't play total woman with me, Meg, i
isn't necessary. Riley and Mignot—"

"No. Riley and Venturi."

They had stopped in front of the door to he
room, but when she reached for the knob h
caught her hand and made her turn to face him
"Wrong again. Venturi and Riley."

"We can argue about that later."

Again, and for the last time, he prevented he
from opening the door. "You've got him back
But you've lost her. And that, too, is partly m
doing."

"I lost her a long time ago," Meg said softly
"When she abandoned a child who needed her i
order to drown her guilt in alcohol and depression
I always knew that, though I concentrated m
hatred on him because—because I loved him best
For a while I had lost them both. I don't eve
hate her any longer; I've become, I hope, mor
tolerant of human weakness. God knows I'v
made plenty of mistakes myself. If I could onl
be sure she didn't—that she wasn't. . . ."

He could have offered her the false comfort c
denial. But as she had learned—and learned t
love—soothing lies were a variety of insult Rile
would never offer her. "She must have know
on one level of consciousness at least. It was ju
too much of a coincidence—the same motel, th
same name. . . . But do her justice; she didn't l
him get away with it because she was too coward
to confess her own fault; there was no way sh
could prove what she suspected. She couldn't fac

ieorge again, though. She couldn't even stand to tay in the same world with him. If there are de- rees of suffering, hers was so far beyond anything ne had coming to her. . . . Are you crying? I idn't mean to make you feel bad."

"I don't feel bad. I love you, Riley."

"Oh yeah?"

"Riley!"

"I love you too."

He let her open the door. "Don't let the decor nhibit you," Meg said, smiling at his expression 'hen he saw the frills and ribbons and lacy pil- ows.

"It would take more than that to inhibit me. 'his is for real, Meg—Mignon. I'll never let you nange your mind now. All the same . . . didn't ou go a little overboard on the roses?"

Laughing, she drew him into the room and shut ie door, closing in the roses, closing out the snow nd the winter cold forever.

X